FAITH ARISING

The Crowning Crescendo:
Season of Miracles
Book 8

RACHAEL C. DUNCAN

CKN Christian Publishing
An Imprint of Wolfpack Publishing
1707 E. Diana Street
Tampa, FL 33610

www.cknchristianpublishing.com

Paperback ISBN: 978-1-63977-478-4
Ebook ISBN: 978-1-63977-477-7
LCCN: 2024947854

NOTE FROM THE AUTHOR

When I began researching for my first novel, I was blown away by the vast array of resources available concerning anything and everything biblical! It was thrilling to discover such a wealth of information regarding topics that have always intrigued me.

Because I write Bible-based novels, please allow me to state this simple disclaimer: The novels I write are categorized as biblical fiction, which means I have taken some literary license in instances where the Bible story itself remains silent, unclear, or disputed. As you can imagine, a *lot* of controversy and differing opinions regarding certain biblical characters, settings, dates, etc. So just a reminder, while based on the biblical narratives, this is indeed a work of fiction.

As I tackled this exciting new project, I sought to honor the Word of God, and then I asked the Lord to help me fill in the blanks in a way that will reach my readers, touch their hearts, draw them closer to Him, and bring these beautiful Bible stories to life, inspiring each reader to dive headfirst into the precious Word of God!

Thank you for purchasing this novel. I hope you are blessed page after page!

FAITH ARISING

CHAPTER 1

Tabitha

Circa A.D. 36, Joppa

Tabitha awakened with a start.

Heart pounding, she sat up in bed, her warm blanket slipping off her slender shoulders and pooling in her lap. Dragging in a shaky breath, Tabitha grasped at the blanket's soft folds, drawing it up to her chin and attempting to compose herself without awakening Laurel, her three-year-old daughter, still sleeping soundly beside her.

She'd had the dream again. But this time, it was so *real*, so very lifelike, she'd awakened with a sharp gasp of disbelief, trembling all over.

For several weeks now, her sleep had been haunted with visions of her late husband, Stephanos—the handsome and fiery evangelist who'd been murdered by a hate-crazed mob goaded on by disgruntled religious leaders and spearheaded by the redoubtable and vindictive Saul of Tarsus.

Clenching her luminous hazel-green eyes shut,

Tabitha attempted to ward off the lingering remnants of the painful dream. For in it, she'd seen once again her beloved's brilliant smile and reveled in the sound of his voice, the tenderness of his touch, the heat of his skin.

Would she ever stop missing him? Needing him? Longing for him with every fiber of her being? Would this incessant, nagging pain ever cease, or rather plague her aching soul for the rest of her days?

Releasing a sigh of frustration, Tabitha tossed aside her blanket and swung her legs over the side of her canopy bed. True, there were times when she was quite certain her broken heart was *almost* mended—typically on her busiest days, when she was completely immersed in local mission work or tending to the orphans and widows in her care. On those days, she could almost believe she was ready to move on, to gently and reverently close the chapter of her life which had included the wonderful evangelist whom she had loved so deeply. And yet, just when she thought she had succeeded in overcoming the rending heartache, the troubling dream returned full force!

Tiredly massaging her aching temples, Tabitha evaluated her own turbulent thoughts and emotions, troubled at heart.

True, the Lord had graciously helped her overcome her bitterness and fury toward Saul of Tarsus and those who had propagated Stephanos' cruel death. By His grace, God had led her to Joppa, granting her shattered life both purpose and meaning. Here, she'd won the hearts of dozens of locals—including her stubborn grandfather and her closest friend, Tirzah—patiently leading them to the Lord.

And after her uncle's sudden death, Tabitha had

received yet another unexpected calling when she inherited the entirety of Joram's shipping business and estate. In the ensuing months, she had completely thrown herself into the renovation of the stately mansion, transforming it into a home for the numerous widows and orphans of the region in addition to providing a worthy meeting place for the local church.

Undoubtedly, everyone around her would say she was fine. In fact, more often than not, *she* would say she was fine. After all, her gracious Father in Heaven had enabled her to overcome insurmountable odds, making an impact on countless hearts and lives. Furthering Christ's kingdom. Making a difference.

And yet, at times, the heartache persisted.

Like today.

Reaching for the soft robe dangling from a gilded hook on the wall, Tabitha rose quietly and slipped into the comforting folds of the silken garment. She'd discovered it in the wardrobe closet and was certain it had belonged to her kindhearted aunt, Pennie. She felt privileged to wear it now, residing in the room that had once belonged to the gracious and compassionate woman.

Crossing the bedchamber on tiptoes, Tabitha gently pulled back the elegant chair parked in front of her aunt's vanity, casting a cautious glance over her shoulder to be certain she hadn't awakened her daughter. Satisfied, she slowly lowered herself onto the cushioned chair, allowing herself a moment to gaze into the polished glass framed by a gold-encrusted mirror. Lifting wooden fingers, she began unbraiding long strands of her honey-colored hair, noting how the unusual shade had lightened considerably in the salty sea air and Mediterranean sunshine. Her bright hair starkly contrasted with her bronzed complexion, high cheekbones, and striking hazel-green eyes. Pursing her lips in deep thought, Tabitha reached for an ivory comb, dragging it somewhat listlessly through her tumbling tresses.

While part of her wished to beg the Lord to bar the troubling dream from ever occurring again, another part of her longed to experience it every night. For in it, her cherished husband was restored to her, even if only for one breathless moment.

Oh, Lord, I'm so conflicted! She groaned inwardly, setting aside her comb and gazing into the mirror with bright eyes snapping her frustration. *Shall I ask You to take the dream away? And if You do, will I forever lose my memories of Stephanos? Will I forget the features of his handsome face, the curve of his smile, the fire in his eyes, the warmth of his embrace?*

One thing Tabitha knew with the utmost clarity: Her recurring dream made the obvious attentions of a certain attractive young merchant all the more unsettling.

Well, perhaps this was the Lord's way of reminding her that she wasn't ready to move on. Perhaps she never would be. Or, could it be that the patient interest of yet another godly man merely provoked tender reminders of the husband she had loved and lost?

Shaking her head forcefully, Tabitha pushed back her chair and rose to her feet, unwilling to waste these precious early morning hours tempestuously brooding and feeling sorry for herself.

After all, she had work to do.

CHAPTER 2

Mary

Jerusalem

"These are turbulent times, Mary! I fear we may all perish with these rising tides of change, for they resonate like a swirling abyss or a seething mount of fire."

"A seething mount of fire, yes?" Mary echoed, one corner of her graceful mouth tipping as a slender brow arched sharply in question. "What a riveting description, dear Agabus."

"What? You mock me?" the young Pharisee declared in disbelief, pausing his agitated pacing long enough to cast her a gaping stare.

"Of course not," Mary assured him, leaning back in the throne-like chair perched behind her desk. "I am simply amused."

"You find our imminent demise *amusing*?" Agabus demanded, open-mouthed.

"I find your dramatics entertaining."

"There is nothing dramatic about me stating the cold, hard facts!"

"The facts, yes," Mary nodded, reaching for an elegant stylus and tapping it thoughtfully on the polished surface of her desk. "But your concerns are not legitimate, Agabus. Your reaction is disproportionate, as your concerns are based solely on hearsay."

"Hearsay?" Agabus declared, appalled. "Far from it!"

"And how so?"

"Our nation has been rocked by both religious and political upheaval, and that's a *fact*!" Agabus reminded her, resuming his mad pacing again and clasping his hands before him in the manner of his stern-faced religious peers. With his long robes fluttering behind him, he added, "Why, we've scarcely entered the new year, and already, the governor, Pontius Pilate, has been summoned to Rome. We all know what that means. His demise is indisputable, and then the emperor shall appoint a new governor, one that may prove even less favorable than Pilate!"

"Or, perhaps, the emperor shall appoint a new governor who will sympathize with our cause."

"Unlikely," Agabus declared with a graceless snort.

Smiling faintly, Mary watched the recent convert as he nearly wore out the swirling floor tiles with his restless pacing. The hour was late, and smoldering mounted torches cast the Pharisee's troubled features in chiseled shadow, further emphasized by his trailing black-and-white head covering.

"As if that isn't enough to cause alarm," Agabus continued, anxiously running a hand over his neatly trimmed beard, "rumors abound regarding Marcellus, a cruel and insolent man. Most believe he is the likeliest candidate to take Pilate's place as governor. If my sources can be trusted, he is in Jerusalem even as we speak. Should this man win the emperor's approval, we can expect little aid from him. On the contrary, he will likely oppose us at every turn."

"Possibly."

"And to make matters worse, the high priest, Caiaphas, has been deposed! And given the fact that he was replaced by his own brother-in-law and longtime rival, Jonathan, our situation will undoubtedly worsen."

"Caiaphas was no friend of ours, Agabus."

"Yet his brother-in-law may prove even more hostile than he!"

"What do you know about this new priest called Jonathan?"

"He's the son of Annas."

"Ah, yes, Annas," Mary mused, setting aside her stylus. "The former high priest and the father-in-law of Caiaphas. He, too, participated in the deliverance of our Lord unto death upon the cross."

"Annas is a fearsome and cunning man, rather like a dark bird of prey just waiting to descend upon its unsuspecting victims."

"And his son, Jonathan? What is he like?"

"I've encountered Jonathan but a few times," Agabus admitted, wringing his hands. "But, already, the Temple resonates with rumors about how he intends to upstage Caiaphas in every way possible. Why, it'll merely be another notch in Jonathan's belt to exterminate a troublesome sect which his brother-in-law failed to subdue. In addition to that, I fear he may prove inexperienced, possibly even incompetent. Those traits become dangerous when combined with a burning zeal to upstage one's predecessor."

Mary nodded briefly, recognizing his concerns but unwilling to fear them.

"So now we are dealing with a new governor and a new high priest, all in the same year!"

"It sounds rather like a season of new beginnings, does it not?" Mary mused, unperturbed by Agabus' rising angst.

"A season of new beginnings?" Agabus scoffed, peeved. "Is *that* what you're calling it?"

"Undoubtedly, doors are opening, Agabus," Mary responded staidly. "This unprecedented era may very well usher in a season of miracles, don't you see? Have you so soon forgotten the miraculous conversion of our former adversary, Saul of Tarsus?"

Agabus crossed his arms, casting her a sideways glance but unable to refute her argument.

"Ever since Saul's conversion, the church has experienced a blessed reprieve, a season of peace."

"Only to be followed by religious and political upheaval on all sides, which will undoubtedly end in disaster!" Agabus proclaimed with an air of doom.

"We needn't relinquish our peace about future troubles that may or may not occur," Mary reminded him with a beatific smile. "God has called you to do mighty things, Agabus. Don't let fear and dread stifle the power of the Holy Spirit working in you."

Feeling somewhat chastised, Agabus dropped onto the upholstered chair across from Mary's desk, defeated. "Recently, I have been wrestling with a difficult decision."

Mary raised a brow in interest.

"I believe God may be calling me out of my old occupation and into something new."

"And is that so hard to believe?" Mary smiled. "Our God delights in doing new things, wonderful things, things beyond our wildest imaginings."

"But I've trained my entire life to become what I am—a Pharisee, a scholar, a learned man. Traveling the torchlit corridors of the synagogue's inner rooms once thrilled me. Studying the Law for hours on end, sequestered in quiet libraries and surrounded by like-minded scholars, was like a slice of heaven on earth. But now..." His voice trailing off, Agabus clasped his hands, his eyes distant. "My former peers have become my foes. In conforming to the traditions of the elders, I am unwittingly promoting an age-old system that opposes the Way at every turn. When I first accepted Christ's message, I thought perhaps I was called to remain, to be a light to my brothers in the Temple and in the synagogue. But the longer I stay, the more glaringly obvious it becomes that I no longer fit. It just isn't the place for me anymore, Mary."

"And what *is* the place for you, friend?"

"How I wish I knew," Agabus sighed, shaking his head.

"Have you prayed about this?"

"Without ceasing."

"And have you experienced any further visions since Damascus?"

"None, not even one." Shaking his head again, Agabus released a frustrated sigh. After experiencing his first vision in the house of Judas on Straight Street, he'd been convinced of his calling as a prophet. The only problem was his extraordinary visions were, apparently, limited. He hadn't the slightest idea about when he might receive his next heavenly revelation. So, then, what exactly was he to do with himself while awaiting direction? Surely there was more to his life than simply sitting around, waiting to receive another divine revelation!

"Sometimes, when we are unsure about how to best proceed, it helps to evaluate our present circumstances and asses if there is a need."

"A need?" Agabus asked her, confused. "What do you mean?"

"God calls us to be useful in His kingdom by meeting the needs of those around us. Have you taken a moment to ask yourself—and the Lord—where help is currently needed?"

"Well, no," Agabus confessed, wrinkling his brow in deep thought. "But where is help most needed? As you've just pointed out, the church here in Jerusalem has indeed experienced a blessed reprieve. And believers continue to share all that they have, gladly meeting the needs of the poor among us."

"Have you considered joining Philip and Kelila in Caesarea Maritima for a time?"

"Caesarea Maritima?" Agabus gasped, jarred by her outrageous suggestion. "Why, that's a godless city!"

"Not for long, if Philip has anything to say about it," Mary grinned.

"Why, a man could be defiled by merely setting foot within the borders of that place," Agabus protested, drawing his shawl further about his shoulders as if to protect himself from Mary's preposterous ideas.

"That sounds rather like the old man speaking

and not the Spirit-filled prophet eager to participate in the salvation of souls," Mary pointed out with a wry smile.

"But…but Caesarea Maritima, Mary? *Really?*"

"Philip and Kelila have recently welcomed their first child into the world, a beautiful baby girl named Nessa," Mary proudly informed him. "And while Philip remains completely devoted to the Lord's work, I imagine he would greatly appreciate your help as he learns to navigate two of God's greatest gifts and responsibilities to man—both ministry and fatherhood."

Releasing a troubled sigh, Agabus contemplated Mary's suggestion, sensing the Spirit's leading in the most bothersome way. After a long pause, he met her gaze, his own riddled with pained resignation. "I think you might be right."

"Pray about it, friend. The Lord will make His way plain to you."

"I fear He already has," Agabus grimaced, none too enthusiastic about embarking on yet another journey so soon after returning from Damascus.

"You needn't fret." Clasping her hands on the desk, Mary rewarded him with a knowing smile. "If you follow God's will, you'll never regret it, Agabus."

The Pharisee's expression indicated a sliver of disbelief.

"Trust me, and even more importantly, trust God," Mary encouraged him, her lovely features appearing enigmatic in the wavering lamplight. "And always remember that *His* way is best."

CHAPTER 3

Tabitha

Joppa

"Knock, knock."

Distracted, Tabitha glanced up from the parchment scrolls scattered somewhat haphazardly across her desk. She was quite certain that Eli had deposited at least a dozen new documents since the previous evening, all of them demanding her immediate attention.

Naturally.

For the umpteenth time, she wondered how on earth Mary had overseen not one, but dozens of business ventures over the years. Somehow, she made it look easy.

Now, Tabitha knew firsthand that it wasn't.

"Adam, hi." Managing a welcoming smile, Tabitha stacked the parchment scrolls on the center of her desk by order of importance.

Slipping past the heavily curtained entrance,

Adam strolled into the spacious office library, his gaze falling knowingly upon her crowded desk. "You look busy."

"Always," Tabitha confessed with a wry smile. "Sometimes there's so much to do, I wonder how on earth I'll ever accomplish all of it."

"Through Christ," Adam reminded her, dropping casually onto one of the straight-backed chairs across from her desk and tossing her a playful wink.

Quickly averting her gaze, Tabitha made a study of the paperwork on her desk, deeply unsettled that her heart quickened in response to the young merchant's handsome smile. Images of her late husband flashed across her mind unbidden, searing her heart. Her recurring dreams about Stephanos still weighed heavily on her mind.

Too heavily.

Fleetingly, Tabitha considered asking Adam to leave, but then thought better of it. Adam had shown her nothing but kindness since the day they had met at the market stalls down by the docks. His behavior toward her brimmed with compassion and understanding. Not once had he conducted himself in a manner that was improper or inappropriate toward her. And it certainly wasn't his fault that her emotions were a roiling mess.

Somehow, she needed to get that under control.

"I dropped by to see if there's anything I can do to help," Adam said cheerfully, interrupting Tabitha's brooding thoughts.

It had become a habit of his, dropping in to see if she needed anything. Adam was always ready to lend a hand with any heavy lifting around the manor, and he was incredibly handy at repairing just about anything. His willingness to assist in any way possible had proven invaluable to Tabitha, especially during those harrying early weeks when she had first opened her doors to those in need.

"It seems there's always plenty of work demanding attention around here," Tabitha managed, flashing a smile she hoped appeared genuine. "I'm so thankful Joram arranged for the household staff to remain employed here after his death. I don't know what I would do without them."

"How are they adjusting to all the changes around here?" Adam asked her, wisely keeping the conversation practically casual. "I'm sure their workload has increased considerably."

"Oh, it has," Tabitha admitted, folding her hands on the desk. "Though Joram was a demanding employer, he was but one man. Now, the staff serves dozens of women and children in need on a daily basis. There's always food to be cooked and served, garments and bedding to be washed, rooms to be cleaned...you understand."

"Everything seems to be running smoothly."

"Even more so than I'd thought possible," Tabitha admitted, relieved. "But God has been so faithful to provide the assistance I need. Eli has become my right-hand man, entirely irreplaceable. He knows the ins and outs of this manor like the back of his hand. I certainly couldn't do this without him. And Martha runs the kitchen like clockwork, while her husband, Jonas, oversees the bookkeeping. Tirzah continues to assist me with Laurel. Your father and Simon have helped many of these women learn trades and secure hired positions so they can eventually support themselves and their children, which is almost unheard of. And you…" Her voice trailing off, Tabitha blushed slightly, hoping not to give him the wrong impression but wishing to demonstrate her appreciation toward him. "Your help has been so appreciated, Adam. Truly, I couldn't have done this without you."

"I'm just glad to be a part of something so clearly God-ordained," Adam said sincerely. "What you're doing here, Tabitha—it's amazing. Not only have you sacrificed your entire inheritance to provide a home for widows and orphans in need, but you're also training and equipping them to become self-sufficient, so they, too, can then assist others in need."

"I believe strongly that we are to help those in need, but we must also equip them to flourish long-term," Tabitha explained with great feeling. "None of these women desire to simply lounge around and receive free handouts for the rest of their lives. Their desire is to become fully equipped to provide for themselves and their children."

"I love it."

"Hopefully, this will allow for even more orphans and widows to be reached," Tabitha continued, passionate about the work the Lord had assigned her to do. "Teaming up with kindhearted locals like Simon the tanner, your father Josiah, and many of his merchant friends at the docks, these women are learning how to earn wages and make ends meet. Did you know that Tirzah has taken several women under her charge? She's teaching them to make pottery and lending them time on her potter's wheel when it isn't in use."

"I'm not the least bit surprised," Adam chuckled, amused. "I'm sure her instruction proves entertaining."

"Oh, I'm sure it does," Tabitha agreed with a knowing smile. "But as these widows gain the confidence and experience needed to be self-sufficient, they will be free to move forward with their lives, allowing space for new occupants. Once one fatherless family is fully equipped to support themselves and move on, a new needy family is already in line to take their place here at the refuge," Tabitha further explained, her eyes alight with anticipation.

"So I heard you finally convinced Ruth to move in as a permanent resident," Adam grinned fondly, pleased for the crotchety old woman.

"It wasn't easy," Tabitha laughed, recalling how stubbornly the old widow had dug in her heels when she'd tried to persuade her to leave the rickety old tenement apartment and relocate to the spacious seaside manor. "But Tirzah has long been concerned about Ruth's health and safety. Her living conditions were deplorable. And since she lived alone and had to travel so many flights of steep steps every day, we were terribly concerned about her taking a hard fall or having an accident of some sort. It might be too late before anyone discovered her plight."

"Is she happy here?"

"She insists that if she's going to live here, then she must make herself useful," Tabitha grinned. "She seems to enjoy working with Martha in the kitchen and ordering around the rest of the household staff. The orphans appear to be both fascinated and taken by her, and Ruth can't help but love them despite the fact that she'd never admit it."

Adam laughed, pleased and amused, as Tabitha shuffled through additional paperwork on the corner of her desk, accidentally bumping a narrow scroll and sending it rolling over the side of the desk.

"Allow me," Adam grinned, easily lifting himself from the chair, retrieving the scroll, and presenting it to the pretty young widow with a bit of dramatic flair.

Laughing, Tabitha accepted the scroll, turning it over to inspect the seal. "Why, this letter is from Mary!" she exclaimed, delighted. "I must have missed it, somehow."

"Well then, shall I leave you alone to enjoy your letter?" Adam chuckled knowingly, aware of how deeply Tabitha looked forward to each letter from her beloved mistress in Jerusalem.

"Oh, no. Please, stay," Tabitha smiled, using the scroll to indicate the chair he'd been sitting in. "I can update you on the news concerning the Jerusalem church, and you can pass along the information to the other deacons, if you don't mind."

"Well, I was hoping you'd say that," he grinned, settling back onto the chair as if ready for a nice, long chat.

Breaking the red wax seal with eagerly trembling fingers, Tabitha quickly unrolled the parchment scroll, her discomfort regarding the handsome deacon temporarily forgotten in her eagerness to feel connected to her beloved church family in Jerusalem. Smiling warmly, her bright eyes scanned the contents of the letter, right to left, in rapt fascination.

"It would seem Mary and her family are doing quite well," Tabitha announced, relieved. "Her son, John Mark, is excelling as he studies to assume leadership in the family business. And her brother, Barnabas, continues in his travels, encouraging the believers scattered across the empire."

"Someday, I hope to meet Barnabas again," Adam mused, eternally grateful to the man who had led him to the Lord.

"I'm sure you will," Tabitha assured him. "Barnabas will likely circle back to Joppa at some point. He doesn't stay put for long."

"So I noticed."

Returning her attention to Mary's letter, Tabitha suddenly gasped in shock, covering her mouth with one hand.

"Tabitha?" Leaning forward in his chair, Adam's brown eyes studied her carefully, concerned. "What is it? Are you all right?"

"I'm just..." Tabitha managed weakly, setting aside the letter and shaking her head in amazement. "I'm just...stunned, that's all."

"Bad news?" he asked gently, worried for her.

"Well, no..." Tabitha responded a bit mechanically. Lifting wide eyes to meet Adam's concerned gaze, she said blankly, "It's about Saul. Saul of Tarsus."

"Who?"

"Saul of Tarsus," she replied weakly, strangely impacted by Mary's miraculous news—news that should have been glorious, and yet left her unsettled.

"Who is Saul of Tarsus?" Adam asked her innocently, wondering at the effect the name had upon the lovely young widow.

"He's the man responsible for the torture and imprisonment of countless believers in Jerusalem—the one who organized the fierce persecution against the Way," Tabitha told him, her gaze distant as she contemplated the stunning news Mary had revealed to her. Taking a calming breath, she added quietly,

"The one who murdered my husband in cold blood."

Adam stared at Tabitha, his expression conveying his shock and sympathy. "Oh, Tabitha. I'm sorry. I had no idea—"

"It's fine," she said quickly, rolling up the letter and pushing it away from her as if allowing herself some distance from the troubling news. "I'm *fine*. It's just, well…"

"We can talk about this later," Adam suggested, sensing her inner turmoil.

"No, it's all right," she said quickly, squaring her shoulders in resolve. "Apparently, there's been an unexpected turn of events."

"An unexpected turn of events? How so?"

"Saul of Tarsus has been converted," she responded, shaking her head in awe. "Our deadliest foe is now a fellow believer."

CHAPTER 4

Tabitha

Joppa

The peaceful garden nook was the perfect place for prayer and quiet reflection. Drawing her knees up to her chest, Tabitha perched on a smooth marble bench placed against a lovely stone wall splattered with verdant ivy tendrils and blossoming spring flowers. A soothing fountain bubbled in the center of the garden respite, and every now and then, small birds alighted upon its elegant marble ledge to sample a taste of the cool, clear water before spreading tiny wings and taking flight.

Breathing deeply of the salty air, Tabitha lifted her gaze, impressed by the canopy of palm fronds high overhead. This was but one of many garden nooks nestled within her uncle's seaside estate, but it had fast become her favorite. Many a misty morning, she had savored her quiet time here, sequestered within the graceful stone walls housing deep greenery bursting with colorful, fragrant blooms. Strategically spaced openings placed in the farthest wall allowed for a dazzling view of the Mediterranean seascape, while towering palms provided a welcome canopy of shade even amidst the heat of the day, sheltering one from the sun's blazing rays.

It was a quiet morning, for which Tabitha was immensely grateful. She needed a moment to process Mary's letter and the unexpected news it had contained about Saul. She scarcely remembered the mumbled excuse she had offered Adam before rising from her chair and slipping away for a breath of fresh air.

He must think her rude, indeed.

She'd simply needed a moment alone to process the shocking news about her husband's killer, the wicked and vindictive Saul of Tarsus. Surely Adam understood that. Surely he wouldn't hold that against her.

Frankly, she was annoyed that the thought of disappointing him bothered her so much.

"May I join you?"

Heart springing into her throat, Tabitha turned her head in time to see the young merchant emerging from an arched stone entryway, an easy smile lighting his handsome features as he approached her bench.

"Forgive me for slipping out so soon after expounding upon Mary's letter," Tabitha said a bit ruefully, readjusting her position on the bench to provide more room for Adam. "It was a bit of a shock, that's all. I needed some time to think and pray about it."

"Perfectly understandable," Adam assured her,

dropping easily onto the bench beside her.

Unsettled when his broad shoulders brushed slightly against hers, Tabitha quickly shifted a bit further toward the other side of the bench, nearly falling off in the process. Smoothing her simple garment, she glanced sideways at Adam, hoping he hadn't noticed her graceless blunder.

If he had, he graciously decided not to mention it.

"Must have been quite a shock about Saul's conversion," Adam observed, clearly sensing her need to sort through troubling thoughts and contrary emotions. "How are you feeling, Tabitha?"

"A bit puzzled by my own reaction, I suppose," Tabitha finally answered, her eyebrows drawing thoughtfully together. "According to Mary's letter, Jesus has handpicked Saul as His own chosen vessel to promote the gospel. But I'm having a difficult time reconciling the hardened, hate-crazed Pharisee I knew in Jerusalem with the entirely new version Mary has described in her letter."

"I can see why," Adam agreed.

Squeezing her hands in her lap, Tabitha released a wobbly sigh. "Stephanos said this would happen," she revealed, biting her lower lip in dismay. "He was so certain God had a plan for Saul."

"How could your husband have possibly known that?"

"The Holy Spirit must have revealed it to him," Tabitha sighed, perplexed. "As for me, I didn't believe it. Not for a moment. I was convinced Saul was a hopeless cause. And yet, somehow, to the very end, Stephanos believed in him."

"Your husband sounds like a remarkable man, Tabitha."

"He was."

Sensing her swelling sadness, Adam asked her gently, "Are you struggling with this unexpected turn of events?"

"Surprisingly, yes," Tabitha responded frankly, a faint sheen of tears glistening in her eyes as she met Adam's gaze. "Until now, I truly thought I had forgiven Saul. Earnestly, I've prayed for his salvation daily, just as Stephanos would have wanted. And yet, now that Saul's been forgiven...and not only *forgiven* but *selected* by God to carry out a special purpose, well, it doesn't seem just. At least, not to me."

"I can understand that."

"Without even knowing it, I suppose I've simply been waiting for Saul to receive the justice he deserves," Tabitha confessed with a shake of her head. "And yet, it would seem the Lord had entirely different plans for Saul than I did."

"Our God is merciful, Tabitha," Adam reminded her, carefully watching her expression. "His desire is salvation for all men, even the worst of sinners."

"Well, *clearly*," Tabitha grumped. "Saul is a shining example in that respect."

"Isn't this what Stephanos would have wanted for Saul? His death was not in vain."

"In vain, no," Tabitha agreed. "But it still *happened*, Adam. And as miraculous as Saul's conversion is, it won't bring my husband back. Nor lessen the pain of his loss."

Adam simply waited, sensing her need to vent and to organize her thoughts.

"And yes," she continued, the frustration evident in her tone. "I should be *happy* that the man responsible for the death of my husband—not to mention, countless others—has seen the light. And yet…how can I simply *accept* the fact that Saul has been ushered into the Kingdom with open arms and awarded a special place in ministry, even after all that he has done?"

"These are tough questions," Adam agreed, one hand massaging his dimpled chin. "We all wrestle with them at some point in our lives."

"Perhaps it's possible to forgive someone, and yet still secretly harbor hopes that the offender will receive what he deserves."

"I think that's very possible," Adam nodded in agreement. "God is our vindicator, and it's only natural to hope that He will avenge the wrongs committed against us and those we love."

"And when He doesn't?" Tabitha asked him, her large eyes frank. "Then what?"

"Then we trust that God's mercy has triumphed over judgment for a very specific purpose," Adam responded steadily, his eyes never leaving hers. "Remember, prior to his conversion, Saul was simply a tool in the hands of the great deceiver. But now, Saul has seen the error of his ways. We must remember, Tabitha, that our battle isn't against visible flesh and blood. Ultimately, it was the enemy who took your husband, not Saul. And now his conversion has dealt Satan a cruel blow, one from which he may not recover. We must see beyond the obvious and the physical, into the heavenly realms. The battle for souls isn't over. On the contrary, it's just begun."

Surprised, Tabitha nodded slowly. She hadn't even considered the fact that God's justice had, indeed, prevailed. Just not in the way she had expected.

"Your husband played a crucial role in propagating salvation unto all mankind," Adam continued earnestly. "And now Stephanos' prayer has been answered. Now Saul will pick up the torch and carry on your husband's great work."

"Perhaps the problem isn't that I haven't forgiven Saul," Tabitha decided. "I believe that I *have* forgiven him. But perhaps I've failed to place his fate in God's hands. I always thought that the Lord would avenge my husband's death. But I can't imagine a greater legacy for my Stephanos than the conversion of our fiercest foe, possibly even resulting in the salvation of countless souls."

"I think you're on the right track there," Adam smiled, tweaking her shoulder in encouragement.

Cheeks warming at his touch, Tabitha clasped her hands in her lap, grateful for the opportunity to sort through her emotions. "Thanks for listening without judgment, Adam. I appreciate that."

"Anytime," he assured her, and Tabitha knew that he meant it.

"According to Mary's letter, Saul spent some time preaching in Damascus immediately following his conversion on the road," Tabitha mused, deep in thought. "But after that, he simply disappeared. Barnabas thinks he went to Arabia, but no one knows for sure. And no one has heard from him since."

"Perhaps he was eaten by a hungry camel along the way."

"Adam!"

"Just a wild guess."

"Wild, yes," Tabitha laughed, feeling better in the presence of the kind and lighthearted young man.

"But likely? No."

"So what are you thinking? Did he get spooked and head for the hills?"

"I suppose we'll find out soon enough," Tabitha said. "But I hope he isn't afraid to embrace his calling. That would be a shame."

"Based on what you've told me about him, I don't imagine Saul is afraid of anything."

"If he has any sense at all, he will be," Tabitha observed, her tone and expression enigmatic. "After all, now he's alienated himself from his peers and the entire academic and religious community. And as for the believers, they won't wish to get near him with a ten-foot pole after all the trauma he's inflicted upon us. At this point, he's made enemies of both sides."

"Sounds like a man whose days are numbered."

"Apart from God's protection," Tabitha said, "they surely are."

CHAPTER 5

Mary

Jerusalem

The hour was late. Too late for supper, but Mary had been far too involved in her business ledgers to retire any sooner.

Reclining staidly upon an upholstered settee in the smallest and most modest of the two triclinium-style banquet halls located in her home, Mary reached for the elegant goblet of fruit-infused water a servant had placed before her. Taking a thoughtful sip, she allowed her gaze to graze the sophisticated chamber with its gracefully gilded furniture, lavishly curtained windows, and brightly painted marble pillars. Though she employed some of the most highly skilled chefs in Jerusalem, the steaming spread upon the table was simple and unadorned, just as she preferred.

How long had it been since she had shared this table with her beloved husband Mark and their laughing, teasing son, dining together as a family? How she missed breaking bread with her own family, and what she wouldn't give to share that experience once more. She hadn't thought much about it then. But now, finding herself dining alone after a long and tiring day, she recalled those happy memories with a pang to her heart.

Typically, John Mark would have joined her at the table, but he was currently staying with his mentor, Simon Peter, visiting the former fisherman's boisterous relatives in Capernaum. Smiling to herself, Mary imagined that he was having a wonderful time. Her son was always eager for an adventure and accompanying the fiery apostle to Galilee certainly qualified.

"Dining alone tonight?"

Glancing up in astonishment, Mary set aside her goblet and rose to her feet, clasping her hands delightedly as a smiling young man donning lavish Greco-Roman attire emerged through the curtained entryway, entering the triclinium. "Luke! What a pleasant surprise!"

"I do hope so," Luke quipped with a wry smile, uncharacteristically devoid of the leather satchel he typically carried with him.

"This must be a social call," Mary teased, stretching out her arms in greeting. "Seeing as you have arrived without your medical supplies."

"Strictly a social visit, I assure you," Luke confirmed, tossing her a wink. "That is, unless you or a member of your household requires medical attention. But I must say, you look vibrant and healthy as ever, despite the rumors reaching Antioch regarding worsening persecution in Judea." Crossing the distance between them, he briefly took her hands in his, offering them a friendly squeeze before releasing them and stepping back to survey her with a fond smile.

"Please, join me." Gesturing toward one of the upholstered couches near the table, Mary revealed indulgently, "Much has transpired in recent weeks, and I believe you'll find the report rather fascinating."

"I always do," Luke attested wanly, accepting her gracious invitation and lowering himself onto the Roman-style couch which she had indicated. "My apologies, Mary. It would seem I have interrupted your supper."

"Nonsense," Mary quickly assured him, gracefully taking her place across the table. "I hadn't yet begun, and I am delighted by your unexpected arrival."

"Greetings, my lady and Doctor Luke." Rhoda entered at that moment, her brown eyes shining with excitement at the arrival of the beloved physician. "Shall I speak with the kitchen staff, presenting any special requests on behalf of your guest, my lady?"

"As always, you are so thoughtful, Rhoda," Mary warmly acknowledged the young maidservant, pleased. "You think of everything."

Beaming at her lady's praise, Rhoda patiently awaited further instruction from Mary, a serving tray tucked carefully beneath her slender arm.

"Now, now, you needn't make a fuss over me," Luke quickly interjected, waving aside Mary's generous intent. "I shall happily and gratefully partake of the fare your staff has already presented here."

"Nonsense," Mary rebutted stoutly. "You've journeyed a great distance. Far too great to partake of simple brown bread and steamed lentils."

"That sounds hardy enough to me," Luke grinned.

"Rhoda," Mary said with her usual air of graceful authority. "Please alert the kitchen staff as to our guest's arrival. And instruct them to prepare a meal worthy of the finest physician in the entire province."

"Yes, my lady," Rhoda nodded her agreement, quickly slipping away to perform her lady's bidding.

"You flatter me," Luke told Mary with an amused smile, only partially lounging on the lovely couch, one arm propped on the gracefully curved and upholstered backing. It was obvious he was accustomed to being interrupted and summoned in a great hurry, for he was always ready to depart at a moment's notice at the first sign of a medical emergency.

"But flattery hints at deception," Mary reminded him, an enigmatic smile touching her lips. "But I speak truth when I say I possess the highest regard for you, Luke."

"I'm honored, though I can't imagine why," Luke confessed with a small chuckle. "Thank you, Mary."

"You have always been kind to us, Luke. How could I harbor anything but the utmost respect for you?"

Rhoda must have acted quickly in alerting the kitchen staff, for several maidservants entered bearing refreshments to be enjoyed while a suitable meal was being prepared.

"So," Luke observed, accepting the full goblet a maidservant offered him with a gracious nod. "You mentioned having a fascinating report to divulge.

Believe me, I'm all ears."

Mary nodded, reaching for her own goblet and taking a thoughtful sip. "Do you remember hearing about Saul of Tarsus, the man responsible for spearheading the persecution against followers of the Way?"

"I think everyone has heard of him," Luke chuckled. "From what I've heard, he's quite the character. Should he ever decide to channel his determination toward something productive rather than destructive, he might actually accomplish something noteworthy."

"That may happen sooner than you think," Mary revealed, her gray eyes glowing. "Saul has experienced a miraculous change of heart. He's one of us now."

"What?" Luke declared in disbelief, his goblet clanking loudly as he replaced it on the table's polished surface. "You're serious?"

"I wouldn't jest about something like this."

"Amazing!"

"Now that Saul has undergone a drastic change of heart, there has been a distinct lull in the persecution against us. These last few weeks have ushered in a season of peace unlike anything the church has ever experienced," Mary explained, both her tone and her expression colored with thanksgiving. "For the first time since the martyrdom of our beloved Stephanos, followers of the Way have assembled for prayer and worship without fear of reprisal."

"I couldn't be happier for you, Mary," Luke said, and he clearly meant it. "You have faced brutal opposition far longer than anyone ought to be forced to endure."

"And yet, God has strengthened us through it."

"That's exactly what I would expect you to say," Luke said fondly. "Finding good in every trial and circumstance."

"Oftentimes, the Lord allows hardships to strengthen our character and draw us closer to Him. This has indeed been true in this instance."

"May I ask if you expect the peace to continue?" Luke asked her, his logical mind always several steps ahead of the present situation.

"It's unlikely," she confessed, her lips tipping ruefully. "Saul was but one of many enemies set against the Way. But presently, the Sanhedrin remains occupied with various endeavors and pursuits, including the appointment of a new high priest. Saul's absence has yet to be noticed. But once his leadership against the church becomes evident among the Sanhedrin, I imagine others will rise to take his place."

"Even so, we can hope and pray against that."

"Indeed, we can."

Their conversation was momentarily interrupted as maidservants bearing steaming trays of food entered the triclinium, smiling welcomingly as they arranged various dishes upon the table, careful to be sure every entrée was within easy reach.

"Mary, this truly wasn't necessary," Luke insisted as the maidservants hastened away after accomplishing their task.

"Oh, but it was," Mary smiled, motioning toward the liberal feast with a graceful hand. "You will always be welcome at our table, Luke."

After the blessing was pronounced over the feast, Luke appeared to relax a bit more on his couch, grateful for the sumptuous fare Mary had provided. "So I must ask," he grinned, breaking off a piece of flatbread and dipping it in a rich, creamy sauce. "What in the world brought about the conversion of a man as hardened and incorrigible as the infamous Saul of Tarsus?"

"He was stopped dead in his tracks on the road to Damascus," Mary indulged, selecting a glistening bunch of grapes from the tray of fresh fruit set before her.

"How so?"

"The Lord Jesus appeared to him just before reaching the city."

"Wait," Luke stopped her, nearly choking on his bread. "Jesus of Nazareth *appeared* to him?"

"In all His radiance, splendor, and majesty. Yes."

"Are you saying he saw a *vision* of this Jesus?" Luke expounded, puzzled.

"No, not a vision. He saw Jesus Christ Himself."

"Impossible!" Luke protested in disbelief. "Jesus of Nazareth was crucified on a Roman cross. Death is inevitable, in that instance. I've carefully perused every single record imaginable. No man has ever survived a crucifixion. Not one."

"I wouldn't disagree."

"But you're saying this Jesus presented Himself alive to Saul!"

"He did."

"I beg your pardon, Mary, but I must question your logic on this matter."

Chuckling good-naturedly, Mary set aside the grapes to lean forward on her couch, meeting the methodical doctor's gaze with an amused twinkle in her gray eyes. "You've known about followers of the Way long enough to know what we believe, Luke."

"You *still* believe this Jesus rose from the dead?"

"Our faith is built upon that glorious resurrection."

"But you do recognize that a resurrection is impossible?" Luke gently reasoned with her. "I respect you greatly, Mary. I do. But one simply *cannot* rise from the dead!"

"And how can you be so sure?"

"True, there have been myths and legends about such fantastical happenings, and even mistakes and misdiagnoses in the medical community," Luke elaborated, appearing troubled. "But we have no confirmed cases of a true resurrection. None. Not one."

"I find that most physicians aren't habited to chronicling the occurrence of miracles," Mary pointed out with an enigmatic smile. "And the resurrection of our Lord and Savior was entirely that—a miracle, indeed."

"It simply isn't feasible."

"And do you believe that I would lie to you?"

"Of course not," Luke assured her, his brown eyes softening in patient understanding. "You couldn't lie, Mary. You simply don't have it in you."

"Well, then?"

"But you could very well be deceived," Luke confessed a bit sheepishly. "And I don't blame you, Mary. Not for a moment. People have always longed for miracles, to believe the impossible. It's ingrained in our human nature."

"That alone should tell you something," Mary reminded him with a knowing smile.

"Well, we're all a bit prone to wishful thinking," Luke finally said, a wistful look in his kind eyes. "I myself rather fancy the idea of life everlasting and eternal bliss."

"Well, it's yours for the taking," Mary informed him with a knowing smile. "It is our Lord's desire that none perish, that all be saved."

"Even a skeptical Gentile doctor from Antioch?" Luke teased, taking another thoughtful bite of flatbread.

"God has already chosen you," Mary said with great conviction, generating a look of surprise from the humble physician. "You may be unaware now, but He will get your attention, Luke. Mark my words."

"I'm a practical man, Mary," Luke reminded her, wondering why her words struck a chord deep within his soul. Shifting a bit uncomfortably on his couch, Luke realized that the fire kindling in his heart was also a phenomenon beyond explanation, defying both logic and reasoning. "I simply cannot accept the resurrection of a dead man as fact. I have been trained to reach logical conclusions based on fact, not on theories or conjecture."

"And if, with your own eyes, you saw a dead person raised to life by the power of the Holy Spirit, then would you believe?"

Luke stared at her, aghast. "What an odd question to ask. Why, the likelihood of my ever experiencing such a thing is next to noth— "

"But would you?" Mary pressed, her eyes glowing with deepening intensity. "It's a simple and practical question, after all. And it deserves an answer."

"Well, yes. I suppose it does." Stroking his clean-shaven chin in avid amusement, Luke grinned, admiring the widow's spunk. "All right,

Mary. Should I witness the resurrection of a dead person by the might of this mysterious Holy Spirit in whom you believe—and with my own two eyes, no less—then yes, I suppose such power would be impossible to deny."

Mary leaned back on her couch with a wry smile, satisfied.

"But," Luke emphasized, shaking his index finger in protest, "that will *never* happen!"

"Well, I suppose we shall see," Mary responded with a graceful lift of one shoulder. Ignoring his look of complete and utter consternation, Mary gestured toward the elaborate feast on the table before him. "I suppose we should move on to lighter subjects as you resume your meal, good doctor. After all, I wouldn't want you having to treat yourself for indigestion."

With a good-natured chuckle, Luke nodded his agreement, relieved to dismiss the troublesome subject at hand.

At least, for now.

CHAPTER 6

Tabitha

Joppa

"Ahem, my lady? A word, please."

Pausing midway through the long corridor which she traveled, Tabitha quickly spun around to see Eli peeking his turbaned head around the corner.

"Hello, Eli," she smiled as he hurried toward her, his tablet and stylus in hand. Noting his somewhat frantic expression, she assumed he must have news to share.

"Well, I'm glad I found you, since you weren't in your office," Eli said a bit stiffly, subtly indicating that she had some nerve vacating the office library where she could have been more easily located.

"I was checking on a few new arrivals," Tabitha told him, smiling over the tall stack of neatly folded linens in her arms and ignoring his obvious chagrin. "We've had three new widows join us this week, and two of them have young children."

"I know all about the new arrivals."

"Well, of course you do, Eli," Tabitha chuckled, amused. Her overseer knew what transpired in every nook and cranny of the sprawling seaside estate. And Tabitha was convinced that nothing escaped his watchful scrutiny. "You know everything that goes on around here, and I appreciate your diligence."

Leaning in and glancing nervously around to ensure they wouldn't be overheard, Eli said under his breath, "You really shouldn't be doing that, you know."

"Doing what?" Tabitha asked him blankly.

"Waiting upon the residents like a common servant," Eli hissed, peeved. "You are no longer a maidservant, Miss Tabitha. As the lady of the estate, you must differentiate yourself from the household staff—"

"Oh, but I shall always be called to serve, Eli."

"You must demand respect if you wish to be respected!"

"I wish to be *obedient* to the Lord, first and foremost. And He has commanded us to *serve*."

"I was afraid you might say that."

"So, how can I help you, Eli?" Tabitha asked him patiently, indifferent toward his mounting aggravation.

"I've received word from Joram's silent partner—the investor from Greece. He's set sail and should arrive here in Joppa within two or three weeks' time," Eli informed her, receiving a wide-eyed stare from Tabitha. "Your expression is concerning, my lady. Surely you're not surprised? You knew this was coming!"

"I suppose I did," Tabitha conceded, her stomach tightening in the most unpleasant way. "I simply didn't expect him to arrive so soon."

"It is crucial that we be prepared to meet with him upon his arrival," Eli declared emphatically. "Your uncle believed this man to be capable of aiding us in the monumental task of running the business and estate. We must not frustrate him with needless delays."

"And we will be prepared," Tabitha promised, lightly touching his arm. "You needn't worry, Eli."

"*You* look quite worried for someone urging another not to worry!"

"I'm just a bit nervous, that's all," Tabitha quickly assured him, hoping to convince herself, as well. "I've never had business dealings with a man of this investor's caliber. But I've witnessed my lady in Jerusalem do so on numerous occasions. Hopefully, I've learned a thing or two from her."

At that moment, the sound of children's lithe and playful laughter met their ears, drifting through the air and floating down the hall like happily chiming bells.

Eli's expression sobered as he tucked his tablet beneath one arm, peeved. "I have a sneaking suspicion this investor isn't going to like what you've done with the place."

"Well," Tabitha shrugged, shifting the linens in

her arms and propping them against her hip. "That's simply a risk we're going to have to take."

"And if he refuses to offer his aid?"

"Then God will provide the help we need."

Shaking his head in perturbation, Eli didn't look convinced.

***

Rhoda

Jerusalem

It had been a trying day, to say the least. Typically, early summer in Jerusalem ushered in a glorious lull in the frenzied activities associated with the spring festival season, providing much-needed recovery time for masters and servants alike.

Not so this time. If anything, the pace had increased as the apostles doubled down on missionary efforts within the holy city, taking advantage of the unlikely peace initiated by Saul's conversion. Countless Judeans accepted Christ as Savior, eagerly joining ranks with the followers of the Way. And Mary's lavish Upper City villa fairly buzzed with activity as a result.

Today had proven particularly trying, in Rhoda's opinion. As new believers flooded Mary's home, the workload increased exponentially. Though Rhoda rejoiced at the presence of so many new believers, she'd been racing around like a mad thing the entire day, attempting to keep up with all the added chores. Unexpected guests had dropped by repeatedly throughout the day, requiring attendance, foot-washings, and refreshments. Doctor Luke had also paid the household a farewell visit before returning to his practice in Antioch. In addition to that, her lady was currently hosting an important business meeting in the banquet hall, which required careful attention to detail and the utmost diligence on the part of her wait staff.

It didn't help that a searing heat wave had swept across Jerusalem even earlier than expected, taking its toll on the entire city and souring the moods of its residents. The late afternoons were particularly unbearable. And this one was certainly no exception.

Feeling sticky and miserable, Rhoda used her cream-colored sleeve to swipe at the beads of sweat on her delicate forehead before bending to lift two heavy earthen pots filled to the brim with dirty water. Undoubtedly, the cloudy water had been utilized for foot-washing. With a heavy jar propped on each hip, Rhoda used her slender back to push open a creaky wooden door, slipping out into the blooming garden enclosed by high stone walls at the back of the estate.

Pausing before a magnificent bed of flowering plants, Rhoda set down one jar, carefully emptying the water from the first onto the lovely foliage sheltered by palms. In this heat, frequent watering would prove essential. And her lady preferred to recycle used water rather than waste fresh water on indoor or outdoor plants.

After emptying the first jar, Rhoda set it aside and proceeded to empty the second one. Despite her weariness, her movements remained graceful and carefully measured. She didn't wish to make a soppy mess of her lady's lovely garden.

Feeling sweaty and disheveled, she couldn't help but contemplate her chances of retiring early to bathe and freshen up. But she decided it was quite unlikely, given that her lady's business meeting would soon end, and the banquet hall would need to be tidied and tended to. The hour was growing late. Soon, the sun would begin its steady western descent.

Bending to retrieve the first urn she had placed on the ground, Rhoda was too absorbed in thought to detect the sound of eager footsteps traveling the stone path behind her.

"Long time, no see."

Oh, no. John Mark! Slowly straightening, Rhoda froze in place, heart pounding, clutching the empty jars like a lifeline. She didn't dare turn around. Writhing inwardly, she considered her ruddy cheeks, tousled hair, and creased, crumpled garments. Humiliated, she clenched her eyes shut, contemplating an escape plan.

No such luck. Hemmed in by impressive stone walls on all sides, she knew that she was trapped. She was going to have to face him!

Wishing she could disappear into thin air, Rhoda finally managed through her embarrassment, "Hello, John Mark."

"Perhaps it's simply my imagination, but you don't seem particularly thrilled to see me," the young man observed, his tone tinged with rueful good humor.

Groaning inwardly, Rhoda didn't dare confess the true state of her feelings. For the fact of the matter was that she had missed John Mark's easy smile and teasing gaze far more than she cared to admit—even to herself. The days had ticked by at an unbearably slow pace during the weeks of his absence. She'd found herself counting down the days since his departure more than once, mentally calculating when he would likely return.

So, yes, she was indeed thrilled by his homecoming. But she couldn't possibly explain that *this* certainly wasn't how she wished to present herself to him after several weeks apart!

"Well?" John Mark prodded, gently touching the back of her arm. "I thought you would be happy to see me. Was I wrong?"

Even as she gloried at his touch, Rhoda couldn't help but pray he didn't feel the damp sweat seeping through her garment!

Gently turning her around to face him, John Mark searched her delicate features, smiling fondly at the sight of her.

"I am happy to see you," she acknowledged shyly, self-consciously lowering her gaze. "It's just that, well..."

"What?" John Mark teased, sensing that something was amiss but now convinced that she had, indeed, missed him in his absence.

"I must apologize for my untidy appearance, John Mark," she finally confessed, her cheeks blossoming with color. "It's been a very busy day, and—"

"Is that all that's bothering you?" John Mark asked her. She couldn't possibly understand how lovely she looked with her large brown eyes, flushed cheeks, and shy smile—even at the end of an exhausting workday. "You always look wonderful to me."

Rhoda lifted her gaze then, astounded by his

candor.

Realizing that perhaps he had spoken a bit too freely, John Mark quickly changed the subject. "I've just arrived with Simon Peter. Tobias informed us that Mother is still barricaded in the triclinium with stuffy old business partners."

"Her meeting should adjourn any moment now."

"Excellent," John Mark grinned, reaching out to take the heavy earthenware from Rhoda's arms. "In the meantime, allow me to assist you."

"Oh no, my lord," Rhoda quickly insisted, mortified. "You mustn't assume my responsibilities. You have fare more important matters to—"

"What did I say about calling me that?" John Mark laughed, amused by her reaction. "I'm not *my lord* to you, Rhoda. I'm simply your friend."

Rhoda studied him, still hesitant.

"Besides, I do have ulterior motives," he grinned, tossing her a playful wink. "I'm famished from hours on the dusty road today. Think you can assist me in finding something to eat, since Mother's kitchen staff is currently occupied serving her guests?"

Heart fluttering nervously in her chest, Rhoda rewarded him with another shy smile. "I suppose that can be arranged."

CHAPTER 7

Tabitha

Joppa

"My lady! My lady!" Bursting through the curtained entrance of the quiet office library, Eli's eyes came to rest upon Tabitha seated behind the desk. Studying an open ledger, she appeared to be busy tracing a long line of numerical figures with an elegant stylus.

"Eli," Tabitha acknowledged him. Glancing up in surprise, a hint of concern touched her attractive features. "Is everything all right?"

"No!" Eli gasped, pausing at the entrance to catch his breath. "I mean, yes! Well, I do hope so."

Lifting a brow in question, Tabitha simply waited, allowing her panting overseer a moment to compose himself.

"A ship from Greece has docked at port, just this morning," Eli finally explained, his expression conveying his panic.

Tabitha studied him blankly, clearly wondering

what all the fuss was about.

"From *Greece*!" Eli repeated forcefully, staring at her as if she'd lost her mind. "Don't you see?"

"I see you're quite excited about this particular ship," Tabitha replied slowly. "But this is *Joppa*, Eli. Ships arrive at port every single day. Is there something special about this one?"

"Oh, I'd say there is," Eli responded, an edge of sarcasm sharpening his tone. "Considering the fact that it's highly likely Joram's silent partner is aboard."

"What?" Tabitha gasped, jumping out of her chair. "So soon?"

"I've deployed messengers each morning to check in at the docks. Apparently, ships are making good time right now."

"Clearly," Tabitha murmured, casting a nervous glance toward the paperwork scattered across her desk.

"Not to mention the fact that it's been nearly two weeks since we received word that the investor had set sail," Eli pointed out. "Undoubtedly, the letter arrived here in Joppa quite a bit after his departure."

"Are we ready for this, Eli?"

"As ready as we'll ever be, I suppose," Eli grumped, his tone of voice far from encouraging.

"We have compiled every last scrap of paperwork, every legal document, and every imaginable ledger—even ledgers decades old—pertaining to the business and the estate to present to this investor, Eli," Tabitha said, attempting to convince herself as well as her nervy overseer. "I'm not sure we could be any more prepared than we already are."

"Oh, one can *always* be more prepared."

"Then what do you suggest we do?" she asked him, trying to mask her annoyance. Surely, Eli could have brought this up before the man's trading vessel docked at port!

"I suspect the man will make an offer on the business and estate, my lady."

"An offer?" Tabitha repeated weakly, caught off guard. "He wants to buy the Refuge?"

"In his opinion, this estate is no house of refuge. It's a moneymaker, pure and simple."

"I am not operating this widows' and orphans' refuge as a moneymaker!"

"And he isn't going to like that."

"Frankly, I don't particularly care what he likes," Tabitha shot back, crossing her arms in disgust. "This is what God has called me to do, Eli. I cannot sell my uncle's estate to a greedy investor who will undoubtedly destroy everything we've built for the widows and orphans here."

"Remember, you don't want to upset him. You are going to need his help!"

"I don't need any help from him," Tabitha huffed, feeling anxious and frustrated. "Perhaps I should simply cancel our appointment. Yes, perhaps this was a mistake. It's obvious he and I won't see eye to eye on—"

"My lady," Eli cut in, exasperated. "One does not simply *cancel an appointment* with a man of his status and importance. He is a powerful figure in Greece, one to be reckoned with, and quite dominant in the shipping industry—the industry upon which our livelihood depends, might I remind you."

"I know that, Eli."

"Trust me when I say it would be a mistake of the

utmost proportions to make this man an enemy."

"Then I shall ask again—what do you suggest we do?"

Surprisingly, Eli stopped to consider her pointed question.

Relaxing slightly, Tabitha waited, willing to accept whatever feedback the overseer had to offer her.

"The way you present yourself to this man is highly important, not to be underestimated," Eli finally decided, looking her over as a parent might inspect a child before taking them somewhere important, like the synagogue. "Men like this investor are trained to detect weakness and uncertainty a mile away."

Tabitha nodded slowly, wishing she'd had more experience relating to businessmen of the investor's caliber. Her former mistress, Mary, conducted herself flawlessly in such instances, fairly radiating with confidence and authority. Closing her eyes, Tabitha tried to remember everything she had learned during the years she had served her lady in business settings.

"My suggestion to you is this," Eli continued, his speech careful and intentional. "Don't walk into this meeting without knowing exactly what you want out of it, exactly how much you are willing to compromise, and exactly how you must stand your ground."

Nodding again, Tabitha assumed that Mary would have offered her the same counsel. She was a brilliant businesswoman, typically several steps ahead of everyone else in the room. She wouldn't dare step into a meeting without knowing the desired end.

"You are a strong and personable young woman," Eli said, and the unexpected compliment wasn't lost on Tabitha. "I imagine you'll do well, my lady."

"Thank you, Eli," Tabitha replied meaningfully.

"Though it's against my nature to state this, I suppose we must try not to worry," Eli informed her, shifting his tablet beneath his arm so he could adjust his impressive-looking turban. "For many years, this investor has greatly profited by partnering with Joram. It is certainly in his best interest to cooperate with his niece now."

"Let's hope he sees it that way."

"I suppose we'd best prepare to meet him at port," Eli sighed. "Knowing his ego, I highly doubt he would approve of being welcomed by a common servant."

"I'll check with Tirzah and make sure she can stay with Laurel in my absence," Tabitha informed him, preparing to take her leave. "Have I time to change and freshen up, Eli?"

"Please do, my lady."

Tabitha stared at him, lifting a questioning brow.

"Oh, I meant no disrespect, my lady!" Eli quickly stammered, embarrassed. "It's just that, well, as mentioned before, the way you present yourself is vastly important, and currently, you are wearing a servant's attire—"

"No, no, it's all right, Eli," Tabitha chuckled, rolling her eyes in amusement. "Say no more. I understand."

"One last thing," Eli quickly amended, surveying his writing tablet with a practiced air. "As you converse with Joram's silent partner, rest assured that I will be listening to every word and taking fastidious notes. We will want to review the information privately before drawing up any paperwork or signing any documents. So don't agree to anything until—"

"Oh, yes," Tabitha interjected knowingly. "Not until I've had the chance to pray about it."

"Actually, I was going to say, not until we've had the opportunity to discuss it privately," Eli responded blankly, receiving a rueful smile from his young mistress.

"But, yes," he affirmed at the look his lady gave him. "I imagine a bit of prayer couldn't hurt."

CHAPTER 8

Tabitha

Joppa

The Greek shipping vessel docked at port was a gargantuan breed fashioned after the Roman merchant ships with a smooth, sleek body, majestic sails, and a sharp stern capable of slicing through the water with surprising speed.

Drawing nervously alongside Eli, Tabitha never ceased to be amazed by the chaos at port. Overhead, gulls soared majestically in the deep blue sky, releasing gusty, plaintive cries and observing the cacophony below as half-clad sailors scurried over the ship decks, scrambling up swaying rope ladders and securing the billowing sails.

Slaves and servants alike scampered up and down the gangplanks spanning the gaps between massive ships and the docks below, their bodies glistening with sweat as they unloaded heavy cargo, while wealthy travelers descended with a cosmopolitan air, casting disdainful glances toward the slaves toting their cumbersome trunks and personal belongings.

Observing the frenzied commotion with wide hazel-green eyes while at least a dozen garbled languages met her ears, Tabitha reached for her graceful head covering as gusty sea breezes whipped at her hair and shawl. She couldn't possibly begin to count the number of nationalities represented here, as coveted wares from all over the world arrived via foreign merchant ships.

"You're sure this is the one, Eli?" Tabitha asked, her tone tinged with nervousness as she awaited the imminent appearance of her potential business partner.

"Well, this *is* the only ship from Greece, isn't it?" he reminded her a bit curtly.

"And how will we recognize Joram's investor when he disembarks?"

"Though it's been many years since your uncle met with him, I still remember him well," Eli said, and it didn't sound like a compliment. "He was a formidable businessman, not easily forgotten. I imagine I will recognize him when I see him."

Nodding slowly, Tabitha bit her lower lip, attempting to compose herself. She knew she mustn't come across as a nervous, indecisive woman. No, Joram's business partner would expect a seasoned lady of business, one who knew exactly what she was about. Carefully adjusting the attractive linen sash belted around her slender waist, Tabitha inspected her own apparel, hoping she had chosen her garments wisely. Since she hadn't more than two garments to her name, she was incredibly grateful she had taken the time to mend and refurbish several of the lovely gowns she'd found hanging in her Aunt Pennie's wardrobe. Had she not done so, she would have possessed absolutely nothing fitting to wear to this appointment. Though the exquisite emerald gown fit her like a glove and the accompanying gold-embroidered head covering greatly complimented her sandy-colored hair and large hazel-green eyes, she would have far preferred her own simple tunic and work apron. She felt rather like an imposter, sporting the elegant attire belonging to a wealthy lady of leisure.

Even so, Eli had insisted she dress for the occasion. Further argument would have only proven futile.

Straightening to her full height—which she couldn't help but wish was just a bit more impressive—Tabitha lifted her chin firmly and uttered a silent prayer for guidance and wisdom. She would not cower in the presence of the powerful man soon to meet her. She would place her fate in God's hands.

That's where it belonged, anyway.

"I suppose I should have long since asked by what name to address this man we are about to meet," Tabitha suddenly realized, wondering how something so important could have slipped her mind. Up to this point, Eli had merely referred to Joram's silent partner as *the investor* in a rather ominous tone.

"There, my lady," Eli breathed, lightly touching her wrist. "That's him now, descending the gangplank with his manservant. His name is—"

"Amal!" Tabitha gasped, her hand flying to her throat in absolute shock.

"Why, yes," Eli affirmed, casting her a sideways glance in puzzlement. "How ever did you know that?"

Pulse pounding loudly in her own ears, Tabitha's stunned gaze swept the lengthy gangplank as streams of weary and impatient humanity trickled forth from the great ship. Battling waves of emotion far more turbulent than the foamy turquoise waters battering the ancient wooden docks, Tabitha's wide eyes never left the stern but familiar face of a man she'd thought she would never see again.

"I know because that man is a relation of mine—my father-in-law," Tabitha breathed, steeling herself against the opposition she knew was coming. "The father of my beloved Stephanos."

***

Mary

Jerusalem

Mary stood upon the graceful balcony overlooking the sprawling stone court below, watching grimly as silly girls attempted to snag her seventeen-year-old son's attention. The group of young people had clustered around the monumental stone fountain gracing the center of the outer court, laughing and talking easily after the evening prayer service. While the young men appeared deeply immersed in their own good-natured ribbing, the young women seemed single-mindedly determined to capture the attention of the handsome and jovial John Mark.

Arching a dark, well-shaped brow, Mary attempted to curb her annoyance as the girls became increasingly obvious in their attempts to outdo each other and gain the bulk of her son's attention, their shrill voices and high-pitched giggles grating on her nerves.

"Ah, to be young and reckless again."

Mouth tipping in amusement, Mary acknowledged her older brother with a wry smile as he joined her on the balcony. "Hello, Barnabas."

"Greetings, dear sister."

"To be young again may indeed possess some merit," she mused, her consuming gaze lingering upon John Mark and his friends still gathered around the splashing fountain below. "But to be reckless? Heaven forbid."

"I knew you'd appreciate my comment," Barnabas teased, tweaking his sister's arm.

"You have always harbored a thirst for adventure, Barnabas," Mary continued. "But you were never reckless. Thank God for that."

"I sense the same thirst for adventure in your young charge," Barnabas observed, carefully gauging his sister's reaction.

"I blame you for that, you know," Mary candidly informed him, glancing at him sideways. "John Mark has always adored you."

"Need I remind you that your own thirst for travel and adventure rivals my own?"

"I've scarcely set foot from Jerusalem since the founding of the church here."

"Ah, yes. But the desire undoubtedly still stirs in your veins."

"Occasionally," Mary confessed with a wistful sigh. "But this is where I belong now, unless the Lord sees fit to place me elsewhere."

A particularly loud burst of giggles from the outer court below drew the brother and sister's attention from the course of their present conversation. Stealing a glance at a somewhat perturbed Mary, Barnabas hid a knowing smile.

"It would seem your son has quite the little flock of admirers," he grinned.

"I wish I could say I was pleased."

"You do realize the boy is nearly grown?" Barnabas pointed out. "You can't avoid arranging his betrothal forever, Mary."

"I'm aware," Mary responded resignedly.

"You are not one to procrastinate," Barnabas observed, watching her closely. "You tackle issues head-on with the force of a battering ram."

"And?" Mary prodded, lifting a delicate brow.

"This tells me that something quite serious must be keeping you from making the proper arrangements for a betrothal."

"Indeed, there is," Mary nodded, mentally reviewing the girls she knew to be around John Mark's age. "How can I arrange a suitable marriage for my son, when a suitable girl cannot be found?"

"Surely of all the young women in Jerusalem, at least one of them would make a worthy wife for your son."

"I've yet to discover a smart match for him. And it isn't for lack of trying, Barnabas."

"Forgive me, Mary, but perhaps your standards are simply too high."

"I want the very best for John Mark, as does the Lord," Mary shot back a bit more tersely than she intended.

"Well, I certainly wouldn't argue that point."

"Though it pains me to say it, even among the believers, young women of marrying age tend to be silly and shallow. They are far too consumed with trivial matters to bother with the important things in life. And I want more than that for John Mark."

"I needn't ask if you've prayed about this, Mary. I know you have."

"Without ceasing."

"Then God will provide," Barnabas assured her, resting sturdy hands upon the balcony's railing, his light-brown eyes panning Jerusalem's golden skyline beyond the sturdy walls of the outer court. "The Lord knows the right girl, and He shall bring her to our attention at the proper time."

"I've decided to have a conversation with John Mark," Mary informed her brother after a thoughtful pause. "I'd like to speak with him and determine the kind of girl he's interested in marrying."

"Are you supposing he has someone in mind?"

"I've closely observed his interactions with all the believing young ladies who attend services here with their families—"

"I have no doubt you have," Barnabas chuckled, receiving a look of correction from his sister.

"And yet, he seems entirely unimpressed by any of them."

"Sounds like his mother," Barnabas quipped, tossing her a playful wink.

"Well, it's certainly not for lack of their interest in him," Mary sighed, shaking her head. "If only I had the ability to see into the human heart, to recognize the deep and hidden motives within. Then I would know if any of these girls were interested in my son for the right reasons."

"And not simply because he's the best-looking young fellow in town?" Barnabas teased.

"The fact that he shall inherit his father's entire estate certainly doesn't help matters, either," she added, annoyed by her own skepticism.

"I suppose good looks and financial means may not always play in one's favor in a situation like this," Barnabas chuckled.

"Not when you wish to know if a young woman has pure motives," Mary sighed in resignation. "John Mark has grown immensely this last year, pursuing his walk with Christ and immersing himself in his studies. He needs a wife who will support him in his calling, not distract him from it. And a girl like that is difficult to find."

"I've noticed John Mark's commitment to attending prayer services and church meetings, his study of Scripture, and his faithfulness in learning the ropes of the family business," Barnabas nodded, proud of the boy. "He seems to be flourishing under the mentorship of Simon Peter."

"John Mark adores him like a father. And Peter loves him as a son."

"It seems to me," Barnabas divulged, turning to meet his sister's troubled gaze, "that the most important matters have been settled. John Mark loves the Lord and has committed his life to serving Him. He is committed to his church, his family, and his calling. Now, we must simply wait for God to arrange the remaining details."

"You make it sound so simple," Mary sighed with a knowing smile. "And yet, I know your words to be true."

"Truer words were never spoken," Barnabas reminded her, turning and offering her his arm.

Accepting her brother's proffered arm, Mary smiled wanly and followed his lead.

CHAPTER 9

Tabitha

Joppa

"Your *father-in-law*!" Eli hissed, fluttering about the triclinium-style banquet hall like an agitated bird. "Amal ben Stephanas, master of the shipping trade in Greece, is your *father-in-law*!"

"Yes, Eli," Tabitha sighed wearily, watching as a flurry of servants hastened to ready the banquet table for the ensuing feast which would be hosted that evening in Amal's honor.

"First, upon your arrival here in Joppa, I learn you are the niece of Joram! And now, I discover that you are the daughter-in-law of the infamous Amal!"

Resisting impatience, Tabitha simply crossed her arms, awaiting his final remarks.

"Are you related to every major shipping tycoon in the empire?" Eli demanded, his agitation evident upon his face.

"No, Eli," Tabitha responded, nodding her assurance toward the servants as they expertly arranged items on the banquet table.

"Any other surprises I should know about?" Eli demanded tersely, appearing even more agitated as he adjusted his large, colorful turban.

"Not that I'm aware of," Tabitha informed him, mentally reviewing all that had transpired at the docks less than an hour ago.

It hadn't gone well. Not at all.

To her great surprise, Amal had recognized her instantly after disembarking from the ship.

And he had *not* been happy to see her.

"You!" he'd nearly bellowed the moment he had reached the docks. "What are you doing here?"

"Greetings, Master Amal," Eli had declared, bowing excessively in his overwhelming nervousness. "May the Lady Tabitha and I extend our warmest greetings to—"

"The *Lady* Tabitha?" Amal had boomed incredulously, drawing the attention of half the merchants and shoppers located near the docks, while his faithful manservant, Dorian, stared unblinkingly ahead, attempting to mask his shock.

Lifting her gaze to meet his head-on, Tabitha had merely smiled, thanking God for the unexpected calm she'd experienced in the face of Amal's blatant animosity. After recovering from her initial shock, of course.

"It is my utmost pleasure to meet with you today, Master Amal," Tabitha had somehow smiled graciously, artfully overlooking his disgust.

"I was informed I would be meeting with Joram's niece," Amal had informed her coldly, his eyes narrowing in disdain. "And I demand to speak with her at once!"

"This is she," Tabitha had assured him, her eyes twinkling in amusement. "At your service, my lord."

Amal's round eyes had nearly fallen out of his head at her shocking disclosure. "*You're* Joram's niece!"

"In the flesh."

"Preposterous!"

Tabitha had only smiled, amused by his reaction.

"And how, may I ask, did you manage to ascend from the rank of a destitute and widowed pauper to a respectable woman of means?" Amal had sneered, clearly unsettled by her unruffled sense of calm.

Bravely, Eli had attempted to convince the obstinate businessman of Tabitha's legitimate relation to her deceased uncle and her subsequent inheritance of his estate. Amal had loudly and blatantly trumped his disbelief, garnering the attention of the people clustered nearby. By some miracle, Eli had somehow convinced him that Tabitha was indeed Joram's niece, the heiress of his entire business and estate.

It had only gone downhill from there.

And now, Tabitha was to host a banquet in Amal's honor, welcoming him to Joppa! She certainly wasn't looking forward to dining with him, even if the conversation remained centered around preliminary matters of business. She knew that Amal would prove obstinate and difficult to work with.

With a wry half-smile, Tabitha realized she shouldn't be surprised that her uncle had partnered with Amal. The two greedy shipping tycoons were like two peas in a pod.

Standing in the elegant triclinium and overseeing the elaborate preparations for the feast which would soon ensue, Tabitha released a wistful sigh, her stomach churning in the most unpleasant way. It had been the shock of a lifetime, discovering that her uncle's mysterious, silent partner was, in fact, the father of her departed husband.

To make matters worse, she had been completely unprepared for the unexpected wave of emotion battering her like a relentless tidal wave the moment she had come face to face with Amal. Her husband's grave was still fresh the last time she had laid eyes upon the man, and the sight of him now sent daggers into her heart. Even more so, the sight of Amal's faithful manservant, Dorian—now a fellow believer—who had greatly encouraged Tabitha during her time of despair. The stoic but kind servant had tutored her husband when he was but a child, and Stephanos had loved him deeply.

It had taken everything in her power to remain calm and professional at the sight of faithful Dorian standing at Amal's elbow on the pier, for she had longed to throw her arms around his neck and weep with both joy and sadness. Somehow, she'd held it together. And Dorian, bless his serious heart, hadn't missed a beat. He'd remained steadfast and stoic as ever, gazing unblinkingly ahead as servants were trained to do.

Tabitha seriously doubted that Amal was aware of her ongoing correspondence with his trusted manservant. They had written to each other until the time she left Jerusalem, with Dorian humbly serving as the middleman between Tabitha and Daphne. Since leaving Jerusalem, they'd lost touch, somehow. She'd often wondered if her letter explaining her move to Joppa had gotten lost enroute, never reaching Athens. Regardless of the circumstances, she knew she must not betray their carefully concealed secret, for it could cost Dorian a great deal—possibly even his livelihood.

Amal was not a kind nor compassionate man. She had visited him and his wife, Daphne, shortly after her husband's martyrdom. Amal hadn't spared an ounce of sympathy, but rather hurled insults and accusations, eventually demanding that she leave.

Placing a hand over her heart, Tabitha squeezed her fingers into a tight fist, wondering if the pain would ever cease. Haunting dreams of Stephanos were bad enough. But to have to face her dead husband's household, to host them indefinitely in her own home, was enough to rend her heart in two.

A bit snidely, Tabitha noted that Amal was more than happy to lodge with her when she had an entire seaside mansion at her disposal! When he and Daphne had visited her and Stephanos in Jerusalem, he had obstinately refused their hospitality, making it abundantly clear that their Lower City "hovel" was far beneath him. Instead, he had arranged to rent a plush Upper City mansion during his stay.

Cheeks burning with indignation, Tabitha could still recall his scathing insults.

Steeling herself against the resentment now rearing its ugly head, Tabitha committed her case to the Lord. Though every ounce of her being balked at the thought of partnering with the man who had mocked and ridiculed the love of her life and welcoming him into her home, she recognized that surely God's hand must be in this.

What were the odds of encountering Amal again, apart from the will of God? Perhaps this was the opportunity her beloved Stephanos had longed for, prayed for, unto his dying breath.

All right, Lord, Tabitha prayed, relinquishing her frustration, resentment, and concerns to God. *You've brought this stubborn man into my life again. So, I will thank You for yet another opportunity to reach him with Your truth.*

CHAPTER 10

Mary

Jerusalem

Mary wasn't looking forward to this conversation.

Pausing just outside the combination office library where her son busily apprenticed under Tobias' knowledgeable tutelage, Mary placed a steadying hand on one brightly painted marble pillar, deep in thought.

What mother truly desired to broach the subject of betrothal and marriage with her child? Was there a mother in all the universe who actually enjoyed the thought of urging her only son to consider taking a wife? Once John Mark took a bride of his own and became a married man, his time would be consumed with his new wife. And once children came along, his attention would be even further divided. The tender dynamics of the relationship between mother and son would undoubtedly change.

As it should, Mary sadly reminded herself. After

all, the Scriptures were inexplicably clear: *Therefore a man shall leave his father and mother and be joined to his wife, and they shall become one flesh.*

Mary had absolutely no desire to become the meddlesome mother-in-law who dominated her son's time, attention, and affection. No, when the time came for John Mark to take a wife, she would do everything in her power to bless the marriage and encourage growth—not division—in the relationship.

Even so, she knew it wouldn't be easy.

Squaring her shoulders in deep resolve, Mary slipped past the rows of painted pillars and entered the bibliotheca, her gray eyes adjusting to the dimly lit atmosphere as low-hanging lamps smoldered somberly in neatly suspended rows, vaguely illuminating the austere workspace.

Heart constricting just a bit, Mary's gaze landed upon her handsome son, seated behind the massive desk stationed before the shelves harboring hundreds of neatly organized scrolls and ledgers. An oil lamp burned at the corner of the great desk, lighting the parchment page he appeared to be inspecting with a gilded stylus in hand.

Detecting his mother's graceful footfalls, John Mark glanced up from the document, his brown eyes teasing as he met her gaze. "Well, well, Mother. What a pleasant surprise."

"Greetings, John Mark," Mary smiled, her heart aching just a bit as she closed the distance between them. Taking a seat in the upholstered chair closest to the desk, she braced herself for the discussion at hand.

"Have you come to rain praises upon my worthy

head regarding my matchless abilities and unrivaled work ethic?"

"I certainly haven't come to commend you for your humility," Mary teased him, always ready to give back as much as her mischievous son dished out.

"Fair enough," he responded good naturedly, setting aside his stylus. "Then to what do I owe the pleasure?"

"There's something I wish to discuss with you. It's rather important."

Sensing the seriousness of his mother's tone, John Mark folded his hands on the desk and leaned forward in his chair, listening intently.

***

Rhoda

Balancing a stack of heavy ledgers in slender arms, Rhoda timidly approached the bibliotheca. Her duties seldom brought her to this distinguished chamber, but today, Tobias had requested that she deliver several ledgers to her lady's desk while he oversaw other matters.

Heart fluttering in her chest, Rhoda wondered if she would stumble upon her young master, hard at work behind his mother's stately desk.

Pausing at the border of the inner court at the threshold of the quiet office, Rhoda drew a steadying breath before entering. Part of her exulted at the prospect of encountering her young master at work, even as the other part of her hoped he wouldn't be there. What a strange swirl of emotions John Mark stirred in her! It was as if the mere sight of him turned her tongue to lead in her mouth when she most desperately longed to greet him, to converse with him, to hear him laugh.

Cheeks warming in embarrassment, Rhoda quickly dismissed such thoughts, focusing instead on the task at hand. Treading softly, Rhoda slipped into the dim bibliotheca, her senses filling with the heady scent of fresh ink, parchment scrolls, and the smoke from burning lamps. Passing the first row of towering marble pillars, she paused as the sound of muffled voices met her ears, floating gently upon the air.

Apparently, her master wasn't alone.

"I wish to discuss the matter of your betrothal, John Mark."

His betrothal! Heart pounding furiously in her chest, Rhoda froze, unable to move, scarcely able to breathe.

Recognizing the woman's voice as belonging to her mistress, Rhoda suddenly realized that Mary must have sought out John Mark to discuss a serious matter.

His betrothal, she thought again, heart constricting. Had Mary arranged a marriage for her son? With whom? And how soon would it happen?

Though Rhoda knew she should turn promptly on her heels and exit the quiet chamber, fear had nailed her sandaled feet in place. Heart breaking, she realized she was about to lose him—the one her heart had loved from the very first moment he'd flashed her that boyish smile.

Slowly, painstakingly, Rhoda placed the ledgers on a nearby stand. Quaking inside, she somehow managed to turn and flee the scene in silence, woodenly placing one sandaled foot in front of the other.

Stepping out into the inner court, she braced herself against the blinding light of the late afternoon sun slanting through the colorful drapes and canopies of the stone courtyard. Placing a trembling hand over her heart, she paused long enough to gather her wits and regain her composure.

John Mark was betrothed. Soon, he would marry a girl and begin a life with her.

Will he leave us to marry his bride? Rhoda wondered, blinking back warm tears of disappointment. *Or will he bring her here to reside with him at his mother's estate?*

As painful as it was to consider, she hoped John Mark would leave. She simply couldn't bear the thought of watching him fall in love with someone else.

Heartbroken, Rhoda slipped past the inner court, tears gliding down her cheeks.

***

Mary

"My betrothal, Mother?" Leaning back in his chair, John Mark crossed his arms behind his neck, arching a brow in amusement. "I wasn't even aware of the fact that I was seeing someone."

"Don't be silly," Mary chided him, equally amused by his antics. "You won't be *seeing anyone* until a betrothal is officiated, and you know it. We believers don't casually *try out* various romantic partners, as the Romans are prone to do."

"You needn't worry, Mother," John Mark grinned, pleased he'd elicited a reaction from the typically composed woman. "I haven't any interest in trying anyone out."

"No?" Mary asked him, a slender brow lifting in question.

"As you're all too aware, I wasted far too much time chafing against my lessons the last few years," John Mark confessed, his lips tipping wanly. "Now, I'm having to make up for lost time learning the ropes of the family business, which I intend to run in a way that would've made Father proud."

"I have no doubt that you will, John Mark," Mary responded, her voice catching just a bit at his earnestness.

"That being said, I'm in no position to take a wife anytime soon," John Mark stated as calmly as if they'd merely been discussing the weather.

"Perhaps not," Mary nodded, willing to hear him out. "But a betrothal certainly isn't out of the question, even if you aren't ready to take a bride immediately. Depending on the terms and conditions of the arrangement, a marriage may not follow for over a year after the betrothal is officiated—possibly even longer."

Her son's only response was a wry smile.

"Have you a particular girl in mind for your future, John Mark?" she asked him, bracing herself for his response. After all, it was possible he'd noticed someone she had overlooked. Unlikely, but possible. Or worse, he may have taken an interest in someone of whom she didn't approve.

"Actually, yes," John Mark responded breezily, taking her aback. "There is."

"There is?" Mary repeated, taken aback.

"Indeed."

"Well?" she asked him, completely puzzled. "Who is it?"

"You mean you don't know?" he grinned.

"Are you merely poking fun at your mother's expense, John Mark? This is a serious subject."

"On the contrary, Mother," he assured her, his brown eyes growing uncharacteristically sober. "I've never been more serious in my entire life."

"Well, then?" she demanded, leaning forward in her chair. Checking her own eagerness, she forced herself to reclaim her graceful posture, lightly folding her hands in her lap. "Who is it?"

"It's Rhoda."

"Rhoda?" Mary asked him blankly, blinking in shock. "*Our* Rhoda?"

"Yes, our Rhoda," John Mark laughed, tickled by his mother's reaction. "Is there any other?"

Shaking her head in amazement, Mary wondered at her son's certainty. "But... are you sure?"

"Surer than I've ever been."

Nodding slowly, Mary attempted to process her son's shocking disclosure. She certainly wasn't against the idea. She was simply...stunned. Rhoda had been part of their family for years, serving ever quietly, ever faithfully, always in the background, more than happy being behind the scenes rather than center stage.

In fact, the girl was the complete opposite of what Mary had expected her son to fall for!

"You object?" John Mark asked her, closely watching her expression.

"No," Mary quickly assured him, meeting his

gaze with clear gray eyes. "On the contrary, I applaud your decision."

"But?"

"Actually, I have no objections," Mary told him, surprising even herself. "None whatsoever. Frankly, I'm wondering why I didn't consider it before now."

John Mark flashed his boyish smile, pleased.

"May I ask what it is about Rhoda that has captured your attention?" Mary finally asked him, wondering at the strange swirl of emotions in her heart. This conversation certainly hadn't gone as she'd expected!

"Rhoda has always desired my best, Mother," John Mark responded without missing a beat. "Even when I strayed and nearly forsook my faith, she stood firmly beside me, praying for me constantly. She never gave up on me."

Mary nodded, both pleased and satisfied that her dashing young son had noticed the pretty young maidservant for the right reasons. "We shall earnestly seek the Lord regarding this matter," Mary promised him, surprised to find herself blinking back tears. "But I am proud of you, John Mark—proud that you've sought a godly woman to be your mate."

"I can't imagine being with anyone else," John Mark confided, his boyish heart upon his sleeve.

"Then, unless the Lord intervenes, I shall make the proper arrangements for an official betrothal." Heart aching just a bit, Mary rose gracefully from her chair, offering her son a reassuring smile.

Rising as well, John Mark came around the desk, arms outstretched. Touched, Mary went into his arms, wondering when and how her son had managed to outgrow her. But a short time ago, she had cradled him in her own loving arms.

"Thank you, Mother."

Moments later, as Mary stole past the tall pillars upholding the somber chamber, she couldn't help but marvel at all that God had wrought over the years. Quietly. Unassumingly. And she, completely unaware as He had crafted the events of their lives, shaping both tragedy and triumph into something beautiful.

All those years ago, she couldn't have possibly known that when God called her to rescue a pale, skinny, and frightened little Cypriot girl from ruthless slavers, that she was inadvertently securing a worthy wife for her son, as well!

Well, Mary decided, pausing with one hand placed thoughtfully upon the final pillar framing the entrance, *I suppose it's a good thing it matters not what others think of me. Won't the locals talk when they discover that the son of the wealthiest woman in Judea has taken an orphaned Gentile serving girl to wife!*

CHAPTER 11

Tabitha

Joppa

The banquet hall appeared as something from a storybook, with tall bronze lamps burning festively and casting a cheerful glow upon the steaming feast spread upon the polished, triclinium-style table. Maidservants had strung lovely garlands of fresh flowers upon the ornately frescoed walls, the colorful blossoms both festive and aromatic. Servants bustled to and fro, slipping in and out of the swinging door adjoining the kitchen, bearing large trays of sizzling dishes and heavy platters of ripe, succulent fruit. Gleaming golden goblets glistened upon the table like a string of gems, ready to be filled, their contents savored over lingering conversation.

Hiding a smile, Tabitha watched as Eli fussed over the various arrangements, frantically directing the servants just as a matronly mother hen might cluck at her scampering chicks. Despite his swelling consternation, Tabitha knew that Eli's motives were kind. His desire was to achieve the best possible outcome with the investor, and a show of liberal hospitality had proven quite effective upon many a wealthy businessman.

Tabitha could only hope that Amal's unfair prejudice toward her wouldn't hinder the chances of a working business relationship. After all, her Uncle Joram had handpicked Amal to become her one and only silent partner.

What shall I do if Amal refuses to work with me? she wondered, her heart rate picking up speed. *Who, then, will help me navigate and steer my uncle's booming shipping business, an industry which I know next to nothing about?*

Tabitha's thoughts were cut short when the entry curtains parted and a tall man partially emerged, his focused hazel-brown eyes scanning the room and swiftly coming to rest upon her.

Dorian! Tabitha's heart lurched with joy at the sight of him. How challenging it had been to remain professional in his presence! How she had longed to bombard him with all manner of questions about his growing faith and that of his mistress, the Lady Daphne!

"My lady," Dorian said politely, his tone crisp and controlled. "May I have a word with you?"

Eli shot her a warning glare from across the vast chamber, but Tabitha wasn't dissuaded. She knew Eli would consider it improper for her—as the lady of the estate—to share a sequestered conversation with a lowly manservant.

Well, Eli would simply have to fret and stew.

"Of course you may," Tabitha responded to

Dorian's polite request as properly as possible. Ignoring the expressive daggers Eli cast her way, Tabitha slipped gracefully past the sprawling table, following Dorian through the curtained entrance and into the narrow vestibule from which he had emerged. Closing the curtains behind her, Tabitha turned to face the Greek manservant, her eyes shining with happiness.

"Dorian!" she breathed, careful to keep her voice low enough to evade her nosy overseer's pricked ears.

"*Lady* Tabitha," Dorian remarked with the closest thing to a smile she'd ever seen upon his serious features. His tone betrayed his amusement despite his stoic manner as he added, "How far the Lord has brought you."

"I couldn't have possibly imagined my life would unfold this way."

"Could any of us have guessed what life held for us?"

Unprepared for the warm sting of tears in her eyes, Tabitha touched his forearm, her eyes conveying her fondness toward the trustworthy manservant. "How are you, Dorian? How are you *really*? And Lady Daphne? How is she?"

"Firm in her faith as ever, as am I," Dorian assured her, and Tabitha noted with relief that he no longer seemed uncomfortable conversing with one he considered above his class. Clearly, his time walking with the Lord had broken down the barriers between his previously rigid social expectations. In his former life, a manservant wouldn't dare request a private audience with the wealthy mistress of a fine seaside estate!

"Have you encountered any fellow believers in Athens?" Tabitha asked him, her eyes bright with interest.

"My lady has been rather reluctant to vocalize her faith as of yet, given her husband's uncompromising stance on the matter," Dorian confessed. "As such, we are currently unaware of any likeminded believers in the area. But I have spoken with fellow servants in spaces of safety, such as the public baths or the local gymnasium. Some of them haven't been entirely closed to the concept of salvation through faith in Christ."

"Oh, how wonderful!" Tabitha exclaimed, clasping her hands in delight. "Surely men will eventually note your witness, Dorian, and they will believe!"

"I pray it may be so."

"Oh, yes!" Tabitha nodded emphatically. "I shall join you in that prayer."

"Thank you, my lady."

"Now what about the local synagogues? Do Amal and Daphne frequent any places of worship in Athens?"

"I'm afraid Amal has forsaken matters of faith entirely after—" At this, Dorian paused, his serious eyes grazing hers knowingly.

"After Stephanos died," Tabitha finished softly with a pang to her heart.

"Yes, my lady."

"I see." Wisely, Tabitha refrained from voicing that Amal's devotion to the Jewish faith of his fathers had been slight at best, even before Stephanos' passing. Even so, she'd hoped his exposure to the Scriptures in a synagogue might eventually break through his stony heart, affirming his son's testimony regarding

Christ as the Messiah.

"It would seem you have not received my recent letters, my lady," Dorian decided, noting Tabitha's sorrow and surprise at his disclosure. "And neither have we received yours, not for over a year now. We hadn't the slightest idea you had relocated to Joppa."

"I penned a letter explaining why I had to leave Jerusalem before I departed," Tabitha assured him, perplexed. "Perhaps it was lost in transit."

"Ah, yes. And I have been directing our letters to Jerusalem, which explains why you have not received them."

"Thankfully, we know how to find each other now," Tabitha said with great feeling. "When you return to Athens, let's keep in touch."

"Agreed, my lady."

"I suppose I must return to Eli and oversee the banquet preparations," Tabitha sighed, reluctant to end the conversation so soon. "Will Amal be ready to join us in the triclinium within the hour?"

"I shall ensure that he is."

"Dare I inquire about his mindset concerning me?"

"Ah, perhaps not." Dorian's firm mouth tipped in amusement.

"He's that unhappy to see me?"

"You needn't concern yourself about his reception of you, my lady. In light of Master Amal's lust for wealth, his hatred toward you pales in significance."

"Amal *hates* me?" Tabitha blinked, stunned. She—along with everyone else at the port—had certainly been aware of his keen distaste toward her upon his arrival. And, true, he had furiously ordered her off his rental property in Jerusalem during their last encounter. But to *hate* her? Surely over a year had provided sufficient time for his loathsome anger to simmer down a bit!

One anxious glimpse of Dorian's sober features convinced her otherwise.

"Stand your ground and trust God," Dorian directed her firmly. "God's will shall prevail in this situation, as with all else."

Smiling warmly, Tabitha watched Dorian as he turned smartly on his heels to vacate the narrow vestibule in which they had shared their sequestered conversation—and promptly collided headfirst with a harried, rushing Tirzah! Clearly, she hadn't been watching where she was going.

Startled, Tirzah released a cry of trepidation as she nearly toppled backward, but Dorian was at the ready. Swiftly grasping her arms, he steadied her, his intense gaze searching her large brown eyes and lovely face in question.

"I beg your pardon, miss," he apologized, though it was obvious to Tabitha that the carelessness had occurred on the part of her impetuous friend. "Are you all right?"

Wide-eyed in her surprise, the typically outspoken Tirzah merely stared at him, perplexed.

"Miss?"

"I'm fine." Suddenly regaining her wits, Tirzah responded somewhat curtly, never one to appreciate being caught off guard. But clearly taken with the handsome and dignified stranger, Tabitha noticed.

"Tirzah, this is Dorian," she quickly asserted, noting the confusion—and fascination—on both their faces. "He is Amal's most trusted servant and also a dear friend and boyhood mentor of my Stephanos."

"I see," Tirzah nodded, attempting to appear composed and nonchalant, but doing a rather lousy job of it, in Tabitha's opinion.

"Dorian," Tabitha added for the sake of clarity. "Tirzah is my dearest friend here in Joppa. She assists me with my daughter, Laurel, when I'm engaged in business affairs."

"It is a pleasure to meet you, my lady," Dorian assured her, his tight features softening just a bit.

"And you, as well," Tirzah shot back, a rueful smile touching her lips. "Though I was somewhat in fear of my life for a moment there. Glad you're fast on your feet."

Flushing slightly, the typically staid Dorian appeared at a loss for the proper response.

And it was then that both suddenly noticed Dorian's steadying hands still upon her. Instinctively, they swiftly separated—rather like the parting of the Red Sea, Tabitha noted with a hidden smile—taking several steps back to place some distance between each other.

"Master Amal is undoubtedly awaiting my return," Dorian finally managed, his usually crisp tone taking on a hint of nervousness. "Please, do excuse me." With a stiff bow, Dorian made haste to vacate the scene, his Roman-style sandals *clack-clacking* upon the marble floor tiles as he made his swift retreat.

Tirzah parted the crimson curtain veiling the vestibule's entry, watching him go. Lifting a curious brow, she seemed entirely unaware of Tabitha's observant gaze upon her. Slowly releasing the curtain, it fluttered back into place as Tirzah turned to face her friend once more.

"What?" she demanded, clearly peeved by Tabitha's knowing grin.

"Well, you certainly made quite the impression on Dorian," Tabitha observed, tilting her head to one side with a hint of mischief.

"Well, I'm not surprised," Tirzah snorted, annoyed. "A stampeding elephant would've proven less conspicuous and far more graceful than I."

"He didn't seem to mind."

"And what, exactly, are you implying?" Tirzah demanded, crossing her arms over her chest.

"He seemed to make a bit of an impression on you, as well," Tabitha pointed out, amused by their obvious chemistry.

"Nonsense," Tirzah huffed, waving a hand in dismissal. "I simply wasn't expecting a head-on collision with a handsome Roman, of all things, in this house."

"Dorian is Greek, not Roman," Tabitha supplied.

"He *looks* like a Roman."

"That, he does," Tabitha chuckled, remembering how very Roman he'd appeared, clean-shaven with a close-cropped haircut and donning a crisp toga and expensive sandals, upon their first meeting in Jerusalem. "So you think he's handsome?"

"Tabitha! I didn't say that."

"Actually, yes, you did," Tabitha laughed, entertained by the look Tirzah gave her.

"Well, I didn't mean it the way you're taking it."

"No?" Tabitha asked with a lift of her brow. "How did you mean it, then?"

"I was simply stating a fact, nothing more," Tirzah huffed, turning to leave. "On that note, I'd best let you return to your supper preparations."

"Um, Tirzah?" Tabitha called after her, her eyes shining with fun. "Wasn't there something you needed to tell me?"

"Tell you?" Tirzah repeated blankly, casting a glance of confusion over her shoulder.

"Well, you came all the way down here to find me," Tabitha pointed out. "Surely there was something you intended to tell me."

"Oh...yes!" Tirzah stammered, her eyes suddenly lighting with recognition.

"I suppose it must have simply slipped your mind somehow," Tabitha teased.

Ignoring her glee, Tirzah said rather curtly, "I've bedded Laurel down for the night in your suite, but she insists upon telling you good night before your supper commences."

"Very well," Tabitha nodded, aware of the lateness of the hour. "I'd best kiss her good night and wish her sweet dreams before the banquet begins. If Amal is half as stubborn as he used to be, then this meeting may drag late into the night."

CHAPTER 12

John Mark

Jerusalem

Feeling almost giddy after Mary had agreed to arrange his betrothal, John Mark was relieved when it was finally time to shut the last ledger and close up shop for the day. Forcing himself to pay attention to what he was doing, he tidied the surface of his mother's sprawling desk, neatly stacking parchment paperwork and returning heavy business ledgers to their proper locations. He knew he needn't bother with cleaning the large chamber or dimming the burning lamps, as servants would tend to those tasks shortly after he vacated the office library.

Rubbing the back of his neck, John Mark squared tense shoulders after replacing the final stack of ledgers, wondering why he was always sorer after a workday bent over laborious paperwork than after an entire day of physical exertion. Though he was grateful for the opportunity to take over the family business someday, he often found himself wishing it involved a bit more physical activity. He'd never been one to sit still for long.

Slipping out the entrance and emerging in the inner court, John Mark felt the welcome whispers of evening breezes upon his cheek, cool and refreshing. Nightfall typically ushered in much fairer temperatures, even amidst these stifling summer months.

Attempting to suppress the telling spring in his step, John Mark played it cool as he crossed the stone court, his pulse quickening as he contemplated the discussion he'd shared with Mary just a few hours earlier. He could scarcely believe he would soon be betrothed—and to a wonderful young woman he cared deeply about. His feelings for Rhoda hadn't hit him with the force of an explosion, as some described the concept of falling in love. Nor had he expected to develop feelings beyond brotherly fondness toward her. And yet, somehow, tender desire for her had descended upon him unaware. She was so sweet, so graceful in her movements and in her speech. And he was drawn to her in a way that far exceeded physical desire, though he'd always thought she was a pretty girl. No, his feelings for her were tender and sweet, loving and protective. He wanted to cherish her heart, to dispel her fears, to shield her from the hurts and harshness of the world in which they lived.

He wanted to *love* her, and to spend the rest of his life doing so.

He couldn't help but wonder how she would respond if she knew the depths of his love for her. Did she even suspect it? And would she readily return his affections when Mary eventually broached the subject of a betrothal with her?

Suddenly apprehensive, John Mark realized that he hadn't any way to know how she felt about him. Sure, he'd suspected that she'd always harbored feelings for him. In fact, there'd even been times when he'd felt slightly annoyed by it when she had been a gangly eight-year-old girl staring upon him with starry-eyed wonder. His friend, Simon, had teased him about it on more than one occasion over the years.

But what if Rhoda's girlish fancies had faded over time? Did she even desire to wed and raise a family of her own? What if someone else had caught her attention? It certainly wasn't impossible.

Quickly casting such thoughts aside, John Mark reclaimed his confidence as he strolled through the first level of the house, eager to freshen up and relax after a long day's work. Passing through the grand reception hall, he was about to take the broad steps two at a time when he noticed a slender form across the room, meticulously dusting the elegant wall fixtures framing the vestibule entry.

There she is. Heart pounding, John Mark paused with one hand resting on the marble banister, watching her graceful movements. Her slender back was facing him, and he knew she remained unaware of his presence as she worked. Her cream-colored garments were simple and delicate, conveying the same humble grace as the girl who wore them. Dark-brown hair pooled about her shoulders, modestly veiled with a creamy white head covering.

Swallowing hard, John Mark was rocked by his desire to love and protect this girl. He wanted to cross the distance between them, take her in his arms, and kiss her sweet face. And yet, he knew he must wait. He knew their betrothal would likely span at least one year's time, and he hadn't the slightest idea when his mother would make it official. It could be two, even three, years before Rhoda became his wife.

His wife! Heart pounding, John Mark realized

that his bravado had completely flown out the window. Should Rhoda notice him standing there, staring at her like a blundering fool, what would he say to her? He hadn't the slightest idea.

Suddenly wishing to disappear, he was about to travel the steps as stealthily as possible when Rhoda must have sensed his eyes upon her. Turning her head, she glanced over her shoulder, her large brown eyes soft and poignant, her rosy lips slightly parted in surprise.

Mentally kicking himself, John Mark wondered what to do. Should he approach her? Drop a hint about the important conversation he'd shared with his mother? Or simply act casual and offer a breezy greeting?

But then he noticed the expression on Rhoda's gentle face, and his stomach dropped in response. Her countenance had grown uncharacteristically clouded, her features pinched as her soft eyes flickered with hidden pain.

Heart pounding in his chest, John Mark was about to ask her if she was all right when she turned swiftly on her heel and hurried away, leaving him standing alone in confusion.

***

Tabitha

Joppa

Amal stared coldly at Tabitha across the elegant dining table, his dark eyes narrowing as his jaw tightened in displeasure.

Resisting the temptation to shift uncomfortably on her upholstered lectus, Tabitha forced a quiet smile she was far from feeling. She could feel Eli's eyes upon her as he stood obediently behind the couch on which she reclined, though she was quite impressed at his ability to mask his usual nervousness in the presence of the important investor. Surprisingly, his seeming calm promoted her own sense of security and well-being. After all, Eli had undoubtedly observed dozens upon dozens of such meetings under Joram's employ. He would certainly know if and when there was due cause to panic.

Even more encouraging was Dorian's staid presence as he stood stiffly beside his master's sprawling lectus, appearing rather like an indomitable Roman statue of chiseled marble. Though his emotions remained expertly concealed, Tabitha knew he was praying for her throughout the dinner meeting. His unshakable faith bolstered hers, as well.

"I trust the meal has met with your approval, my lord?" Tabitha inquired with a gracious smile after nearly half an hour of glaring silence.

Amal's only response was a patronizing smile as he stroked his well-kept beard.

Refusing to be intimidated, Tabitha was reminded of many unpleasant suppers shared with this pompous father-in-law and his far more gracious wife, Daphne, when they had hosted the younger couple in their extravagant rented villa during their brief stay in Jerusalem. She'd felt under inspection as Amal had studied her critically over the rim of his lavish golden goblet night after harrowing night.

Lifting her chin and strengthening her resolve, Tabitha refused to be cowed. How often had she witnessed her mistress, Mary, face opposition regarding her own family business? Not once had Tabitha ever seen her shrink back in fear or cower in the presence of a bully. No, Mary addressed issues head-on, refusing to compromise or back down if she knew the Lord was leading in a certain direction.

At this point, Tabitha wasn't entirely sure where God was leading—at least, where the shipping business was concerned. Instead, she drew upon what she *did* know. She *did* know that God had provided a home for dozens of orphans and widows in the region, and the estate she had inherited was a crucial part of that ministry. Not only that, but the mansion had also provided a safe space for the fledgling church in Joppa to meet each week. For both ministries to continue to flourish, her inheritance must be protected and maintained. Which meant her uncle's shipping business must continue producing income to fuel both ventures.

And Amal's help was certainly needed, as she hadn't the slightest idea how to oversee an operation of such massive proportions.

Not only that, Tabitha reminded herself, *but God has brought this stubborn man back into my life for a reason. What are the odds of encountering him again, especially given all the impossible circumstances?* She couldn't help but assume that God had provided her a second chance to reach the father of her beloved Stephanos. And she intended to embrace that calling wholeheartedly—for the sake of her departed husband, yes. But also in obedience to the God who desired to save everyone, even the most obnoxious and pompous of sinners.

"So, exactly what kind of operation are you running here?" Amal demanded, his strident voice jarring her from her thoughts.

Sensing Eli stiffening behind her, Tabitha prayed for wisdom in her response. "You know all about this business, my lord," she replied, addressing his animosity with a clear gaze. "It would seem you have been my uncle's silent partner for many years."

"Joram and I were partners before you were born," he huffed, offended at the thought of negotiating with someone he considered ignorant in business matters and far beneath him—and a woman, at that!

"So I needn't waste your time delving into the inner workings and daily operations of this venture," Tabitha reminded him calmly. "My uncle's last will and testament was clear: He desired for this shipping business to remain in operation even after his death. He specified that you should be the one to help me oversee the day-to-day operations. As you know, I have little experience in the shipping industry—"

"You have *no* experience!"

"But I'm willing to work with you to ensure the welfare of this business," Tabitha finished, undeterred by his animosity.

"I imagine you're not only willing, but desperate, to work with me," Amal observed, toying with the rim of his goblet and staring at her just as a cat might taunt an unfortunate mouse. "Without my aid, you'll undoubtedly run this business into the ground."

"I do wish to work with you, my lord," Tabitha affirmed, striving for calm. "But I am not desperate. If you wish to break free of your ties with this business, I shan't stop you."

"You couldn't stop me even if you wanted to."

"Neither of us are free to control the other," Tabitha pointed out, raising his ire with her boldness. "You are free to do as you wish, as am I."

"Good luck finding another investor."

"Eli has already located several local and foreign

investors willing to work with us, should you decline my uncle's invitation to do so."

"You're bluffing."

"I wouldn't lie to you."

Amal studied her fiercely, clearly wrestling with the facts. Much to her surprise, he seemed to trust her word.

"According to my uncle's will, he wished for you to assign someone to oversee the daily operations of the shipping business," Tabitha explained. "This would be done in exchange for a percentage of the business and profits."

"I already own a percentage of the business and profits."

"You would own more," Tabitha pointed out. "And I am willing to negotiate the matter."

"You wouldn't know how to negotiate a fair deal if your life depended on it."

"Well, there's only one way to find out."

"I've been making careful observations and gathering evidence since my arrival here," Amal smirked, changing the subject. "You've turned this beautiful estate into a common hostel for riffraff."

"Are you referencing the orphans and widows lodging here?" Tabitha asked him, ready to defend her cause.

"Orphans and widows!" Amal shook his head in awe. "Unbelievable!"

"There are many poor here in Joppa, all of them in need of sanctuary."

"And exactly how much are you charging them for this *sanctuary*?" he sneered.

"They live here free of charge."

"Free?!" he demanded, his color deepening in fury.

"This is a ministry, Amal," Tabitha informed him. "I'm not taking advantage of the destitute for my own personal gain."

"You should be charging them a premium to live here!" Amal declared, outraged. "This is prime real estate. It should cost a fortune to rent a suite in this fine home!"

"These widows haven't a shekel to their names, much less a fortune."

"And how is that *our* problem? We should be concerned with the welfare of this business—not the financial state of strangers!"

"We *are* concerned with the welfare of this business," Tabitha reminded him. "Which is why we're having this discussion."

"If you were truly concerned about the financial stability of this venture, you'd be utilizing and leveraging every inch of the estate," Amal argued impatiently. "It's not a bad idea—converting the empty rooms into suites and renting them out. We could be making a killing, providing the only suitable lodging in the city!"

"I suppose we could," Tabitha humbly conceded. "But I have no doubt that God has called me to minister to these women and children, Amal. They need a home, and I'm more than willing to provide a place for them."

"Free of charge," Amal huffed, red-faced and agitated. "You're a fool for passing up an opportunity to make so much easy money," he ground out.

"In the eyes of men, perhaps," Tabitha said quietly. "But I wish to be justified in God's sight rather than seeking the approval of man."

Eyes flashing dangerously, Amal reached for his goblet, emptying it of its contents in one fell swoop.

Slamming it down on the table, he met her gaze, his own kindling with resentment. "Fortunately for you, my interest revolves around the shipping business—not the house."

Tabitha could have pointed out that the house was rightfully hers and he hadn't any say in what she did with it. Legally, Joram had left the house entirely to her. But she held her peace instead, awaiting his response with an enigmatic smile.

"I need time to think," Amal announced coldly, clearly relishing the power he believed he held in his hands. "Tonight, I shall mull over the financial ledgers and the information presented to me, thus far."

Tabitha nodded, unwilling to grovel or beg. Not that it mattered. Ultimately, God was in charge, not Amal.

Rising with the air of an unhappy prince, Amal tossed his cloth napkin on the table with a hint of disdain. "We shall reconvene in the morning."

Exchanging a secret look with Dorian, Tabitha read the message in his glittering eyes and bit back a knowing smile at his silent communication: Amal hoped she would fret and stew late into the night, worried that he would walk away from the shipping business. But he'd already made up his mind. And he wasn't going anywhere.

Clearly, Dorian had been right about his master's love of wealth.

CHAPTER 13

Mary

Jerusalem

It was a lovely summer morning, the blue sky overhead dotted with lazily floating clouds. The early morning sun felt warm on Mary's back as she was ushered past a simple but elegant stone court gracing the front of her brother's attractive home. It was rather early for a friendly visit—early enough, she hoped, to converse with her older brother before he was needed elsewhere.

A simply clad manservant officiously opened the double doors, permitting her entrance with a wide sweep of his muscular arm.

Nodding her gratitude, Mary slipped past him, stepping into the welcome coolness of a frescoed grand foyer checkered with colorful floor tiles. Pausing to assess her surroundings, Mary folded graceful arms, tilting her head to one side as she studied the dizzying patterns of a large hanging tapestry mounted upon the nearest wall, awaiting her brother's arrival.

"Greetings, dear sister!" Barnabas' welcoming voice boomed through the impressive reception hall as he emerged from the nearest entrance, his arms outstretched as he approached her with a broad smile.

"Barnabas." Mary smiled, pleased to see him. "Good morning, my brother."

"It is now," he grinned, taking her hands in his and giving them a brotherly squeeze. "To what do I owe this unexpected pleasure?"

"I have news, Barnabas."

"Your expression renders it difficult to judge whether this news is welcome or not," Barnabas teased.

"Perhaps a bit of both," Mary confessed, allowing her brother to guide her toward the flowering central court nestled within the heart of the large house. As they stepped past rows of tall pillars and into the golden sunshine, Mary followed her brother toward a bench placed before a bubbling stone fountain in the center of the garden court.

"Please, be seated," he offered kindly, allowing her to be seated first before lowering himself onto the bench beside her.

Smiling faintly, Mary was relieved that Barnabas had directed her to the serene garden courtyard rather than convening with her in his office. Apparently, she'd approached him at a favorable time. He frequented the tranquil garden court only when he had time for a leisurely chat.

Or perhaps he merely sensed her need to share her news—and her heart—with him. Barnabas had always been highly intuitive and sensitive to the needs of others.

"Last night, I spoke with John Mark about the possibility of arranging a betrothal."

Barnabas' brows lifted in surprise. "And?"

"And he caught me entirely by surprise, Barnabas."

"Catching *you* by surprise—that's no small feat," Barnabas chuckled, amused.

"He wants to marry Rhoda."

"Rhoda?"

"I see he caught you by surprise, as well."

"Rhoda," Barnabas repeated, shaking his head with a small smile.

Mary simply nodded, her hands folded in her lap.

"I must say, Mary," Barnabas revealed. "I'm impressed with John Mark. He's made a wise decision."

"Yes, I believe he has," Mary agreed, wondering at the strange mix of emotions tugging at her heart.

"And yet, you don't seem pleased," Barnabas prodded gently, not condemning but rather seeking to understand.

"I'm pleased about the arrangement," Mary confirmed, her gaze uncharacteristically downcast. "I love John Mark, and I love Rhoda. Frankly, I can't imagine why I didn't think of it before. They're a perfect match."

"My, my," Barnabas chuckled, shaking his head in amazement. "She was right there all along, Mary!"

"God certainly knows how to provide," Mary acknowledged with a small smile. "Rhoda is a sweet, godly young lady. I have no doubt she will love and serve my son selflessly and with the utmost devotion."

"But?" Barnabas coaxed, sensing her need to unburden her thoughts.

"Truly, I couldn't be happier for my son," Mary finally said, lifting her serious gaze to meet his. "But things will change, Barnabas. The dynamics will change when John Mark takes a wife. I must pray and ask God to give me strength to encourage my son in this new season of his life."

"You are wise to seek the Lord's help in this," Barnabas encouraged her with a knowing smile. "I can't imagine it's easy for any mother to see her son take a bride and begin a life of his own. But if the marriage is destined by God, the result will ultimately be sweet for everyone involved. It is indeed true that you're not losing a son, Mary, but rather gaining a daughter, as well."

"And for that, I am truly thankful."

"So when shall this happy betrothal take place?"

"Since the girl is still quite young, I've decided to wait a year and a half to legally arrange the betrothal, though I plan to speak with Rhoda right away to make sure she, too, wishes to marry John Mark."

"That girl has adored John Mark from the moment she laid eyes on him," Barnabas grinned, happy for both of them. "Trust me, she'll say yes."

"And if she does, then we shall follow through with the betrothal and marriage," Mary nodded. "I will arrange for the customary year-long betrothal period, as I wouldn't wish to initiate a marriage before Rhoda's sixteenth birthday. And this will also allow John Mark the time to master his work and assume his role of leadership in the family business."

"It would seem you've thought it all through, though that doesn't surprise me in the least."

"Barnabas," Mary asked him, turning serious eyes upon her brother and taking his hands in her own. "You know Rhoda is an orphan, with no father to oversee these sacred proceedings. It saddens my heart, and yet, it also thrills me to ask if *you* would be willing to assume that position, to stand beside her and give her away when the time comes."

It was obvious Barnabas was deeply touched by Mary's request. "I can think of no greater honor, Mary," he smiled, his soft brown eyes reflecting the depths of his feelings. "I was there the day you rescued her from the slave traders and the day you brought her into your home. She has confided in me when she felt she had no one else to turn to, and I have watched her miraculous transformation from a wide-eyed and frightened little girl into a lovely, God-fearing young woman. It would be my honor to present her to my nephew in marriage when the time is right."

Squeezing his hands tenderly, Mary blinked back an unexpected sheen of tears.

***

Tabitha

Joppa

"Here's what I propose."

Seated behind her uncle's imposing desk, Tabitha folded both hands on top of an opened ledger, hoping she appeared steadfast and confident before Amal as he presented his case to her and Eli.

Exchanging a swift glance with her overseer,

who stood dutifully at her elbow, writing tablet in hand, Tabitha offered a silent prayer for guidance and forced a calmness she was far from feeling. "I'm listening."

"I will partner with you," Amal said, a brow raised in challenge as he gauged her reaction.

Resisting the urge to release an enormous sigh of relief, Tabitha's gaze grazed Dorian's—standing calmly, ever at the ready, beside his master's chair—ever so slightly before locking eyes with her arrogant father-in-law.

"For fifty-one percent of your uncle's holdings," Amal added, his dark eyes narrowing dangerously.

Feeling Eli visibly stiffen beside her, Tabitha hid her surprise as best she could, keeping her tone even. "Fifty-one percent?"

"You heard me," Amal barked, gripping his gilded armrests and leaning forward in his chair. "Fifty-one percent, and not a shekel less."

Leaning back in her own plush chair, Tabitha contemplated the offer given. If Eli's stiffening body language and Dorian's smoldering stare were any indication, Amal's surprising offer was a bad deal, unworthy of consideration. But how should she counter? What should she say?

Stomach churning, she realized she hadn't the slightest idea how to proceed.

"Well?" Amal growled, eager to seal the deal and be on his way. "I haven't got all day."

Eli cleared his throat, conspicuously enough for Tabitha to look his way. Catching his gaze, she read the clear message in his eyes and suddenly remembered his prior remonstration to discuss any potential deals in private before making it official.

"Thank you for your offer, my lord," Tabitha finally acknowledged, surprised at how calm she sounded. "I have asked my kitchen staff to prepare a lovely breakfast for you and your manservant. Please allow my overseer to escort you to the banquet hall. I shall consider your offer while you dine, and then I shall join you in the triclinium once you have partaken of your meal."

Stunned by her quick thinking and seeming calm, Amal's eyes narrowed in suspicion as Eli set aside his writing tablet, came around the desk, and gestured graciously toward the curtained entrance. "This way, my lord," he said, his eyes darting toward his lady still seated behind the desk as Amal reluctantly rose from his seat.

"You have until the close of the morning meal," Amal said coldly, peeved by the obvious fact that Tabitha possessed the upper hand. "I won't wait around for weeks while an ignorant and uneducated widow woman ponders what should be a very clear decision. You'd be a fool not to accept my offer."

Tabitha simply waited, watching as Amal grudgingly rose from his chair and followed Eli out of the room. Dorian, too, followed suit, tarrying slightly when he reached the curtained entrance. Casting a knowing glance in her direction, his expression warned her to be cautious and thorough regarding his master's offer.

Without a word, he slipped from the resplendent office, leaving her to breathe an immense sigh of relief once she was finally alone with her thoughts. And prayers.

CHAPTER 14

Tabitha

Joppa

Eli returned within moments of getting Amal and Dorian settled at the table in the triclinium. He discovered his lady pacing before her uncle's desk, her brow furrowed in deep thought.

"My lady?" he dared, wondering if he should allow her to walk off a bit of her nervous energy before diving headfirst into business dealings.

"What should I do, Eli?" Tabitha asked, crossing her arms over her chest. "I could tell neither you nor Dorian approved of Amal's offer."

"You needn't concern yourself with the opinion of a Greek *manservant*," Eli informed her, peeved. "He works for Amal. He cannot be trusted."

"I told you, he's a fellow believer. I trust him implicitly."

Eli's expression conveyed his annoyance.

"But our time is limited, so I shall ask again," she

plunged ahead, perching on the corner of her uncle's large desk and crossing her legs at the ankles. "So what should I do about Amal's offer of a partnership in exchange for fifty-one percent of my uncle's business holdings?"

"Counter at forty-nine percent," Eli shot back, surprising her with the speed and surety of his response.

"Offer him forty-nine percent?" Tabitha repeated, mulling it over. "Would he not be more likely to accept a deal if we agreed on at least a fifty-fifty split?"

"If we're wise, we won't relinquish more than forty-nine percent of our holdings," Eli told her bluntly. "According to your uncle's wishes, this is now *your* business and estate. But if you grant Amal half the business, then he becomes an equal partner and may possibly even sell the business and estate. Should he do such a thing, where would your widows and orphans go? They would be back on the streets, without shelter or sustenance."

Tabitha did a double take, surprised by Eli's obvious care and concern for the very tenants he had once been so reluctant to allow into the mansion.

"We cannot let that happen," he said quickly, brushing aside her surprise. "You must maintain control."

Nodding slowly, Tabitha recognized that he made a valid point. "All right," she said, furrowing her brow as she mulled over all he had suggested. "I shall do as you say."

"My lady," Eli dared, watching her closely as he spoke. "I believe there's one more thing you should consider before reaching an agreement with this investor."

***

"Well?" Amal leaned indolently back on his couch, impatiently fingering the stem of his elegant goblet. "Have you enough sense to accept my offer or not?"

Smiling wanly, Tabitha refused to be cowed into a quick decision. "I'm honored that you wish to partner with me, my lord, and I have given your offer much consideration."

"And?" Amal demanded, arching a sardonic brow. "You'd be a fool to reject an opportunity like this."

Ignoring Amal's scathing pronouncements, Tabitha straightened on the couch across from him, glad for the polished table between them. Though the conniving businessman appeared relaxed on his lavish, upholstered couch, Amal's body language was disturbingly reminiscent of a viper poised to strike its hapless prey. Sitting upright and rather stiffly on the couch adjoining his was Dorian, who was clearly unaccustomed to dining at the same table as his master. Seated ramrod straight like an unbending steel pole, his large, well-shaped hands folded between his knees, Dorian's muscled calves were tensed beneath his interwoven leather sandal thongs.

Standing dutifully behind Amal's couch, writing tablet in hand, was Eli, strategically located to communicate silently with his mistress, if needed. As before, his anxiety remained carefully concealed behind a seemingly casual expression.

"Here's what I propose, my lord," Tabitha stated, keeping her voice as even as possible. "I am willing to relinquish forty-nine percent of my uncle's business holdings—and we're solely discussing the *shipping business*, not this house or estate, which my uncle's will clearly left to me as an inheritance."

"Forty-nine percent?" Amal sneered, surprised she'd had the wherewithal to see through his bid for absolute control. "I want more."

"I am unwilling to impart more than that," she said frankly, almost expecting him to walk. "Do you still wish to partner with me?"

Taking a slow, careful swig from his goblet, Amal studied her with cold eyes, clearly weighing his options.

"Fifty percent," he finally said, his flashing, fiery gaze daring her to defy him.

"No, my lord. I cannot give you fifty."

"I want fifty."

"Forty-nine percent is the highest I shall go."

As a thundering silence lingered in the air, Tabitha sensed that both Eli and Dorian held their breath along with her, awaiting Amal's response.

Jaw tightening in dismay, Amal finally slammed down his goblet and gave his daughter-in-law a curt nod. "I shall accept your conditions. For now."

Stunned, Tabitha hoped she didn't look too amazed. She could hardly fathom that Amal had agreed to her stubborn counter. Sensing Eli's dark eyes intensifying upon her, she fleetingly met his gaze. At his nod of encouragement, she suddenly remembered that it wasn't over yet.

"I do have one condition to state before the paperwork is drawn up," she said, hoping she sounded firm enough.

"You do realize that you're in no position to demand anything from me?" Amal sneered, ruffled by her seeming audacity.

"But I imagine you'll agree with my line of thought once you hear me out," Tabitha assured him, praying that she sounded far more confident than she felt. "As you know, my uncle hoped you would partner with me, receiving a higher percentage of the profits in exchange for guidance in the operation of his shipping business."

"So?"

"So we've agreed that, from this point forward, you will receive forty-nine percent of the profits, which is a much higher percentage than you have received up to this point. In exchange, I request the presence of a qualified steward whom you trust to oversee the daily operations of this shipping business. As you can imagine, this is all new to me, and professional guidance is essential."

"And why would I relinquish one of my very best men to babysit an ignorant widow who's bitten off far more than she can chew?"

"Because doing so will double and possibly even triple revenue, which, in turn, will raise your own profits considerably."

Amal gave her a long, hard stare, clearly unable to argue her logic. Moving his jaw back and forth, he reached for his goblet again, allowing himself a long, leisurely sip, his eyes never leaving the gutsy widow's.

"Done," he finally said, setting aside his goblet with a loud *thud.*

Done? Cutthroat Amal had actually agreed to her terms and conditions, just like that? Tabitha stared at him, open-mouthed. Quickly realizing her gaping expression, she promptly closed her mouth and forced a wobbly smile instead.

"Then it would seem we have reached an agreement," she stated, half expecting him to interrupt and change his mind partway through her triumphant statement. "I shall contact my uncle's attorney so the paperwork can be drawn up."

"Do it now. I haven't endless time to waste!"

"I shall see to it this very moment, my lady," Eli promised even before she could address him.

"Thank you, Eli," Tabitha told him, her sincere expression conveying her gratitude.

"Accompany him, Dorian," Amal commanded with the air of one who lived to order others about. "From this point forward, you will be my man in Joppa. And when I return to Greece, you shall stay and oversee my operations here."

Nearly falling off her couch, Tabitha shot a glance toward the startled manservant, who looked every bit as shocked as she felt.

"My lord?" Dorian questioned, clearly wondering if he'd heard his master correctly.

"You heard me! I want you handling all my affairs here. There's simply too much at stake to appoint someone less qualified."

"Then...then Dorian shall remain here...in Joppa...indefinitely?" Tabitha questioned, scarcely daring to hope that such an arrangement could be true. Why, the thought of her dear brother in Christ—and one who had been so close to her beloved Stephanos—residing in Joppa nearly filled her heart to bursting with joy!

"Are you two deaf? Hard of hearing?" Amal barked, mistaking their surprise for resistance. "Or merely dumb as a box of rocks? I don't want to hear a word of protest from either one of you! I've made up my mind. What's done is done."

Somehow stifling a huge sigh of relief, Tabitha intentionally avoided Dorian's gaze. If Amal so much as suspected her great joy, he would surely change his mind and assign someone else to the post in Joppa just to spite her. Casting a cautious glance toward Eli, she saw that he appeared every bit as surprised as she.

"Well?" Amal demanded, fast losing the shred of patience he still possessed. "Are we merely going to sit here gawking at each other? Or shall we summon an attorney and get this matter settled?"

"Yes, my lord, of course." Swiftly rising from the couch, Dorian met Eli at the door. Tabitha couldn't help but note the stark contrast between the two of them as Eli—with his colorful garments, large turban, and somewhat condescending manner—led the tall, stoic Dorian toward the exit. Eli appeared even more thoroughly Jewish in the presence of the crisply dressed, dignified Greek manservant.

Pausing at the exit, Dorian cast the faintest hint of a rueful smile in Tabitha's direction before calmly slipping out the door.

CHAPTER 15

Tirzah

Joppa

Gingerly stepping into the large, silent kitchen, Tirzah lifted her lamp a bit higher, surprised by the eerie solitude of the typically bustling chamber. The hour was late—certainly too late for one to be snooping about the empty kitchen, searching for snacks. But she had tossed and turned for hours, unable to calm her racing mind long enough to drift into blissful slumber.

Perhaps a midnight snack would take the edge off and settle her enough to sleep. Having stayed with Laurel while Tabitha met with Amal and Joram's former attorney late into the evening, Tirzah had neglected to partake of the evening meal. Despite the fact that Tabitha had insisted she indulge in the lavish leftovers of the feast she had provided for her business associates, Tirzah had declined, feeling too uneasy to eat. She knew what was tugging at her mind, rendering her unable to concentrate on her work, her meals, or really anything else, for that matter.

Even so, she didn't care to think about that right now. She was far too busy regretting the fact that she had skipped the evening meal. Her growling stomach loudly protested against the blatant injustice. And now, she could only hope to glean some of the leftovers she had refused earlier in the evening.

Placing her lamp on the large stone counter in the center of the great kitchen, Tirzah wandered over to the large kiln, still glowing with burning embers. Martha often stoked the fire shortly before retiring, which kept the kitchen warm and faintly lit with an orange glow through the midnight hours.

Ah, there! Near the kiln was a basket of freshly baked loaves, gleaming golden brown in the faint firelight.

Delighted, Tirzah made a beeline for the large basket on the counter. In her haste, she failed to notice the kitchen stool, which hadn't been tucked back under the central stone counter. Smartly barking her shin, Tirzah yelped in pain as the stool went flying across the kitchen, clattering loudly to the floor.

Grasping her shin in keen displeasure, Tirzah froze, scarcely breathing. Surely, her unfortunate accident had awakened the entire household. In fact, she was quite certain her noisy antics could have awakened the dead. But after several moments of ensuing silence, Tirzah decided that, somehow, the crisis had been averted. She hadn't awakened the sleeping household, after all. Now she could safely proceed with her late-night snack, undisturbed.

Eagerly snatching a soft loaf from the basket, Tirzah raised it to her nose, delightedly inhaling the tantalizing aroma of freshly baked bread. And Martha's bread was inarguably the best in the entire province!

Opening her mouth, Tirzah allowed herself a very generous bite, far too generous to be ladylike.

"I beg your pardon, miss. But are you well?"

Tirzah froze, instantly recognizing the crisp, dignified voice. Groaning inwardly, she slowly lowered the large loaf, her cheeks overly full like a chipmunk storing leftovers for later.

"Miss?" Dorian stepped into the kitchen then, looking quite regal even in his sleepwear. Blushing, he averted his gaze when he realized that the lovely young woman prowling about the kitchen also donned the form-fitting undergarment in which she slept, her rich chestnut brown hair devoid of its covering. "My apologies," he stammered, his gaze just barely grazing hers. "I heard someone bumping around in the kitchen and supposed I ought to ensure that all was well."

Bumping around in the kitchen? Peeved, Tirzah furrowed her brow, her embarrassment regarding their questionable attire forgotten in her heated chagrin. "I don't typically sneak around the kitchen in the middle of the night, you know."

Dorian did a double take, caught off guard by her defensive response.

"Well, I don't!" Tirzah insisted, her ire further aroused. "In fact, I don't even live here. I have my own house just down the lane."

Though Dorian wisely held his tongue, his expression indicated that he wondered why she was raiding someone else's kitchen if she had her own.

"Tabitha insisted that I stay the night rather than walk home after dark," Tirzah plunged ahead, wondering why she even cared to explain herself to an uppity Gentile stranger. "I was watching Laurel upstairs while Tabitha finalized the legal documents with Joram's attorney this evening. And the meeting went so long that I missed taking supper. Which is the *only* reason why I'm here now. As previously stated, I don't usually sneak around the kitchen at midnight searching for snacks."

"No?"

"No!"

Dorian's only response was a wry smile, his amusement evident upon his handsome features.

The nerve of that man! Galled, Tirzah took a fierce bite of bread, her flashing brown eyes daring him to say something smart.

"Well?" Tirzah demanded around a mouthful of bread. "You've seen that all is well here. Not that the goings-on in this house are any of your concern. You are but a guest, and Tabitha wouldn't expect you to run guard duty, as well. You may return to bed now."

"On the contrary, I am more than just a guest."

"Oh, are you now?" Tirzah asked him with a lifted brow. Was he about to sputter off some preposterous explanation of his own elevated sense of self-importance?

"As of today, this is my home as well."

"*What?*" Tirzah nearly choked, stunned. Why hadn't Tabitha said anything about this? She made a mental note to chide her about her negligence later. "How? Why?"

"My master has assigned me to remain in Joppa

to oversee the shipping business here," Dorian explained, his expression revealing nothing about his opinion on the matter. "The Lady Tabitha kindly offered to house me in one of her spare chambers."

"She *is* very kind," Tirzah mumbled her agreement, wondering why Tabitha had said nothing about this new arrangement. Her friend had a lot of explaining to do, that was certain!

"Until you explained otherwise, I thought you abided here as well."

Eyeing the tall, handsome Greek with suspicion, Tirzah assumed he wasn't one to extend a conversation for the mere sake of it. But she couldn't imagine why her whereabouts would interest him.

"I'm not sure why you assumed that," she corrected, a bit more brusquely than she intended.

"Ah, well. I must have assumed falsely since you appear so at home here."

Tirzah supposed she did, prowling around the kitchen in her sleepwear in the middle of the night, searching for snacks. Annoyed by his obvious amusement, her hackles rose in defense. "I possess a house of my own just down the street," she assured him, waving her loaf at him to emphasize her point. "I don't typically stay the night here, but Tabitha insisted. Her meeting ended later than expected, and since I was here watching Laurel, she didn't wish for me to travel home after dark. I stayed the night just to humor her, though I would've been fine walking home. I can take care of myself."

"I imagine you can, miss."

Arching a suspicious brow, Tirzah couldn't decide if he was being serious or facetious. His expression was like a closed book.

For *his* sake, she hoped he was being serious.

"I should turn in now," Dorian stated in his clear, succinct manner.

"Yes, you should."

"I heard a rather boisterous clatter before entering. I should ensure that you are, in fact, all right before I depart."

"I'm fine," Tirzah shot back, impatient for him to disappear so she could finish her bread and nurse her humiliation in peace.

His gaze coming to rest upon the large, upturned wooden stool across the room, Dorian's mouth tipped knowingly. "The perpetrator?" he asked, his mouth twitching ever so slightly.

"Someone left it out in the middle of the room," Tirzah protested, refusing to confess her own clumsiness.

"I see." Turning smartly on his heel, Dorian left the kitchen with a very proper, "Good evening, miss."

She couldn't be certain, but she thought she detected a muffled, "Enjoy your snack," tossed over his shoulder in departure.

Annoyed that she even cared what a snobbish Greek manservant thought of her, Tirzah tossed the half-eaten loaf back in the breadbasket.

She didn't even want it anymore.

CHAPTER 16

Tabitha

Joppa

Standing upon the wharf, Tabitha watched with a strange mix of emotions as Amal walked up the gangplank and boarded a mammoth ship, all set to return to Greece before the dangerous stormy season commenced in the fall. Clearly, he had no desire to risk being stranded in Joppa until the following spring.

"You look sad, my lady," Dorian said quietly, stationed faithfully at her elbow.

Turning to look at him, Tabitha was relieved for Dorian's staid presence as they saw Amal off. The truth was, she felt both disappointment and relief at Amal's departure, swiftly followed by needling guilt for feeling relieved. For, despite his belligerence and intolerable pride, Amal was still her father-in-law. And still in need of forgiveness.

She should be longing for more time with him rather than inwardly exulting at his departure.

Suddenly realizing that Dorian was awaiting her response, Tabitha managed a wobbly smile. "These last few days have seemed like a whirlwind," she confessed, thankful that Joram's attorney had gotten everything squared away.

Dorian simply waited, sensing she had more to say.

"I suppose I'm regretting the fact that we had little time to discuss anything but business," she sighed, feeling as if she had failed Stephanos' father. Again.

"My master knows no other language," Dorian told her.

"But this situation was undoubtedly God-ordained," Tabitha went on, feeling worse by the minute. "Was it merely my imagination, or did Amal stonewall and redirect the conversation every single time I attempted to discuss anything personal?"

"It wasn't your imagination. He didn't wish to be proselytized."

Glancing up in surprise, Tabitha noted the corner of Dorian's mouth tipping ruefully. "But how can I share the gospel with him when he refuses to stay in Joppa even a moment longer than necessary and doesn't allow any discussion to transpire that isn't strictly business?"

"The same way you've been sharing the gospel since you met him, my lady."

"But how is that?" Tabitha asked him, perplexed.

"By the way you live."

***

Rhoda

Jerusalem

John Mark seemed to be popping up everywhere, much to Rhoda's great consternation. It was almost as if he was *trying* to bump into her fifty times a day. Which was agonizing, given the circumstances and her present pain. The mere sight of him sent a sharp pang to her heart.

After another unwelcome encounter in which John Mark *just happened* to stumble into the quiet garden where Rhoda worked diligently, plucking weeds from among the summer flowers, the maidservant had mumbled a weak apology and promptly fled the scene, leaving John Mark to stand in puzzlement, alone, in the middle of the garden.

Pressing her back against a cold stone wall in the dim chamber which the servants utilized to venture between the house and outdoor grounds of the estate, Rhoda released a shaky breath, her heart pounding anxiously in her chest. Closing her eyes, she struggled to regain control of her emotions.

Heart swelling with sadness, Rhoda reminded herself that her feelings toward John Mark were entirely inappropriate. Very soon, he would marry someone else. He would establish a life, a home, and a family with a wife of his own.

Rhoda certainly hoped the girl—whoever she was—recognized how blessed and fortunate she was. John Mark would make a worthy husband. Any young woman would be privileged beyond measure to become his wife.

Blinking back tears, Rhoda bit her lower lip, feeling overcome. *Precious Lord,* she prayed, her heart heavy with sorrow. *I am overwhelmed with grief. How can I bear it?*

Another thought assailed her, one that filled her with trepidation. For it was quite likely she would soon have to *meet* the girl to whom John Mark would be betrothed. Even worse than that, she'd probably have to attend the betrothal, and then the marriage ceremony, as well! Mentally scrambling, Rhoda wondered if she could be dismissed from attendance, somehow. She supposed she could honestly say she was unwell when the dreadful day arrived, for indeed, the thought of John Mark marrying another woman sickened her.

Clasping her hands over her heart, Rhoda strove for calm. Somehow, she must return to her chores, and she must do so with a cheerful spirit. And yet, in her present state, all she wished to do was drop into a miserable heap on her pallet in the servants' quarters and have a nice long cry.

Oh Lord, she thought, weeping inwardly. *I couldn't help but think that maybe, just maybe, John Mark had feelings for me. But clearly, I couldn't have been farther from the truth. Was I wrong, Lord? Did I play the fool?*

Swiping away a stubborn tear, Rhoda straightened, adjusting her head covering with purpose. Regardless of how she felt, it didn't matter. Even if John Mark had felt something for her, he could do so much better than to wed her. After all, he deserved the world. He was fun, smart, loyal, and most importantly, seeking after God in truth and sincerity. Someday, he would inherit his mother's business empire and estate, possibly even step into the shoes of his Uncle Barnabas or his mentor, Peter, and become a powerful leader in the church. He certainly deserved far better than an orphaned Gentile serving girl for a wife.

Drawing another calming breath, Rhoda pushed herself off the stone wall and determined to get back to work. She certainly hadn't time to mope around in dark corners, childishly nursing her griefs. Instead, she would resolve to be happy for John Mark. After all, he deserved every happiness in the world. And if she truly loved him, she would rejoice to see him happily married to a woman of his own choosing.

Yes, that's what I'll do, she decided, purposefully squaring slender shoulders. *I will be happy for him. Even if it kills me. Which it very well might.*

She couldn't help but wonder if it was possible for one to die of a broken heart.

CHAPTER 17

Tabitha

Joppa

"It would seem that the Lord has worked everything out for the best," Tabitha disclosed, strolling with Adam through the flowering grounds of Joram's estate. "Amal has left a capable aide to help me manage my uncle's shipping business. God has truly provided a worthy mentor to help me."

"You sound surprised," Adam teased, strolling easily beside her, his hands folded behind his broad back as he walked in step with her.

"I shouldn't be," Tabitha confessed with a rueful smile. "God always does what is best."

"Tell me more about Dorian."

"Oh, where to begin?" Tabitha chuckled fondly. "He's a wonderful man. What's more, he's a fellow brother in Christ."

"You seem to think very highly of him."

"Oh, I do. Not only was he a dear friend and mentor of my late husband, but he was also there for me at my darkest hour. After Stephanos died."

"The two of you seem close."

"You could say that," Tabitha nodded, wondering why Adam's posture had stiffened just a bit. Though his easy smile remained in place, it seemed slightly forced. "I can't imagine a worthier mentor than Dorian. Though I daresay Amal's motives were less than gracious when he assigned Dorian to this task, he's done me a very great favor by doing so."

"To keep an eye on you?" Adam grinned.

"Most likely," Tabitha chuckled. "Clearly, Amal doesn't trust me. By assigning Dorian to oversee operations here, Amal is also seeing to his own best interests."

"Clever."

"But it works in my favor, as well," Tabitha assured him, taking in the quiet beauty of the garden scene as they strolled. "I'm glad for Dorian's presence for the exact same reason—as my brother in Christ, I trust him completely. He wouldn't swindle or misguide me. He will look out for my interests, as well."

"What exactly will he be doing here?"

"Basically, he'll handle everything pertaining to the business, with the help of Eli, of course. And Martha's husband, Jonas, who oversees the books," Tabitha explained. "He'll also teach me the ropes, so that I'm capable of running the business independently, if needed."

"Sounds like a sturdy plan."

"I hope it is," Tabitha answered honestly. "And it will free up a considerable amount of time for me so I can focus on the ministries I've begun here in Joppa."

"Like the orphans and widows here."

"Yes. And the church body, which now meets in my home."

"Has anyone ever told you that you're a busy lady?" Adam teased, playfully tweaking her shoulder as he lowered himself onto a curved marble bench placed in an ivy-strewn stone enclave.

Recognizing his silent invitation, Tabitha lowered herself onto the space beside him, careful to keep an appropriate amount of distance between them. Though she knew her relationship with Adam entailed nothing more than friendship, she'd noticed several churchgoers eyeing them curiously during recent interactions.

Best to keep any unwanted suspicions at bay.

"I wish you could've seen Tirzah's first interaction with Dorian," Tabitha divulged with a mischievous smile.

"This sounds interesting. Didn't they get along?"

"Oh, perhaps a bit too well," Tabitha chuckled, bemused. "I daresay Tirzah was rather taken with him, and I was shocked. In all the time I've spent with Tirzah, not once have I seen her display the slightest interest in anyone."

"You're telling me our feisty, independent Tirzah has actually taken a shine to someone?" Adam declared in disbelief.

"Not only that, but Dorian was rather taken with her, as well!"

"Dorian is interested in Tirzah?"

"Without a doubt," Tabitha grinned, wondering why Adam appeared to visibly relax at the disclosure. "In all the years I've known him, I've never seen him flustered before… until now."

"Well, I can't wait to see where this goes," Adam grinned, shaking his head in amusement. "I must confess, I have a hard time imagining our spunky potter woman opening her heart to anyone, ever. Especially given her fiercely independent nature."

"And considering her past, as well," Tabitha sadly agreed. "Her first marriage wasn't a positive experience, to say the least."

"I suspected as much."

"Perhaps we should be praying for them, Adam. Regardless of what the future holds for Dorian or for Tirzah, I'm afraid that she might close her heart to love again, even if the Lord ordained it."

"It's a thoughtful prayer, and one I shall join you in praying."

"Thank you, Adam," Tabitha said, knowing he meant it.

"But what of you?" Adam asked her, his gaze growing serious. Too serious for Tabitha's liking. "What if God brought someone into your life, Tabitha? Would *you* open *your* heart to the prospect of love again?"

Feeling trapped, Tabitha met his gaze with anxious eyes as visions of Stephanos danced in her mind. The searing pain of loss remained all too real, though she tried not to dwell on such feelings. Still, the oozing ache resurfaced at the most inconvenient of times.

Like now.

"Tabitha?" Adam gently prompted, sensing her inner turmoil.

"I—" Tabitha stammered, wondering how to best answer his question truthfully. She saw the hope reflected in his eyes, shadowed with deep concern for her. Was he simply asking the question for the sake of her future well-being, or was his inquiry fueled by more personal intent?

"I'm not asking you to marry me, Tabitha," Adam chuckled, tucking a stray strand of her golden hair behind her ear. The gesture felt natural, but tender. "I'm simply asking if you would ever be open to the concept of loving someone again."

"I love *many* people, Adam," Tabitha tried to object. "I love my brothers and sisters in Christ, the widows and orphans of this region, those of my home church in Jerusalem—"

"I'm speaking of a deeper love," Adam gently interjected. "I think you know what I mean."

Yes, I'm afraid I might, Tabitha thought, near panic. Though she had no desire to obliterate the friendship she shared with the handsome young merchant, how could she truthfully say when—or *if*—she would ever be ready to move on?

And how could she? How could she do such a thing without betraying the memory of her wonderful Stephanos?

"It's all right," Adam assured her kindly. "We don't have to talk about it."

"I'm sorry, Adam—"

"No, no," Adam smiled, gently hushing her by placing a finger before her lips. "There's no need to be sorry. I value your honesty."

With a sinking feeling, Tabitha watched him as he rose from the bench. Turning around to face her, he offered his hand.

Tentatively accepting his assistance, Tabitha rose from the bench, wondering why she felt so discouraged.

"The believers will begin arriving for prayer service any moment now," Adam told her, his cheerful tone almost masking the disappointment in his kind eyes. "Shall we head that way?"

Nodding her agreement, Tabitha fell into step beside him and the two returned to Joram's mansion in silence.

CHAPTER 18

Rhoda

Jerusalem

The late summer heat wasn't the only thing that had become unbearably oppressive in recent weeks.

Going about her chores as cheerfully as possible, Rhoda felt like a fraud. Her heart was heavy, despite the halfhearted smile that remained fixed in place.

It had been several weeks since she'd stumbled upon the private conversation between Mary and John Mark. Rhoda imagined most of the details pertaining to the betrothal had already been worked out. And as the autumn months and ensuing festival season drew nearer, Rhoda couldn't help but agonize over what was to come.

Would John Mark's betrothed be invited to share the holidays and feast days with them? Would she have to serve the glowing couple as they lounged together at the table, planning and dreaming about a future together?

The only thing Rhoda knew to do was to distance herself from John Mark. In her present state, it hurt far too much to be near him, even to see his handsome face. When he flashed her that boyish smile, her heart melted in sorrow.

She wished he would just marry the girl already and move far, far away. She could only hope and pray he wouldn't bring his bride to live in his mother's house.

Turning her attention back to her dusting, Rhoda steeled herself against the tears that had been stubbornly trying to surface for weeks.

She hadn't the slightest desire to waste any more time sorrowing over what might have been. Especially since it would never, ever be.

***

John Mark

John Mark was utterly perplexed.

For weeks now, he'd sensed Rhoda's quiet withdrawal. Clearly, something had changed. But *what*? And *why*?

Nearly driven to distraction with doubt, John Mark's mind buzzed with a thousand different questions about what could've gone wrong. Had he offended Rhoda in some way? Was it something he'd said or done? Mentally backtracking the last few weeks, he contemplated his behavior toward the quiet maidservant, but couldn't think of anything problematic.

Which actually concerned him even more. If he could've recalled a thoughtless word or careless deed, then he would know exactly what the rapidly growing rift between them was about. And he would feel qualified to apologize and hopefully mend things between them. But this? This dreadful, glaring silence between them for seemingly no reason at all? The concept of vengefulness or passive aggression was entirely foreign to Rhoda, so he knew her uncharacteristic behavior was far from petty. If anything, he had hurt her deeply.

He just didn't know how.

But the worst of it all was the niggling fear pounding at the back of his mind, the only logical conclusion he'd been able to reach over the last few weeks.

What if Rhoda had somehow learned of his intentions to marry her and was pushing back now? What if she had no desire whatsoever to marry him?

Had he been entirely wrong about her feelings toward him?

Unwilling to endure the dreadful suspense a moment longer, John Mark squared his shoulders in deep resolve.

It was time to confront the matter head-on.

***

Rhoda

"Rhoda, we need to talk."

Wheeling around in surprise, the shy maidservant's pulse quickened as John Mark approached her with purposeful steps, his brown eyes burning with...something. Determination? Frustration? Zeal? She couldn't quite place what it was.

"We should really talk," he repeated with even more urgency this time.

Anxiously toying with her dust rag, Rhoda wondered what she had done to elicit such a reaction from her young master. In her present state of distraction, had she overlooked one of her chores? It was unlike her to do so, but with this emotional turmoil plaguing her thoughts, she wouldn't be entirely surprised if she had. Lately, her mind had been entirely on John Mark and his upcoming betrothal. Even despite her best efforts to cast such thoughts aside and focus on her work.

"M—may I assist you, my lord?" she stammered nervously as he drew before her in the reception hall, his heavy footfalls pounding on the marble floor and echoing loudly through the vast chamber.

"Yes," he answered shortly, causing her head to come up in surprise at his clipped tone. "What's going on between us, Rhoda? What happened, anyway?"

"What do you mean, what happened?" Rhoda echoed, anxious and perplexed.

"Don't dodge the question. You've been avoiding me for weeks. Why?"

Heart pounding in her chest, Rhoda stared at him with round brown eyes. Surely he had the decency and common sense to recognize that she was simply being *respectful*, keeping a modest distance between them since he was soon to be betrothed!

"Is it something I said?" he pressed, determined to get to the bottom of it. "Or something I did?"

"Well," Rhoda stuttered, wondering how much she could tell him without looking silly. "I suppose it's something you're about to do."

"About to do?" John Mark repeated, perplexed. "How can you be mad at me for something I haven't even done yet?"

"I'm not mad at you, John Mark," Rhoda quickly assured him.

"Well, you could've fooled me. In fact, you did."

"I had no intention of doing so."

"It doesn't matter," John Mark quickly asserted, hoping perhaps they were finally getting somewhere. "I need to know what I'm *about to do* that's upset you so much?"

Biting her lower lip, Rhoda looked away, tears stinging her eyes. Lowering her head in embarrassment, she hoped her pained expression was fully shadowed by her cream-colored head covering. She didn't wish to make a fool of herself in front of John Mark.

"Rhoda?" John Mark prodded, overwhelmed with the desire to soothe her pain and ease the tension between them. "What is it? You can tell me."

Daring a glance at her beloved's face, Rhoda saw nothing but tenderness reflected in his gaze. Which only made her heart ache all the more.

"I overheard you talking with your mother a few weeks ago."

"All right..." John Mark nodded slowly, wondering where this was going. Had he inadvertently said something hurtful about the gentle maidservant? He certainly couldn't imagine doing so!

"Forgive me for overhearing, my lord. I certainly didn't intend to stumble on your conversation," Rhoda apologized, too humiliated to meet his gaze. "But I heard the two of you discussing, well...your *betrothal*, my lord."

Rhoda's whispered admonition was like a punch in the gut, stopping him short.

So that's what it is, he realized, suddenly going cold inside. *Rhoda knows I want to marry her. And she's upset because she doesn't want to marry me.*

Wondering at the strange expression flickering across her beloved's face, Rhoda thought he must be angry at her for eavesdropping. "I truly apologize for overhearing, my lord. Once I realized what was happening, I left. I didn't wait to hear the details."

"Wait, you left?" John Mark repeated, hope surging within him. Perhaps Rhoda didn't realize that he intended to marry her, after all! Was it possible that she was upset because she thought he was going to marry someone else? Had he accidentally broken her heart?

"How much did you overhear?" he asked her, hope returning full force.

"Very little, my lord," Rhoda whispered honestly, mortified. "I left the bibliotheca as soon as your mother mentioned a betrothal."

Oh, I must appear so foolish to him, she thought, her cheeks burning in shame. *Here I am, pining away for him, and he doesn't even want me. He probably still thinks of me as a clumsy, annoying little sister.*

"Ah," John Mark nodded, his hopes confirmed. "And you think I've chosen a girl to marry?"

"Haven't you?"

"Yes, actually," John Mark informed her soberly, the corners of his mouth twitching slightly and betraying his hidden amusement. "I have."

Sensing his sudden merriment, Rhoda glanced up at him, confused.

"Here, come sit with me," John Mark said, taking

her by the elbow and guiding her toward the slanted staircase. Helping her take a seat at the base of the marble stairs, he lowered himself beside her, easily propping his elbows on the step behind them.

Feeling flustered and uncertain, Rhoda folded her hands in her lap, her serious brown eyes searching John Mark's face.

"I believe the Lord has led me to the perfect young woman," John Mark revealed. "It's as if she was tailor-made made for me, Rhoda. I love everything about her."

Squeezing her hands together, Rhoda resisted tears. She couldn't cry in front of John Mark, not when he was so ridiculously happy about his upcoming betrothal. Clearly, she'd misread his signals all along. John Mark wasn't in love with her. He'd found someone else—someone who was perfectly suited for him.

Trembling inside, Rhoda knew she should be happy for him. Perhaps, in time, the Lord would help her achieve such a feat.

But she certainly wasn't ready to be happy for him *today*.

"Mother will make all the arrangements for my betrothal at the proper time," John Mark was saying, his voice reflecting the excitement mirrored on his handsome and aristocratic features. "Though I must confess, I'm impatient. I can't wait to marry her and take her as my bride."

Balking inwardly, Rhoda rose from the steps, unable to stomach another moment of listening to John Mark singing the young woman's praises. Mumbling a weak excuse about needing to return to her chores, she prepared to flee.

"Wait," John Mark exclaimed, clasping her hand and drawing her back to him. "Where are you going? Aren't you going to ask me who this girl is?"

Delicately shaking her hand free from his grasp, Rhoda simply stared at him, astonished by his glaring inability to sense her resistance. How could he be so blind? Didn't he know he was tearing her heart to shreds?

Was he intentionally being cruel? Did he want to see her suffer? Or was he simply the densest young man on the planet?

Neither option was comforting.

"Well?" he persisted, flashing his famously boyish smile.

"Who is she, John Mark?" Rhoda finally asked him, feeling defeated but sensing that he wasn't going to let it go. Forcing herself to keep it together, Rhoda stood rooted at the base of the stairs, hands folded in front of her, simply waiting.

"Frankly, I can't believe you even have to ask me, Rhoda," he told her, smiling tenderly and rising to stand before her. Taking her hands in his, he didn't release them when she stiffened and drew back. Instead, he held them captive, fully meeting her gaze, his own filled with promise. "I've fallen deeply for a priceless, wonderful girl, and I fully intend to marry her someday…if she'll have me."

Heart pounding as realization dawned like a startling explosion, Rhoda wondered at the intensity in his gaze, the intentionality of his tone. Surely he didn't mean…

"It's *you*, Rhoda," John Mark told her.

Stunned to her core, Rhoda couldn't speak. She couldn't move. She could scarcely breathe. Heart pounding furiously in her chest, she could only stare at him, her rosy cheeks blooming with color.

"It was always you," John Mark told her again, his eyes conveying everything she needed to know for the rest of her life. "From the very first, from the day we met, it was always you."

CHAPTER 19

Tabitha

Joppa

There were very few things in the world that Tabitha enjoyed more than gathering with her brothers and sisters in Christ to hear the Scriptures, to worship through song and praise, and to enjoy godly fellowship along with spiritual accountability. And the number of believers in Joppa increased by the day as more locals began to wonder about the strange meetings hosted in the luxurious mansion. While many attended the meetings merely to satisfy their growing curiosity, Tabitha was delighted that most returned night after night, hungry for the joy and peace the believers shared. Dozens received Christ as their Savior each week, fervently joining the growing ranks of believers in Joppa.

Now transformed into a modest but spacious gathering place, the former reception hall was sweetly reminiscent of Jerusalem's Upper Room with its rows of simple wooden benches, warm lamplight, and a low wooden platform positioned at the front for the deacons to address the assembly.

Seated on a bench near the front of the gathering with Laurel nestled contentedly on her lap, Tabitha listened as Adam's father, Josiah, addressed the believers from the speaker's platform. She always enjoyed listening to Josiah's animated preaching. His lusty voice and excited gestures kept the entire gathering engaged from start to finish. She often found herself pondering the Scriptures he shared many hours after the service had ended.

"Sorry I'm late," Tirzah whispered breathlessly, slipping onto Tabitha's bench. Fidgeting somewhat nervously with her head covering, Tirzah glanced a bit too casually over her shoulder.

Intrigued, Tabitha followed her friend's gaze.

Dorian stood at attention near the door, ever ready to jump to her assistance. Even in the middle of a church gathering.

Not bothering to hide an amused smile, Tabitha tweaked Tirzah's shoulder. "The speaker is *up there*, on the platform. Not at the back door."

"I know that," Tirzah hissed, peeved at Tabitha's obvious insinuation.

"If only you had eyes in the back of your head," Tabitha whispered teasingly, her own fixed innocently upon Josiah. "Then you could watch the speaker and stare at Dorian all at the same time."

"I'm not staring at Dorian," Tirzah shot back under her breath.

"You've never been so enthralled by the back door until now."

"Hush," Tirzah hissed again, bristling. "Pay attention to the sermon."

I could say the same to you, Tabitha thought, too entertained by Tirzah's uncharacteristic behavior to take offense. Wouldn't it be something if Tirzah and Dorian's obvious attraction for each other blossomed into something more? They were both kind, thoughtful, wonderful people. Both served the Lord with reckless abandon. Surprised by her sudden realization, Tabitha decided they were a perfect match—Tirzah with her feisty temperament and steely determination, and Dorian with his endearing humility and quiet dignity.

Perhaps they'd balance each other out, in a way, Tabitha thought, amused.

With a bit of effort, Tabitha directed her thoughts back to the sermon. Cuddling her daughter close, Tabitha placed her own cheek against Laurel's, rejoicing in the togetherness of the church body. She was delighted to see so many friends and neighbors in attendance, as well as the clean, shining faces of the orphans and widows hungrily soaking up the Word of God.

It's all so sweetly reminiscent of my time with the Jerusalem church in Mary's home, she thought, her heart constricting just a bit as bittersweet memories crowded her thoughts. How many times had she shared a bench in the Upper Room with her beloved Stephanos, her hand captive in his own as one of the apostles had addressed the gathering. Often, they would discuss the sermon the entire way home, deeply impacted by what they had heard.

Smiling faintly, Tabitha recalled their brief season of courtship before Stephanos had taken her to be his wife. She could still remember the way he often cast her that knowing smile from across the room. Oh, how her heart had raced at the sight of him! And how deeply she missed him now.

Releasing a wistful sigh, Tabitha decided it would be a far wiser use of time to listen to Josiah's sermon rather than mulling over the painful past. Glancing up, she saw Adam across the room, standing beside the platform while his father delivered the sermon.

He was watching her intently.

Instantly unsettled, Tabitha averted her gaze, her heart pounding uncomfortably in her chest.

Sensing Tirzah's eyes upon her, Tabitha drew a steadying breath. She had no desire to dwell upon troubling thoughts. Why shatter the serenity of this perfect evening? Dismissing her unease, Tabitha determined to focus on the sermon instead.

***

"So what's going on between you and Adam?"

"Me and Adam?" Tabitha blinked, unprepared for Tirzah's pointed question.

"Yes, you and Adam," Tirzah emphasized, pausing amid the cobbled street, planting both hands on her hips and staring her down.

"Nothing," Tabitha answered with a twinge of conscience. Resuming her stroll along Joppa's main thoroughfare, she wondered if she could honestly say there was nothing going on between her and Adam. While Tabitha avoided Tirzah's gaze, her friend's glaring skepticism wasn't lost in her peripheral vision.

Apparently, Tirzah was far from convinced.

"Oh, nothing my eye," Tirzah muttered, catching

up to Tabitha as she strode rather stiffly alongside the bustling roadway. "That was quite a display between the two of you during the church service last night."

"Adam and I didn't even speak to each other last night," Tabitha shot back, inspecting the fresh produce in her basket to evade Tirzah's knowing stare. "And there was certainly no display."

"Neither did you speak to him at the fruit seller's booth just now," Tirzah pointed out, unwilling to back down. "What's going on, Tabitha? You and Adam were such good friends."

"We still are."

"Friends who never speak to each other? Who avoid each other like the plague?"

"Adam certainly hasn't been avoiding me," Tabitha told her, peeved. In fact, she'd feel somewhat relieved if he was. Lately, Adam had been too straightforward with her, too honest, his warm brown eyes communicating a far deeper message than she wished to receive.

"Besides, we were at the fruit seller's to purchase produce, not to wile away the entire morning in conversation."

"That never seemed to bother you before."

"There's much work to do at the mansion today, Tirzah. The place certainly won't run itself."

"Come now," Tirzah exclaimed, unwilling to be put off. "With Dorian now on board, you have even more help than you know what to do with! There was more than enough time to catch up with Adam this morning. You just didn't want to."

"Speaking of Dorian," Tabitha huffed, surprised at her own level of annoyance at Tirzah's incessant prying. "Perhaps *I* should be asking *you* about *him*."

"Nice way to change the subject."

"I'm not changing the subject. You brought him up!"

"All right, then," Tirzah acknowledged, never one to back down. "Ask me whatever you want. I assure you, I have nothing to hide."

"Fine," Tabitha said, accepting her challenge. "If you're so enamored by Dorian, why act as if you don't care?"

"I've only been enamored by a man once in my entire life, and it's the biggest mistake I've ever made," Tirzah hotly responded. "I'd sear my own eyes with burning coals before going down that path again!"

"Your first husband."

"Yes. Who else?"

"Clearly, you've noticed Dorian," Tabitha told her, relieved to no longer be under perusal. "I can assure you, he's absolutely nothing like your first husband."

"You didn't even know my first husband."

"You've told me enough about him for me to draw my own conclusions."

"Which seems to be exactly what you're doing concerning Dorian and me," Tirzah shot back, miffed.

"I'm simply saying that I noticed your interest in Dorian when you met him, Tirzah. And this is the first time I've seen you even remotely interested in someone," Tabitha told her. "Dorian is a wonderful, God-fearing man. So why do you insist upon studying him from afar rather than getting to know him as a fellow brother in Christ?"

"Men are great deceivers," Tirzah said, the pain of

her past evidenced in her tone. "And I have no desire to be deceived by one again."

"But Dorian is a fellow believer!"

"He's a Gentile who has spent much of his life serving a greedy, self-centered, materialistic fool," Tirzah spouted, noticing Tabitha's shocked expression a bit too late. "No offense to your father-in-law, of course."

Nodding slowly, Tabitha had to admit that Tirzah's summary of Amal was accurate. There was no point in taking offense.

"Listen, I've been just fine living alone as a widow for more years than I can count," Tirzah declared, her tone uncompromising. "I'm content—even happy—as I am. So why on earth would I toss a man into the mix and ruin everything?"

"But if the Lord led Dorian to pursue a relationship with you, would you be open to it?"

"Now why on earth would the Lord do that?"

"I find that our God is often full of surprises," Tabitha smiled.

"I don't like surprises."

"Is that a no?"

"Yes," Tirzah harrumphed. "That's a no."

"So you'll simply spend the remainder of your days observing Dorian from afar?"

"Of course not! You make me sound like a desperate, foolish woman. And I can't say I appreciate it much."

"I just care about you, Tirzah," Tabitha insisted as Joram's mansion loomed ahead. "If I didn't care, I would hold my tongue."

"Well, the same goes for me," Tirzah told her, emphatically. "If I didn't care about you, it certainly wouldn't matter to me if your friendship with Adam went up in smoke."

"Well, at least we both care about each other," Tabitha huffed, thinking that they'd shared a rather heated discussion for two people who cared about each other! With a twinge of conscience, she touched Tirzah's forearm, a pacifying smile softening her features. "I think we've been a bit silly, goading each other on like this. Perhaps we should simply agree not to talk about it for now."

"I can agree with that," Tirzah chuckled a bit sheepishly. "My, we're touchy today, aren't we?"

"God, forgive us," Tabitha sighed, resolving to better corral her emotions the next time an uncomfortable discussion caught her off guard.

If only she could sort out the tumultuous emotions limiting her patience and sharpening her tongue so often these days. But this was when one was forced to lean on God, to rely upon Him for strength to clear the confusion and to bring contrary feelings under His subjection.

Tabitha knew that feelings could be dangerous. And she had no desire to let them jeopardize God's plan for her future.

CHAPTER 20

Mary

Jerusalem

Waiting patiently at her guard's elbow, Mary watched as he unlocked the iron gate, throwing back the grate with the metallic clash of metal and ushering her into her own outer court with a bow and a chivalrous gesture.

It had been a trying day. Mary had spent the entire morning awaiting access to believers incarcerated in the common prison. As usual, the guards hadn't made it easy for her. She was grateful for the presence of Crassus, her only Roman ally at the prison. His help had proven irreplaceable as she sought to meet the needs of imprisoned believers. As had the presence of her own trained guards. The keepers of the prison were far less likely to bully or intimidate a woman accompanied by a fleet of strong, armed men.

"Thank you, Daniel," she said, hoping her smile didn't appear forced or strained.

"It is my pleasure to serve you, my lady."

Passing beneath the impressive stone arch framing the iron gate, Mary entered the outer court, her gaze sweeping about the attractive garden space. She welcomed the serenity of the peaceful scene. The cheerful chirping of tiny birds, the whistling of the summer breeze, and the gentle splashing of the stone fountain was like music to her ears.

Unexpectedly, girlish laughter penetrated the air—a bit discordant amidst the tranquil backdrop, in Mary's opinion. Her gaze traveling toward the bubbling fountain, Mary saw Rhoda seated on the semi-circular marble bench encircling the fountain, all smiles, scrub cloth in hand, her bucket of warm, soapy water neglected and forgotten a few short paces away. John Mark—also all smiles—stood before the maiden in a confident but leisurely pose, clearly teasing her.

At her approach, they quickly glanced her way, their expressions a bit sheepish, both clearing their throats in discomfiture.

"Hello, John Mark."

"Greetings, Mother."

"Rhoda."

"Greetings, my lady," Rhoda said, quickly scrambling from the bench and effecting a swift but delicate curtsy.

"How was your trip to visit our brethren, Mother?" John Mark asked her, appearing just a bit like a child who'd been caught in mischief. "How do they fare?"

"They're in *prison*, John Mark," Mary reminded him, uncharacteristically nettled. "They don't fare well."

"Ah, yes. Of course."

"Our brothers and sisters asked about you," Mary informed him a bit more crisply than she intended.

As always, she had extended the invitation for him to accompany her to the common prison, but John Mark had insisted he had too much work to do to go along this time.

He looks hard at work, all right, she thought, peeved.

"Ah.," John Mark nodded, clearing his throat again. "I would have loved to visit with them, Mother. But I was buried in work."

Mary's response was a sharply lifted brow.

"Somehow, I wrapped up my work far earlier than expected."

"So I see."

Shifting a bit nervously, John Mark appeared uncharacteristically lost for words.

"Though you seem to have blown through your daily work allotment, I imagine you are keeping Rhoda from her chores," Mary told him, noting the way Rhoda's color deepened in mortification.

Aware of the gentle rebuke, Rhoda quickly offered a shy apology and hurried away to retrieve her water bucket.

Watching as Rhoda hoisted the heavy bucket and prepared to scrub the far side of the courtyard, Mary turned her attention upon her son, her expression enigmatic.

"Apologies, Mother," John Mark said, though his tone was far from apologetic. "I certainly didn't intend to keep Rhoda from her chores."

"Rhoda is a diligent girl," Mary told him once the maidservant was out of earshot. "But I'm afraid she's a bit too shy to speak up if someone is interfering with her work."

"I don't understand why you had to scold her like that, Mother."

Brows lifting in surprise, Mary found herself

instantly on the offensive.

"She did nothing wrong," John Mark continued hotly. "I'm the one who kept her from her tasks."

"But she made the choice to engage," Mary reminded him, attempting to cool her flaring emotions. "And I didn't scold her, John Mark. My reminder was very, very gentle. And gracious."

"I should see if there's any more work to do in the bibliotheca," John Mark muttered as he stormed off, miffed.

Watching him go, Mary resisted the urge to call after him and have the last word. She certainly hadn't appreciated his manner or his tone with her. For the first time, she realized how John Mark's up-coming betrothal could complicate her relationship with him—and Rhoda.

Clearly, her son was already taking Rhoda's side. And it was likely he would continue to do so if issues arose in the future.

And the young lovers weren't even married yet.

Wisely curbing her annoyance, Mary decided to spend some time seeking the Lord on the matter. She certainly didn't wish to allow tension to build in her household.

***

Tabitha

Joppa

"I'm glad I found you!"

Glancing up in surprise, Tabitha set aside her sewing project, feeling somewhat dismayed at the sight of Adam approaching her with his broad, welcoming smile.

"Do you typically do your sewing in the washroom?"

"Only when absolutely necessary," Tabitha quipped a bite ruefully, adjusting herself on the rickety wooden stool and folding nervous hands in her lap. "I needed a bit of peace and quiet, and the servants have finished the day's allotted washing."

"You sure you're not hiding from anyone in particular?" Adam asked her, his expression indicating that he had his suspicions about from whom she was hiding.

Laughing nervously, Tabitha was about to insist that his suspicions were absurd—until she realized that such a statement would be untrue.

The fact of the matter was, she *was* in hiding. But, clearly, she hadn't done a very good job of it.

"You've been nearly impossible to locate lately," Adam informed her, pulling up another rickety old stool and casually seating himself across from her.

"Have I?" Tabitha asked him, shifting slightly.

"Have you been avoiding me?"

Tabitha stared at him, mouth agape, completely caught off guard by Adam's blunt question.

"I'll take that as a yes," Adam surmised with a wry smile. "So my next question, then, is this: Why have you been avoiding me?"

"Adam," Tabitha protested, her cheeks growing warm. "It's not like that—"

"Have I hurt you, Tabitha? Or caused offense in some way?"

"Of course not!"

"Because if so, I would want to make it right," Adam assured her, his brown eyes earnest.

Unsettled by the intensity of his gaze, Tabitha looked away. Inexplicably troubled, she wondered what she should say to him. She knew he'd done absolutely nothing deserving of the cold shoulder she'd been giving him in recent weeks. After all, he was a kindhearted servant leader among the believers in Joppa—not to mention, a very good friend. He'd been there for her from the start, helping her kickstart her ministry with the local orphans and widows by gaining Ruth's trust, and renovating Joram's mansion into a worthy refuge for them. Not only that, but he'd become a pillar of strength for the flourishing young church in Joppa. As a deacon alongside Josiah, Phineas, and the newest appointed deacon of the local church, Simon the tanner, Adam served his community heartily and selflessly.

"You haven't done anything wrong," Tabitha finally said a bit lamely, wishing she better understood her warring emotions. She'd spent many evenings in prayer about the situation, asking the Lord to help her sort through it.

On the one hand, she adored Adam. He was a wonderful person, and it was impossible *not* to like him. On the other hand, she feared perhaps that she liked him a bit too much. And she felt it was likely that their friendship could easily develop into something deeper if she didn't remain on guard.

And the thought of betraying her beloved Stephanos by falling for another man ripped her heart to shreds. She couldn't do that to him. She just couldn't.

Daring a tentative glance in Adam's direction, her heart jumped. He seemed to be carefully reading her, as if hoping to decipher her thoughts. She couldn't help but wish she knew what *he* was thinking, as well.

Perhaps I'm reading far too much into this, she thought, attempting to set her own fears to rest. *Adam is gracious and friendly with everyone. He may not have any interest in anything but friendship with me. I could be overthinking this.*

But when she nervously met his gaze, his own seeking to know her heart, her confidence was shaken yet again.

Had she ever seen him look at anyone else that way? She didn't think she had.

"Have I made you uncomfortable, Tabitha?" Adam finally spoke again, breaking the lingering silence between them. "Do you feel as if our friendship is inappropriate?"

"No, not at all," Tabitha repeated, feeling miserable and humiliated. How could she possibly explain to him what was in her heart without making a complete fool of herself?

"Tell me what's on your mind," Adam offered gently. "I won't be upset."

Studying him closely, Tabitha decided it was safe to do so. Adam had always been completely open with her. It was only fair to reciprocate.

"I think…" she began, her voice trailing off in nervousness. "Well, I think perhaps certain boundaries may be in order for our friendship."

"Boundaries?"

"I respect you immensely, Adam," she plunged ahead, eager to be done with the awkward conversation. "But you're a man, and I'm a woman—"

"That tends to be a winning combination," Adam teased, though his eyes were beginning to reflect his concern.

"What I'm saying is, our friendship should have healthy boundaries in place," Tabitha finished in a rush. "It's not like my friendship with Tirzah, or the female believers, or the widows. I'm afraid we could fast find our friendship becoming...well, something *more*. If we're not careful."

"And, based on your response, I imagine you'd be entirely opposed to the idea?" Adam asked her, watching her carefully.

"I treasure your friendship, Adam," Tabitha told him, feeling broken inside. "But I love my husband, Stephanos. He will always be my husband, in life and in death. Can you understand that?"

"Of course I can," Adam nodded, his voice laced with compassion and understanding. Even so, Tabitha knew she would never forget the hurt and disappointment he so bravely attempted to conceal. "I promise to respect any boundaries you may establish between us."

"Thank you, Adam," she said quietly, feeling as if she'd just stabbed her closest friend in the back. Staring at her hands folded anxiously in her lap, she could almost see the blood on them.

"Well, I'd best be off," Adam announced, rising and flashing a casual smile. "The deacons are meeting within the hour, and I shouldn't be late."

Nodding her understanding, Tabitha watched as Adam turned and slipped out the washroom door, leaving her completely alone with her thoughts.

And far too many doubts.

CHAPTER 21

Adam

Joppa

Slipping quietly through the door of his father's modest house, Adam closed it softly behind him, pausing long enough to take a deep breath to steady his composure. Facing the closed door, he placed his hand on the wood's grainy surface, feeling tired. And defeated. He was surprised by the depth of his keen disappointment, bordering despair. And yet, he knew he needed to keep a clear head as he met with the deacons in his father's humble home. It wouldn't be fair to them, allowing his raw emotions to cloud his logic and judgment as they discussed important matters of the church.

"Adam?"

Turning his head, Adam saw his father, Josiah, across the room, watching him intently.

Forcing a broad smile, Adam turned to approach his father, running a hand through his abundant brown hair.

The weary gesture wasn't lost on Josiah. "Everything all right?"

"Everything is fine, Father," Adam assured him, After all, the world wasn't coming to an end. Even though it felt a bit like it was. "I see that Ida has graced our table with fresh bread and olive oil for our guests," he remarked, hoping to change the subject.

"Mm-hmm," Josiah agreed, his eyes narrowing instinctively as he watched his troubled son. "She's become a diligent housekeeper after embracing Christ as Messiah."

"And we're blessed by her hospitality."

"Indeed," Josiah surmised, watching as Adam strolled around the low table, hands folded behind his back, inspecting the simple but tantalizing spread.

"What happened, Adam?"

"What?"

"What happened?"

"Father, it's nothing—"

"*I said*, what happened?"

Meeting his father's steely gaze, Adam saw the flinty determination reflected in the burly man's eyes. To deny his father's pointed inquiry certainly wouldn't end well. Unfortunately, Josiah knew Adam like the back of his hand.

His plan to retire early to privately nurse his wounds was no longer an option.

"It's a long story, Father," Adam sighed, not particularly desiring to talk about it.

"Phineas and Simon won't arrive for another half hour," Josiah pointed out. "I have time."

Crossing muscled arms in front of his chest, Adam met his father's gaze in resignation. "I just spoke with Tabitha."

"About?"

"About my feelings for her."

Josiah's brows rose in surprise.

"It didn't go well."

"I can see that."

"I'm not sure what I was expecting," Adam sighed, catching himself running his hand through his hair again. "It's obvious she still grieves the loss of her husband every day."

"Then perhaps your discussion today was a bit premature," Josiah pointed out, never one to hold back punches.

"It doesn't matter," Adam said, a bit more forcefully than he intended. "I fell in love with Tabitha the moment I laid eyes on her. But she'll never be ready to move on. Never."

"You don't know that."

"Oh, I know that," Adam told him, somewhat embarrassed by the sympathy softening his father's gaze. "She's still deeply in love with her first husband and probably always will be."

"Give her time, Son," Josiah counseled him, folding burly arms across his chest. "Just give her time."

"No," Adam disagreed, squaring his shoulders in resolve. "If I truly love Tabitha, then I will respect her wishes. And that simply means I won't pursue her anymore." Releasing a sigh of resignation, Adam went around the table, pausing at the foot of the dim staircase. "If you'll excuse me a moment, Father, I have a few things to tend to before the deacons arrive."

Deeply saddened, Josiah watched as his son jogged up the narrow staircase, taking the steps two at a time. His heart went out to Adam—and Tabitha. But how could he possibly help his son understand that, ultimately, God's will would prevail? If it was God's plan to bring Adam and Tabitha together, then He would do so. And if, for some reason, it wasn't meant to be, then God simply had something else—something even better for both of them—in mind.

Smiling faintly, Josiah decided that his son would undoubtedly reach the same conclusion after a bit of seeking and earnest prayer.

***

Mary

Jerusalem

Mary spent much time in prayer concerning her son's upcoming betrothal to young Rhoda, not to mention the family dynamics that would undoubtedly shift after the wedding. She had no desire to become a jealous mother-in-law, competing with the new bride for her son's affections. And that could easily happen if she allowed her emotions to go unchecked. She also recognized the need to uphold certain boundaries and expectations between the future bride and groom prior to the wedding. She knew her son well—John Mark was impetuous and passionate. She certainly didn't wish for him to behave in an unseemly manner toward the pretty maidservant. Undoubtedly, his patience and discipline would be sorely tested during this exciting new season of his life.

Based on recent interactions she'd observed between John Mark and Rhoda, Mary suspected that her son had already overstepped, usurping a task that should have fallen to *her* as the one responsible for arranging the betrothal.

Mounting the graceful staircase which would take her up two stories to the Upper Room, Mary's steps were purposeful as she made her steady ascent. Emerging at the last flight of steps, she paused at the entrance to the Upper Room as the sound of silvery laughter met her ears.

Across the room, Rhoda kneeled on the wooden floor, diligently scrubbing the old planks with a soapy sea sponge. Propped indolently on the bench behind her was John Mark, clearly enjoying watching her work.

Rhoda didn't seem to mind. Smiling shyly, she glanced over her shoulder to acknowledge whatever witty remark John Mark had dropped. And then her gaze fell upon Mary, now in her line of sight. The beautiful woman stood gracefully at the threshold, still as a statue, observing their conduct, her gray eyes solemn.

Quickly pushing herself to her feet, Rhoda offered a swift curtsy. "Greetings, my lady."

John Mark's head swiveled around then, his playful expression vanishing.

"Hello, Rhoda," Mary acknowledged the maidservant, her elegant sandals clacking gently upon the wooden floor as she approached the sheepish pair. "I'm glad to see my son hasn't kept you from your work. The floors are fairly shining. You've done wonderful work."

"Thank you, my lady," Rhoda smiled shyly, beaming at her lady's praise.

"But I'm afraid I must request a moment alone with John Mark," Mary continued, sensing her son's rising angst. "Please see to something else for now, Rhoda. I shall summon you to finish your scrubbing after I've spoken with my son."

"Yes, my lady," Rhoda said quickly, her gaze flitting nervously toward her suitor. Apparently, John Mark wasn't the only one who sensed his impending doom.

"Thank you, Rhoda." Mary nodded, mindful of her tone toward the sensitive maid. "You are dismissed."

With another anxious curtsy, Rhoda hurried away, disappearing down the curved stairwell.

Mary imagined the poor maidservant was probably taking the steps two or three at a time in her hasty retreat.

"Hello, Mother," John Mark quipped, flashing the easy smile that so often melted maidens' hearts.

Fortunately, Mary was a lot tougher than the average maiden.

Standing at the foot of her son's bench, Mary tipped her head, her sheer blue head covering shimmering in the natural sunlight peeping through rows of open windows. "Rhoda seems quite happy, does she not?"

"She does, indeed."

"Excessively happy, one might say."

"Rhoda's always happy," John Mark shot back, his tone tinged with annoyance.

"John Mark," Mary said, placing a graceful hand on her hip. "I've known Rhoda most of her life. I know when her behavior is out of the ordinary."

Lifting his brows, John Mark shrugged in dismissal.

"She knows about the upcoming betrothal, doesn't she?"

Her son's guilty expression told Mary everything she needed to know.

"John Mark," Mary sighed, lowering herself beside him on the bench. "It wasn't your place to say anything to her about the betrothal. In fact, it was entirely inappropriate."

"I didn't mean to tell her," John Mark insisted, feeling cornered. "I certainly didn't *plan* to tell her."

"And yet, that's exactly what you did."

"And now you're mad at me."

"It's not about being *mad* at you, John Mark," Mary told him, striving for calm. She was sorely tempted to remind him that he was *seventeen* years old, not *seven*. He had no business behaving like an errant child. "It's about being *frank* with you. I'm very happy for you and Rhoda, but everything must be done properly and honorably."

"I have always conducted myself honorably toward Rhoda."

"But have you?" Mary asked him, feeling him stiffening in indignation beside her on the bench. "The betrothal hasn't even been arranged yet, and already you have begun interfering with her work and keeping her from her chores. In addition to that, you told her about the betrothal, as well. That wasn't your place, John Mark."

"But you don't understand. Rhoda thought I was betrothed to someone else," John Mark hotly insisted. "It nearly broke her heart, Mother. I *had* to say something."

"Or you could have come to me, and I would have quickly resolved the matter and cleared up any confusion."

John Mark looked away.

"And I believe you know that."

His only response was stubborn silence.

"I'm not against this marriage, John Mark. I believe Rhoda is a smart match," Mary said, placing a placating hand upon his wrist. "But you have a long wait ahead of you before the two of you are wed. The official betrothal won't be arranged for another year at least, possibly longer. Followed by another year in between the betrothal and the wedding ceremony. It's only proper that you conduct yourself in an honorable manner while you wait. Do you understand?"

"Yes, Mother," John Mark sighed, slightly appeased by the gentleness of her tone. "I may not like it," he added ruefully. "But I understand. And I will not shame you."

"Though I truly appreciate your desire to uphold our family's reputation, John Mark, it is the *Lord's* honor that should be first and foremost in your mind," Mary explained. "We must honor Him in the way we conduct ourselves in all matters of life—in our work, our business, our pursuits, and our relationships. And this includes the way a young man relates to his betrothed."

"I have no intention whatsoever of behaving inappropriately toward her, Mother."

"I know you don't," Mary assured him. "But sometimes, a plan is in order. It's best to *plan* not to fail, rather than simply hoping that you won't."

"You're saying not to place ourselves in a compromising situation?" John Mark asked her, amused. "It seems that would go without saying."

"Yes, that," Mary nodded. "But it goes even beyond that, John Mark. Consider this: once Rhoda becomes your wife, you shall assume the spiritual headship of your family. And *now* is the time to begin practicing that spiritual leadership."

"I recognize that," John Mark insisted. "And I shall take that role very seriously."

"Encouraging Rhoda to shirk her responsibilities by interfering with her work isn't taking that role very seriously," Mary stated plainly.

John Mark's jaw twitched ever so slightly, but he didn't argue. "It won't happen again."

"You're a wonderful young man, John Mark," Mary told him affirmingly. "And you shall be a worthy husband and father someday."

"I've never been particularly good at receiving constructive criticism," John Mark admitted wanly. "But I love you, Mother. And I appreciate your concern for me. And Rhoda."

Heart constricting just a bit, Mary patted his arm before rising from the bench to return to her work.

CHAPTER 22

Mary

Ten months later, Jerusalem

Feeling buried alive in ledgers boasting endless rows of mind-boggling numbers, Mary decided she would be relieved when John Mark finally took over the bulk of the business operations, eventually succeeding her. She'd spent many years performing the job of five men, much less one untrained woman. Even so, the Lord had mercifully sustained her through it.

Wondering if she dared turn in for the night, Mary leaned back in her chair, gripping the claw-like armrests. Tilting her head back, she closed her eyes, enjoying the sound of crackling torches, softly burning lamps, and the low howl of the night wind rustling through the canopies just beyond her opened double doors.

Even as endless numerical equations swirled through her tired mind, Mary's thoughts were crowded with additional cares and concerns. But unlike the opened ledgers before her, she was unable to do anything about the outcome of such thoughts. The start of a new year had ushered in a tumult of both political and religious upheaval. Contemplating the turbulent and riotous setting of the current world stage—which included yet another new governor, a new high priest, and a new Roman emperor upon the throne—Mary couldn't help but wonder what the future held for the believers.

Unfortunately, it was highly likely that this blessed season of peace was about to come to a crashing end.

"Shall I return after you've had your nap?"

Eyes snapping open, Mary smiled wanly as a handsome, mild-mannered young man approached her in the bibliotheca.

"Greetings, Luke," she acknowledged knowingly. "I wondered when you would come to see us again."

"You know I never leave Jerusalem after the festival season without a proper farewell," Luke grinned, lowering himself onto one of the chairs across from her desk and setting his leather satchel down beside him.

"And when shall you return to Antioch?"

"I set sail upon the morrow, as I prefer traveling by sea rather than overland."

"Undoubtedly, your patients will be relieved to have their beloved physician return to them."

"Ah, the rascals give me nothing but trouble.," Luke grinned good-naturedly, rolling up his fitted sleeves and leaning back in the chair as if settling in for a nice long chat. "I often wonder why my patients bother coming to see me. They never do what

I prescribe."

Noting the fondness in his tone, Mary was warmed by the young Gentile's obvious affection for his patients. "They're blessed to have you, Luke."

"And I, them," Luke assured her.

Mary smiled at him, her gray eyes twinkling.

"Now, tell me," Luke grinned, leaning forward in his chair. "Do you intend to stir up much trouble here in Jerusalem while I'm gone?"

"I was just pondering that very thing."

"Stirring up trouble?"

"No, not stirring up trouble," Mary chuckled, propping her elbow on the desk and resting her chin on her delicate hand. "But the possibility of trouble rising against us. It could surely happen, given the current state of affairs—both locally and nationally."

"Ah, yes. I see," Luke acknowledged knowingly. "Are you aware of the rumors circulating concerning Caligula's role in Emperor Tiberius' death?"

"Well aware, yes," Mary nodded grimly. "It's been said that Caligula violated the late emperor's will. Apparently, Tiberius had demanded joint leadership between his grandson, Tiberius Gemellus, and his nephew, Caligula. And yet, only Caligula ascended the throne."

"It wouldn't surprise me one bit if poor Gemellus soon undergoes an unfortunate *accident*," Luke said dryly. "Caligula clearly has no interest in sharing his rulership with his cousin. Nor with anyone else, for that matter."

"We can only hope that Caligula will prove to be a fair-minded ruler like his predecessor."

"If rumors can be trusted, it's not looking good."

"I fear you may be right," Mary sighed in resignation. "I have received word from my dear friend, Lady Claudia Procula. She recently arrived in Rome with her husband, Pontius Pilate, by order of the former emperor."

"I imagine the capital city is a madhouse."

"Oh, worse," Mary sighed. "Its inhabitants are torn between rowdy celebrations and dangerous riots, as some rejoice over the appointment of a new emperor, and others mourn the death of Tiberius."

"I can imagine."

"Claudia is terribly concerned about the current state of affairs in Rome," Mary explained, contemplating the information contained in the noblewoman's letter. "She and her husband had set sail for the capital city because Pilate was summoned by Emperor Tiberius. Unfortunately, the emperor died before their arrival. And now, Claudia fears for Pilate to go before Caligula. She senses him to be a ruthless man."

"And I imagine she is correct in her assessment," Luke grimaced, pitying the anxious wife.

"Claudia says that the summons Pilate received was regarding a reprimand. He's been cruel and heavy-handed with the people of his jurisdiction. She'd hoped Tiberius would extend grace, or merely assign him to a new posting. But now..." Mary's voice trailed off rather than simply stating the obvious.

"But now she fears that Caligula will have Pilate executed or order him to commit suicide," Luke finished for her.

"Yes," Mary agreed sadly. And Claudia would be devastated if her husband was put to death without the saving knowledge of Christ.

"Unfortunately, it's not looking good for him,

either."

"While Caligula's rise to power is daunting to some, it would seem others are taking full advantage of his ascension."

"You must be referring to Herod Antipas and his wife, Herodias."

"I heard they recently set sail for Rome."

"Yes," Mary nodded, amused. "Apparently, Herodias' brother, Agrippa—who also happens to be her husband's nephew—was appointed king over the territories formerly governed by her daughter's husband, Philip."

"Roman families," Luke chuckled, shaking his head. "Brother, husband, nephew, daughter... how can we possibly keep track?"

"Well, all the Herods claim to be Jewish, not Roman. But they certainly follow in the Roman way."

"An understatement, if ever I heard one."

"Apparently, Herodias was infuriated when Philip's former regions were assigned to her brother, Herod Agrippa, rather than her husband, Herod Antipas. So she has convinced Antipas to go to Rome seeking a royal crown—and title—from the new emperor."

"Seems a bit risky to me."

"Oh, I imagine Herodias' notorious scheming will eventually go awry."

"One can only hope," Luke grinned. "And what's this I'm hearing about a new high priest?"

"The former high priest, Annas, has kept the priesthood in the family somehow. His son, Theophilus, has recently been appointed high priest."

"That Annas is a crafty one."

"Crafty and dangerous, I'm afraid."

"I imagine he's the one pulling the strings, even if his relatives claim the lofty title of high priest."

"It wouldn't surprise me in the least."

"Amidst all this religious and political upheaval, I can see why the church has cause for concern. Though I daresay you know how to hold your own, Mary."

"It is our gracious Father who upholds us, Luke," Mary gently reminded him. "But I've been thinking about Nehemiah and the great task God assigned him to do. He was called to rebuild the walls of this very city—the walls surrounding Jerusalem. And even when many came against him, he stood firm."

"That legend has always fascinated me," Luke confessed.

"It's not a legend, Luke. It's history."

Brown eyes twinkling, Luke waited for her to go on.

"When Nehemiah suspected that trouble was brewing, he prayed *and* assigned an armed guard to keep watch. He had faith *and* works—prayer *and* action. I think it would be wise for the believers in Jerusalem to do the same."

"How so?"

"We need a reliable contact in the heart of the empire," Mary stated with conviction. "The political winds and tides have the potential to greatly affect the church and the furtherance of the gospel."

"True," Luke agreed solemnly. "But have you any contacts in Rome, Mary?"

"The Lady Procula has agreed to correspond with me for now, but she suspects their stay in Rome will be brief," Mary sighed. "She has agreed to seek out potential contacts while there, but the likelihood of encountering a fellow believer in Rome is minuscule, at best."

"I'd say impossible."

"Nothing is impossible with God," Mary said with an enigmatic smile.

"So I've noticed.," Luke chuckled, shaking his head in amusement. "You seem to have a divine connection, Mary."

"Shall I remind you again that you, too, can have a divine connection?"

"I think you just did," Luke pointed out with a knowing smile.

"Well, good. Keep that in mind, Luke."

"Speaking of divine connections…" Luke mused. "Have you received any word about your former archnemesis, Saul of Tarsus, after his supposed supernatural encounter on the road to Damascus?"

"Not a word," Mary confessed, curious about the matter herself. "Last I heard, he had vanished into Arabia. No one has heard from him since."

"Perhaps he was ambushed by thieves along the way."

"No, not with God's calling on his life."

"*If* he was truly called."

Mary responded with an enigmatic smile.

"Does the man have any friends or relatives here in Jerusalem? Anyone who might know what has become of him?"

"Saul's own sister, Leah, is a devoted member of the church here," Mary informed him. "But she has received no word whatsoever from her brother."

"Strange indeed," Luke murmured, always curious. Clearly, his practical mind sought the missing puzzle pieces in vain.

"Perhaps Saul simply doesn't wish to be disturbed at the present time," Mary suggested knowingly.

"It's been at least a year and a half since the incident on the road," Luke reminded her in the practical tone of an experienced doctor. "It's highly likely something happened to him, or he changed his mind. Otherwise, you surely would have heard something by now. One doesn't simply receive a divine calling from on High, only to sequester himself in the wilderness never to be heard from again."

"I disagree," Mary rebutted with an impish smile. "It would seem most heroes of the faith experience a season in the wilderness—if Moses, Elijah, David, John the Baptist, and even Christ Himself are any indication,"

"Ah, well," Luke chuckled, entertained. "It would seem I stand corrected, my lady."

"I've prayed long and hard for our brother Saul," Mary revealed, her gray eyes conveying the depths of her fervency. "And though it seems as if he's vanished off the face of the earth for now, mark my words: The time will come when the entire world knows his name."

CHAPTER 23

Tabitha

Joppa

"Something on your mind?"

"Ah, greetings, my lady," Dorian acknowledged a bit sheepishly, rising from behind the massive office desk. "Forgive me, I was a bit distracted. I did not hear your approach."

"I can see that you're distracted," Tabitha chuckled in good humor. It was highly unusual for anyone to catch the vigilant manservant off guard.

Dorian's color deepened ever so slightly, revealing his embarrassment.

"Please, be seated, Dorian," Tabitha smiled warmly, always cheered by his valiant and noble presence. "You needn't rise on my account."

"Oh, but I must," Dorian insisted chivalrously, clearly reluctant to resituate himself in the throne-like chair in his lady's presence.

"Shall I command you to be seated then?" Tabitha teased, pausing before the large desk and placing a hand on her hip.

"That won't be necessary, my lady," Dorian assured her, lowering himself onto the chair again in a rather dignified manner. "I shall do as you ask."

"That's better," Tabitha chuckled, dropping onto another chair across from the desk. "I thought someone ought to check on you to see that you're still alive. Martha said you've been working in here for hours without taking a break or even a meal."

"Ah, yes, that," Dorian murmured, his intense gaze scanning the mounds of work upon the desk. "I do apologize, my lady. I seem to be having difficulty concentrating today."

"And for what are you apologizing, Dorian? For working too hard? Or for being too competent? Too diligent? Too trustworthy?" Tabitha arched a brow in question.

"My lady, you are too kind."

"No, I'm *honest*," Tabitha stoutly informed him. "It's no wonder Amal has depended so heavily upon you all these years. Ever since you joined us nearly a year ago, my uncle's shipping business has run like a well-oiled machine."

"Don't you mean *your* shipping business, my lady?"

Still taken aback by the shocking realization every time the matter was brought to her attention, Tabitha wondered if she would ever see the shipping business as *hers*. Or the stately desk behind which Dorian sat. Or the office in which they convened. Or even the elegant roof over their heads. In her mind, all of it still belonged to her stubborn old uncle. At times, she even expected to find him seated behind the elegant desk, his silvery brows furrowed in agitation. Or standing upon one of the balconies overlooking the sea, clenching the wrought-iron railing with white-knuckled fists. It was hard to believe he was gone.

Oh, how I miss that ornery old soul, she thought with a flicker of emotion. Though he'd nearly driven her mad in the process, Joram had ultimately found Jesus in the end. And someday, uncle and niece would be reunited again, under far better circumstances.

"You *do* know that this business belongs to you now, my lady?" Dorian reminded her again, the corners of his mouth teasing a small smile.

"Only by God's grace, Dorian," she said quickly, reminding herself as much as him. "His mercies truly never cease, and I am overwhelmed by His tender provision." Not only had He supplied a breathtaking seaside home for her and her young daughter, but along with it, He'd enabled her to provide a refuge for dozens of impoverished orphans and widows— every last one of them precious in the sight of God. Joram's mansion, once a cold, dismal place, now rang with the laughter of happy children. The great halls resonated with the hymns and prayers of the saints as they convened daily to study the Word and immerse themselves in prayer. What drastic changes had taken place in such a short amount of time!

Equally astonishing was the fact that God had also provided a booming business to fund Tabitha's ministerial endeavors, a financial partner to back it, and a worthy brother in Christ to help her with the daily operations.

It left her breathless every time she allowed herself a moment to ponder it.

"Now, about this distraction that's been plaguing you all day," Tabitha challenged, already convinced she knew what his agitation was about. "Is there anything I can do to help?"

"I'm afraid not, my lady."

"No?"

"No, my lady."

"Would you care to discuss it?" she prodded with a teasing smile. "Perhaps I *can* help. Even if it's only to lend a listening ear."

"My lady, I suspect you already know what is on my mind."

"I do have my suspicions," Tabitha admitted, her hazel-green eyes lighting with mischief.

"Forgive me, Lady Tabitha," Dorian said, his color deepening a bit further. "I really should be focusing on work right now—"

"Nonsense," Tabitha cut in, holding up her hand to stop him. "You're a workhorse, Dorian. Even *you* must take a moment to pause and breathe on occasion."

Dorian's expression indicated that he strongly disagreed.

"It's about Tirzah, isn't it?" she dared, tickled when his smooth olive complexion turned yet another shade of scarlet.

"I have no business daydreaming about a beautiful young woman like Tirzah, my lady," Dorian said, lowering his tone. "What must she think of me?"

"If she has any brains inside her head, then she deeply respects you," Tabitha said stoutly. "You are a kind, godly man with a servant's heart of gold. She would be crazy not to notice."

"I imagine she's a great deal younger than I," Dorian added. "She may not be interested in an older man."

"Dorian, you're not *old*," Tabitha harrumphed. "And, frankly, Tirzah's no spring chicken herself. She's at least ten or fifteen years my senior."

Dorian looked at her in surprise. But that wasn't unexpected—Tirzah had aged very gracefully. The attractive woman appeared at least a decade younger than she actually was.

"Tirzah is only about ten years younger than you," Tabitha proudly informed him.

"But wouldn't she prefer someone closer to her own age?"

"My wonderful Stephanos was about fifteen years older than me," Tabitha assured him. "Trust me when I say that didn't stop me for a moment."

Dorian didn't appear convinced.

"Besides, since when do my people—or yours, for that matter—marry within their own age bracket? Most men take brides who are quite a bit younger than they are."

"My lady," Dorian assessed, folding his large, well-shaped hands under his chin. "One might think you were trying to convince me to pursue her."

"Perhaps I am," Tabitha flung back at him, an impish smile playing about the corners of her lips.

"And if I should attempt such a daring feat, do you believe she would receive it well?"

Dorian's practical question gave Tabitha pause. How *would* Tirzah receive it if Dorian decided to pursue her? It had been at least a year since Tabitha had discussed the matter with Tirzah, as both women had agreed it was best not to squabble about Dorian's obvious attraction to Tirzah, nor Adam's interest in Tabitha. The touchy subject merely led to heated tiffs between them, and neither of them wished to jeopardize their friendship in that manner.

Yet, while Tabitha had wisely refrained from asking Tirzah any questions about the handsome Greek manservant, she had been actively observing the chemistry blossoming between them. And while Adam's interest in Tabitha had seemingly waned in recent months, Tabitha couldn't help but notice

Dorian's admiration for Tirzah growing with every passing day. The man was entirely smitten, bless his proper and dignified heart!

And Tabitha couldn't help but feel certain that her two dear friends were perfectly suited for each other. How, then, could she simply step back and say nothing when they clearly needed her help? Frankly, Tirzah was far too scarred from her first marriage to encourage Dorian's affections, and Dorian was far too reserved to pursue her without a clear sign.

"My lady?" Dorian dared, interrupting her train of thought. "I must confess, your lingering silence hasn't bolstered my confidence."

"Oh, it's not like that, Dorian," Tabitha insisted, shaking herself from her mental reverie. "I was merely lost in thought, considering how perfectly suited you and Tirzah seem to be for each another."

"But does she agree?"

"There's only one way to find out," Tabitha reminded him, praying that she wasn't overstepping or leading him astray. *If Tirzah shuts her heart to this wonderful man, so help me*—she thought, peeved. Surely, her friend was capable of seeing a perfectly good thing standing right in front of her! *But some women never do,* she realized, feeling a slight twinge of conscience as Adam's kind eyes and broad smile flashed across her subconscious mind. *Now, now,* she argued with her own conscience. *This is different! Besides, Adam has clearly lost interest in me. He rarely seeks me out anymore. And on the unusual occasions when he does, our conversations are casual to a fault. Perhaps he's finally met someone else and forgotten all about me.*

Annoyed, Tabitha wondered why that bothered her so much.

Dismissing her train of thought, Tabitha rose

from her seat. Crossing the short distance between her gilded chair and the large cedar desk, she paused before it, placing an encouraging hand on Dorian's muscled forearm. He looked up at her with searching eyes, sensing that she wanted to say more. *If only he understood the hurt and betrayal Tirzah experienced with her first husband,* she thought sadly. *Then, he would better understand her reservations.* But she knew she mustn't tell him Tirzah's story, not now. Probably not ever. And certainly not without her friend's permission.

But how much could she say to Dorian without betraying Tirzah's trust? She felt he needed to know.

"Tirzah has had a very difficult life, and she's experienced a great deal of loss," she said slowly, touched by the understanding flickering in Dorian's eyes. "The best advice I can offer you is to let her see who you really are, because she won't be able to help falling in love with you. Allow her time to see your character, your heart. And don't give up on her. She'll come around, I'm quite sure of it."

"All right, then" Dorian nodded, his heart uncharacteristically upon his sleeve. "I trust your judgment, my lady. And I shall do as you suggest."

CHAPTER 24

Tirzah

Joppa

Reaching for the swinging back door utilized by the kitchen staff, Tirzah hoisted a heavy wooden box a bit higher, propping it against her hip as she struggled to push open the uncooperative door. Impatiently blowing her brown bangs out of her eyes, she wished she had a free hand to swipe the sweat on her brow. Summer was fast approaching, and her added cargo made her even more keenly aware of that unpleasant fact. Feeling sweaty and irritable, she was already regretting her refusal to allow Adam to carry the cumbersome crate to Tabitha's mansion, recently dubbed *the Refuge,* by the orphans and widows residing there.

It had certainly been a ponderous trip from Josiah and Adam's dockside booth all the way back to the Refuge, toting the laborious wooden crate overflowing with hand-carved toys lovingly crafted by father and son for the orphans at the Refuge.

Bless them, Tirzah thought, still struggling with the swinging door. *They have such a heart for Tabitha's orphans.*

And she ought to know. She'd become the designated go-between, of sorts, for Tabitha and Adam ever since they'd decided to start avoiding each other like the plague. She'd made more trips back and forth between Josiah's house and his market stall than she cared to admit, as he and Adam often had donations for the Refuge. Usually, it was toys they had designed by hand or *surplus* produce from Josiah's fruit vendor's stall—although Tirzah knew better. The two deacons always gave generously whether they had extra or not. Even if it meant they had less for themselves.

Typically, Adam insisted on helping her carry the boxes back to the Refuge. This time, however, she'd argued adamantly against it. She wasn't in the mood for company, nor for the cheerful small talk Adam would make on the way back, heroically pretending that Tabitha hadn't broken his heart into a thousand pieces.

Well, it would've been worth enduring the sadness in his eyes today, Tirzah decided as the box nearly slipped from her grasp. Was it just her imagination, or was the crate much heavier *now* than it had been when she left the docks? Well, Adam had been eager enough to help. It was her own blamed foolishness that had prevented him from doing so. After vehemently refuting his help multiple times, Adam had finally backed off and allowed her to shoulder the crate herself.

Oh dear, she realized a bit too late. Adam had

probably assumed that Tabitha didn't want to see him. In fact, he probably thought Tirzah had refused his help to keep him away from the Refuge.

Well, I probably just increased the tension between them, she realized. It wasn't the first time she'd regretted her impulsivity.

Unfortunately, it probably wouldn't be the last, either.

"Ha!" she declared, finally succeeding in pushing open the door with her rear end. It wasn't the most ladylike method of making a grand entrance, but who was watching, anyway?

"Oh no!" she cried out, suddenly losing her grasp on the heavy crate. Sickened, she knew it was about to crash to the unforgiving flagstones below, probably shattering the lovely toys Adam and Josiah had so lovingly crafted.

"Steady now." Seeming to materialize out of nowhere, Dorian appeared in the nick of time, catching the box in strong arms and stopping the swinging door with his foot just before it could hit her.

Open-mouthed, Tirzah met the tall manservant's gaze, his own just a bit too intense for her liking.

"Shall I carry this inside for you, my lady?" he asked her, appearing even more chivalrous than usual.

"I believe I can handle that myself, thank you," she responded tersely, reaching for it.

Stepping just beyond her reach, Dorian lifted a brow in question. "Forgive me, my lady, but you very narrowly escaped disaster just now. Please, allow me to carry it for you."

"I almost dropped a box," Tirzah shot back, miffed. "I hardly call that a disaster."

"Had you been injured, or had these lovely little toys suffered harm, you might feel otherwise," he crisply informed her, surprising her with his grit.

Clearly, her fuming didn't bother him in the least.

"Fine," she muttered, crossing her arms in indignation. "If you insist, I shall allow you to carry it."

"Thank you, my lady, for the privilege of carrying this heavy box."

Surprised, Tirzah did a double take. Was he teasing her, or being sarcastic? Swiftly perusing his handsome features, she realized his expression was impossible to read.

Swallowing her pride with quite a bit of effort, she allowed him to hold the door for her and entered the vestibule ahead of him, biting her tongue until she thought it would bleed.

Even so, she somehow managed to still the sharp retort threatening to escape her lips.

***

Tabitha

Joppa

Tabitha was surprised when Dorian entered her office toting a large crate of wooden toys. But she was even more surprised when Tirzah rounded the corner, trailing behind him, her lovely features pinched.

"Well, hello, you two," Tabitha beamed, extremely pleased to see them together. "Dorian, did you accompany Tirzah to the docks this morning?"

"I would have gladly done so had I known she was

in need of assistance," Dorian assured her, placing the box on the edge of Tabitha's desk.

"I didn't need any assistance," Tirzah interjected crossly.

Glancing questioningly at Dorian, Tabitha saw the corners of his mouth twitching slightly and suspected he had something to say about Tirzah's stubborn denial. Even so, he held his peace, standing patiently before her desk while awaiting further orders.

Rising from her chair, Tabitha lifted a toy from the box—a delicately carved, hand-painted wooden lion with a full mane and an open mouth complete with sharp little teeth. Turning it this way and that, she held it up for them to see, smiling delightedly. "Aren't these wonderful? Josiah is such a talented craftsman."

"Adam, too," Tirzah reminded her, amused. "Might I remind you that he made at least half of these."

"Yes," Tabitha nodded, blushing. "Adam certainly takes after his father."

"Like father, like son," Tirzah agreed. "Both of them, a blessing."

"Indeed," Tabitha supplied a bit lamely, placing the lion back in the box. "The children will love these. I hope you thanked them heartily, Tirzah."

"It wouldn't hurt to thank them yourself," Tirzah shot back pointedly. "*Both* of them."

"I certainly will," Tabitha said quickly, sensing Tirzah's hidden reprimand. A bit embarrassed, she realized that she probably deserved it. "Dorian," she added, intentionally changing the subject. "What's on your agenda for today?"

"First and foremost, I plan to meet with Jonas to discuss the monthly budget," he told her. "Even with profits increasing, I would like to evaluate the possibility of practically cutting costs."

"Have I mentioned how glad I am to have you on board, Dorian?"

"Only every day, my lady," he responded, his eyes twinkling despite his serious expression.

"Well, I am."

"And I am glad to be here, as well."

"I suppose I should let you get to work with Jonas now," Tabitha chuckled, lowering herself back onto her chair behind the desk. "I have kept you long enough."

"Thank you, my lady," Dorian said. With a respectful nod, he turned and strode past Tirzah, pausing at the entrance long enough to cast her a knowing smile.

Still a bit nettled, Tirzah ignored him.

Slipping out of the office, Dorian disappeared, the *clack-clack-clack* of his sandals echoing and floating down the marble hall.

CHAPTER 25

Tabitha

Joppa

Tirzah waited until Dorian's sandaled footfalls ceased before turning to look at Tabitha, her expression conveying her annoyance. "The nerve of some men," she harrumphed, strolling further into the office and resting her arms on the back of the chair facing Tabitha's desk.

"What do you mean, the nerve?" Tabitha laughed, shaking her head in amusement. "Dorian is a perfect gentleman."

"No one's perfect," Tirzah huffed. "And especially not a *man*."

Tabitha wondered at Tirzah's vehemence. It would seem her friend's contrary feelings toward a certain Greek manservant were reopening some old wounds, sharpening her tongue and her demeanor.

"You know," Tabitha said carefully, clasping her hands on the desk. "I recognize there are plenty of bad men in the world. But Dorian isn't one of them."

"And how can you be so sure?"

"Because I know him," Tabitha insisted gently. "He's a wonderful person, Tirzah. And if I'm not mistaken, you suspect I might be right."

Coming around the chair, Tirzah dropped heavily onto it, crossing her arms.

"May I speak freely with you, Tirzah?"

"Don't you always?" Tirzah asked her, arching a brow.

"How do you feel about Dorian? I mean, *really* feel about him?"

"How do I feel about him?" Tirzah repeated, feigning indifference. "I feel nothing at all."

"And in saying that, are you being entirely truthful with yourself?" Tabitha prodded gently, concerned for her friend.

"Yes!" Tirzah insisted. "And even if I did have feelings for him, I certainly wouldn't let them rule over me. Feelings are dangerous. And they can land a person in an awful lot of trouble."

"I completely agree," Tabitha nodded. "Feelings can be dangerous. But you've never been one to be swayed by girlish fancies when it comes to men. In fact, Dorian is the first man I've ever seen you notice. That tells me that perhaps there's something to it."

"You say I've never been swayed by feelings or girlish fancies?" Tirzah repeated, cocking her head in annoyance. "Have you forgotten about my late husband?"

"Tirzah, that was ages ago!" Tabitha pointed out. "And you learned from that mistake. I think it's safe to say you won't make it again."

"You're absolutely right, I won't," Tirzah said

forcefully, shaking her head in dismay. "I swore I never, ever would. I know the cost of falling head over heels for a handsome face masking a demon within. And I'll live alone for the rest of my days before I'll risk doing that again."

"I recognize your concerns, Tirzah. I really do," Tabitha assured her. "But I've been praying about this for weeks, and I feel certain that perhaps your fear of failure is preventing you from accepting and receiving a truly wonderful gift."

"Ah, you've been praying for *me*?" Tirzah asked her with lifted brows. "Well, hear this: I've been praying for *you*, too! And you know what? I think I could say the exact same thing to you."

"To me?" Tabitha blinked, perplexed. "How so?"

"You're one to talk," Tirzah clapped back, peeved. "You say I've failed to receive a wonderful gift? Well, Adam's been in love with you for ages and you pretend you don't even see it! But you do. I *know* you do. Otherwise, you wouldn't be so busy pretending that the poor man doesn't even exist!"

"Tirzah, that's different," Tabitha exclaimed, shocked by her friend's painful honesty. "I loved my husband deeply, and he was *murdered*. If I let myself fall in love with someone and then lose him, how can I bear to endure that kind of pain again? Not only that, but to remarry would be disloyal to Stephanos' memory. How could I do that to him? How could I betray him like that?"

"It's not different, Tabitha. You could take the leap just as well as I could."

"Well, based on this conversation, it doesn't seem as if either one of us will be doing so," Tabitha sighed, wondering why they simply couldn't discuss this topic without argument. Perhaps they were both too raw, too scarred from their respective pasts, to discuss the future calmly.

Saddened, she realized that certainly wasn't what God desired for their friendship. As sisters in Christ, they were called to peace, regardless of past experiences or raw emotions.

"Tirzah, I'm sorry," Tabitha sighed again, feeling deeply convicted. "It isn't my place to tell you what to do. I suppose it's just much easier to look at *your* situation and decide what *you* should be doing, rather than examining my own life."

"Well, perhaps I owe you the same apology," Tirzah admitted wryly. "Funny how easy it is to tell *someone else* what God's plan is for *their* life, isn't it?"

"Well, I guess we should just be grateful we've both been praying for each other," Tabitha muttered. "Clearly, we need it."

"That, we do."

Lost in deep reflection, both women pondered the troublesome conversation that had passed between them. Tirzah was the first to break the lingering silence in her usual frank manner. "Is it just me, or are we both wrestling with the same fears and doubts?" she asked, thoughtfully leaning back in her chair and grasping the curved armrests with both hands.

"I think maybe we are," Tabitha sighed. "What are the odds of this happening to both of us at the same time?"

"Either it's a cruel joke, or the Lord's hand is in it," Tirzah observed with a rueful smile.

"And which do you think it is?"

"I'd be terrified to guess."

"As would I," Tabitha sighed. "But based on the facts, what do you suppose it is?"

"I don't know, Tabitha," Tirzah said, shaking her head. "The truth is, I've prayed for you without ceasing. But as for my own circumstances, I've scarcely prayed at all. I'm ashamed to admit this, but it's almost as if I'm afraid to pray because I fear what God may tell me to do."

"I felt that way at first, too," Tabitha confessed. "Nearly a year ago, I started praying much more intentionally about my own situation."

"Is that when you felt led to place some distance between yourself and Adam?"

"Well, honestly, I may have acted a bit hastily," Tabitha sighed, feeling a twinge of conscience. "I'd been praying for clarity, for guidance, regarding my friendship with him. But even after quite a bit of praying, I still felt as if I had nothing from the Lord, no answer whatsoever. Just silence, dreadful silence."

"That reminds me of something Josiah said during our last prayer meeting," Tirzah pondered. "Remember? He said that, sometimes, God refrains from revealing His will to us until He knows we'll be willing to receive it and act upon it."

Tabitha looked at her, her eyes widening in recollection. She hadn't even considered how that profound statement might apply to her life, although she remembered thinking that Josiah had made a very good point, at the time.

"Perhaps that's why I felt like I hadn't received an answer from the Lord," Tabitha thought aloud, knitting her brows together. "Even though I was still actively praying about my friendship with Adam, I wasn't truly ready to accept God's will if it contradicted my own. Perhaps I wasn't truly waiting on the Lord. Rather, I was just hoping He would agree with me and condone the plans I'd already made."

"Unfortunately, I'm afraid I may be guilty of the same mistake," Tirzah acknowledged. "So what happened during that time, Tabitha? Did you have a lover's quarrel with Adam? Clearly, something changed between the two of you—basically overnight."

"We talked," Tabitha responded, feeling a bit embarrassed. "Adam sought me out and made his intentions clear. He was hoping for a future together, something far deeper than friendship. But I shut him down, Tirzah. I told him that my loyalty is to Stephanos and always will be."

"Tabitha," Tirzah said gently, kindly. "Stephanos is *gone*. He's in the arms of Jesus, awaiting the hope of the blessed Resurrection. Don't you see that?"

"Knowing that doesn't help me feel any less disloyal when I consider giving myself to another man," she whispered, blinking back tears.

"Based on everything you've shared with me about your late husband, it's obvious that he loved you deeply," Tirzah ventured cautiously, praying for wisdom even as she spoke. "Do you truly believe he would have wanted you to endure the remainder of your days alone? You were only nineteen years old when he died. And it's likely you have many more years ahead of you now."

"Stephanos was selfless in every sense of the word," Tabitha said with a fond, teary smile. "He would have sacrificed his own feelings in a heartbeat to do what's best for me."

"Then I think that tells you everything you need

to know about what he would want for you now."

"But even if Stephanos was willing to deny himself for me, why should he have to?" Tabitha asked, her large hazel-green eyes growing serious. "Stephanos sacrificed his *life* for the sake of others. He shouldn't have to sacrifice *everything*."

"Stephanos has already received the victor's crown, Tabitha. He'll never be in want again. His fate is sealed—an eternity in perfection with Christ, his first love."

Biting her lower lip, Tabitha looked away. She knew Tirzah spoke the truth, and yet, her mind cried out against it. How was it even possible for a human being to feel as torn as she did? Much more of this, and her fragile heart would surely be ripped to shreds.

"I suppose I shouldn't have spoken so rashly with Adam that day," Tabitha admitted wearily. "I should have held my peace until I knew what the Lord desired."

"It's not too late to turn this over to the Lord, Tabitha," Tirzah reminded her. "Ask God to forgive you for speaking to Adam apart from His leading, and then entrust the entire situation to Him."

"I will do so," Tabitha promised, feeling as if a weight had lifted from her tired shoulders. "That's what I should have done in the first place."

"I should do the same," Tirzah sighed, her expression indicating that her confession was costly to admit. "Concerning Dorian."

"We can do it together.," Tabitha smiled, encouraged. "And we can pray for each other as we learn to entrust even the scariest parts of our lives to God."

"True," Tirzah nodded. "Because I'll confess,

the thought of trusting another man fills me with trepidation."

"I can understand that, especially after what you endured with your late husband," Tabitha nodded. "But the key is allowing God to lead you to the *right* man. The problem isn't trusting a *man*—the problem is trusting the *wrong* man, someone outside of God's will for you."

"Well said," Tirzah admitted.

"If a man truly loves you, he will have no desire to walk all over you, Tirzah," Tabitha reminded her, her heart aching just a bit as memories of Stephanos' tender protection and provision surfaced in her mind.

"And how can you know if a man truly loves you?" Tirzah asked her, a skeptical brow raised.

"First, he must love God," Tabitha mused, reaching for her stylus and tapping it thoughtfully on her desk. "A man must love his bride as Christ loves the church, but how can he do so if the love of God isn't in him?"

"Dorian *claims* to love the Lord, but how can I know that he truly does?"

"By observing him closely," Tabitha told her. "Actually, you're already quite good at that."

"Oh, stop it," Tirzah retorted, holding back a smile.

"I've known Dorian a long time, Tirzah," Tabitha said. "And I've seen much spiritual fruit in his life. I believe that's how you know if a man's faith is genuine."

"What kind of fruit have you observed?"

"First and foremost, Dorian has remained steadfast in his faith, even while employed by an unbelieving master in a godless city," Tabitha told her. "In addition to that, he has served his master and mistress with diligence. And he has helped my mother-in-law, Daphne, stay in touch with me all this time, as she cannot read or write. Without his faithful help, she and I would have completely lost touch. And Dorian has risked doing this, knowing it could arouse the wrath of his master and ultimately result in losing his favored position with Amal. But it's important to Dorian to help his lady stay connected with the church in Jerusalem, even if it means putting himself at risk."

Tirzah simply nodded, taking it all in.

"Ultimately, only God can reveal His plan for you regarding Dorian or anyone else," Tabitha continued. "But if you ask the Lord to reveal a man's character, I believe He'll be faithful to do it. A potential suitor must demonstrate genuine faith through his *actions* over a long period of time. This is how he earns trust."

"In this case, it may require an especially long period of time," Tirzah muttered. "I'm just not willing to be deceived again."

"And the Lord doesn't want that for you, either," Tabitha said encouragingly. "He desires your best, Tirzah. Allow Him to lead you in this area of your life, and you won't regret it."

"Neither will you, you know," Tirzah reminded her seriously.

"I know," Tabitha nodded, releasing a quiet sigh.

"So…" Tirzah prodded, curious. "What will you do about Adam?"

"Pray," Tabitha responded. "I will pray until I know what God desires in this. Until then, I have no answer."

Tirzah simply nodded. What more was there to say?

"In Jerusalem, the Apostle John was always quick to remind us that there's no fear in love," Tabitha mused, setting aside her stylus and folding her hands on top of her desk. "I often wrestled with that statement. How can one truly love another without hesitation or reservation? Without worrying about what may or may not happen in the future?"

Biting her lower lip, Tirzah waited, sensing that what Tabitha was about to share was very important.

"And then it hit me, the solution to this dilemma," Tabitha continued, her gaze distant as she pondered the surprising answer. "As John says, there is no fear in love, because perfect love—*true* love, which is only the love of God Himself—casts out fear. So we needn't dread it. If God has arranged the union between a man and a woman, then it's *His* love that sustains it."

CHAPTER 26

Tabitha

Joppa

Stepping into the quiet waters of the mikveh housed deep below the stately mansion, Tabitha slowly descended the stone steps, one at a time, until she was waist-deep in the cool, refreshing water. Sinking onto a stone bench at the far side of the mikveh, Tabitha relaxed under the soothing water, leaning her head back against the stone ledge and closing eyes.

In recent months, the mikveh had become her safe haven, the only place she could disappear for an hour, undisturbed. Alone with her thoughts and prayers. Alone with God. Even the servants knew that the underground chamber was off limits, unless she had instructed the maidservants to ready the mikveh for her bath.

The dim, candlelit chamber was inexplicably calming to Tabitha, with its arched stone ceiling, mounted wall lamps, swirling mosaics, and dozens upon dozens of candles burning brightly, framing the underground pool.

Above ground, Tabitha was in high demand at the Refuge. The orphans adored her, and somehow they—along with Laurel, their ringleader—always found creative ways to rope her into their play. She adored her time with the children and wouldn't trade it for anything in the world, even though she often found herself scrambling to accomplish her tasks afterward. She also invested quite a bit of time getting to know the widows in residence, often encouraging them with Scripture and prayer time together. And she was in the process of teaching many of them how to sew, hoping the skill would enable them to provide income to support their children. Then, there was the instruction of the household staff, overseeing the operations of the shipping business, and hosting daily church meetings, as well. Most importantly, she was Laurel's mother, and longed to faithfully train her in the ways of the Lord. The girl was nearly five years old now and full of restless energy. And, of course, Tabitha felt terribly inadequate assuming the role of both father and mother to the formerly abandoned child.

She deserves better, Tabitha thought, wondering if Laurel ever felt cheated without a father. *But perhaps being surrounded by fatherless children here at the Refuge will help her feel less disadvantaged.*

Dismissing the troubling thought, Tabitha settled even more comfortably on the bench, enjoying the cool water upon her flushed skin. After all, she had come here to *pray*—not to worry, fret, and stew.

And there was certainly plenty to pray about.

Her daughter's upbringing, the care of the orphans and widows, her faithful staff, the thriving church in Joppa, the Jerusalem church, her fellow believers scattered across the empire, Eli's refusal to accept Christ, Tirzah's reluctance to receive Dorian's overtures of friendship…and then there was Adam.

Oh Lord, what am I supposed to do about him?

She'd been earnestly praying about the situation for several weeks now. And still, she had no answer.

One thing she did know, regardless of how her friendship—or lack thereof—with Adam unfolded. She owed him an apology for the way she had treated him.

The question was, how difficult would it be to humble herself enough to deliver it?

***

Tirzah

It was a picturesque walk to the village well, and Tirzah always enjoyed the stroll. Overhead, the deep blue sky loomed larger than life as billowy white clouds drifted lazily across the vast expanse. At this early hour, the sun was just beginning its steady ascent heavenward after cresting the shimmering waters of the Mediterranean, casting a cheerful glow on the cobblestone streets and ivory-strewn walls below.

With her earthenware vessel propped casually on one hip, Tirzah adjusted her head covering, pushing it back ever so slightly. She wanted to feel the fresh sea breezes upon her face, fancying the way it tickled her nose and tugged at her bangs. Every so often, she crested a smooth hill, allowing the turquoise waters of the Great Sea to pop into view like a charming game of peekaboo.

"Good morning to you, my lady."

Speaking of peekaboo... Swinging around sharply, Tirzah saw Dorian strolling a few paces behind her, his long-legged strides swiftly catching up to her much shorter ones.

Why is he *here?* Feeling the familiar surge of emotions at the sight of the handsome Greek manservant, Tirzah offered a swift, silent prayer heavenward. She knew that her old habit of building impenetrable walls around her heart at the mere sight of a potential suitor had to go. Instead, she hoped to learn to trust God to reveal the truth to her regarding any man interested in pursuing her.

And it was rather difficult to see the truth through self-imposed walls thicker than Jericho's.

"Hello," Tirzah said slowly, attempting to curb her suspicions. Had Dorian followed her? Or had Tabitha sent him, knowing she would be out to draw water at this time? As he closed the distance between them, Tirzah realized he, too, held a stone water jar, his much larger than hers.

Did he truly intend to draw water? He would look utterly ridiculous, a very tall, masculine man drawing water surrounded by a bevy of chatty women congregating at the village well!

Noticing that Tirzah's skeptical gaze rested upon the jar he cradled in the crook of his arm, Dorian's lips twitched slightly as he held back a smile. "Somehow, Martha ran out of water for the kitchen."

"And she sent you to fetch it?" Tirzah asked him, arching a brow. "She has an entire fleet of kitchen staff at her disposal to get her water. Why would she send *you* trotting after it?"

"Actually, I volunteered."

"You volunteered?" Tirzah repeated, perplexed. "Why?"

"With the influx of new residents at the Refuge, Martha and the entire staff are hard-pressed to meet all the needs and keep everyone fed. I'd stepped out of the office a moment when she discovered she was out of water, and I offered to assist," he explained. "Thought a breath of fresh air would do me some good."

"It's a lovely stroll to the well," Tirzah informed him, monitoring her own tone with a bit of effort. Feeling slightly unsettled and out of place, she knew she could easily fall back into her old pattern of scathing sarcasm.

"It is, indeed," Dorian agreed, looking surprised that she remained cordial even after multiple sentences had passed between them. "As we seem to be headed in the same direction, may I join you?"

Heart pounding in her chest, Tirzah wanted to refuse him. She considered telling him that she wasn't going to the well, but the empty jar propped against her hip was a dead giveaway.

"Very well," she finally sighed, her voice sounding stilted in her own ears.

"Excellent."

Second-guessing herself, Tirzah forced an awkward, lopsided smile—one she was far from feeling.

"Allow me to carry your jar, my lady," he offered, further surprising her.

All right, now you're pressing your luck, she thought, peeved. "I can carry my own jar, thank you."

"I insist."

"So do I." As amusement twinkled in Dorian's eyes, Tirzah realized she was quickly reverting back to familiar habits. She was shutting him out. Again.

Humbling herself with great effort, Tirzah released a frustrated sigh and held out her jar. "Actually, that would be lovely."

Accepting the jar with a bit of flair, Dorian tucked it under his free arm. Ruefully, Tirzah decided she was glad his arms were full. Kept a bit more distance between them.

"After you, my lady," he stated politely with a slight dip of his head.

"As you wish." Clearing her throat in discomfiture, Tirzah strolled ahead of him, hoping she appeared far more at ease than she felt.

CHAPTER 27

Tabitha

Joppa

"Adam, may I request a moment of your time?"

Halting mid-conversation with several of the men, including his father and Dorian, Adam looked at the pretty, earnest young widow as if he'd just been unanimously elected emperor of Rome.

"Tabitha," he finally managed, exchanging a look with his father, Josiah. "Yes, yes. Of course."

"Shall we speak in the courtyard adjoining my office?" she asked him, feeling her face flush with embarrassment as the men encircling Adam exchanged telling expressions. Clearly, they were all busily speculating about what she wished to discuss with the handsome young deacon.

"Yes, of course," he repeated, his gaze darting questioningly toward Josiah. The look of encouragement the father gave his son wasn't lost on Tabitha.

"Thank you," Tabitha managed, quaking inside. "I appreciate your time." Turning on her heel, she led Adam past throngs of believers congregating in her home after the prayer service, through a curtained entrance, down a maze of frescoed corridors, and finally, through her office and out the adjoining door leading to a small, quaint outer court.

"This is a surprise," Adam quipped with a wry smile, stepping into the outer court behind her.

Wheeling around to face him, Tabitha blurted out before she could stop herself, "I owe you an apology."

"An apology?" Adam's eyebrow lifted in question. "Why?"

"Because…because of the way I've treated you." Raising troubled eyes, Tabitha dared to meet Adam's gaze. He stood directly across from her in the smoldering torchlight, appearing confident as always, but also confused. She realized that the outer court felt quite a bit smaller with his broad frame filling the center of it. Suddenly, she wondered if she should have merely spoken to him back in the house, surrounded by fellow believers. It felt a bit too cozy in the elegant garden court with just the two of them.

Sensing her unease, Adam took a thoughtful step back, placing some distance between them. His features appeared even more handsome, bathed in the warm glow of flickering torchlight. He smiled, sending her heart racing in the most inconvenient fashion. How was she supposed to gather her thoughts while he smiled at her like that, anyway?

"Um…" she stammered, the apology she'd rehearsed so fastidiously completely flying out of her head. "I'm afraid I may have been distant...with you. Ever since, well...since the uncomfortable discussion we shared in the washroom...it happened about a year ago, I suppose. Do you know which conversation I'm referring to?"

"Ah, yes, that," Adam nodded. "I do remember. But, yes, that was a long time ago."

"And I should have apologized long before now," Tabitha rushed ahead, feeling awkward and bumbling as she spoke. "Even if I wasn't ready to move on, I shouldn't have handled the situation the way I did."

"You were honest and open with me, Tabitha," Adam tried to reassure her, sensing her distress. "And you needn't apologize for that. I would prefer to hear the truth from you, rather than be misled by false hopes."

"I never meant to hurt you, Adam," Tabitha breathed, frustrated when hot tears pricked her eyes. He must think she was a blubbering fool! "You have been nothing but kind to me from the moment we met. I shouldn't have let fear and apprehension destroy our friendship. I hope you can forgive me."

"You have every right to protect your heart, Tabitha," Adam told her gently. "You were concerned that our friendship might develop into something more, and you weren't ready for that. I understand why you felt the need to place some distance between us."

His compassion only made her feel worse. Why

couldn't he just be angry with her? That would make her feel so much better! If he responded in anger, perhaps that would dash the frightening feelings arising within her, unbidden. Feelings she wasn't ready to consider or accept.

Oh, why did he have to be so understanding? Why couldn't he be furious instead?

"Please," Adam spoke again, shaking her from her present anxiety. "Don't apologize. Like I said, I appreciated your honesty. And I still do."

"I've been doing a lot of praying about us," Tabitha ventured, turning to pace the narrow courtyard. "That's what I should have been doing from the start. And I certainly shouldn't have spoken to you as I did without the Lord's guidance. Though I can't say what God may desire for us in the future, I do believe He has orchestrated our friendship here in the present."

"I believe that, too," Adam said quietly, watching her restless movements and wishing for a way to ease her anxiety.

"You still do?" Tabitha asked him, her large hazel-green eyes hopeful as she paused to look at him.

"Of course I do."

"And you forgive me?"

"I told you, there's nothing to forgive."

"You're far more generous than you should be, Adam. But I'm grateful to hear you say that."

"Friends again?" Adam teased, tossing her a wink.

"Absolutely."

"Good," Adam grinned, offering her his arm.

"Now that the matter is settled, shall we return to your guests? We wouldn't want to disappear too long and give them something to talk about now, would we?"

Blushing deeply, Tabitha accepted his proffered arm, allowing him to steer her out of the garden court.

***

Mary

Jerusalem

Mary couldn't remember the last time she'd requested the services of a religious leader.

Seated across from one now in a dim office buried within the bowels of a local synagogue, Mary folded her hands in her lap, waiting patiently. The house of worship possessed all the charm of a fortress, with its unadorned stone chambers and dark halls haunted by somber men dressed in dark robes and head coverings.

The Pharisee was seated behind a cedar desk, looking both regal and severe in his black-and-white striped garments. Mary thought he appeared rather ghostlike, cast in the dim lamplight as fingers of smoky haze hung heavily in the air, which wreaked of incense. Once inside the grim office, one wouldn't have the faintest idea the sun still burned brightly in the sky just beyond the thick gray walls.

Reviewing the parchment paperwork in front of him, the Pharisee's dark eyes carefully scanned the lines, right to left.

"Everything appears to be in order," he stated after what felt like an eternity to Mary. "The signature of a high priest is required, along with signatures of the bride and groom and their parents or guardians."

Mary breathed a sigh of relief. It was becoming increasingly difficult for believers to obtain the legal documentation required for the most basic occurrences like betrothals, marriages, purchasing a home, or business arrangements. Having been ostracized from the religious communities of their peers, believers were having to jump through ridiculous hoops to obtain even the simplest of documents. Mary was grateful that Barnabas had recommended the services of this particular Pharisee. She was abundantly thankful this man was willing to assist her.

"Have you a priest in mind to conduct the ceremony?" the Pharisee asked her, jarring Mary from her train of thought.

"Can you recommend anyone who would be willing to do so?" Mary asked him, hopeful. The sympathetic old priest who had proven so helpful on many past occasions had recently been laid to rest with his fathers. Finding a replacement certainly wouldn't be easy.

Stroking his long beard, the Pharisee appeared to ponder her request. "You are the sister of Joses and a friend of Agabus, yes?"

"Indeed," Mary nodded, smiling to herself at the now unfamiliar use of her brother's given name. To her, he would forever and always be *Barnabas*. Joses no longer existed.

"Joses arranged this meeting," the Pharisee went

on, watching her. "He seems well."

"He is, indeed."

"And Agabus? How is he?"

"He is well," Mary told him, careful not to disclose too many details. "He recently went to assist a good friend in a coastal city." She intentionally left out the part about the coastal city being Caesarea Maritima, and the friend in need of assistance being an evangelist of the Way. She would undoubtedly lose the Pharisee's sympathy should she be so careless in speech.

"I know of a priest willing to legalize the betrothal and marriage ceremonies," the Pharisee decided, handing her the paperwork across the desk. "He does not squabble over religious differences if he deems the payment acceptable."

"I see," Mary nodded, understanding.

"He will charge a hefty fee."

"Money is no object."

"Very well," the Pharisee nodded, rising from behind the desk.

Taking that as her cue, Mary rose as well. "Thank you for your time," she said graciously, receiving a staid nod from the Pharisee in return. "You have been most helpful."

CHAPTER 28

Tabitha

Joppa

Setting aside a letter from Mary, Tabitha smiled, warmed by the good news it contained. The Jerusalem church continued to thrive, experiencing relief from persecution despite the turmoil brooding in Rome. Many imprisoned believers had even been released to allow space in the common prison. Apparently, murderers and thieves were finally considered a bit more dangerous than the followers of the Way.

In addition to that, Mary had recently acquired the paperwork needed to officiate the betrothal between John Mark and Rhoda. Deeply moved, Tabitha remembered how the former slave girl had followed her around like a sweet little shadow after Mary rescued her and brought her to Jerusalem. Tabitha could hardly believe the girl had already blossomed into a godly woman of marriageable age, soon to be engaged to a wonderful young man.

Inexplicably happy for them, Tabitha's mind was flooded with bittersweet memories of her own wedding day. What precious moments had transpired between her and her beloved husband. She would never forget the love shining in his eyes the moment he had lifted her veil, nor the way her heart had soared when the priest pronounced them husband and wife. At the time, she had been overjoyed at the thought of forever with the man she adored.

She hadn't known that their love story would be so violently cut short.

Glancing up as the sound of a woman's laughter drifted over the quiet garden enclave, Tabitha felt like the happy sound was strangely discordant with her tragic thoughts. She had sequestered herself in the solitude of the gardens eager to savor every bit of news contained in Mary's letter. But somehow, her thoughts had drifted to a place of keen discouragement.

Again.

Shaking herself out of it, Tabitha' surprised gaze fell upon the unexpected form of Tirzah as the lithe potter woman entered the garden enclave many paces away. Dorian was at her elbow, his aristocratic features bearing the slightest traces of a smile as he strode alongside her in a dignified manner.

Tabitha couldn't help but smile at the sight of the two of them together. They were like a fascinating study in contrasts—Dorian, with his reserved and steady manner, and Tirzah, with her carefree and free-spirited nature. She imagined the two would balance each other out wonderfully, if the Lord intended to bring them together.

"There you are," Tirzah exclaimed, swiftly closing the distance between herself and her friend and leaving Dorian to hurry after her as quickly as his dignified strides would allow. "Laurel is asking for a trip to the wharf to see the big boats on the water. I told her we must ask her mother's permission first."

"Why doesn't that surprise me," Tabitha mused, a wry smile tipping her lips. "That girl is full of energy."

"Like someone else I know," Tirzah grinned. "Who somehow manages to perform the tasks of at least seven women daily."

"If only," Tabitha chuckled softly. "If I could bottle my daughter's energy and take a dose of it each day, I would be unstoppable."

"I think you're already unstoppable."

"Down to the wharf, you say?" Tabitha repeated, thinking it over. She wasn't thrilled about the idea. The roads were congested this time of day, and she hadn't time to accompany them, as Eli had already made it quite clear he awaited her in the office to review some important paperwork. And she'd learned not to keep him waiting.

"I overheard the little one's request," Dorian informed her, eventually drawing alongside Tirzah. "And I shall gladly accompany them, if it will set your mind at ease, my lady."

"Oh, Dorian, I couldn't ask you to do that—"

"I insist."

Casting a quick, questioning glance toward Tirzah, Tabitha attempted to gauge her friend's reaction to the idea. Surprisingly, Tirzah didn't seem the least bit disturbed about allowing Dorian to accompany her and Laurel to the docks. But then again, Laurel had the potter woman completely wrapped around her cute little finger. Tirzah would put up with almost any discomfort to please the bubbly little girl.

"Thank you, Dorian," she agreed, relieved he was willing to accompany them. "I know they will be safe in your care."

The expression flickering over Tirzah's face indicated that she wished to argue against needing his protection. Instead, she wisely held her peace.

"Enjoy the lovely day and have a nice time" Tabitha smiled at them, wishing she was free to go as well.

"Laurel will be ecstatic," Tirzah grinned, turning to go tell the little girl the exciting news.

Dorian lingered ever so slightly, exchanging a knowing look with Tabitha. It would seem that Tirzah was slowly warming up to him. Nodding her encouragement, she chuckled to herself as the manservant turned sharply on his heels to follow Tirzah.

Watching them go, Tabitha retrieved the letter from Mary, lovingly rolling it back up and clasping it close to her heart.

***

Tirzah

"Look! Birdies!" Squealing her delight, five-year-old Laurel pointed heavenward toward the snowy white seagulls dipping and swaying in the sky. Darting ahead of her guardians on the cobbled path, the girl was feverishly excited about every single sight and sound along the way to the docks.

"Don't get too far ahead of us, Laurel," Tirzah cautioned, picking up her pace a bit to close the distance between herself and the exuberant little girl. "Stay close, please."

"Yes, Auntie Tirzah."

Warmed by the title of endearment, Tirzah smiled, pleased to see the child enjoying herself.

"To be young again, and so full of life and wonder."

Tirzah glanced sideways at Dorian, surprised by his unexpected remark. And even more surprised by how deeply it resonated within her heart. Watching young Laurel skipping and laughing delightedly, reveling in the simple glory of the morning, made her heart ache just a bit.

Her own childhood had been riddled with heartache. What she wouldn't give to do those years over again.

Sensing the wistfulness in Dorian's statement, Tirzah wondered if he could relate to her own life experiences.

"Have you ever wished you could go back?" Tirzah finally asked him, half expecting the private manservant to dismiss the personal question.

"Quite often, yes."

Surprised again, Tirzah did a double take, reevaluating the man strolling confidently alongside her. Despite his stoic demeanor, he was quite handsome with aristocratic features and a strong build. Prominent cheekbones framed serious but thoughtful eyes. She thought he looked very dignified with his clean-shaven features and short Roman haircut, which emphasized the smattering of salt and pepper colored hair at his temples. Perhaps there was something tragic about his demeanor, though he concealed it well. Suddenly curious, she resisted the urge to bombard him with questions.

"And you?"

Jarred back to the present by his question, Tirzah blinked in question. "What about me?"

"Have you ever wished you, too, could go back? Begin anew?"

Ah, right. That's what we were talking about. "I suppose you could say that," she answered carefully, unwilling to get into details.

"Then we have something in common."

Daring to meet his gaze, Tirzah was shaken by the meaningful look he gave her. For one powerful moment, she couldn't look away.

"Look! Look, Auntie Tirzah! The boats, the boats!"

Relieved for the sudden distraction, Tirzah grasped Laurel's hand as the little girl excitedly pointed a finger at the merchant ships lining the harbor up ahead. "I see them," she chuckled, allowing Dorian to escort them across the bustling street.

As they drew nearer the docks, Laurel began hopping impatiently up and down, hoping for a better view of the ships with their massive sterns and billowing, cloudlike sails. She was a bit short to see over the throngs of humanity crowding the docks.

Swooping her up in strong arms, Dorian lifted the girl as she squealed in delight. Clinging to his chest, the child gazed upon the frenetic activity of the busy harbor, her brown eyes wide with wonder and excitement.

Standing at his elbow, Tirzah watched the two

of them, strangely moved by the scene. Fleetingly, she wondered if this is what it would be like to have a family of her own. It was certainly what she had hoped to experience someday. But one careless decision she had made as a young woman had dashed her dreams to pieces like angry waves battering against a rocky cliff face.

Now, she was far past the age of most *marrying* women. Without a husband. Childless. And petrified to trust a man again.

Get yourself together, Tirzah! Startled by the hot tears suddenly stinging her eyes, she quickly blinked them back, redirecting her thoughts to safer subjects.

CHAPTER 29

Mary

Jerusalem

"Greetings, Sister!" Extending both arms in welcome, Barnabas took Mary's hands in his, giving them a brotherly squeeze.

"Barnabas," Mary smiled, warmed by the endearing sight of her older sibling. "How do you fare, my brother?"

"Even better now that my little sister has come to see me," he grinned, looping her arm though his and guiding her through the reception hall toward the elegant outer court.

"May I suggest we convene in your office rather than the courtyard, Barnabas? I have brought some paperwork for your review."

"Ah, a business call."

"Not exactly."

"Well, now you've piqued my interest," Barnabas teased, taking a sharp turn and guiding her down a frescoed hall toward his private office.

Entering the familiar chamber, Barnabas released

his sister's arm, gesturing toward a comfortable chair across from his desk. "Please, be seated, Mary."

Mary did so, slipping her dainty leather satchel off her shoulder, opening the flap, and retrieving a rolled-up document from inside.

"Is that what I think it is?" Barnabas asked her, his light-brown eyes twinkling with anticipation.

"The paperwork to officiate John Mark's betrothal."

Leaning back in his chair, Barnabas shook his head in disbelief. "When did that boy grow up on us, Mary?"

"I can scarcely believe he's nearing his eighteenth birthday."

"My, that must mean we're getting older, too," he teased, his curly beard twitching in merriment. "But I'm happy for him, Mary. Rhoda is an excellent match."

"I agree," Mary nodded, handing the important scroll over the desk to him. "The Pharisee you recommended was willing to render aid drawing up the paperwork. Your signature will be required as well, since you've agreed to give Rhoda away as her guardian. I have arranged for the ceremony to be officiated at the end of the year."

"And you believe both of them will be ready to take such a big step by then?"

"I do," Mary nodded. "John Mark has been working tirelessly to master his trade in the family business. He's also renovating a private suite on the second floor, where they shall abide together as husband and wife. You'd think that boy was Jacob serving seven years for Rachel, given how furiously he's working to make it happen."

Barnabas chuckled heartily. "And young Rhoda?"

"Rhoda was born to be a wife and a mother, Barnabas. I have no doubt about that."

"How old is she now, Mary?"

"We can't know for certain, since she was rescued from slavers," Mary replied. "We can only go by what age the slavers estimated her to be when she was sold. But based on that, she will have likely reached her fifteenth birthday once the betrothal is officiated."

"And will you follow the customary one-year waiting period after the betrothal before conducting a marriage ceremony?"

"Yes, I believe that's wise."

"It seems like a sturdy plan."

"I believe that God orchestrated the details long ago," Mary nodded. "It was no accident that we just happened to be in Cyprus when the slavers put Rhoda up for sale. And it was certainly no accident that God led me to rescue her and set her free."

"As always, our God knows what He's doing, Mary," Barnabas encouraged her. "You can rest in that."

"Yes," she smiled, feeling slightly emotional at the thought of her only son taking a bride and establishing his own life, his own family. "Indeed, I can."

***

Tabitha

Joppa

The autumn air was brisk as Tabitha hurried down a quiet lane after making a few purchases at the merchant stalls near the docks. Typically, a servant would have been sent to retrieve any supplies, but

Tabitha had tried to make a point of visiting the marketplace herself after patching up her friendship with Adam. She didn't want him to think that she was still avoiding him.

Several months had passed since she had apologized to him in the solitude of the courtyard. And their friendship seemed none the worse for the wear. She was thankful for Adam's merciful spirit. In some ways, he was so much like her Stephanos had been.

At times, just being in Adam's presence sent shards of pain through her heart, reminding her of tender moments shared with her fiery evangelist before he was so cruelly taken from her.

Oh, Lord, she thought, praying silently as she went. *What is Your plan for my future? And for Laurel's? Whether or not I marry again greatly impacts her, as well. You know how anxious I feel about allowing myself to love another man. And yet, it seems as if You've placed one in my life for that very purpose. Adam is a good man, a godly man. And I think he loves me.*

What am I to do, Lord? How do I know what's best?

"Well, top of the morning to you, Miss Tabitha!"

Wheeling around in surprise, Tabitha saw Adam's father, Josiah, approaching her with his long, upbeat strides, a broad smile on his bearded face. "Josiah," she smiled, warmed by his cheerful greeting. "How do you fare this lovely morning?"

"Splendidly," he grinned, drawing alongside her in the narrow lane, his broad shoulders bumping against her as they strolled. "Even better now. It's good to see you, dear little sister."

"And you, as well," Tabitha said with great feeling.

This big, burly man with his swelling joy and larger-than-life personality had fast become near and dear to her heart. In fact, he'd become much like a father to her, with his kind words of encouragement and his eagerness to assist her at the Refuge, no matter what the task might be. Even during a year of estrangement between herself and his son, Josiah had remained steady and kind as ever. Not once had he been petty or vindictive.

Even when she herself had been unkind to Adam.

"Are you headed back to the Refuge?" Josiah asked her, folding his arms behind his back as they strolled along together.

"Yes, I've just returned from the market stalls," she nodded, lifting the basket on one arm. "Adam was there, manning the booth. It was good to see him, as always."

"Ah, it does my heart good to see your friendship flourishing once again."

"Mine, as well," Tabitha agreed, blushing slightly. How much did Josiah know about Adam's feelings for her?

"You appeared very deep in thought when I stumbled upon you," Josiah pointed out, his eyes twinkling knowingly.

"I suppose I was," she confessed, hoping he wouldn't ask any more questions.

"Ah, is something heavy on your heart, dear one?"

Something about the way Josiah spoke, the compassion and understanding saturating his tone, brought tears to her eyes. Mortified, she blinked them back, to no avail. The tears kept coming.

"Oh, dear sister," Josiah said gently, taking her by the elbow. "Come, sit with me a moment."

Allowing Josiah to guide her off the cobbled lane and toward a quiet stone enclave with curved benches surrounding a gently lapping fountain, Tabitha sat down on the nearest bench, her cheeks flushed with humiliation.

"Forgive me, Josiah," she said, swiping at her tears as he sat down beside her.

"There's nothing to forgive," Josiah told her, reaching into his tunic and retrieving a neatly folded cloth. Handing it to her, he allowed her a moment to dab at her wet eyes and compose herself.

"Now, what is it that's troubling you, Tabitha? How can I help?"

Wondering how much she should say, Tabitha nervously fingered the handkerchief, lowering her hands to her lap. She greatly respected Josiah. He was a powerful man of God and a dedicated leader of the church. How often had she benefited from his great wisdom and knowledge of the Scriptures? If anyone could provide godly counsel, it was Josiah. And hadn't she just been asking the Lord for wisdom when the kindhearted deacon had bumped into her on her way back to the Refuge?

Perhaps that wasn't a coincidence, after all.

"Forgive me if I'm wrong, Tabitha," Josiah said gently, sensing her inner struggle. "But would it be safe to assume that perhaps your distress has something to do with your late husband?"

"I miss him," Tabitha confessed, biting her lower lip as her eyes filled with tears again. "It's been over three years since I lost him, Josiah. And yet, he still haunts my dreams. And thoughts of him fill my waking hours."

"You loved him," Josiah reminded her, his eyes

utterly devoid of judgment. "It's only natural to grieve the ones we love when we lose them."

"Sometimes I worry it's a lack of faith on my part," Tabitha voiced aloud for the very first time. "If I truly trusted God, wouldn't I be overjoyed that Stephanos achieved the greatest victory imaginable, rather than wallowing in my grief day after day?"

"I've known you for quite a while now, Tabitha," Josiah assured her. "And I've yet to see you *wallow*. You are a dedicated follower of Christ and a very hardworking woman. You have devoted your life to caring for the orphans and widows of your community, not to mention opening your home to the family of God. Nothing about your life demonstrates a lack of trust."

"If that is true, then why do I feel so uncertain so often these days?" Tabitha asked him frankly.

"May I ask a few questions, Tabitha, that may help us get to the bottom of your uncertainty?"

Tabitha nodded slowly, thinking that Philip had done well to appoint Josiah as a deacon of the church in Joppa. He was born for ministry work. Rather like his son, Adam.

"All right," Josiah said, carefully watching her as he spoke. "After your husband passed away, did you eventually reach a point when you felt as if your season of grief had drawn to a close?"

"I did," Tabitha nodded, her brows furrowed in confusion. "Naturally, there were still moments when I missed him terribly. But I trusted that God had a plan in all things, even Stephanos' death. And I believed that He still had good plans for me."

"And that peace remained with you for quite some time?"

"It did."

"But then, suddenly, your peace was disrupted," Josiah mused. "It is possible that perhaps you feel a bit confused, possibly even a bit guilty, for being drawn to someone else?"

Tabitha stared at him, stunned. He'd read her like an opened book. And, somehow, hearing him state the truth aloud made it sound even more terrible.

"You know, Tabitha," Josiah continued, watching her with warmth and compassion. "The human heart is a strange but beautiful thing. God designed our hearts to expand, to grow, to fill with all our loved ones."

Bowing her head, Tabitha allowed Josiah's words to sink in, sensing that they were important.

"Stephanos will always be a part of you, beloved. And he will always claim a very special place in your heart. No one can replace him, nor should they try," Josiah said gently, allowing her a moment to receive his encouragement. "I understand your grief, child, and my heart goes out to you. I, too, lost my dear wife, and the anguish I experienced at that time was unlike anything I could have prepared myself for. But God is gracious. He has filled my life with many people to love and to serve. And He has given us all the promise of a sweet reunion with those we have lost."

Tabitha nodded, understanding. The Lord had done the same for her, as well.

"In a way, I think I understand exactly how you're feeling, Tabitha," Josiah continued, his eyes earnest. "You see, very few people know this story. But before Adam was born, his mother and I had a son."

Tabitha's head came up then. In all the conversations she'd shared with Adam, he'd never told her about this.

"Isaac was a beautiful child, always happy, and so bright. The religious leaders said he was a promising boy and predicted that he would become great. As you can imagine, his mother and I were ecstatic. We loved him dearly. And then, when he was three years old, he died."

Struck by the horror of the story, Tabitha touched his arm. "Oh, Josiah, I'm so sorry."

"We suffered terribly, his mother and me. It was an inexplicable loss, one from which I feared we wouldn't recover. I had never known such grief, nor did I understand how to cope with it," Josiah paused, thoughtfully stroking his beard. Clearly, it cost him to share this very personal part of his life. "And then, about a year later, we discovered that my wife was with child. I can't even begin to describe the conflict of emotions I experienced when she told me."

"You weren't happy?"

"Oh no, not at first," Josiah said emphatically. "In fact, I felt guilty. As if this second child would somehow *replace* the son we'd lost. You can certainly understand how I felt—no one could replace Isaac, no one! And the thought of another child coming into our home, sleeping in Isaac's little bed, playing with his little toys, sitting at his place at the table—it was almost too much to bear."

Heart going out to him, Tabitha realized that Josiah did, indeed, understand exactly how she felt.

"And then, as the months ticked by and my wife's belly began to grow, something happened inside of me," Josiah went on, offering her a faint smile. "I started to sense the wonder of the little life being nurtured in her womb. And without even trying, I began to anticipate the birth of the child. Which only further increased my tension. Because then I found myself feeling guilty for being happy. After all, I shouldn't be happy! How could I gladly welcome another child into my life, when Isaac was dead and buried? It was a miserable time, and I was utterly conflicted. Until my good friend, Phineas, who had also experienced the loss of a child, recognized my grief and misery. At that point, he graciously took me aside, and we shared a very helpful conversation."

"What did Phineas say?" Tabitha asked him, amazed at how well she could relate to Josiah's tragic story.

"Kindly, patiently, Phineas reminded me that the child on the way was a gift from God, evidence of His tender mercy and provision," Josiah said, smiling faintly. "And in that moment, it hit me like a ton of bricks: the new baby couldn't possibly replace our first child. Isaac would always hold a very special place in our hearts, and the tender memories we made with him would be with us forever. Instead, God had graciously provided yet another tiny person for us to love and cherish, just as He loves and cherishes us. My wife and I realized that we had a very important decision to make. Our loving Father was trying to give us a very special gift. But it was up to us whether or not we would receive that gift from Him."

"And did you receive it?"

"Oh, yes," Josiah nodded, warmed by the memory. "And by accepting that gift from God, I learned more than I ever thought possible about the tender love and mercy of our heavenly Father."

"And then what happened? After you decided to accept the gift you had been given?"

"My wife and I welcomed Adam into the world with open arms, thanking God for His mercy and provision."

Blinking back tears, Tabitha shook her head in amazement. Fully aware of the precious friendship between father and son, she was so thankful that Josiah hadn't spurned Adam when he was born. Imagine all the blessings that would have been lost had he done so!

"So, you see, dear one," Josiah finished, leaning forward and clasping his hands together. "Our God has a way of arranging gifts when we need them most. Sometimes, we aren't even aware that we need them. But He knows. The important question we all must ask ourselves pertaining to the will of God, is this: Will we receive His will and His gifts with open arms?"

With tears slipping softly down her cheeks, Tabitha bowed her head, pondering Josiah's words of wisdom. He had certainly given her much to think about.

CHAPTER 30

Mary

Jerusalem

Mary sank into bed, both physically and emotionally drained.

John Mark is betrothed, she thought, pulling her blanket up to her chin and settling comfortably on the plush mattress. *In a year, he shall officially have a wife. My son shall be a married man.*

She could scarcely believe it, even though she'd witnessed the betrothal herself earlier that evening. It had been a quiet ceremony, occurring in the solitude of her office library. Only five people had been present—Barnabas and herself, John Mark and Rhoda, and the balding, somewhat shifty-eyed priest who had overseen the ceremony. The Pharisee at the synagogue hadn't been joking when he said the little man would charge a hefty fee. Cringing, Mary considered the fact that he would undoubtedly demand another fee when he later conducted the marriage ceremony.

Closing her eyes, Mary thanked the Lord for the comfort of her bedchamber, the soft blankets enshrouding her, and the plush mattress upon which she reclined. She knew it was a privilege to enjoy such luxuries at the end of a wearying day.

It wasn't that she was disappointed about her son's betrothal. She kept reminding herself that Rhoda was perfect for him. The girl had loved him since the moment she entered their home, and she had served him selflessly and graciously ever since. No, she couldn't be happier about her son's choice of a bride. But her mother's heart ached just a bit as she considered how drastically things would change once John Mark became Rhoda's husband, and she, his wife.

Precious Lord, she prayed, eager to commune with her Maker before the sweetness of sleep overtook her. *Thank You for blessing John Mark's betrothal this evening. I pray that You will prepare him and Rhoda to be kind, patient, faithful, and understanding in their marriage. May this waiting period bring great spiritual growth for both of them. Right now, they are experiencing the wonder of young love. But may their love be strengthened and grounded in You. May they stand firm in their resolve to honor You in their relationship.*

Releasing a steadying sigh, Mary silently added, *And please help me as well, Father. Make me a worthy mother-in-law to Rhoda. Help me to respect the love they share. Help me to seek to strengthen their marriage at all times, rather than becoming a divisive factor between them.*

Rolling gently to one side, Mary tucked her hands

under her cheek, smiling softly as she recalled the details of the betrothal ceremony. Appearing more handsome and confident than she ever remembered seeing him, John Mark had beamed as he had presented Rhoda with a delicate golden ring, a token of his affection and promise of his love. Wearing a special ruby-colored gown that Mary had presented to her as a gift, Rhoda had shyly accepted the ring, her face shining with joy as John Mark had placed it on her finger. Though the priest had droned the proper words and phrases to officiate the ceremony, it was obvious both Rhoda and John Mark were lost in each other's eyes, reveling in the wonder of the moment. Mary doubted that either of them had heard a word spoken by the priest the entire time.

Mary released a small sigh, but this time, it was a happy one. God had supplied the wisdom and strength she needed to secure the perfect bride for her son. As always, the Lord had proven faithful.

Finally ready for sleep to claim her, Mary's last thought of the night was a whispered prayer of thanksgiving to her righteous Father in Heaven.

***

Rhoda

Lying awake on her soft pallet in the servants' quarters, Rhoda cradled her hand close to her heart, scarcely able to comprehend that John Mark's promise of love was sealed upon her finger. The vast chamber was quiet and still, as it should have been at that hour of the night. And she was grateful. Some girls may have delighted in being flocked by the other servants and bombarded with dozens of questions about the betrothal that had taken place that evening. But Rhoda preferred to treasure these sacred memories in her heart. She knew she would never forget all that had transpired in the bibliotheca that day. The one she had loved since childhood had pledged his heart to her. The mistress she adored as a mother had stood beside her, smiling her encouragement. And Barnabas, the man she treasured as a father, had agreed to give her away.

Could she possibly be more blessed?

Sweet Savior, Rhoda prayed, curling up on her pallet and closing her eyes. *Only You would notice a shy, orphaned servant girl like me. Only You would rescue her from ruthless slavers to bring her farther than she could ever dare to dream. And only You can fulfill my heart's desire, Lord. John Mark is a gift indeed, but please help me to remember that I cannot love him well if I do not love You first.*

***

Tabitha

Joppa

Elbow deep in bread dough, Tabitha plunged her hands into the fine flour, sending a smoke-like puff of flour into the air, which delighted the giggling children surrounding the large stone counter in Martha's kitchen.

"I said it's time to *knead* the dough," Martha huffed, pretending to be peeved as she planted her hands on ample hips and stared at the playful widow. "Not play with it!"

"Ah, but isn't that what I'm doing?" Tabitha asked her, pounding at the dough as if she intended to kill it and eliciting even more excited giggles from the orphans, Laurel's laughter being the loudest of all.

This was a new concept at the Refuge, teaching the children valuable life skills like cooking, sewing, and bread making. It had been Martha's suggestion, and Tabitha had been pleased the older woman was so eager to assist the children. A firm believer that it was best to keep oneself busy, Tabitha had jumped at the idea. As Martha was already training the widows to bake their own bread, it wasn't too challenging to toss in an additional class to teach the children, as well.

"This is a bread making session, not a lesson in self-defense," Martha harrumphed, drawing more giggles from around the stone counter. "Children, children, please. Disregard Lady Tabitha's antics and allow me to show you how it's done." Tossing a discreet wink at her mistress, Martha stepped around her, ready to show the children what to do next.

Backing away from the counter, Tabitha allowed Martha room to instruct the children. She thoroughly enjoyed tag-teaming with the talented cook. And the children adored the playful banter they exchanged throughout the process.

Pushing open the swinging door leading out of the kitchen, Tabitha caught a glimpse of Dorian and Tirzah near the dining hall entry. Halting mid-step, Tabitha watched as Tirzah leaned with her back against a painted marble pillar, her arms folded across her chest, her head tipped inquisitively to one side as Dorian spoke with her. Dorian's posture was more relaxed than Tabitha ever recalled seeing him as he spoke earnestly with the woman he clearly cared about.

Fascinated, Tabitha wondered what the two were discussing. But considering the fact that Tirzah was fully engaged in the conversation without the slightest trace of skepticism or animosity, Tabitha resisted the urge to join them.

It would seem the independent Tirzah was finally warming up to the noble Dorian.

Shaking her head in amusement, Tabitha smiled, pleased. Backtracking toward the kitchen, she silently shut the swinging door behind her.

CHAPTER 31

One year later, Arabia

Darkness fell swiftly in the Arabian desert, bringing with it a surprising chill that seeped into one's very bones, especially after enduring the scathing heat of the daylight hours.

Barricaded in a private room on the highest level of a colorful establishment catering to desert sojourners, a young man sat hunched at a desk as ancient as the inn itself, studying a parchment scroll with smoldering intensity. Oil lamps flickered in the gathering darkness, illuminating furnishings that appeared far more Arabian than Jewish. Mystical music floated upon the air, filling the entire inn, even though the musicians brandishing stringed, wind, and percussion instruments were limited to the first level of the establishment.

Glancing up from his scroll, the young man raised steely dark eyes toward the open window across the room, his gaze grimly observant as the tapestries fluttered in the chill night breezes, ushering in the mournful desert song.

As his gaze hardened with recognition and determination, Saul of Tarsus acknowledged the Holy Spirit stirring within his breast.

His years of study and contemplation had ended. It was time to resume his calling.

***

Mary

Jerusalem

Sequestered in the bibliotheca at dusk, Mary slowly unrolled the thin scroll that would change her son's life forever. In her opinion, the fulfillment of the marriage document was long overdue. It had been over a year since the betrothal had taken place, and John Mark was biting at the bit to take his bride.

Unfortunately, the priest who had agreed to perform the ceremony had relocated without bothering to inform her. And now she was without a man to legalize the ceremony. Again.

Releasing an impatient sigh, Mary rolled up the document and tossed it back on her desk.

"My lady."

Glancing up from her brooding, Mary saw Tobias hurrying toward her, appearing troubled. "What is it, Tobias?"

"I'm afraid you have a visitor."

"A visitor?" Mary repeated, warned by his manner and tone. "I'm not expecting company, Tobias."

"Shall I send him away?"

"First, tell me who it is. Then I shall decide."

"We haven't the slightest idea. The fellow is very

secretive, I'm afraid. The guards remain quite skeptical."

"Hmm," Mary mused, intrigued. Her first thought was to assume that Alexander had returned to Jerusalem. She also considered Luke but quickly dismissed both options. Her household staff would recognize both young men by now. "A diversion might serve me well this evening," she quipped, a wry smile tipping her lovely lips. "Send him in."

"But, my lady—"

"It will be fine, Tobias. Send him in."

"As you wish." Hurrying away, Tobias' annoyed manner informed her that he considered her decision a rather foolish one.

Tapping her long, manicured fingernails on the top of her desk, Mary awaited the arrival of her guest, her curiosity aroused. Resounding footfalls echoing across the inner court informed her that the visitor approached swiftly with purposeful steps. A moment later, the powerful form of a man emerged, his dark cape covering most of his face and trailing behind him with an air of mystery.

Mary knew she should have been alarmed. Instead, she was intrigued. Folding her hands beneath her chin and tipping her head to one side, she noted the visitor's determined strides and his muscular build despite his less-than-average stature. Surely this couldn't be…

The guest drew before her desk, flinging back his hood.

"Well, well," Mary observed, a small smile playing about the corners of her mouth. "Saul of Tarsus. We meet again."

CHAPTER 32

Mary

Jerusalem

Mary could scarcely believe that Saul of Tarsus stood before her desk, his dark eyes resting enigmatically upon her. In his flowing black robes and hooded cape, he appeared more like a specter from the underworld than a respected Pharisee of Judea.

"Mary of Jerusalem," he said, his voice tinged with amusement.

"You've changed," Mary remarked, fascinated, as her observant gray eyes swept the former Pharisee's person. Whereas before, burning fury had seethed just below Saul's well-presented façade, he now exuded a powerful energy, a burning zeal, that intrigued her. As if all his rage had been channeled into a new, productive outlet, now filling him with a relentless drive to embark upon his sacred mission. Previously, his every word and every move had been carefully planned, calculated, and executed to affect his audience. And while he appeared far more authentic now, years of polished practice still rendered him a bit theatrical, in Mary's opinion. Even Saul's appearance was altered, quite unlike the rigid Pharisee she remembered so well. No longer did he proudly bear the showy robes of a religious leader. Relieved, Mary noted the keen absence of the ostentatious jewelry he had once displayed, as well.

Frankly, the robes and jewelry weren't needed to capture the imagination of anyone within a Roman mile of Saul. *This man would still stand out in a stadium full of people,* Mary realized, admiring the confidence emanating from his form. *And, someday, he very well might.*

"So, I've changed?" he acknowledged, the slightest hint of the old sardonic humor edging his tone. "Do you still think I am a bad fish?"

"That is yet to be seen," Mary informed him, unwilling to make any pronouncements until she'd gotten to know the man personally. "Tell me, can the rumors be trusted? Did you experience a divine encounter while on the road?"

"About three years ago, yes," Saul responded. "Your brother, Barnabas, knows the tale by heart. Surely he revealed it to you."

"I just wanted to hear you confirm it with your own lips. And so you have."

"Surprised?"

"Quite the opposite," she shot back. "If anything, I'm surprised it took you so long to come around."

"Now I remember why I didn't like you," Saul muttered, partially in jest. "You have a tongue like fire."

"Fire purges impurities and reveals the truth."

"Ah."

"Do be seated, Saul," Mary said, gesturing toward one of the chairs across from her desk.

With a wry smile, Saul lowered himself onto the chair nearest her desk, watching her with flickering eyes. "I thought perhaps you might tremble in fear of me after all the trouble I've caused here in Jerusalem. Clearly, I was wrong."

"I fear God alone, nothing else," she readily replied. "Even before your conversion, you could do nothing apart from His permission."

Saul looked away, his expression pained, his mouth forming a grim line. Clearly, he had many lives upon his conscience.

"I am delighted you have come to see me," Mary informed him, softening her tone. "I wondered if this would happen. Where have you been, Saul? We've all wondered about you many times."

"I spent three years in study and prayer, preparing to take up my calling."

"And what calling is that?"

"I plan to take the world by storm," Saul told her, leaning forward in his chair, his dark eyes flashing fire. "Jesus Christ cannot be silenced, and neither can I. The message must go unto the ends of the earth. And I intend to take it there."

"Praise God. How can we help?" Mary asked him, sensing the Holy Spirit burning mightily within him. This man—the unlikeliest of all candidates—was on fire for God. She had no doubt that his testimony would turn the world upside down.

"Actually, there is something you can do for me," Saul said, and Mary could tell that the confession cost him. "I have come to Jerusalem seeking an audience with your nephew by marriage, Simon Peter."

"Oh? And why not go directly to him yourself?"

"I'm no fool. I recall the influence you have with the apostles."

Mary's only response was a knowing smile.

"Can you arrange a meeting?"

Heart pounding, Mary considered the kind of reception Saul would undoubtedly receive from the Jerusalem church. Many family members and loved ones of the local congregation had perished at his hand. It was highly unlikely that he would be received with open arms among the brethren, although she intended to do her best to pave the way.

"Well?" Saul asked her, resisting the old impatience. Clearly, he was still a work in progress.

"Frankly, I'm surprised you came to me rather than seeking out my brother, Barnabas."

"I would have gladly sought your brother if he would remain in one place long enough to be located!" Sail pointed out. "The man can't stay put for ten minutes."

"He does enjoy his travel," Mary chuckled, amused.

Saul shook his head, miffed.

"All right," she supplied, leaning forward on the desk. "I'm sure I can arrange an introduction for you, Saul."

Saul breathed a bit easier, grateful she hadn't made it difficult.

"On one condition," she added, resisting the urge to laugh out loud at the exasperated look he gave her.

"What is it?"

"First, I must ask. Are you qualified to officiate a wedding ceremony, Saul?"

Saul simply stared at her, scratching his head in confusion. "Of course. But why?"

"Perfect," Mary replied, her eyes sparkling with a hint of mischief. "I have a small favor to ask of you. Just consider it restitution for all the trouble you formerly caused around here."

"And if I take the bait, shall I prove to you that I'm no bad fish?"

"It's highly likely," she grinned, awaiting his response.

"All right." Releasing a sigh of frustration, Saul leaned forward in his chair. "Now tell me, what is this favor of yours?"

CHAPTER 33

Mary

Jerusalem

"Wait, you're telling me that you hired a *killer* to conduct our wedding?"

"Would you prefer no wedding at all?" Mary responded a bit more tersely than she intended, nettled by John Mark's obvious prejudice against Saul.

"Of course not," John Mark declared vehemently.

"Well, currently, those are our options," Mary informed her son, watching him as he impatiently shuffled through paperwork at her desk. Her announcement had clearly agitated him.

"I can't believe that villain stood in this very room last night, and I didn't even know it."

"John Mark, Saul has given his life to the Lord. He's one of us now."

"Or so he says."

"Time will surely tell," Mary reminded him, preparing to take her leave. "But I believe he is sincere, and so does your uncle."

"Uncle Barnabas believes the best about *everyone*."

"But he isn't naïve," Mary told him, surprised by the vehemence of her son's reaction. "And don't forget, Barnabas grew up with Saul. He knows him better than any of the rest of us. He would know if Saul was bluffing."

"I hope you're right, Mother."

"Just before returning to Jerusalem, Saul was nearly murdered by angry Jews in Damascus. He very narrowly escaped with his life. His former colleagues stirred up such a ruckus that Aretas, the Nabataean king, became involved, stationing soldiers at the city gates to prevent Saul's escape. Does that sound like someone still working for the religious leaders?" Mary asked him pointedly.

"Any storyteller could have woven that story," John Mark grumped, dismissing the evidence.

"Yes," Mary agreed. "Excepting the fact that Barnabas' good friend, Ananias of Damascus, witnessed the whole ordeal and described it in detail in his most recent letter. In fact, Ananias was one of the believers who aided Saul in his escape. I spoke with your uncle about it this morning. The account is indeed true."

"And exactly how did he manage to escape with soldiers posted at the gates?"

"Apparently, one of the believers residing in Damascus owns a home on the furthest city wall. Local followers hid Saul in a large basket and lowered him out of a window placed in the wall."

"A pity they didn't drop the basket."

"John Mark!"

"Forgive me for being skeptical, Mother, but this is the man responsible for the imprisonment and deaths of countless fellow believers," John Mark declared, and he didn't sound particularly apologetic. "I find his conversion highly suspect."

"It's been three years, John Mark," Mary reminded him. "Surely if his conversion was false, Saul would have come after us by now."

"Maybe he just wants us to think that."

"I think that's doubtful."

"So when do you plan on showing him off to the rest of the church?"

"I won't be *showing him off,* John Mark," Mary argued, maintaining her peace with a bit of effort. "Saul shall be presented to his fellow brothers and sisters in Christ, a changed man. We must pray that the brethren will be receptive."

"Well, this should be interesting," John Mark muttered, closing an open ledger with a loud thud. Coming around the desk, he prepared to take his leave.

Watching him go, Mary released a sigh of frustration.

John Mark hadn't even asked when the wedding would occur.

Shaking her head, she decided to allow him some time to acclimatize to the idea of Saul officiating the ceremony. John Mark certainly wasn't a fan of the former Pharisee.

She couldn't help but wonder, if it was this challenging to convince her own son of Saul's sincerity, how would she ever convince the church of it?

***

Tabitha

Joppa

"This reminds me of the good old days," Tabitha smiled, wiping a clay dish dry and handing it over her shoulder to Tirzah, who retrieved it and set it up in the cupboard. "When we used to host church meetings here in your home for the widows and orphans."

"Ah, yes," Tirzah grinned, receiving another clay dish. "Before you became a lady of means."

"I'm still the same woman I was then."

"Except for one minor detail—you now have an entire shipping business and seaside estate at your disposal."

"Well, there is that. But that doesn't mean I'm any different," Tabitha smiled, used to Tirzah's constant ribbing.

"You know, you're one of the few people whom I can actually say that wealth has not changed," Tirzah told her, putting away the last dish. "How many wealthy women do you know who would have supper at the home of a lowly potter woman and wash her dishes afterward?"

"It's an honor and privilege to share supper with

you," Tabitha assured her, dipping her rag in the wash water, swirling it around, and wringing it out. "And it's very nice to escape the Refuge for a few hours. You know how it is, Tirzah. I'm usually needed for something."

"Those children run roughshod all over you," Tirzah grinned, joining Tabitha at the counter.

"And I love every minute of it."

"The orphans adore you, Tabitha. I don't know how you do it. I couldn't handle one child, much less two dozen of them!"

"Nonsense," Tabitha told her, laughing. "Look how beautifully you interact with Laurel. She treasures you."

"Well, Laurel is different."

"Oh, speaking of children, I received a letter from Kelila this morning," Tabitha remembered, her features lighting up.

"Oh, Tabitha, that's wonderful! How is that sweet little baby girl of hers?"

"Nessa is growing like a weed, apparently. Can you believe she's nearly three years old?"

"No! How is that even possible?"

"I ask myself the very same thing every time I look at Laurel."

"And how is life in Caesarea Maritima?" Tirzah asked, anxious to hear about their dear friends. "Do they fare well?"

"They do," Tabitha nodded, setting aside her rag and lowering herself onto a stool near the glowing kiln. "Agabus is still with them, assisting Philip in his ministry. Apparently, he and Philip have become very close."

"Oh, that's wonderful. Especially since Philip

lost his best friend," Tirzah said, realizing too late how that must have sounded to Tabitha. "Not that Agabus could ever replace Philip's friendship with Stephanos. You know what I'm saying."

"I do," Tabitha said, dismissing the wave of sadness that threatened to wash over her. "As Josiah taught me, God designed our hearts to expand, to fill with loved ones. Philip needs a friend. And I'm thankful God sent Agabus to him."

Tirzah nodded, relieved by the emotional growth she saw in her friend.

"The news I found most exciting is that Kelila is expecting another baby," Tabitha smiled, warmed by the thought of it.

"Is she thrilled?"

"Well, she will be," Tabitha chuckled. "Though she's excited to welcome another little one into their home, she still has vivid memories of the traumatic labor and delivery she endured with Nessa. She has asked us to pray for peace of mind as she prepares to do it again."

"I've heard that the first child can be the most difficult to deliver. Perhaps this one will be easier."

"I'm not sure childbirth is ever easy," Tabitha sighed. "But, yes, we must be praying for a smooth pregnancy, labor, and delivery. We want everything to go well with this baby, and for Kelila."

"Amen to that."

"Childbirth is one thing I'm glad I missed out on," Tirzah remarked, drawing another stool around the counter and taking a seat across from her friend. "You couldn't pay me to go through that now."

"I've been told it's worth it," Tabitha pointed out with a sad smile.

"I don't know if anything is worth that amount of misery!"

"I imagine you'd feel very differently after holding a newborn child in your arms."

"That's one sensation I'll never experience," Tirzah quipped with a rueful smile.

"I wouldn't be so sure about that," Tabitha teased, folding her hands in her lap. "You can't fool me, Tirzah. I see the friendship blooming between you and Dorian."

"It takes more than friendship to have a baby, Tabitha," she pointed out a bit crossly.

"Well, obviously," Tabitha chuckled, amused. "I'm just saying, don't completely write off the possibility of motherhood. It could still happen."

"I'll be just fine if it doesn't."

"May I ask how things are going with you and Dorian, Tirzah? How are they *really* going?"

Sighing, Tirzah leaned her head back as if pondering how much she should reveal. "I've had the privilege of observing his character for over two years now. And frankly, I was determined to find hidden flaws."

"And did you?"

"Not a one," Tirzah breathed, shaking her head in amazement. "Obviously, I'm not naïve. I know he isn't perfect. No one is."

"That's true."

"But his character is impeccable," Tirzah said, still taken aback by the realization. "I never guessed such a man even existed."

"But he does," Tabitha told her with an encouraging smile. "And his heart is entirely yours, Tirzah—if you'll have it."

"Well," Tirzah acknowledged after a reflective pause. "I suppose that's up to him. *I* certainly won't be proposing to *him*."

Sharing a laugh, the two women rose from their stools, ready to get back to work.

CHAPTER 34

Mary

Jerusalem

Crossing her arms, Mary sat ramrod straight upon a long bench in the Upper Room, praying silently as Saul stood upon the speaker's platform with Simon Peter and James, the Lord's brother. The tension in the air was so thick it could've easily been cut with a knife as church members sat rigidly upon their benches, discussing Saul's presence among them as if he weren't right there listening.

"He has no place here!" one man shouted, anger tinging his tone. "He does not deserve to fellowship among us."

"He's a liar and a murderer," another shouted as murmurs of agreement rippled through the congregation. "How can we trust him after all he has done?"

"Brothers and sisters, please," Peter shouted over the din, raising a large hand to still the restless crowd with little success. "Let's discuss this in a rational manner."

Despite Peter's admonition, Mary knew her nephew well enough to recognize the frustration and unease boiling just beneath the surface. She was proud of him for remaining objective, regardless of the fact that the man with whom he now shared the platform was responsible for his own imprisonment, persecutions, whippings, and beatings. Allowing her gaze to travel over the faces of her fellow believers, Mary saw obvious concern on all of them.

Would no one accept the truth about Saul's conversion? Was no one willing to extend mercy, a second chance? Isn't that what the body of Christ was called to do?

Glancing over her shoulder toward Saul's younger sister, Leah, who shared a bench with Rhoda and John Mark a few rows back, Mary's heart went out to the poor girl as her brother's fate was loudly and publicly debated. The serious young woman sat with her hands knotted in her lap, her features taut.

As the din rose in the Upper Room, reaching a swelling chorus as believers argued about what should or shouldn't be done about the former Pharisee and his desire to join their ranks, Mary could take it no longer. Propelling herself to her feet, she turned and faced the entire congregation, extending one graceful hand toward a deeply humbled Saul, who stood grimly beside Peter upon the platform with his head bowed, regret etched upon every line of his bearded face.

"Brothers and sisters!" she shouted to be heard above the uproar. The chaos quieted ever so slightly as the believers stopped to look at her, blinking in surprise. "How many years have we prayed for the salvation of this man? And how long did we earnestly seek his repentance and restoration? How many prayer meetings and services did we host on his behalf?" Breathing heavily, her gray eyes swept over the gathering, reflecting the intensity kindling in her heart. "The answer is *far too many to count*. So let me ask you this: Is it really too difficult to believe that God has answered our prayers? That He has touched the heart of this man? And that He has a plan far greater than any of us could truly imagine?"

The silence lingering in the vast chamber was laden with guilt, but suspicion and mistrust hung even more heavily in the air.

"And by what evidence do we believe Saul's report?" someone angrily demanded. "We have nothing but his word to go by! And what's the good of a murderer's pledge?"

"Not so." At that, Barnabas rose from his seat, turning to face the angry congregation. "I, too, am a witness. I was in Damascus when the Lord rescued Saul on the road. And though I wasn't traveling alongside him when Jesus appeared and spoke to him along the way, I was there when his sight was miraculously restored by the Holy Spirit, through the willing hands of my good friend, Ananias. I was there when Saul was baptized in the name of the Father, the Son, and the Holy Spirit. And I was there when Saul preached boldly in the name of Christ, turning many of his former peers against him. This man's conversion is sincere. I witnessed far too many miracles in Damascus to believe otherwise."

Barnabas' impassioned proclamation was followed by lingering silence as the believers mulled over his words. It was obvious that the perspective of many of the brothers and sisters remained torn. Some were clearly fearful, and others, angry. While still others simply appeared extremely uncomfortable with the entire situation.

Finally, a man stood near the back of the room, his eyes flashing fire. Mary instantly recognized him as one whose father had been imprisoned early in Saul's death campaign. The young man's old father had eventually perished of a wasting illness in prison. "Perhaps God has forgiven Saul," the grieving son spat out, his voice quaking with hurt and pain. "But how is it that we're supposed to just drop everything he's done to us? Everything he's done to our families and loved ones? How many of our brothers and sisters have suffered torturous deaths at his hand? Saul of Tarsus has blood on his hands! He's covered in it. I can almost see it from here."

Murmurs of agreement rippled through the Upper Room, along with the soft sounds of women weeping and children fidgeting in fear.

Turning and approaching Saul with purposeful steps, Barnabas slowly, silently, mounted the platform, dropping a merciful hand upon the former tyrant's shoulder. Locking eyes with the anguished young man across the room, Barnabas' gaze softened in understanding. "Yes," he said gently, his tone saturated with the love of God. "You speak well when you say that Saul is covered in blood. As are you, my friend. As am I. We are *all* covered in the precious blood of Jesus Christ. Forgiven. Redeemed."

The room grew eerily silent as Barnabas' words settled over the gathering, piercing, convicting, true.

"Praise God, the enemy has lost his relentless

battle for the soul of this man," Barnabas continued, and Mary shook her head in firm agreement,
offering a strong, resounding *amen*. "Now, shall we,
as the body of Christ, praise our God for this victory
in the faith? Or shall we allow bitterness and fear to
rob us of this great joy?"

"Forgive me." The entire gathering appeared
shocked when Saul spoke, his powerful voice resounding through the crowded chamber. "There are
no words to remedy the wrongs I have committed
against you. But you have my word that Saul of Tarsus is dead and buried. From this day forward, I am
no longer Saul, but Paul."

Paul, Mary thought, smiling faintly. Meaning
small or *little*, it was a fitting name for one who had
been so thoroughly humbled before God and men.

As a soothing calm descended upon the crowd,
Mary closed her eyes, thanking God for moving
upon the frightened hearts of His children. Undoubtedly, it would be a long, hard road for Paul. But
God was in control, paving the way for the blessed
light of the glorious gospel message.

***

Tabitha

Joppa

"I have news, my lady."

"News?" Tabitha glanced up from behind her
desk at Dorian's unexpected entrance. Noting the
parchment scroll he bore in one hand, she assumed
it must be from his master, Amal.

"We've just received word from my master," he continued, confirming her suspicions. "It would seem he has decided to grace us with his presence once again."

"I see," Tabitha nodded slowly, not entirely surprised. Amal liked to be in control. It would be unlike him to wait much longer before dropping in for a surprise visit to monitor his holdings. "I imagine he will set sail from Greece sometime after the stormy season then?" she confirmed, grateful it wasn't the proper time to travel by ship. After all, that would buy her some time. She wanted to be fully prepared to convene with her father-in-law this time.

"On the contrary," Dorian countered, catching her by surprise. "According to this letter, he plans to travel overland from Caesarea Maritima, where he has been overseeing a few investments."

"So Amal is already in the region?" Tabitha asked him, stunned.

"Apparently so," Dorian mused, his brow furrowing as he scanned the full contents of the letter. "I imagine he could arrive any day now."

"Oh my," she exclaimed, rising from her desk. "I suppose we must prepare then!"

"I beg your pardon, my lady, but what is it we must prepare?"

"Well…" Tabitha murmured, glancing around the office in confusion. "I'm not entirely sure. What does he desire from this trip?"

"He'll wish to see the ledgers, which I can easily review with him. I'm sure he's also curious about what you've done with the place since he saw it last."

"So there's nothing I need to do to prepare?"

"You need to pray," Dorian told her, his eyes

twinkling ever so slightly. "It would seem the Lord has presented us another opportunity to win the old badger for Christ."

"And pray, I shall!" Tabitha nodded, her heart pounding in nervousness. Amal had a way of making her feel like the smallest human in the universe. She certainly wasn't looking forward to sharing more lingering suppers in the triclinium with him as he glared at her over the rim of his goblet. "I suppose I shall have the servants ready a suite for him. He'll undoubtedly wish to stay here with us, rather than at one of the local drinking establishments."

"Oh, yes. Undoubtedly."

"I shall do so this very instant," she decided, coming around the desk. "Perhaps I should prepare my remarks for him, as well. If I present the gospel in such a way that might actually snag his interest this time—"

"My lady," Dorian interrupted, holding up a gentling hand. "Might I remind you that our actions shall prove a far greater testimony than our words."

Nodding slowly, Tabitha released a nervous breath. How desperately she longed to see Stephanos' father saved! And wouldn't Daphne rejoice if her husband returned to her a changed man!

"There is a slight chance that my master will order me to return to Greece with him after this trip," Dorian said quietly, looking down.

"Dorian, no," Tabitha argued, feeling as if the wind had been knocked from her lungs. "You cannot leave! What would I do without you?"

"Obviously, my fate is in the Lord's hands," he said, though she could see it cost him to say so. "And it isn't likely. But you know my master. He is unpredictable. I think we should brace ourselves in advance for every possibility."

"Oh, Dorian," Tabitha breathed, falling onto one of the chairs in front of her desk. "I don't even want to think about losing you. You are so dear to me, to all of us!"

"And you have all become dear to me, as well."

"I suppose this is one more thing to pray about," Tabitha sighed, unwilling to relinquish this loyal, kindhearted manservant without a fight. She resolved she would do whatever it took to keep him in Joppa, even if it meant going toe-to-toe with his master.

"Given this possibility—as unlikely as it may seem—there's something I wish to discuss with you," Dorian added, his color deepening slightly.

Intrigued, Tabitha glanced up at him, her large eyes brimming with questions.

"There's something I must do before I lose the opportunity—or the nerve—to do so," he continued, lowering himself onto the chair across from her. "But, first, before I proceed, I'd like to seek your blessing."

CHAPTER 35

Tirzah

Joppa

Tirzah awakened with the distinct impression that God had whispered her name. Rising slowly from her sleeping pallet, she cast aside her covering as delicious sunlight streamed in the open window, slanting across her form and bathing her face in warmth and light.

Like the sun's soothing and gentle rays, something about this morning held warmth and promise. She sensed the Lord's presence filling her heart, her home. And though she knew the Lord was always with her, she savored these rare moments when it felt like a tangible force, so close she could almost reach out and touch the nail-scarred hands of her beloved Savior.

Lord, You are so good to me, she prayed, rising from her pallet and preparing to begin her day. *Your presence is like a healing balm. I sense You have wonderful things in store today, though I cannot guess what those things may be. Lead me in Your will today. Protect me from my own stubborn will and guide me in Your Way instead.*

After slipping into her simple garments and fastening an apron around her slender waist, Tirzah dunked her hands into her freshwater jar, splashing her face with the cool, refreshing water. Reaching for a soft washrag, she gently dabbed her face dry before hanging it back up on the rope line. Hurriedly combing her hair, she swept her bangs to the side and reached for her head covering, adjusting it on top of her smooth brown hair.

It was time to head to Tabitha's, where she would spend several hours playing with Laurel and the orphans before returning home to work at her potter's wheel.

Slipping out the door, she closed it and fastened it carefully behind her, locking it and then dropping the key in a pocket sewn in her apron.

As sunlight streamed down upon the outer court, Tirzah lifted her face heavenward, enjoying the sun's warmth on her skin. It felt far more like spring than winter, and she didn't mind one bit.

"I thought I would find you here."

Nearly jumping out of her skin, Tirzah's eyes snapped open as she jerked her attention toward the far end of the stone court. There, seated on a bench carved into the wall, was Dorian, appearing handsome and regal as always in his attractive Greco-Roman apparel.

"Well, naturally, you'd find me here. I *live* here," she declared, placing a hand over her pounding heart.

Dorian's response was an enigmatic smile.

"Did Tabitha send you for something?" Tirzah asked him, recovering from her surprise.

"No," he responded with an easy smile. "I came of my own accord."

"Oh?" she asked him, puzzled. "But...why?" It seemed very strange for Dorian to seek her out at her home, despite the budding friendship between them. Not once had he done so before.

"Walk with me?" he asked her, rising from the bench and offering his arm.

Blinking in surprise, Tirzah stared at his proffered arm, balking inwardly. "It's a very kind gesture," she said, glancing around in embarrassment. "But if the townspeople see us strolling about the village arm-in-arm, well, they might make some assumptions."

"Let them assume what they may," Dorian said, surprising her. "Won't they do so anyway?"

"Well, you have a point."

"Come, walk with me," he prodded, extending his arm once again.

Reluctantly, Tirzah accepted his arm, surprised at how natural it felt to take it. She couldn't imagine what this was about.

She could only hope she wouldn't regret it later.

***

Surprised by how much she enjoyed strolling the cobbled village streets arm-in-arm with Dorian, Tirzah was caught off guard when he eventually led her to her place of refuge, the rocky cleft overlooking the sparkling waters of the Mediterranean.

Much to her surprise, an elegant marble bench had been placed a cautious distance from the ledge, framed on all sides by Grecian urns of wildflowers.

"What is this?" Perplexed, Tirzah looked at Dorian as he drew her toward the bench. "How did you know—" Stopping short, she furrowed her brow. *Tabitha!* Her best friend was the only other person in the world who knew how special this spot was to her. "I accepted Jesus as Lord and Savior here," she said, allowing him to help her get situated on the bench.

"I know." He smiled faintly, sitting beside her, his hazel-colored eyes sweeping over the breathtaking view.

Following his gaze, Tirzah was awed by the beauty of the shimmering waters as the sun rose high overhead, framed by gauzy white clouds. The waves lapping upon the rocky shore far below were gentler than usual, as the day was calm and the wind was mild.

"Several years ago, you made the most important decision you will ever make right here, in this very spot," Dorian said, interrupting her train of thought. Looking at her with earnest eyes, he took her hand, stunning her. "You believed that Jesus Christ is the Son of God, and you pledged your life to Him. You received Him as your ultimate Bridegroom, promising yourself to Him as a chaste, devoted bride."

Tirzah watched Dorian tentatively, wondering where he was going with this.

"Now, I must humbly ask you to consider another important decision, Tirzah," he continued, searching her eyes with his. "And this may very well be the second most important decision you will—or won't—ever make."

Heart pounding in her chest, Tirzah suddenly realized what was coming next. She knew a moment of very real panic… followed by a peace so all-encompassing, so settling, that her fear vaporized in an instant. Like a gentle whisper, she remembered the distinct impression she had experienced that morning, as if Jesus Christ Himself had knelt at her bedside, tenderly stroking back her hair and whispering, *Tirzah, wake up, child. It's going to be a beautiful day.*

Shifting a bit on the bench so she could turn and look Dorian full in the face, she waited patiently for him to continue, already knowing what her answer would be.

"Tirzah," he said, boldly lifting his hand and brushing his knuckles against her smooth cheek. "The moment we met, my attention was completely arrested. I've never known a woman like you—so full of life, and spunk, and purpose. You serve the Lord with all your might, and it's a wonder to behold."

Honored and humbled, Tirzah held his gaze, her heart burning within her chest at the unexpected emotions stirring within her. *I love this man,* she realized, stunned to her core. *What's more, I trust him. I trust him with my heart. I trust him with my future. I even trust him with my life! Righteous Father, will Your miracles never cease?*

"Tirzah, my beloved, will you accept my proposal of marriage and receive me as your bridegroom?"

"Yes," she said, shocking him with the speed and certainty of her response. "Yes, Dorian. I will."

"You will?" he repeated, shocked.

"Of course I will," she laughed, taking his hands and giving them a playful squeeze. "God brought us together, even when I was too frightened to admit it. Not only that, I *love* you, Dorian. And I would be honored to be your wife."

***

Tabitha

Dorian and Tirzah didn't waste any time getting married, and Tabitha was glad. She'd never known two people better suited for one another—*Well, excepting myself and Stephanos, of course*, she thought with a sad smile. *We were perfect for each other. In every way.*

Standing faithfully at Tirzah's elbow, Tabitha watched as her dear friend stood across from her bridegroom on the speaker's platform in the church meeting hall, pledging her life and loyalty to him before God and many joyful witnesses. The bride and groom both wore their finest apparel, but it was their shining faces that so captured the imaginations of those present. Good old Phineas presided over the ceremony, being qualified to perform the marriage rites, while many church members, widows, and orphans huddled around the beaming couple, eager to wish them well on their happy day.

Pulling her gaze from the glowing couple with a bit of effort, Tabitha's eyes swept over those gathered to witness Dorian and Tirzah pronounce their wedding vows. Ruth, Tirzah's former mother-in-law, was there, appearing almost happy. Along with Martha, Jonas, and Eli, who had developed a grudging admiration for Dorian, even if he was still hesitant to trust a Greek. Heart jumping just a bit, she accidentally locked eyes with Adam, who stood with his father and Simon the tanner. He nodded at her, his joy for the newlyweds evident on his handsome features.

Sharing a smile with him, Tabitha was relieved their friendship had been restored. For a fleeting moment, she wondered what it might be like to stand upon the platform with him, pronouncing sacred vows as Dorian and Tirzah now did.

Cheeks warming in embarrassment, she wondered at the course of her wayward thoughts. She and Adam had agreed to carry on with their friendship, nothing more. The matter was too troubling and confusing to think upon, anyway. She had placed Adam in the Lord's hands and decided it was best to leave him there.

"I now pronounce you man and wife," Phineas announced, his voice ringing out over the crowd as he turned Dorian and Tirzah to face their adoring guests.

Cheers rose up from the gathering, affirming the glowing couple as they prepared to begin a new life together.

Heart aching just a bit, Tabitha joined her fellow believers in celebration.

CHAPTER 36

Tabitha

Joppa

Returning from a trip to the market, Tabitha approached the mansion, mentally reviewing all the new residents and their children. She'd had an influx of guests arrive in recent weeks, all of them deeply impoverished and anxious to find help. While she was grateful the Lord had led the widows and orphans to her, it was a lot of work caring for so many. Even the servants were weary, working twice as hard as usual to meet all the needs.

"Pardon me," a small voice said, jerking Tabitha's attention from her thoughts. "Is this the place they call the Refuge?"

Following the sound of the voice, Tabitha's gaze fell upon a young girl huddled against the stone wall encircling the outer court, just barely out of the guards' line of vision. Heart turning in her chest, Tabitha was stricken by the girl's abject poverty.

She gazed up at Tabitha with hollow eyes far too large for her small face streaked with dirt and the remnant of tears. Her greasy, matted hair, torn and soiled clothing, and emaciated form all indicated that she had suffered for quite some time.

"This is the Refuge," Tabitha told her with a warm smile, hoping she sounded less appalled than she felt. "How can I help you?"

"Do you know the Lady Tabitha?" the girl asked her, her voice quavering in hope…and fear.

"Oh, I am Tabitha," she said quickly, realizing she probably didn't look very much like a lady of means, returning with supplies from the market and sporting her former servant's apron and attire.

The girl did a double take, confused, clutching a small, wrapped bundle close to her heart.

"Please, come inside with me," Tabitha invited her, sensing that the girl was in desperate need of help. "You are welcome here," she added, extending her hand in hospitality.

"Oh, thank you," the girl whispered, her large eyes filling with tears. Rising a bit unsteadily, the bundle in her arms began to tremble, mewling like a tiny kitten.

Stunned, Tabitha took a step back, realizing that the tiny bundle contained a *baby* rather than the girl's belongings! "Oh my," she exclaimed, shocked.

"He's very little, and he won't take up much space," the girl plunged ahead, terrified that Tabitha had changed her mind after seeing the baby. "And he is nursing, so he won't require any food or drink, honest. I—"

"No, no, your baby is more than welcome here," Tabitha assured her. "He was just so quiet; I didn't even notice him there." Stepping closer, Tabitha lowered the blanket swaddling the child to chuck his little chin. The moment she saw the baby's face, her heart dropped. The infant was pale as death, clearly sick. Very sick.

"Oh, beloved," Tabitha breathed, fearful for the little one. "How long has he been sick like this?"

"That's why I came," the girl wept, rocking the baby in a desperate attempt to calm his weakened cries. "I can't afford a doctor, but he keeps getting worse. He's been sick for at least a week, maybe longer."

"I'll see what we can do for him," Tabitha encouraged her, wondering at the plight of the poverty-stricken mother, a mere child herself. What was her background story? And how did she land in such a desperate situation? "Come, let us help you," she encouraged, guiding the girl by the shoulders and leading her toward the gated entrance. "We'll get you both all cleaned up with a nice change of clothes, a warm meal, and a comfortable room."

"Oh, bless you," the girl wept, her shoulders shaking with sobs of gratitude. "The stories I heard about you are true. Bless you, bless you, Lady Tabitha."

***

Breathing a frustrated sigh, Tabitha leaned against the doorframe, watching as the third physician she had contacted that week was led away by a very nervous Eli.

"Any luck?" Tirzah asked, coming around the corner with Laurel.

"We don't need *luck*," Tabitha muttered, shaking

her head in aggravation. "We need a *miracle*."

"How many physicians have examined the infant?"

"Three. None of them could help."

A fit of violent coughs erupted from the room behind them, where the young mother and infant were now staying.

Peering through the open door, Tirzah winced. "That baby is very sick, Tabitha. And now the mother is coughing, too."

"I know," Tabitha responded grimly. "I'm afraid the mother is suffering from the same malady. She started having coughing fits late last night."

"My, you'd think the sickness could jump from one person to another," Tirzah groaned, shaking her head.

"It certainly seems that way, even though physicians insist sickness comes from contaminants in the air. Two of the doctors blamed the malady on stagnant seawater."

"What can we do?"

"I haven't the slightest idea," Tabitha sighed, holding out her arms to Laurel. The little girl went into them, sensing that her mother needed comfort. "But I'll confess, I'm worried."

"Did any of the three physicians have any practical suggestions to promote healing?" Tirzah asked her, troubled.

"I was told to keep mother and child as comfortable as possible," Tabitha told her, grimacing as the young mother exploded into another fit of painful coughing spasms in the chamber behind them. "The infant is only a few weeks old, Tirzah. The doctors didn't seem hopeful that he would make it."

"Oh, Tabitha."

"I know. I don't even want to think about that."

"Was the child born sickly?" Tirzah asked, lowering her tone.

"Hannah says her baby was small and frail when he was born, but not sick," Tabitha answered a bit distractedly, clutching Laurel's hand like a lifeline. "That poor girl has endured more tragedy than I can imagine. Last year, her father sold her to a brothel frequented by sailors for a few measly coins. The infant is a result of that decision."

"Oh, that's awful."

"I can't even fathom what she's gone through," Tabitha sighed, her heart breaking for the girl. "She's only fourteen, Tirzah. And she's here because she managed to escape from her master. Should he find her, he would undoubtedly beat her into submission and drag her back to the brothel."

"Then we mustn't let that happen," Tirzah put in stoutly, her eyes blazing.

Another fit of coughs exploded in Hannah's suite, so violent that both women winced. When it continued without reprieve, Tabitha gently placed Laurel's hand in Tirzah's. "Will you take her out for some fresh air, Tirzah? I need to sit with Hannah and the baby. They're burning up with fever. Perhaps I can provide some relief."

"How many families are sharing a room with them?"

"Only two widows with their children," Tabitha replied, her tone laden with concern. "I may need to relocate them to another room if the coughing doesn't let up. I can't imagine they're getting any rest."

"Let me know if there's anything I can do, Tabitha," Tirzah said gently, squeezing Laurel's hand and leading her down the frescoed hall.

Watching her go, Tabitha's heart constricted in her chest. If only she could dismiss the dreadful sense of foreboding in the air, threatening to suffocate her.

She couldn't help but sense that something terrible was about to happen.

Slipping into the sickroom, she forced an encouraging smile she was far from feeling, praying fervently for God's merciful intervention.

CHAPTER 37

Tabitha

Joppa

Sinking onto a wooden chair she'd placed in the hallway just outside Hannah's suite, Tabitha buried her face in her hands, trembling violently. *Oh God,* her heart cried brokenly. *Oh God, help us.*

"Lady Tabitha. A word, please."

Lowering her hands into her lap, Tabitha glanced up with exhausted, bleary eyes as the same physician who had assisted her uncle in his last days emerged from the sickroom, looking very serious.

"What can I do for you, sir?"

"The baby has been pronounced dead," he said, though Tabitha had known the moment she checked on him first thing that morning. Stomach flopping in nausea, she nodded miserably. "My servants will see to everything."

Feeling sick, Tabitha nodded again. *Oh, Hannah,* she thought, heartbroken for her. *That poor girl. How will she recover from this?*

"The young mother is in bad shape," the physician

continued as factually as if they merely discussed the weather. "As you know, she was hysterical upon the death of her infant. I gave her a drought that induced sleep. She should rest, undisturbed, for hours."

"Thank you," Tabitha responded numbly, wondering what in the world she would tell the girl when she finally awakened. How was one to comfort a young woman who had just lost her child to wasting illness? And what if the same fate awaited Hannah, as well? "What can I do for Hannah? How can I help her get well?"

"Very little, unless you happen to be a miracle worker," he quipped a bit snidely.

"My God is," Tabitha whispered as tears stung her eyes.

With a slight flicker of sympathy, the physician released a rather dim sigh. "She needs plenty of fluids. Force broth, if you can, to keep up her strength. And cold compresses to help reduce the fever."

"I will do as you say."

"My servants shall arrive shortly," the physician informed her, preparing to take his leave. "Where shall I collect payment?"

"Eli will meet you in the former reception hall. It's a meeting place now."

"Very well." Turning sharply on his heel, the physician traveled down the quiet, frescoed hallway, eager to be on his way.

Heart pounding, Tabitha rose on wobbly legs, eager to check on the sick young woman. Entering the room, she was stricken by the oppressive spirit within the chamber, as if malevolent spirits hung heavily in the air.

Perhaps they did.

Crossing the room, Tabitha stood at the foot of Hannah's bed. Since it was daytime, the occupants who shared her room were out and about rather than in the chamber. The girl appeared so frail, so alone, her face still wet with tears of anguish even as she slept. Despite the physician's potion, she struggled to draw breath as she slumbered, her lungs heaving and straining in protest.

Tears slipping down her cheeks, Tabitha's gaze strayed toward the small wooden cradle at Hannah's bedside. A blanket had been drawn respectfully over the dead infant's head, but his tiny little outline was prominent beneath the covering, deathly still.

Oh, God. Heart clenching in sorrow, Tabitha covered her mouth with her hand to muffle her sobs. Lowering herself onto the stool beside the bed, Tabitha reached for the girl's cold, pale hand, grasping it tightly in her own. *Righteous Father,* she prayed fervently, bowing her head as tears fell from her eyes. *I opened this refuge to save life, to foster hope. But today, death hangs heavily in the air. Others are now displaying signs of sickness, too. It feels like an ill omen, like a dark plague. I don't know what to do or how to stop it, Lord.*

Drawing a ragged breath, Tabitha lifted her gaze heavenward, squaring her shoulders in resolve. *But You are the Great Physician, Father. Please intervene. Save these women and children from harm. Surround us, as with a shield.*

***

Within a matter of days, the residents who shared Hannah's suite and the servants who had tended the bedchamber were stricken with the wasting illness. As sickness swept through the mansion, the physician ordered Tabitha to seal off the sickroom, where the infected widows, children, and servants were instructed to be kept apart from the rest of the household.

"Select one or two servants to tend the sick," the physician had commanded Tabitha, his tone boding no argument. "Besides that, no one goes in or out. The chamber is defiled, unclean."

Horror-stricken by the sickness ravaging her home, Tabitha decided she would tend to the patients herself. She had no desire to send her staff into a chamber reeking of hopelessness and death. They didn't deserve that.

"You can't do this alone, Tabitha," Tirzah said stoutly, joining her friend in the kitchen as Tabitha collected steaming bowls of broth from an exhausted and harried Martha. "Let me serve the sick with you. I can handle it."

"Tirzah, I can't send you in there," Tabitha told her firmly, lifting the tray bearing the bowls of broth. "What if the sickness claims you, as well? What would Dorian say?"

"My husband knows I'm committed to seeing this through," Tirzah told her, getting the door for her. "I'm not going to leave you alone in this."

"The sickness seems to be spreading," Tabitha said, mounting the stairs and wondering if she even had the strength to climb to the top. "Anyone who gets near it becomes ill."

"The physicians insist it doesn't work that way," Tirzah told her. "You can't catch a sickness."

"I'm not convinced that the physicians know what they're talking about."

"They must know more than *we* do!"

Shaking her head, Tabitha climbed the last step, entering the quiet hallway with purposeful strides.

"I'm going to help you whether you like it or not," Tirzah insisted, trailing behind her in the hall. "You can't serve an entire fleet of sick people by yourself."

"God will provide the strength."

"And He's also provided a *helper*," Tirzah informed her, blocking the doorway once they reached the sickroom. "So, will you accept His gift or not?"

"Tirzah..."

"It's a simple question deserving a simple answer, yes or no."

Searching Tirzah's determined eyes, Tabitha finally nodded, blinking back tears of gratitude.

"That's better," Tirzah huffed, stepping aside. "All right, then. Let's do this together."

***

Tabitha was convinced she'd never been more exhausted in her entire life.

Sinking onto a bench in the meeting hall, she gazed up at the empty speaker's platform. The evening service wouldn't commence for several hours, and for now, the meeting hall provided a quiet place to think and pray. She and Tirzah were taking shifts sitting with the ill residents and servants, and it was currently Tirzah's turn. Tabitha knew she should probably go straight to bed and catch up on some much-needed sleep, but her mind was so crowded with anxious thoughts she imagined that slumber would elude her entirely.

At least here she could pray, beseeching God for help, for answers.

Lifting her tired gaze, she noted the newest addition to the platform—a wooden cross mounted on the wall directly behind the speaker's stand. Josiah had recently fashioned it himself—a reminder of the sacrifice Jesus had made at Calvary.

"How are you holding up?"

Forcing a tired smile, Tabitha glanced over her shoulder as Adam entered the meeting hall, his gaze resting upon her in concern.

"Hi, Adam."

"Father and I have been worried about you," he revealed, crossing the distance between them and joining her on the bench. His broad shoulders brushed against hers as he took his seat beside her, turning to face her with a sympathetic smile.

Tabitha's smile was weak, but she hadn't the strength to muster something bigger.

"You and Tirzah are running yourselves ragged, trying to relieve all the sick," he mentioned, his tone laced with worry. "You can't keep this up forever, Tabitha."

"I pray I won't have to."

"You need more help."

"I can't place my staff in harm's way, Adam."

"*You're* in harm's way," he told her, tenderly tucking a stray hair behind her ear. "And I don't mind confessing, I'm worried sick about you."

"I'll be fine," she assured him, her stomach churning at the look in his eyes. "I cannot forsake these women, these children. They are my sacred assignment."

"You need more help."

"God has provided the strength. And He will continue to do so."

"You look dead on your feet, Tabitha," Adam persisted, ignoring the look she gave him. "I just want you to be careful. You need rest and sustenance. And I fear you may be neglecting both."

"I rest when I can," she told him, too weary to argue. "I'm resting now."

"Not really."

"I'm doing the best I can, Adam," she sighed, shaking her head.

"Let me stay," Adam spoke up, meeting her gaze with determined eyes. "Let me help."

"It wouldn't be proper to send you into the sick-room with all the women and children," Tabitha reminded him. "But thank you, nonetheless."

"Then you take care of *them,* and let me take care of *you.*"

Blushing deeply, Tabitha looked away.

"Listen, Tabitha," Adam insisted, lifting her chin with his finger. "If something happens to *you*, what will happen to your orphans and widows?" He paused, allowing the impact of his argument to fully sink in. "Let me help you."

"All right," she finally consented, seeing the logic in his statement. "I suppose you can stay in Dorian's old quarters. He no longer has need of it, now that he's married to Tirzah and abiding with her."

"Perfect."

"Thank you, Adam. Truly."

"Don't mention it," he smiled, tweaking her cheek. "Another thought. You have enough to worry about right now, without fearing for the life of your daughter. Would you consider sending Laurel to stay at my home with one of your trusted servants? I feel she would be much safer there."

"It's not a bad idea," Tabitha admitted. "Though the selfish part of me wants to keep her close through this."

"I can understand that," he nodded grimly. "But I fear her welfare is at stake here at the Refuge. And ultimately, you'll have greater peace of mind knowing that she's safe."

"I know you're right," she finally managed. The Refuge—meant to be a place of healing and safety—had become a pestilent warzone.

Oh God, she prayed silently, her heart breaking. *Will this ever end?*

"I'll see about packing a few things for Laurel," Tabitha said, rising a bit unsteadily. "Martha can stay with her in your home."

"Won't Martha be needed in the kitchen?"

"The kitchen staff can manage without her for a time," Tabitha decided. "But, other than Tirzah, Laurel feels most comfortable with Martha. Since Laurel will be in an unfamiliar environment, I'd prefer she stay with someone she loves."

"Understood," Adam nodded supportively. "And, of course, my father, Josiah, will be there. You know how he dotes on Laurel. And our housekeeper can stay, as well."

"That sounds perfect. Thank you, Adam."

"Why don't you step outside for some fresh air?" Adam suggested, rising from the bench. "I can speak with Martha and ask her to pack Laurel's belongings."

"No, I should do that myself—"

"Tabitha, you're pale and drawn," Adam argued, his tone boding no argument. "I imagine you haven't set foot beyond these walls in days."

Blinking in surprise, Tabitha realized she couldn't argue with him. He was right.

"Now go enjoy some fresh air and sunshine," Adam instructed, taking her by the shoulders and turning her toward the door. "God knows you need it."

Wishing to protest, Tabitha did as she was bidden, though every fiber of her being cried out against it. After all, she was needed at the Refuge. And Tirzah's shift would end soon. Then it would be her turn to sit with those ravaged by illness.

Forcing such thoughts far from her mind, Tabitha decided to do as she was bidden. Hopefully a walk in the fresh air would do her some good. And it would provide some much-needed time to pray, as well.

Prayer was certainly needed. She could only hope that God would intervene before even more lives were lost.

CHAPTER 38

Tabitha

Joppa

Soon after Adam had bid her to take a walk, Tabitha found herself at Tirzah's favorite spot, standing on the edge of the great precipice overlooking the crashing waves of the Mediterranean Sea. The churning, slate-colored waters reflected the gray hues of the wintry sky high overhead, which in turn mirrored Tabitha's current state of mind: Gray. Anxious. Hopeless. Dim.

Precious Lord, she prayed, her hazel-green eyes gazing listlessly upon the troubled waters below. *I know You are loving. I know You are good. But I must ask, why haven't You intervened?*

As if in response to her anguished question, a particularly large, angry wave crashed against the rocky cliff face far below, sending up sprays of foam.

Righteous Father, Tabitha continued silently,

feeling lost, defeated. *We need help. Hannah is at death's door, and the others aren't far behind her. The Refuge was meant to be a place of healing and restoration, not sickness and death. I know You called me to these women and children, Lord. So why is this happening? Why are You allowing it to happen? Please, Father, intervene. Intervene now!*

Closing her eyes, Tabitha felt the chill winter breeze stinging her face, tearing at her head covering like a demon's angry talons. *It's obvious the enemy is trying to stop me,* she prayed, considering the great spiritual warfare she was up against. *The devil doesn't want the Refuge to survive. He hates everything we stand for, Lord. He desires to crush my spirit and my will to continue. But I cannot let him. Strengthen me, Father. Equip me to stand against the forces of evil coming against me on all sides.*

Fleetingly, Tabitha thought of her Aunt Pennie, whose dream had been to turn the mansion into a refuge for the needy, the lost. But she had perished in her efforts, her dream and heart's desire unfulfilled.

What if my fate is the same as hers? Tabitha realized, slightly panicked. How much power did the enemy have over her? Was she truly equipped to stand against hell's unquenchable fury?

Her aunt certainly hadn't been.

Stepping back, Tabitha lowered herself onto the marble bench Dorian had set up for Tirzah. The wind had blown over the Grecian urns, scattering dead flowers across the grassy knoll. The scene was strangely foreboding, whispering of death.

Gripping her head in her hands, Tabitha prayed furiously. Unlike she had ever prayed before.

***

Tirzah

Joppa

Silver moonlight slanted through the window as soft night breezes tugged at the pale curtains framing the opened shutters. Lying on her back on her sleeping pallet, Tirzah was pleasantly aware of her husband's closeness, his tall, lean form stretched out beside her under their shared blanket. She hoped he was finally asleep, as he needed his rest. She had no idea how long she'd been lying there, wide awake, blinking in the darkness, her mind cluttered with concerns for Tabitha, the Refuge, and those suffering from the virulent malady sweeping the mansion.

"Are you still inspecting the ceiling?"

Surprised, Tirzah turned her head sideways on her pillow to glance at her husband. Since getting married, she had been delighted by Dorian's completely unexpected and often dry sense of humor. "How did you know I was still awake?" she whispered into the darkness engulfing them.

"You are still as stone," he told her, and she sensed his smile even though she could barely detect his features in the dim light of the single oil lamp kindling on the nightstand. "When you are asleep, you move about like a performing acrobat. Something is on your mind."

Resisting the urge to argue about his unflattering depiction of her at rest, Tirzah acknowledged the second half of his statement. "I'm worried about Tabitha. I can't shake this feeling that she could be next."

"Any of us could be," Dorian reminded her, taking her hand and interlocking his strong fingers with hers. "I must confess, I worry about you, as well."

"Me?" Tirzah repeated, perplexed. "Why?"

"You're in the thick of it, just like Tabitha," Dorian said. "I do fear for you, beloved."

Mulling over his words, Tirzah guessed she shouldn't be surprised. It was perfectly natural for a husband to worry over his wife, given the circumstances. But it had been such a long time since anyone had worried about her well-being. She wasn't sure she liked it.

"I'll be fine, Dorian," she assured him, hoping he wasn't about to ask her to stop assisting Tabitha at the Refuge. If so, their first fight would be well underway!

"I do hope so, beloved."

"God will protect me."

"That is my constant prayer."

"Then keep praying," she told him, squeezing his hand. "God is faithful. We have no cause for concern."

"Were it not for His great faithfulness, I couldn't bear to see you enter the dragon's lair each day," he admitted, drawing her into his arms. "I have moments when all I can think about is getting you out of there until this plague burns itself out."

"God has called me to help in this, Dorian."

"I know," he whispered into her hair. "It's the only

reason I haven't protested."

"Thank you," she whispered, sensing it took every ounce of trust he possessed to support her in this dangerous mission. "I couldn't live with myself if I left Tabitha to deal with this alone."

"I know," he said again, kissing the top of her head. Holding her close, he breathed deeply of her scent, praying fervently for her safety, entrusting her to God.

***

Tabitha

Bone weary, Tabitha glanced up as Eli hurried down the hall on the upper floor, appearing as if he'd just had a full-fledged fit. Eyes wild and turban askew, he closed the distance between them with surprising speed.

"My lady, he's here. *He's here!*"

"Who's here?" Tabitha managed tiredly, swiping at beads of sweat on her forehead with the back of her hand.

"Master Amal has arrived from Caesarea Maritima!"

Heart stopping in her chest, Tabitha's eyes widened in dismay. "He's *here*? At the estate?" she asked weakly, hoping perhaps she had misunderstood him.

"That *is* what I just said, isn't it?" Eli shot back, more tersely than was fitting for a servant.

"Oh dear," Tabitha breathed, sinking onto the chair stationed outside the sickroom. "With all the mayhem wrought by this dreadful malady, I completely forgot about him."

"You *forgot* about your most important investor?"

"I've been a bit busy, Eli," Tabitha pointed out, miffed.

"What should we do?"

"I'm going to need your help," she sighed, tiredly rubbing the back of her neck. "First, alert Dorian about Amal's arrival. While Dorian keeps him entertained, visit the kitchen staff and ask them to ready the banquet hall and throw together the fastest feast imaginable. And you—prepare the books and ledgers. Amal will undoubtedly wish to see them after we dine."

"Yes, my lady," Eli breathed, his head bobbing frantically. Hurrying off in a flash, he went to perform his lady's bidding.

Forcing herself to her feet, Tabitha was hit by a sudden wave of dizziness that caused her to rock back several steps. Placing a steadying hand on the cool, frescoed wall, she attempted to orient herself. It felt as if the entire hallway was spinning, careening out of control.

What on earth? She thought, annoyed. *I don't have time for this.* Undoubtedly, she was exhausted from caring for sick patients, forgoing meals and sleep far too many days in a row. Lifting delicate fingers to her forehead, she massaged her warm temples, wondering at the pain pulsing at the base of her neck and traveling steadily upward, promising to develop into a full-blown headache.

Glancing down at her attire, she knew Eli would insist that she dress in her finest apparel to greet their guest, but the thought of changing clothes and readying herself for company was overwhelming. She'd never felt so worn down in all her life. *But I guess I shouldn't be surprised,* she thought, shrugging off her initial concern. *After all, I've been slaving over sick patients for nearly two weeks without reprieve.*

Smoothing down her apron and adjusting her simple head covering, Tabitha decided Amal would simply have to receive her as she was. She was far too tired to bathe, style her hair, and locate a gown worthy of his approval.

Hoping she was capable of keeping a clear head given the circumstances, she slowly descended the stairs, bracing herself for an unpleasant encounter with her critical father-in-law turned business partner. Regardless of how exhausted and worn down she felt, she knew she must muster the strength to be a gracious hostess. Her witness for Christ remained at stake.

Jesus, may this be the trip in which Amal receives You as Lord and Savior, she prayed.

CHAPTER 39

Tabitha

Joppa

"What is the meaning of this?" Amal raged, too upset to accept the comfortable seat Dorian offered him in Tabitha's office. "I arrive at the estate housing one of my prime investments only to find the servants missing, the place a shambles, the lady of the house conspicuously absent, and sickly lowlife occupying every nook and cranny!"

"My humblest apologies, my lord," Tabitha said, standing behind her large desk and watching him pace. Exchanging a nervous look with Dorian, she hoped the feast being prepared in Amal's honor would be ready soon. Perhaps a delectable meal would help appease the ruffled investor.

"You should have had servants stationed at the city gates, scouting out my arrival!" Amal growled, pausing long enough to grip the back of the chair facing Tabitha's desk. Observing the whiteness of his knuckles, Tabitha wondered if the chair's delicate frame would snap in half.

"Forgive me, my lord," Tabitha apologized sincerely. "I do feel terrible about that oversight on our part. We've been deeply burdened caring for the sick—"

"The sick!" Amal sneered, dropping heavily onto the chair across from her. "I warned you, *this* is the kind of thing that happens when you open your doors to filthy ingrates! They're little better than street rats, ravenous and disease-ridden!"

With great effort, Tabitha held her peace, ignoring the accusatory finger he pointed at her. She was thankful for Dorian's steadying presence as he stood stationed by the entry. Though his gaze remained unblinking, carefully concealing his true emotions, Tabitha knew he was silently willing her strength and empathy.

"And to make matters worse, my hostess greets me looking like she crawled out of a garbage dump," Amal continued, eyeing Tabitha's peasant attire with keen distaste. "Is this the kind of business relationship I have to look forward to? If so, I have no issue whatsoever taking my business elsewhere—somewhere I shall be granted the respect I deserve!"

"Again, I must apologize," Tabitha managed, wishing she could crawl under the desk and hide until Amal's seething anger settled. "But I was caring for the sick when you arrived. I didn't wish to keep you waiting any longer—"

"You're caring for the sick?" Amal declared, his eyes growing round with disbelief. "The lady of the house slaving over sickly peasants? Absurd!"

"Someone has to care for them—"

"Might I remind you that's what *servants* are for!" Amal thundered, scandalized. "Or have you depleted all your funds and mismanaged profits so poorly that you can't afford to pay for hired help?"

"No, sir," Tabitha responded, placing her hands on her desk to steady herself. "I simply worry for my household staff. I don't wish to expose them to anything dangerous—"

"Well, by all means, I do hope your servants are comfortable!" he exclaimed, his tone dripping with sarcasm. "Have they any special requests for us? A long, relaxing foot rub? Or perhaps a full body massage and a cleansing scrub with scented bath salts specially imported from the Dead Sea? Maybe even an all-expenses-paid vacation to the former emperor's pleasure gardens in Capri!"

Feeling battered by his sarcasm, Tabitha evenly met his gaze, unwilling to back down or be cowed. "Speaking of servants, the kitchen staff is currently preparing a feast in your honor," she informed him, carefully keeping her tone neutral. "It should be ready within the hour."

"Ah, your servants cook?" he inquired, arching a sardonic brow. "I'm surprised you're not in the kitchen baking the bread yourself while your paid staff enjoys a leisurely afternoon nap."

With a brittle smile, Tabitha gestured toward the doorway where Dorian stood waiting. "We shall summon you the moment supper is ready. In the meantime, please allow Dorian to escort you to your room—we've reserved our finest for you. And we hope the accommodations will be to your liking."

Looking as if he wished to say more, Amal rose from his chair, casting Tabitha a withering glare over his shoulder as he departed.

"This way," she heard Dorian say as he led his master down the hall—and thankfully, away from her!

Slumping onto her desk, Tabitha closed her eyes, trying to shut out the pounding headache. She hoped she had the strength to endure an entire supper at the table with Amal. His animosity was like a tangible force in the room.

Despite her misgivings, Tabitha was not ignorant of the enemy's ploys. It was no coincidence that Amal had arrived when she was at rock bottom, at her weariest point. She shuddered to think how easily her Christlike witness could be destroyed, given her sheer exhaustion and fragile state of mind.

Lifting her head with a bit of effort, Tabitha squared her shoulders in resolve. She refused to squander this opportunity to share the love of Christ. Though her stomach lurched at the thought of food, she rose from her desk, ready to join Amal at the supper table.

***

Supper went a bit better than Tabitha had expected. Despite his hostility, Amal was ravenous after his trip and partook of the feast with gusto. Tabitha was grateful that the meal had occupied the bulk of his attention.

Watching as the servants cleared away the dishes and the remains of the feast, Tabitha remained lounging in the triclinium with Dorian, assessing how the meeting had gone now that Amal had retired for the night.

"My lady, perhaps we should reconvene upon the morrow rather than this evening," Dorian suggested, aware of Tabitha's growing exhaustion. "You need to rest."

"I'm fine," Tabitha assured him, though she didn't sound very convincing. "We need to regroup before meeting with Amal tomorrow morning. He will want to review the ledgers. Is everything ready?"

"Indeed," Dorian promised. "You needn't worry about a thing. Everything is under control."

"There's nothing to discuss? Nothing we must do to prepare?"

"That's what I have been doing while you have been caring for the sick, my lady."

"Dorian, you're a lifesaver." Rising unsteadily from the couch upon which she lounged, Tabitha swayed as the entire room began to spin. Waves of nausea washed over her, nearly bowling her over.

"My lady?" Jumping to his feet, Dorian reached to steady her. "Are you well?"

"I'm...I'm all right," she managed weakly, closing her eyes and attempting to overcome the debilitating nausea. "I'm a bit dizzy, that's all."

"Shall I help you to your room?"

"No, no. I'll be fine."

"You're sure, my lady?"

Releasing a tremorous sigh, Tabitha nodded, overwhelmed by a pounding headache and churning stomach. All she wanted to do was climb into bed and give way to sheer exhaustion, but she knew she must sit up with the sick widows, orphans, and servants until her night shift ended. Tirzah had already sat with them all afternoon and evening. It wouldn't be fair to ask her to stay any longer. She deserved to return home with her new husband.

"I should go," Tabitha murmured, her voice sounding a bit slurred in her own ears. "Thank you, Dorian."

"My lady, I feel rather concerned for you," Dorian confessed, releasing her with obvious reluctance.

"I'll be fine," she said, turning to leave. Waves of nausea overtook her then, battering her like the furious waters of the sea amidst a raging storm. With a frightened yelp, Tabitha reached for something—anything—to steady herself, to no avail. Crashing to the ground, she hit her head against the corner of the table when she went down. She heard Dorian crying out, but his words sounded muffled, as if he spoke to her through a long, dark tunnel or even underwater. The last thing she remembered was his face, crazy with concern, clouding her entire field of vision as he dropped to the ground beside her.

And then everything went black.

***

Adam

Adam was in the corridor just outside the triclinium, waiting for Tabitha to update him about her progress with Amal when he heard the loud crash. Without stopping to think, he flung open the door and burst into the triclinium.

The sight that met his eyes was enough to turn his stomach.

Tabitha was sprawled on the floor like a limp rag doll, her eyes closed, her face pale as death, a large red welt swelling on her delicate brow. An extremely anxious Dorian was kneeling over her, shaking her shoulders, begging her to revive.

Bounding into the room and crossing the distance between them, Adam dropped to his knees beside Dorian, stretching out his hand and caressing Tabitha's pale cheek. Her skin was flushed and clammy. Clamping his hand over her forehead, Adam's heart constricted in fear. She was consumed with fever. The heat of her skin felt as if it would burn a hole through his palm.

"Dorian, what happened?" Adam demanded, attempting to quell his rising panic.

"She was going to turn in," Dorian tried to explain, nearly frantic. "She seemed a bit unsteady when she rose from the couch. And then she came crashing down. It all happened so fast."

"She passed out?"

"So it would seem. She hit her head on the table going down," Dorian winced, his hands trembling as he brushed her hair out of her face to get a better look at the angry welt forming on her brow.

"Let's get her upstairs," Adam commanded, taking charge. Sliding strong arms beneath her, he lifted her with ease, cradling her close to his chest. "Get the door for me, please," he instructed, and Dorian leaped to his feet to assist.

Oh God, revive this precious daughter of Yours. Climbing the stairs with Tabitha in his arms, Adam wondered if his pounding heart would come crashing through his chest. *Heal her. Restore her to health. Don't let this one perish, Lord. The widows and orphans need her. Our fellow believers need her.* Pausing at the top of the stairs, he allowed Dorian to guide him to the proper suite. *I need her, Lord.*

Pushing open the double doors leading to Tabitha's private quarters, Dorian stepped aside so Adam could carry her in.

Reverently entering Tabitha's abode, Adam carried his precious cargo through the cozy bedchamber. Reaching the canopy bed, he gently lowered her onto the soft mattress, tenderly stroking back her hair as he kneeled at her bedside.

"Has she revived?" Dorian asked hopefully, appearing behind him.

"No," Adam whispered, stroking her cheek. "Dorian, we need a doctor. Right away."

"I shall locate the physician immediately. And I will send Tirzah to sit with you and help keep an eye on her while we wait."

"Thank you, Dorian."

With that, the manservant hurried out of the room, anxious to find help.

Folding his hands in prayer, Adam bowed his head, his lips moving silently, fervently, as he begged the Lord to restore the beautiful young woman, once so vibrant and full of life, now lying lifelessly upon the bed.

CHAPTER 40

Tabitha

Joppa

Groaning, Tabitha reached for her head with trembling fingers. Gasping in pain, she withdrew her hand when her slender fingers brushed against a tender welt on her brow.

"Oh, praise God! She's awake!"

Recognizing Tirzah's voice, Tabitha struggled to open her eyes. Her eyelids felt laboriously heavy, as if they had been sealed shut. Persisting in her endeavor, Tabitha eventually managed to crack open her eyes ever so slightly. Groaning again, she clenched her eyes shut as bright light sliced through her vision, causing her aching head to throb even more violently.

"Tabitha! Oh, Tabitha. We've been worried sick," came Tirzah's voice again, and Tabitha felt a woman's cold hands gripping her own like a lifeline. "How are you feeling, beloved?"

Pursing her lips together, Tabitha attempted to form a response. Immediately, she regretted her decision to speak as her throat constricted in sharp, stabbing pain. Biting her lower lip, she wondered if perhaps she had swallowed shards of glass. Or maybe she'd eaten an entire set of pottery. It certainly felt like it. She couldn't imagine what else would cause such an excruciatingly sore throat.

"Adam, is she conscious? I think she's conscious.," Tirzah's voice echoed again, causing Tabitha to wince in pain as her head throbbed in response. "She was stirring, anyway."

Adam? Wishing she could crawl under the bed and hide forever, Tabitha realized Adam must be present as well. Otherwise, Tirzah wouldn't have addressed him.

Oh, what a dreadful sight I must be, she thought, mortified, but too sick to move or do anything about it. *How long have I been lying abed? And how did I get here? What happened?*

"Tabitha?" Now it was Adam's voice that spoke, welling with tenderness and tinged with concern. "Tabitha, can you hear us, dear one?"

Desperate to communicate with her friends, Tabitha managed one slow, painful nod.

"Oh, yes!" Tirzah cried, and Tabitha sensed that she was weeping, though she'd never seen Tirzah cry before. "Oh, thank You, Lord. Praise God!"

"Tabitha, we're here for you, beloved," Adam assured her, and she felt a strong hand caressing her cheek. "We're here. You aren't alone."

"I'll go to the kitchen and get her some broth," Tirzah declared as the sound of her chair legs scraping against the floor caused Tabitha to grimace in pain.

"The doctor said she should eat once she revived."

The doctor? Tabitha had no memory of seeing a doctor. None, whatsoever.

"Great idea," Adam agreed. "She needs to keep up her strength."

The sound of Tirzah's hurried footfalls eventually faded as her friend made her way down the hall.

"Oh, Tabitha," Adam breathed, and something about the way he said her name made Tabitha's heart pound in time with her throbbing head. Forcing her eyes open again, she gazed up into Adam's handsome face, though it appeared bleary and distorted in her feverish vision. Taking her hand, Adam leaned in close, his face just a few inches from hers. "You must be wondering what happened," he said, squeezing her hand. "You passed out in the banquet hall after sharing supper with Amal last night. We have been following the physician's instructions, but we've all been worried sick about you. Tirzah just left to fetch you some broth. It's important that you try to eat, if you can. Proper sustenance will help you recover faster."

Considering the fact that her throat was unbearably raw and swollen, Tabitha couldn't imagine trying to eat anything. But she would do her best, if only to set her friends' minds at ease. As Adam had said, they'd all been worried sick about her.

Tirzah returned a moment later, carrying a bowl of warm broth. "Help her sit up a bit, Adam," Tirzah directed, going around to the opposite side of the bed and drawing up a stool as Adam stood.

Embarrassed, Tabitha tried to work with Adam as he gently lifted her to a sitting position, fluffing the pillows behind her and using them to help prop her up. Smiling warmly, Adam tucked a stray strand of her honey-colored hair behind her ear before sitting down again, ever vigilant over his charge.

Oh, Adam, please don't just sit there and watch me try to eat! Tabitha thought, mortified. But it seemed that was exactly what he intended to do.

"All right," Tirzah said, dipping a wooden spoon into the broth and offering it to Tabitha as one might feed a small child. "I hope you can eat this."

Obediently, Tabitha opened her cracked lips, accepting the broth. But the moment it slid down the back of her throat, it burned like fire, causing her to yelp in shock and pain.

"Let's try just a bit more," Tirzah suggested, dipping the spoon back in the broth. But Tabitha shook her head adamantly, unwilling to endure that kind of pain again. She'd rather go hungry. Even now, the muscles in her throat constricted violently, threatening to cut off her air supply. She had no desire to try that again.

"Oh, Tabitha, you must eat," Tirzah admonished, worried. "Let's try just a few more spoonfuls."

Stoutly, Tabitha shook her head *no*.

"Let's try again later, Tirzah," Adam cut in, recognizing that Tabitha was in pain. "Allow her some time to recover first."

"To *recover*, she needs to keep up her strength," Tirzah shot back, clearly peeved with him. But she didn't argue any further. Setting aside the broth, she reached for a washrag, dipping it into a pail of water on the nightstand. Wringing it out, she placed it on Tabitha's flushed forehead. "I suppose we can simply focus on keeping the fever down, as the physician suggested."

Feeling as if she would jump out of her skin, Tabitha gritted her teeth, jolted by the shocking sensation of the cold compress. It felt like ice on her heated skin.

Gently, Tirzah dabbed at Tabitha's forehead, face, and neck while Adam watched, clearly anxious.

"All right, beloved," Adam said once Tirzah had wrung out the washrag and draped it over the pail. "Do you think you can sleep now? The physician insisted you get plenty of rest."

"The...the others—" Tabitha managed, grimacing in pain as she spoke. Her voice sounded hoarse and gravelly in her own ears.

"The others are fine," Tirzah cut in, sensing the direction of Tabitha's thoughts. "In fact, many seem to be improving today. So you needn't worry about anything except getting better and regaining your strength. Can you do that?"

Tabitha nodded miserably, recognizing she would be no good to anyone in her present condition. She simply had to focus on healing. The widows and orphans depended on her. She couldn't let them down.

Another thought hit her, one that nearly propelled her from her bed. "A—Amal!" she exclaimed, her eyes growing round as marbles.

"He's been informed that you collapsed last night and are currently resting, as per the physician's orders," Tirzah put in stoutly, pushing Tabitha back down in bed. "And you needn't worry about that, either. Dorian is reviewing the ledgers with Amal today. Tomorrow, he will take him to the big warehouse near the port and to inspect the ships docked at the harbor. Dorian will keep Amal plenty busy, trust me."

"Laurel…"

"…is happy as a clam at Josiah's house," Tirzah assured her. "Martha is with her, and apparently, Laurel has already won over the housekeeper, as well. She's the center of attention over there and loving every minute of it."

"Thank…you," Tabitha managed weakly, clutching at her swollen throat with a trembling hand.

"Now get some rest!" Tirzah demanded, drawing the blankets back up to her friend's chin. "Everything is under control."

Daring a glance at Adam, Tabitha saw that his eyes were locked upon her, welling with concern. It made her wonder about how bad her situation must be. Was she in even worse shape than she realized? Regardless, she didn't want him to worry. It took all the strength she possessed to reach for his hand, mustering a smile of reassurance. In response, his brown eyes flickered with intense emotion.

"Get some rest, beloved," he whispered.

Closing her eyes, Tabitha attempted to do so.

***

Tabitha stood alone at the top of the stairs gazing down the upper-level corridor, her pulse pounding loudly in her ears. The darkened hall appeared as lifeless and still as the rest of mansion. The silence was ominous, malevolent. Clasping her hands over her rapidly beating heart, Tabitha attempted to calm herself, and yet her skin prickled with a sense of dread as an air of dark foreboding settled over her.

Inexplicably frightened, Tabitha stumbled down the dark hall, flinging open the first door she en-

countered. The sound of violent coughing filled the air, engulfing her. Horror-stricken, Tabitha's gaze swept the gray chamber filled with rows and rows of sickbeds. Blankets were draped over the still forms of the suffering, the dying. Slamming the door shut, Tabitha moved to the next one. Grasping the gilded knob, she flung it open, only to be confronted with the same dreadful scene. Rows of sickbeds filled with coughing, wheezing women and children, all of them deathly pale with hopeless, hollow eyes. All of them at death's door. All of them looking to her for answers, answers she did not have.

Slamming the door shut, Tabitha fled down the hall, opening door after door, only to be confronted with the same terrifying scene time after time. Slamming the last door, she staggered down the hall, her heart pounding so violently she wondered if it would come crashing through her chest. Picking up speed, she ran, sensing an invisible enemy hot on her heels, chasing her down, intent upon her destruction.

Somehow, the darkness grew thicker, even more oppressive. As if hitting an invisible wall, Tabitha stopped in the middle of the corridor, her wild eyes searching for a way of escape.

What was that? A strange sound filled the air, a hissing sound, growing louder and louder until it resonated throughout the entire hall. Panic-stricken, Tabitha saw a strange, incandescent mist seeping from beneath the doors of the sickrooms lining both sides of the corridor. Filling the vast hall, the mist seeped toward her with alarming speed.

Horrified, Tabitha turned to run, only to find that the mist was approaching from all directions, trav-

eling toward her like the greedy fingers of the evil underworld. Tabitha stood still as stone, her breath coming out in short, hard puffs as panic rose within her breast. Encircling her ankles, the mist closed in upon her, traveling steadily upward, filling her nostrils, burning her eyes, threatening to choke the life out of her.

Dark forces, agents of evil, had stormed the Refuge, and now they were out for blood. Her blood. They wanted to destroy her.

Covering her face with quaking hands, Tabitha screamed in utter terror...

"Shhh! It's all right, it's all right. I'm here."

Tabitha awakened with a start, drenched in sweat and quaking from the dastardly nightmares plaguing her sleep. Eyes snapping open, she realized, deeply relieved, that she was still safe and snug in bed, in her own private quarters. The balcony doors were thrown open wide, allowing daylight and fresh sea breezes to stream in. The suffocating darkness and plaguing mist of her dream was nowhere in sight.

Glancing sideways, Tabitha saw Tirzah still seated on the stool at her bedside, her eyes clouded with concern. Leaning forward, she rested the back of her hand against Tabitha's forehead, wincing at the searing heat of her skin.

"Were you having a bad dream?" Tirzah asked gently.

Tabitha nodded, her eyes stinging with tears.

"Well, it's over now," Tirzah assured her, readjusting her friend's blanket as tenderly as a mother might tuck in her child. "You don't have to think about it anymore."

If only it was that simple. Tabitha knew the nightmare would plague her sleep and her waking hours. She feared, perhaps, there was truth in it. Even though there was no deadly mist seeping into her bedchamber, she knew that the enemy of her soul was working overtime. The devil hated her and everything she stood for. He hated the lives that had been changed at the Refuge. He hated the church gatherings hosted in her home, where dozens of people received Christ as their Savior week after week. And he hated the opportunity she now had to share the love of Christ with Amal.

Clearly, the enemy was doing everything in his power to discourage her, to silence her. Closing her eyes, she mustered every ounce of resolve the Holy Spirit had planted in her heart, drawing upon it for strength.

Glancing up at Tirzah, Tabitha saw the fear reflected in her eyes, though her friend was doing everything in her power to present a brave front. Reaching for her hand, it took all the strength Tabitha had to give it a gentle squeeze. "You...look... worried," she ground out, her raw throat screaming in protest.

"I'm just focused on getting you well," Tirzah responded with a forced smile.

"What's...on...your mind?"

Tirzah furrowed her brow, deep in thought, clearly wrestling with something. Her silence only served as confirmation to Tabitha.

"You can...tell...me."

Sighing, Tirzah leaned forward, meeting her friend's bleary-eyed gaze. "I'm glad I sent Adam out to refill the freshwater. I've desired a moment to speak with you alone."

Tabitha simply waited, worried for her friend.

"I keep thinking about your aunt."

"Pennie."

"Yes."

"Why?"

"I've wrestled about whether or not I should share this with you," Tirzah sighed, appearing more troubled than Tabitha had ever seen her. "But I don't think I could forgive myself if I held my tongue, and then…" voice trailing off, Tirzah refused to complete the sentence. It was too terrible to voice aloud.

"What…is it?" Tabitha managed, her apprehension mounting.

"I cared for your aunt right here, in this very room, during her final days and hours. She lay right here, in this very bed. And she looked so like you, Tabitha—hopeful, patient, to the end." Fighting tears, Tirzah cleared her throat, determined to continue. "Your aunt's dream was so like yours. She desired to utilize this mansion to help those in need, to minister to the poor and the destitute. But that dream was cut tragically short, along with her life."

Heart pounding dully in her chest, Tabitha bit her lower lip as fear seeped in. The parallels were certainly disturbing. She had contemplated the uncanny similarities between herself and her aunt many times since becoming ill.

"I can't help but wonder," Tirzah continued, her pinched features conveying a hint of guilt. "What if this is more than just an illness? What if the enemy is determined to prevent Pennie's dream from happening? What if this is…some kind of curse?"

Tabitha didn't respond immediately. The weight

of Tirzah's words had hit her full force, and she needed a moment to process them. Finally, she managed, "No doubt...the devil hates us. He desires...to thwart...God's plan." Bowing her head, Tabitha was seized by a sudden fit of coughing that burned her lungs like fire. Determined to finish the conversation, she looked up again, weakened from the painful bout. "But Jesus...Jesus conquered the curse of sin and death. He took the curse...upon Himself...so we wouldn't have to. He bore the curse of sin...upon the cross. The enemy...has no power over Him. Nor has he any power over us...unless it has been given to him...from above, just as Jesus told Pontius Pilate...when the governor thought...he had the power...to execute our Lord." Reaching for her throat, Tabitha bent at the waist as another fit of coughing spasms seized her, rendering her unable to speak for several minutes.

Taking Tabitha's exhortation to heart, Tirzah stood, patting her friend's back as she coughed. Reaching for a washrag, Tirzah handed it to her, and Tabitha cupped it over her mouth, coughing inconsolably. When the coughing finally settled, she leaned back against her pillows, her pale face streaming sweat, her eyes and nose running like a fount. Slowly lowering the washrag, her heart jumped at the sight of bright red blood seeping through it.

"Oh, Tabitha," Tirzah whispered, taking the cloth and inspecting it grimly. "Perhaps...perhaps we should just relinquish this mission. If you are no longer operating the Refuge, then perhaps the enemy will back off. And leave you alone."

"No," Tabitha said firmly, shaking her head with

as much vigor as she could muster. "Don't let him win."

"But he's trying to *kill* you."

"The enemy...has no power...over me," she whispered hoarsely, her voice nearly gone. "Nothing can happen...to me...without God's permission."

"Oh, Tabitha," Tirzah groaned, setting aside the washrag and covering her face with her hands. "I admire your faith, but I do hope you're right. I don't want to lose you, too."

"God has...a plan," Tabitha forced the words out as best she could. "We must simply...trust Him. And...stand firm."

CHAPTER 41

Tirzah

Joppa

Seated faithfully beside her charge, Tirzah watched as Tabitha's chest rose and fell with her every labored breath. She had been sleeping more or less peacefully for about an hour, and Tirzah was grateful. According to the physician, sleep was crucial to the healing process.

And you must get well, Tirzah thought, watching her friend with anxious eyes. *I love you like a sister, dear one. We all do. Don't leave us, not now. Not yet.*

Tabitha had insisted that God had a plan, but Tirzah was having some serious trouble seeing it. What was the purpose of so much pain and suffering? Menservants had buried another child just that morning, and the physician seemed certain that Hannah, the young mother who had lost her baby, wouldn't make it, either.

*And now Tabitha…*Tirzah thought, marveling at the injustice of it all. The beautiful young woman had done nothing but love the people of Joppa, welcoming them into her home with open arms. She had invested hours training the widows in important skills like cooking, sewing, and bread making, equipping them to make a living on their own. She had held and cuddled dozens of orphaned children, lavishing love and acceptance upon them. And she had slaved over the sick for weeks on end, expecting absolutely nothing in return.

Why, Lord? Tirzah's heart cried in resistance. *Why did this plague have to come upon her? She didn't deserve it. You know she didn't, Lord.*

If only Dorian was available to sit with her, to minister comfort and strength by his calming presence and quiet sense of trust. But Dorian was needed to assist Amal, as Tabitha was unable to do it. Tirzah knew the consequences could be dire if the greedy businessman was left to his own devices.

Adam's company hadn't proven particularly encouraging either, even though he had remained vigilantly by Tabitha's side the entire time. But the young deacon's overwhelming concern for Tabitha overshadowed all else. Tirzah had begun sending him out to change out the water and retrieve supplies much more frequently, eager for a reprieve from his intense presence. It was depressing.

She was glad he hadn't returned from the latest errand upon which she had sent him. The peace and quiet was far more comforting than Adam's brooding.

At the sound of someone loudly clearing his throat in the doorway, Tirzah looked up in annoyance. Eli stood there, wringing his hands, looking more like a lost puppy than a confident overseer.

"Yes, Eli?" she asked, peeved.

"Ah, I...ahem," Eli stammered, nervously clearing his throat again. "I was just checking on Lady

Tabitha's progress," he announced from the door.

"Again?"

"Has she demonstrated any signs of improvement?"

"She's sleeping," Tirzah hissed, her nerves worn entirely thin. "And she would sleep even better if you'd stop standing in the doorway clearing your throat every twenty minutes."

"Apologies," Eli muttered, his voice sounding even more anxious than usual. "Ah, um... Is there anything I can do?"

"You can make yourself scarce until she recovers!" Tirzah shot back, protective of her patient's welfare.

"Wait!" Struggling to sit up, Tabitha looked beseechingly at Tirzah. "I want...to see...him."

"Eli!" Tirzah huffed, rising from her stool with her hands on her hips. "You woke her up!"

"It's fine," Tabitha managed. "Send him in."

"Tabitha," Tirzah argued. "You need to rest—"

"Please."

"Fine." Releasing a frustrated sigh, Tirzah nodded toward Eli. "You might as well come in. You've already disturbed her sleep."

Eli ventured into the room then, nervously wringing his hands as he approached his lady's bedside. The fact that he had even entered the private suite spoke volumes about how much he cared. It went entirely against his nature to disregard the age-old protocols governing the behaviors between master or mistress and servant.

"Thank you...for checking...on me," Tabitha said laboriously, struggling to form the words.

"We've all been worried sick!" Eli confessed, his eyes shifting nervously under his large turban.

"Thanks for...for holding down...the fort," she said with a tired smile.

"We just want you well."

"Doing my best," she teased. "Eli, I want you to…to consider everything…I've told you…about Jesus. Promise me…you'll do that."

"My lady, you know I can't—"

"Promise me."

Eli stared at his lady, blinking nervously. The last thing he wished to do was to disappoint his mistress as she battled for her life. But how could he agree to do something so foolish and dangerous?

"Promise me," Tabitha insisted, more emphatically this time.

"I shall consider it," he finally responded, drawing a sigh of contentment from her.

"All right, that's enough chatter for now," Tirzah cut in, inexplicably troubled by her friend's serious, heartfelt exhortation to Eli. Tabitha spoke as if she were on her deathbed, with urgent finality. "She needs to reserve her strength, Eli."

Reluctantly, he turned to leave, pausing briefly once he reached the doorway to cast a poignant look over his shoulder.

Tabitha forced a smile, one she hoped conveyed how very dear the anxious little overseer had become to her over the years.

As Eli disappeared down the hall, Tirzah lowered herself slowly back onto the stool, her gaze flickering over Tabitha. The sick young woman was already asleep again, lying with her head cushioned against the pillows, her hands folded over her heart.

Does Tabitha think she is going to die? Covering her dearest friend's hands with her own, Tirzah bowed her head, praying desperately for healing.

CHAPTER 42

Tirzah

Joppa

The new year came and went, but those dwelling in the Refuge scarcely noticed. The air fairly crackled with intensity as friends, fellow believers, widows, orphans, and servants alike fretted for Lady Tabitha, anxious about her fate. While most of those who were formerly ill seemed to be steadily improving—including young Hannah—Tabitha grew worse by the day.

"The physician says she wore herself completely ragged, tending to the needs of the sick," Tirzah said, anxiously pacing Tabitha's office while her husband sat behind the giant desk, tiredly rubbing the back of his neck. "He said perhaps she would've had a fighting chance had she not gone weeks without rest or sustenance caring for those who were ill. When the plague came upon her, her body was exhausted, depleted, and completely defenseless against the attack."

"And there's absolutely nothing we can do?"

Dorian asked her, his eyes conveying his desperation.

"According to that good-for-nothing physician, no. There's nothing we can do at this point, besides keeping her comfortable," Tirzah stormed, pacing like a caged animal. "And how on earth are we to keep her comfortable when she's consumed with excruciating pain?"

"How is she this morning?" Dorian asked, wondering if he would regret voicing the question.

"Worse than ever," Tirzah spat out, furious. "She can hardly breathe, Dorian. She's gasping for breath between brutal bouts of violent coughing. I can hardly bear to sit with her and watch her suffer. Adam is with her now. He doesn't look good, either."

"He hasn't taken ill, has he?" Dorian asked her, concerned.

"No, but I can tell he's worried sick. He's afraid we're going to lose her, Dorian."

"There must be something we can do."

"Well, you tell me. What can we do?" Tirzah challenged, feeling testy in the face of her hopelessness. *God, why is this happening? Why haven't You stepped in? Didn't You heal Adam's father through Philip the evangelist, rescuing him from certain death? Would it really be so hard to do the same for Tabitha?*

"I'm going to write Luke the physician," Dorian stated firmly, reaching for a blank parchment page and spreading it open on the desk.

"Who?" Tirzah asked him blankly, drawing alongside the desk and glancing over his shoulder.

"Luke," Dorian responded, reaching for the small pot of ink and a writing instrument. "I've never met him personally, but both Mary of Jerusalem and Tabitha have spoken very highly of him. He is a skilled doctor, and apparently quite creative in his methods."

"And you know how to reach him?" Tirzah asked him, her eyes brimming with hope.

"No, but I do know he resides in Antioch, though he spends a great deal of time in Jerusalem. I shall pen two letters to him, and I will send one letter to Mary, and the other to Antioch," Dorian decided, the firm set of his jaw indicating that he meant business. "And we shall pray that one of these letters will find him in time."

"Oh merciful Father, may it be so," Tirzah whispered under her breath, sensing a glimmer of hope for the first time in days.

"I'll address the Jerusalem letter to Mary, as well," Dorian said, scribbling furiously even as he spoke. "She is like a mother to Tabitha. She will want to know what we're up against."

Placing a quivering hand on her husband's shoulder, Tirzah watched as his hand fairly flew across the page, pouring out his heart's request to Doctor Luke, the kindly physician he had never met but deeply respected.

***

Mary

Jerusalem

Laughing heartily, Mary leaned back in her chair behind her desk, enjoying Luke's delightful recollection of medical mishaps in Antioch. He was a natural-born storyteller with astute attention to detail and a fun flair for the dramatic and even theatrical.

She always enjoyed listening to him recounting his thrilling adventures, especially when they involved his many travels overland and by sea.

"I must thank you for coming to see me this evening," Mary told him with a genuine smile. "With the Passover drawing near, I assumed you would be arriving in Jerusalem soon. Just not this soon."

"You know I wouldn't miss it," Luke told her with a grin. "Your festivals here in Jerusalem are unlike anything I've ever experienced in Antioch. Not to mention, it's a wonderful excuse to visit you and your delightful brothers and sisters of faith."

"Speaking of faith…" Mary said, casually lifting a stylus from the desktop and twirling it in slender fingers. "Have you contemplated anything I shared with you since your last visit?"

"Ah, still trying to make a convert out of me, are you?"

"Till the day I die, yes."

"You needn't sound so morbid," Luke teased, rolling up his fitted sleeves and leaning forward in his chair. "I may come around long before that."

"I certainly hope so."

Luke's only response was a knowing smile.

"Dare I ask what it would take to convince you that Jesus is Lord, the Creator and Savior of all mankind?" she asked him, setting aside the stylus and resting her delicate chin in one hand.

"It would take a miracle of the century, I'm afraid." Luke chuckled, amused. "I'm a physician, Mary. I deal with statistics, facts, and case studies.

I need cold, hard evidence to be won over to a new theory or an idea. You know that."

"Fortunately, my God has been known to work a mind-blowing miracle every now and then," she told him, her lips tipping in a rueful smile.

"My lady!" Tobias burst into the bibliotheca, a sealed scroll in hand. "You have just received a letter. And according to the messenger, it's quite urgent."

"I see." Mary nodded, accepting the scroll with a serious nod. "Thank you, Tobias."

With a slight bow, Tobias hurried away.

"Sounds rather serious," Luke acknowledged, always inquisitive.

"Let's see what this is about," Mary murmured, breaking the seal and unrolling the thick parchment scroll. As her observant gray eyes scanned the page, her slender brows lifted in dismay.

"Mary? Is everything all right?"

"It's Tabitha," Mary breathed, lowering the scroll and meeting his gaze with anxious eyes. "She's taken ill. The local physician doesn't expect her to make it."

"Great God of Heaven," Luke breathed, gripping the gilded arms of his chair. "Have mercy."

"Her household staff has requested your services," she continued, her heart pounding in her chest. "They believe you can help her, Luke."

Rising from his chair, Luke reached for his leather physician's bag. "Where is she staying, Mary?"

"In Joppa," Mary answered, still processing the shocking news from Tabitha's good friend, Dorian.

"All right then," he said without the slightest hesitation. "Come along, Mary. We must make haste for Joppa. By the looks of that letter, we haven't a speck of time to waste."

Relieved to her very core, Mary jumped to her feet and came around the desk, thanking God for sending Luke—yet again—just in the nick of time.

***

Tirzah

Joppa

"Adam, we have to do something!" Tirzah cried, frightened, as Tabitha thrashed under her blankets, moaning and crying out in pain.

Standing on the other side of the bed, he reached for Tabitha, attempting to still her violent movements. "Tabitha, be still. Be still, beloved."

Consumed with fever and oblivion, Tabitha continued to thrash about violently, groaning in agony.

"Merciful Father, help us!" Tirzah nearly shouted, at her wit's end. "Show us what to do! Help her, Lord!"

As if in answer to her desperate plea, Dorian burst into the bedchamber with a professional-looking young man and a strikingly beautiful woman hot on his heels. "Tirzah!" he exclaimed, nearly shoving the man and woman into the room with them. "Doctor Luke has arrived, along with Mary of Jerusalem!"

"We haven't time for pleasantries," Luke said quickly, his practiced eye scanning the room. "I must tend to her immediately."

"Oh, thank God," Tirzah wept, dashing at her

tears with trembling fingers. "Can you help her?" she pleaded, surprised by the appearance of the handsome young physician. He was much younger than she expected—a Gentile with clean-shaven features and soft brown eyes. The moment his gaze landed on Tabitha, Tirzah knew it was serious. Bounding to his patient's bedside, Luke pressed his hand against her forehead as she continued to groan and thrash, his eyes growing round with concern. "She's consumed with fever," he declared, throwing off her blankets with a rough sweep of his arm. "I need cold water, and plenty of it! And clean compresses. Hurry! I need them now."

Dorian dashed out of the room to perform the physician's bidding.

"She's slipping away," Luke declared as Mary drew alongside him, her lovely features pale and drawn with concern. "All right, I must work quickly. Everyone out of the room, except Mary. Now!"

With hot tears streaming down her cheeks, Tirzah let Adam guide her gently from the suite. Luke closed the double doors behind them with a resounding *thump*, clearly determined to focus all of his attention and energy on his patient.

Dorian returned within minutes, toting a large pail filled with water and a stack of neatly folded washrags. After depositing them in the room with the physician, he returned to the hallway, where Tirzah and Adam waited for him, deeply disturbed.

"Where are you going?" Tirzah demanded as Adam turned toward the stairway, his shoulders set in resolve.

"I'm going to summon all the believers," he said, his tone boding no argument. "We shall pray for Tabitha without ceasing until she is fully restored to us again."

"A prayer vigil?" Dorian asked him, understanding.

"Exactly."

"We'll join you in the meeting hall once everyone is assembled," Dorian assured him, his eyes conveying his deep understanding and sympathy toward the hurting young man.

"Thank you, Dorian."

Waiting until Adam disappeared down the stairs, taking them two at a time, Tirzah turned to her husband, dissolving in bitter tears. Taking his wife in his arms, Dorian held her close, gently running his hand over her hair and whispering soothing words to her as one might comfort a hurting child.

Eyes soaked with tears, she looked up at him, her lovely features tightening in devastation. "I can't do this, Dorian. I can't lose her. She's my closest friend."

"Shhh," he whispered into her hair, pulling her closer. "You haven't lost her yet."

"But what if she dies?"

"She is in the Lord's hands. And He will give you the strength to endure, no matter what happens."

"I can't do this," she repeated, shaking her head in anguish. "I've lost too many loved ones. How can I lose one more?"

"No matter what happens, beloved, God is here. As am I," he reassured her, gently wiping away her tears and cupping her face in strong hands. "He won't leave you alone in this, my darling. And neither will I."

Burying her face in his shoulder, Tirzah wept bitterly.

CHAPTER 43

Adam

Joppa

It seemed as if the entire village crowded into the meeting hall to seek the Lord on behalf of their dear sister, Tabitha.

Standing soberly on the outer fringes of the gathering, Adam watched as his father, Josiah, stepped onto the platform to host the urgent prayer vigil. On the floor, Phineas distributed small wax candles to everyone gathered in the meeting hall. Reverently, Phineas lit his candle, then carefully touched his neighbor's wick with the flaming wick of his own candle. Each attendee followed suit, lighting their neighbor's candle with their own miniature flame. Soon, the entire room was aglow with the light of a hundred candles, burning steadily like the faint flicker of hope burning in each of their hearts.

"Brothers and sisters," Josiah said, his compassionate eyes sweeping the gathering below the platform. "We are here on behalf of our beloved little sister, Tabitha. Together, let us seek the Lord for her healing and restoration."

As the entire congregation bowed their heads, resolutely lifting their candles, Josiah led them in prayer, his powerful voice booming throughout the meeting hall and resounding off the frescoed walls. Adam watched, heart aching, as the believers' lips moved fervently in silent petition, all in heartfelt agreement with Josiah.

Glancing sideways when someone clumsily bumped into his arm, Adam was shocked to discover it was Eli, anxiously clutching his own small candle, his head bowed in desperate petition. Feeling warmth sweeping over him, Adam knew how Tabitha would rejoice if she knew her own crisis was drawing the reluctant overseer closer to the Savior still awaiting him with open arms.

Perhaps there was, indeed, a purpose after all.

Choking up, Adam offered his candle to a small child standing beside her mother and slipped away.

***

With a gentle knock, Adam cracked open the door to Tabitha's suite, reluctantly poking his head into the room. Immediately, his gaze fell upon Tabitha. She lay prostrate on the bed, her beautiful eyes closed, her hands folded delicately on her stomach. If not for her labored breathing, he would have feared she was already gone.

The young physician, standing at her bedside, looked up then, catching his gaze. Raising a finger to his lips, he whispered, "Please, leave us."

Adam was about to put his foot down when the beautiful woman seated at Tabitha's bedside spoke, her dulcet voice conveying her feminine grace and quiet strength. "It's all right, Luke. Let him in."

Brows lifting in surprise, Luke nodded his approval toward Adam.

Impressed that the doctor was humble enough to receive instruction from a woman, Adam slipped into the room, quietly closing the door behind him.

"You must be Adam," the lovely woman whispered as he approached her. "Tabitha has written about you in her letters."

"And you must be Mary," he whispered back, instantly impressed. Not only was she a vision with her waist-length dark-brown hair, bronzed complexion, and aristocratic features, but she carried herself with a queenly air of confidence. Rarely did one encounter a woman so self-assured, and yet still conveying feminine grace and humility with her every word, her every movement. "Tabitha has told me so much about you. It's truly an honor to meet you, though I wish it was under better circumstances."

"I feel the same," Mary assured him, her gaze flicking over to the physician, who watched them with a hint of disapproval. "Luke, take a few moments to partake of a meal and refresh yourself. I will stay with Tabitha, and I shall send Adam to retrieve you if anything changes."

"Are you sure?" Luke asked her, interested in the prospect of a warm meal but clearly reluctant to leave his patient's bedside.

"Go." Mary smiled with a slight wave of her hand. "It will be fine."

"I won't be long," Luke promised, nodding politely toward Adam before slipping quietly out the door.

"Please, help yourself to Luke's stool," Mary offered, gesturing toward the empty stool on the other side of the bed.

As quietly as possible, Adam went around the bed, retrieved the stool, and carried it back around to Mary's side. Situating it beside her, he sat down, wondering at the way her presence somehow comforted him without her having to say a word.

"How is Laurel?" Mary asked him, keeping her voice thoughtfully low.

"She is staying at my father's house with Martha," he told her, keeping his voice equally low. "She doesn't know, Mary."

"Hopefully, she won't have to."

"That is certainly my prayer."

Mary nodded, her calm gray eyes resting tenderly upon her sleeping patient.

"How is she, Mary?" Adam asked her, desperate for a positive report. "Praise our merciful God that Luke was able to settle her and ease her pain."

Biting her lower lip, Mary honestly met his gaze. "She isn't well, Adam. Luke is very concerned."

"Can he save her?"

"Only God can save her at this point," Mary responded frankly, her eyes glistening with a faint sheen of tears. "Luke is doing his best to keep her comfortable, but even he is at his wit's end. It's killing him, I think—feeling as if he cannot save her."

Heart constricting, Adam's gaze fell upon Tabitha's face, appearing so sweet and serene despite her great struggle. "Is she sleeping, or merely unconscious?"

"She's unconscious, Adam. We don't know if she will awaken again."

Mary's softly spoken warning was like a punch in the gut. Closing his eyes, Adam tried to breathe but felt as if the wind had been knocked out of him.

Placing a gentle hand upon his knee, Mary met his gaze with calm, clear eyes. "She is in God's hands, Adam. He won't let her go. Not in life, nor in death."

Death. Shaking his head, Adam battled for faith and strength, but it was swiftly slipping from his grasp. "I love her, Mary," he said hoarsely.

"I know."

Adam looked at her in shock, but quickly realized he shouldn't be surprised. Mary's perceptive eyes conveyed both discernment and intelligence. He imagined very little escaped her notice.

"Now she'll never know," Adam finally said, resisting the urge to weep. "I should have told her. I should have professed my love to her."

"She knew."

Adam blinked at Mary in surprise. "Did she say something in her letters?" he asked her, hopeful.

"No," Mary answered frankly. "But she knew."

"How can you be sure?"

"Because I know Tabitha, Adam. And I can assure you, she knew how you felt about her."

Swallowing hard, Adam looked away, ashamed of the tears threatening to come.

"She loved you too, you know."

Adam's head came up at that, his eyes wide with surprise. And hope.

"The way she spoke about you in her letters..." Mary smiled, shaking her head. "I knew it was only a matter of time before she recognized it. Before she would be willing to accept it. But you have her heart, Adam. She trusts you. And she loves you, deeply."

Shaking his head in amazement, Adam chuckled through his tears.

"I know your pain," Mary told him, her soft gray eyes willing him strength and understanding. "I lost my husband many years ago. But I can tell you—as one who knows and has experienced it—you will get through this. Regardless of the outcome."

"I told her to be careful," Adam said raggedly, watching as the woman he loved suffered through every painful breath. "I told her I was worried when she placed herself in harm's way, right in the midst of this cursed plague. I should have stepped in. I should have stopped her—"

"And would you also tell the sun not to rise? The ocean tides to cease to swell? The birds to hush their singing? The moon to hide its face?" Mary smiled faintly, patting his knee in a comforting, motherly fashion. "You could have no sooner stopped Tabitha from helping those in need. It's her nature. It's who she is. And if I'm not mistaken, it's what you love most about her."

Swallowing hard, Adam nodded, wondering at the injustice of it all.

"There's nothing you could have done to stop this," Mary assured him. "Don't waste another second blaming yourself, Adam. It isn't right to do so."

"Are you always this strong, this full of faith?" he asked her, marveling at her courage.

"I've experienced many life lessons that have taught me to depend fully upon the faithfulness of my God," she humbly confessed, her luminous gray eyes willing him to understand. "I have no strength apart from Him. And neither do you. Lean on Jesus, Adam. His arms are open wide to you. He understands your pain, your suffering. And He suffers with you."

Moved by Mary's strength, Adam rose from the stool, going to Tabitha and taking her hand. "Even if you *knew*, beloved, how I wish that I had told you," he whispered brokenly.

Mary watched him with tears in her eyes, her heart going out to the young man in pain. "It's not too late, Adam. You can tell her now."

Glancing over his shoulder, Adam met Mary's gaze. He nodded in understanding, then turned to look at the woman he loved, his heart constricting in his chest. Adoring every curve of her graceful face, the softness of her mouth once so quick to smile, the way her dark lashes lay upon her pale cheek, Adam held her hand firmly in his own, aching desperately inside. "How I love you, dear Tabitha," he whispered hoarsely. "From the very first day you stepped into my life with all your vibrant beauty, your laughing eyes, and your cheerful countenance, I have loved you. I have always loved you. And I always will."

Heart springing into his throat, he nearly jumped out of his skin when her slender fingers tightened around his hand! Was it just his imagination, or had she squeezed him back? Wide-eyed and open-mouthed, he stared at her, heart pounding, wondering if she would awaken...but to no avail. She lay lifeless and still upon her sickbed, her limp hand resting in his.

Perhaps he had simply imagined it. Wishful thinking was a powerful thing, after all.

Gently releasing her hand, Adam returned to his place beside Mary, lowering himself painstakingly onto the borrowed stool. Grasping his head in his hands, Adam gave in to his swelling grief.

CHAPTER 44

Mary

Joppa

Mary knew something was wrong when Luke sent Tirzah and Adam out of the room. He had been standing beside Tabitha's bedside, monitoring her pulse, his brows furrowing in concentration.

Mary watched Luke closely, trying to stay calm, to keep her peace. Something was wrong. She could see it written all over the physician's face.

"Luke?" she asked quietly, still stationed faithfully on the stool by Tabitha's bed.

Luke waited until the door had completely closed behind Tirzah and Adam. Reaching for the thin sheet at the foot of Tabitha's bed, he lifted it from both corners, slowly, reverently drawing it over the young woman's still body and covering her face.

"She's gone," he said, his voice catching in his throat.

Still as stone, Mary attempted to process Luke's

unexpected, tragic announcement. "Are you sure?" she managed, her tone sounding low and dull in her own ears.

"Yes," Luke said, his shoulders slumping in defeat. "I'm so sorry. So terribly sorry, Mary. I know how much she meant to you."

Lowering her gaze to the sickbed where Tabitha's shape and profile was still vividly outlined beneath the sheet, Mary's gray eyes glimmered with a sheen of tears. As the familiar sensation of loss tightened in her chest, she straightened in her chair, battling against the waves of emotion threatening to steal her composure.

Releasing a tremorous breath, she raised her eyes to Luke. He was standing at Tabitha's bedside, his forehead in his hands, his stance completely, utterly defeated.

And suddenly, Mary's entire being was flooded with compassion…and hope. Straightening in her chair, she folded her hands in her lap. She knew what must be done.

Luke must have sensed her revelation. Lowering his hands, he looked to Mary, confused by the sudden shift in her demeanor.

Lifting her gaze to meet his puzzled brown eyes, Mary stated calmly, "Send for Simon Peter."

***

"Help me understand, Mary," Tirzah demanded, trailing behind the elegantly clad woman in obvious frustration. "Tabitha is dead. Dead! What's the point of summoning an apostle now?"

Turning around to face the angry young woman,

Mary met Tirzah's flashing gaze with calm gray eyes. It had been difficult informing Tirzah, Dorian, and Adam about the death of their dear friend. While Dorian had grown quiet and sorrowfully reflective, his wife had received the news with raging, bitter anger.

And Adam. *Oh, poor Adam*, Mary thought, her heart breaking anew for him. She'd never seen a young man so overcome.

"Well?" Tirzah demanded, planting her hands on her hips. "Why on earth are we sending for your nephew, Mary? What can he do now that Tabitha is gone?"

"I have learned to heed the voice of the Holy Spirit," Mary explained to the furious young woman. "And I have never regretted doing so."

"And the *Holy Spirit* told you to summon Simon Peter?" Tirzah asked brittlely.

"I wouldn't have sent Dorian and Adam to locate him in nearby Lydda, otherwise."

"You've sent them on a wild goose chase," Tirzah huffed, pacing the upstairs corridor like a restless panther. "Dorian has never even been to Lydda. How is he to locate a man he's never even met, in a completely unfamiliar city?"

"He and Adam are working together," Mary reminded her. "They'll be just fine."

"It will take an entire day's journey just to reach the village and then another day to return," Tirzah pointed out, peeved. "In the meantime, Tabitha is just lying there, alone and neglected—" Tirzah's voice cracked then, and she had to pause to compose herself.

Heart going out to her, Mary drew closer to her,

gently touching her arm. "Do you believe our God can work all things together for good, Tirzah? Even this?"

Tirzah stared at her for a long time, seriously considering the question. Finally, she said angrily, "I suppose I should say *yes*. But, Mary, I must confess, my faith is sorely tested right now."

"We all face times of testing," Mary said gently. "But I believe God has a plan in this. I don't know what it is, but I have hope."

"Hope for what?" Tirzah asked bleakly.

"I don't know yet," Mary answered honestly. "But soon enough, we shall see."

***

Mary

"It's utter chaos in the meeting hall," Tirzah exclaimed, barging into the suite in which Mary had been assigned to reside during her stay. "You can hear the commotion all the way up here."

Mary glanced up from the salts and perfumes the servants had delivered to her chamber. It had nearly broken her heart, knowing these items would be used to prepare her beloved Tabitha for burial.

If only we were in Jerusalem, she thought, deeply saddened. *Then, she could be laid to rest beside her dear husband.* It didn't seem right, Tabitha's young life being cut short so soon. Just like her Stephanos. *Oh, God, I trust You. If only I could understand why.*

"Can you hear it?" Tirzah demanded, her features pinched with frustration.

Pausing to listen, Mary's stomach flopped at the

riotous sound swelling on the first floor. "What is happening, Tirzah?"

"Half the village has shown up to mourn Tabitha's passing," Tirzah chafed, frustrated beyond comprehension. "Not only that, but the widows and orphans are demanding to pay homage. They want to see her body."

"Unfortunately, that isn't possible," Mary said firmly. "She isn't washed and prepared for burial yet."

"I informed Josiah, and he's telling them now," Tirzah said, cringing as the uproar grew even more deafening. "It sounds like they aren't taking it well."

"Has someone taken charge?" Mary asked, willing to step in if need be. "Who is corralling the madness downstairs?"

"Josiah is handling it, along with help from Phineas and Simon the tanner. We've stationed guards inside and outside to keep order in the mansion," Tirzah said, her eyes flashing fire. "This is insane, Mary."

"Everyone is grieving," Mary said, her tone laced with sympathy. "Their reaction is understandable."

"Who knew the death of one woman could so impact an entire community?" Tirzah said, her voice catching in emotion.

"She was deeply loved," Mary agreed, turning to lift the tray laden with perfumes and bath salts. "Will you honor me with your assistance in this sacred task, Tirzah?"

Tirzah nodded, blinking back angry tears.

"Come, beloved," Mary said, aching for her. "Together, we shall perform this final labor of love for our dear sister."

CHAPTER 45

Mary

Joppa

Washing and preparing Tabitha's stiff, lifeless body for burial proved far more difficult than Mary could have possibly imagined. Despite her firm resolve, she found herself weeping throughout the entire process, her heart going out to the beautiful young woman who had lived to serve and love others. Her death had left so many in pain. Mary worried about everyone left in the wake of the tragedy, especially Tirzah. The potter woman had worked silently alongside Mary to wash and anoint Tabitha's body, radiating bitterness and fury.

Once the task was done, Mary reverently draped the sheet over Tabitha's still form, relieved to have completed her mission. She was about to thank Tirzah for her help when she noticed the young woman was hunched over, gripping her abdomen as if in pain.

"Tirzah?" Mary asked her, instantly concerned. "Are you all right?"

Stumbling to the corner of Tabitha's suite, Tirzah sank to the ground, her back pressed against the wall, sobbing inconsolably.

"Oh, beloved," Mary whispered, going to the young woman. Kneeling on the floor in front of her, Mary took both her hands, gazing into her tear-streaked face. "This is not the end," she told her, struggling against tears of her own. "You will see her again, Tirzah."

"It's just so wrong," Tirzah gasped through her tears. "Tabitha didn't deserve to die. This shouldn't have happened."

"No, it shouldn't have," Mary agreed, squeezing Tirzah's trembling hands. "But this world is imperfect, beloved. When Jesus returns, He will make everything right. Until then, we must be strong. We must trust Him."

"I can't stop thinking about little Laurel," Tirzah wept, drawing her knees up under her chin and hiding her face. "Oh, Mary. Who will tell her? And how?"

"We needn't speak about this to Laurel yet," Mary decided, her heart breaking for the little girl. "Let's pray first. God will show us what steps to take."

"She's going to figure it out eventually," Tirzah snapped, her nerves worn thin.

"The Lord will show us when to speak and what to say," Mary said. "Until then, why don't you go spend some time with Laurel, Tirzah? It may prove healing for you, ministering to Tabitha's daughter."

"If I can hold myself together," Tirzah groaned, impatiently dashing at her tears.

"I believe that you can," Mary assured her, rocking back on her heels and offering her a faint, encouraging smile.

"I'll go," Tirzah decided. "It's what Tabitha would do—pushing through the pain to minister to those most in need."

Mary nodded in agreement, thankful Tirzah had chosen to do so. The best way to overcome one's own woes was to get busy serving others—a lesson their dear Tabitha had embodied so well.

**

Praying earnestly at Tabitha's bedside, Mary's head came up when the double doors burst open, slamming against the opposite walls. Amal barged into the bedchamber, furious.

"Is it true? Is she dead?" he demanded, his eyes searching the room like a thief scouting out market stalls.

"Master Amal," Mary acknowledged, rising gracefully from her stool. Though she was sickened and appalled by his irreverent display and sheer disrespect toward the deceased, she held her peace. "How can I assist you?"

"You can tell me if it's true," he exclaimed, wheeling around to face her head-on. "Is that her?"

Following Amal's gaze to the still form of Tabitha lying in repose underneath the sheet on the sickbed, Mary responded with a single nod of confirmation.

"Unbelievable," Amal raged, shaking his head. "I demand that an attorney be summoned immediately so the proper paperwork can be drawn up."

"And what paperwork would that be?" Mary

asked him coolly, unwilling to be badgered or bullied by an arrogant businessman.

"I am Lady Tabitha's silent partner," Amal informed her, as if explaining a math problem to a particularly slow student. "Now that she's gone, the shipping business is rightfully mine."

"I beg your pardon, sir," Mary said, refusing to be goaded or cowed. "But that is rather presumptuous of you to assume."

"How dare you!"

"Those of us who loved Lady Tabitha are presently grieving," she said, her tone uncompromising. "Once we've had sufficient time to mourn her passing, we shall summon an attorney to help us sort through the legal ramifications pertaining to the shipping business and estate."

"You have no right—"

"I have every right," Mary returned, unwavering. "Lady Tabitha assigned me to be the executor of her estate. You may confirm that with her attorney, if you wish."

Blinking in shock, Amal's features grew mottled with rage.

"Now, please, return to your chambers and allow us to grieve in peace."

Moving grudgingly toward the exit, Amal paused in the doorway, casting a disdainful look over his shoulder toward Tabitha's lifeless body. "All these years, she tried to sell me on that Savior of hers," he said, his eyes narrowing in disgust. "Some Savior. Couldn't even save His most faithful daughter. Nor could He save my son."

Amal slipped out the door before Mary could even formulate a response. Stunned to her core, she walked to the doorway, placing her hand on the frame and watching as the investor stole down the corridor with angry strides and clenched fists.

Amazed, she realized that, in his own way, Amal was grieving the loss of his daughter-in-law. And his son.

***

Josiah

The first twinkling stars were just beginning to appear in the night sky, as if placed there by a skillful artist's brush.

Emerging at the top of a steep staircase, Josiah stepped onto the flat roof of Tabitha's mansion, eager for a bit of fresh air after a long, trying day. It had been exhausting, maintaining the peace as hundreds of villagers had converged upon the mansion, heartbroken over Tabitha's fate. He'd lost count of how many times he'd explained what happened to weeping widows with their small children. Even now, those who had come to view Tabitha's body refused to leave, spreading their tunics on the floor of the meeting hall and simply bedding down for the night.

What do they think? He wondered, crossing the vast roof and making his way toward the edge. *That she'll miraculously rise from her bed, travel down the stairs, and present herself to them alive?*

Oh, but wouldn't it be nice if she could! His own heart ached at the thought of life without the kind young widow. She had become such a fundamental part of the town. It wouldn't be the same without her, nothing would.

And his heart broke anew for his son, Adam, every time he considered his great loss. It would be a long, hard road to recovery from grief.

Nearing the edge of the roof, Josiah's defenses rose when he saw the dark silhouette of a man painted against the dusky sky. Hearing his approach, the man turned his head, his features etched with pain.

Suddenly, Josiah knew who this was.

"You must be Master Amal, the investor," Josiah decided, drawing alongside him and offering his hand.

Amal stared at his hand for a moment as if debating whether or not to accept the gesture. Finally, he did, though grudgingly.

"I am Josiah, Adam's father," Josiah informed him, leaning comfortably on the tall stone ledge encircling the rooftop. "It's a pleasure to finally make your acquaintance."

Amal said nothing, only turned and redirected his gaze to the sleepy outline of stone houses lining quaint, cobbled ways dotted with towering palms. In the distance, the waters of the Mediterranean glistened like a sea of shimmering glass, reflecting the silver moonlight.

"May I ask what's on your mind?" Josiah asked him in his usual friendly fashion, never mindful of the social barriers erected by haughty men. To him, it didn't matter that he was a lowly commoner working a market stall, and Amal was a wealthy merchant prince. Josiah saw a man in pain. And that was all that mattered to him.

Lifting a sardonic brow, Amal didn't grace him with a second glance.

"I'm a good listener," Josiah pointed out, a faint smile twitching his beard.

Amal looked at him then, and though Josiah could barely discern his features in the growing darkness, he sensed his need to speak.

"I marvel at the faith of you so-called believers," Amal murmured, his voice low and threatening. "Your God stands by and does *nothing*. He allows the very best to perish in agony. And yet, you still insist that He exists. Even worse, you insist that He cares."

"Ah," Josiah nodded, understanding. "I can see your point there."

Amal looked at him in confusion, clearly disappointed he'd failed to nettle the friendly deacon.

"To fully understand the way of things, one must simply go back to the beginning," Josiah mused, his wise gaze traveling over the scenic view before them. "It wasn't meant to be this way, you know. God created a perfect world in which death did not exist. Sin had no place. Righteousness and justice prevailed. But when the devil deceived that first man and woman, when they chose to act upon their own desires rather than trusting the wisdom of God, sin entered this world. And it's been a perfect mess ever since."

"And how is that our fault?" Amal demanded furiously. "I wasn't there. Neither were you. Tabitha and my son didn't fall prey to temptation in Eden. Why, then, must *we* suffer for Adam and Eve's stupidity?"

"Because their decision opened the floodgates for death and destruction," Josiah answered practically. "You see, they were given a choice. And they chose *sin*. But God has been on a quest ever since to redeem mankind, to restore His creation. It will happen, Amal. Mark my words. It will take time. And faith. And patience. But it will happen."

"If your God is as powerful as you say, He could have prevented the deaths of two faithful people who did nothing but serve Him selflessly."

Impressed by Amal's evaluation of Tabitha and Stephanos, Josiah nodded again. "But, you see, we're in a war. The battle rages for the souls of men. And as in any war, there will be casualties. Often innocent ones."

"So the innocent perish while evil men flourish?"

"Again, it won't always be this way," Josiah reminded him, turning to look him in the eye. "We must always remember that when the faithful perish, the loss is temporary. If anything, their struggles have ceased. No longer must they toil and muddle through this world so full of sin and injustice. When a believer dies, it's merely a gateway to a better life. A perfect life. A life in paradise with a faithful God who loves them so much that He sent His Son to redeem them, to make that life possible."

Sensing Amal's angry withdrawal, Josiah touched his arm before turning to take his leave. "Think about what I have said, my friend. I speak the truth to you."

With a friendly smile, Josiah crossed the roof and descended the stone steps, leaving Amal to ponder all he had said.

CHAPTER 46

Mary

Joppa

"You know I greatly respect you, but Mary, we must bury the body! We cannot merely leave her to decompose on that sickbed."

Seated on a balcony overlooking the Mediterranean Sea, Mary watched as Luke paced back and forth, exasperated with her refusal to bury her former maidservant.

"I know it's difficult to bury a loved one," Luke went on, pausing to meet her gaze. "But, Mary, it must be done."

"Once Simon Peter arrives, we can discuss it further," she said, unruffled. Though she couldn't explain why, she sensed that it wasn't yet time to commit Tabitha's body to the earth.

"And what if it takes three weeks to locate him?" Luke argued, disturbed. "Will you still refuse to bury her? You know we can't do that, Mary!"

"Lydda is less than a day's journey from here. And my nephew isn't easy to miss. Dorian and Adam will surely locate him quickly and bring him back."

"Mary," Luke said, respectfully lowering his tone and joining her at the wrought-iron table. "Forgive me for being so frank, but soon, she will start to smell."

Mary simply met his gaze, undeterred.

Further exasperated, the physician ran his hands through his hair in frustration. "You aren't going to budge on this, are you?"

"Not unless the Spirit reveals otherwise."

"The Spirit," Luke sighed. "I see. Well, perhaps the Spirit can hasten the men's return with Simon Peter. We haven't much time to wait."

Curbing her impatience, Mary held her peace, her unperturbed gaze traveling over the vast Mediterranean Sea sparkling beneath the morning sun. "Everything will be fine, Luke."

"I surely hope you're right."

"Greetings, my lady." Dorian stepped onto the balcony, looking far more at peace than he had appeared when he left for Lydda.

"Dorian!" Mary exclaimed, rising from her chair with clasped hands.

"We found your nephew, my lady," he informed her, his eyes conveying a glimmer of hope for the first time in many days. "He has requested to see you and Doctor Luke in Tabitha's suite."

"We really shouldn't be convening in a room with a corpse," Luke said, reaching his wit's end. Although it was obvious he was relieved that Adam and Dorian had returned from Lydda with Simon Peter in tow.

"I can only pass along Peter's request," Dorian said, standing patiently at attention near Mary.

"Come along, Luke," Mary said, hastening past the manservant. Her entire being lurched with familiar anticipation, every nerve ending in her body tingling with expectation, as she sensed the Spirit's gentle stirring.

Reluctantly, Luke rose and followed after her, hoping he wouldn't regret it.

***

As Mary hurried down the corridor toward Tabitha's room, she was surprised to see streams of women trailing into the sickroom, many of them clutching tunics, garments, and blankets close to their hearts. Confused, she pushed her way through the throng, emerging into Tabitha's private quarters with quite a bit of effort and hoping that Luke was still behind her. The women had surrounded the sickbed, many of them weeping and wailing inconsolably.

Trying to see over the flow of women, Mary located Simon Peter standing beside the bed, hemmed in all sides by weeping women. *These must be the widows to whom Tabitha ministered,* Mary realized, wondering why they had been permitted to follow Peter into the room. They were making quite a scene.

"What is the meaning of this?" Luke demanded, pushing through the thick crowd of women and looking around in dismay. "This is unseemly."

Glancing over the heads of many widows, Mary met Luke's gaze, shrugging her shoulders in confusion. She hadn't the slightest idea what was going on.

Many of the women had encircled Peter, weeping softly as they held up lovely garments for his inspection. Mary was utterly perplexed until she realized they were showing him the clothing Tabitha had lovingly sewn for them before she passed away.

"All right," Simon Peter said, his booming voice filling the room and silencing the sea of women. "You have all seen your dear sister in repose and paid your respects. Now, I must ask you all to leave."

Surprisingly, the widows respected his request. Sorrowfully, the women turned and filed out of the room, crying as they stumbled along, clutching the garments Tabitha had made for them.

Standing beside Luke, Mary's gaze swept the large chamber once the widows had departed. The room was strangely, eerily silent after the cacophony had subsided. The balcony doors remained open, airing out the room. And all the furniture remained in place, just as Tabitha had arranged it before she became sick. Gaze flickering toward the canopy bed, Mary saw that the young woman's body was still in repose, her lovely profile prominent beneath the ceremonial sheet.

"Mary," Peter said, graciously extending his arms to her. "How good it is to see you."

Going to him, Mary embraced her nephew, pulling back and meaningfully meeting his gaze. "Thank you for coming to us, Peter."

"Always," he assured her, turning his gaze upon the physician across the room, who was clearly uncomfortable with the situation. "And Master Luke, greetings."

"Greetings," Luke responded politely.

"It's good seeing you apart from needing to be

examined after a beating or stitched back up after getting whipped by order of the Sanhedrin," Peter quipped, eliciting an amused smile from the doctor.

"Likewise," Luke chuckled, a bit more at ease.

"Forgive me for having to send everyone out," Peter said. "They desired to pay homage to this wonderful young woman, but they can't stay for this. Not for what I'm about to do."

"What is it you're about to do?" Luke asked him, clearly getting nervous.

"Well, not I. But the Holy Spirit," Peter clarified, exchanging another meaningful look with Mary.

Heart pounding, Mary felt a surge of hope. She didn't know why, or what it meant. But she knew it was enough to comfort her heart.

"Please, excuse me a moment," Peter said, turning to kneel at Tabitha's bedside, focusing all of his attention on the body.

Stepping back, Mary watched as Peter reverently lowered the sheet, revealing Tabitha's pale, lifeless face.

"What are you doing?" Luke demanded, scandalized by Peter's actions. "What is the meaning of this?"

"It's all right, Luke," Mary said, drawing alongside him and touching his arm.

"But, he's—"

"Shhhhh," Mary soothed, her heart pounding as she watched her nephew. A gentle breeze wafted through the open window, rustling the curtains and the elegant tapestries draped about the canopy bed. Mary could almost imagine the wind bearing healing upon its invisible wings like tender breath from heaven, encircling the still body of the departed young woman.

The Holy Spirit is at work, she realized, tingling with rising anticipation. *Something is going to happen.* She could sense it with every fiber of her being.

Beside her, Luke watched the apostle's every move, breathless, suddenly sweating. One look at the wide-eyed physician told Mary that he had sensed the power surrounding Peter the moment he'd entered the room.

Taking Tabitha's hand, the Apostle Peter bent over her still form, his lips mere inches from her ear. "Tabitha," he spoke, his voice a low whisper yet resounding with unrivaled power. "Arise."

Luke watched with bated breath, heart pounding, palms sweating.

Instantly, Tabitha's eyes snapped open.

Luke cried out in shock, knocking back into a tall bronze lamp and sending it clattering to the ground.

Smiling warmly, Peter grasped Tabitha's hand, helping her sit up.

Laughing through her tears, Mary dashed them away, astounded by the unbelievable miracle she had just witnessed. Tabitha was *alive* and fully restored to them! She could hardly wrap her head around it. It seemed—impossible. But then again, she supposed she shouldn't be surprised.

After all, she served a God of the impossible.

CHAPTER 47

Tabitha

Joppa

Tabitha sat on the edge of her bed, blinking in confusion. The Apostle Peter was kneeling at her bedside, grasping her hand and smiling ear to ear.

The Apostle Peter? she thought, perplexed. What was *he* doing in Joppa?

Looking around, she saw Mary standing beside a wide-eyed, open-mouthed Luke, the physician, just a few short paces away.

Wait…*Mary?* And Luke? What were they doing in her bedchamber? Was she experiencing a vision? Or a hallucination? Had she somehow been miraculously transported to Jerusalem? It wasn't entirely out of the question. The same had happened to Philip the evangelist when he traveled on the road from Jerusalem to Gaza, when he'd miraculously found himself transported to Azotus!

But, no, Tabitha was in her own private quarters—in her very own bed! So, unless the entire mansion had been beamed to Jerusalem as well, she was still in Joppa.

"My lady?" she asked, addressing Mary in the old familiar way.

"Oh, beloved!" Sensing Tabitha's confusion, Mary went to her, arms outstretched, tears slipping down her cheeks. "Oh, you're alive! You're well! Tabitha, you're *restored*!" Sitting beside her on the bed, Mary scooped the young woman up in her arms, holding her close.

Realizing that Mary was, indeed, *real* rather than a vision or the product of wishful thinking, Tabitha hugged her back, weeping softly. "Oh, my lady," she cried, burying her face in Mary's shoulder. "You're *here*! I can't believe you're here! How I've missed you." She hadn't seen her former mistress in nearly five years, since the week her husband had been laid to rest in Jerusalem.

"And I have missed you, beloved," Mary told her, finally pulling away. Taking Tabitha's hands in hers, she looked into her eyes, her expression earnest. "Dear girl, have you any recollection of what happened to you?"

Studying her blankly, Tabitha knit her brows together, deep in thought. Whatever had happened, it must have been serious to bring half of Jerusalem to Joppa! "I was sick…" she suddenly remembered, her eyes growing round. "I was very sick."

"Yes," Mary told her, turning to glance over her shoulder at Luke, who now looked even more pale than Tabitha's corpse had appeared. "Tabitha, beloved, you were so sick that your friends feared for your life. Dorian summoned Luke and I, asking him to help. We came immediately, but it was too late. You were already consumed with fever."

Tabitha looked at her with wide eyes, surprised. "I don't remember that."

"You were unconscious when we arrived," Mary explained, wondering how Tabitha would receive the shocking news. "And then...well, then you died."

Tabitha stared at her, her eyes growing so round she wondered if they would pop out of the sockets. "I...I *died*?" she trembled, stunned to her core.

"You were dead for nearly three days," Mary told her, squeezing her hands. "In fact, you've already been washed and prepared for burial. The entire village has been in mourning, grieving your loss."

"What? How?"

Chuckling, Peter nodded as he rose to his feet. "It's true. We are all witnesses. Including Doctor Luke over there."

Turning to acknowledge Luke, Tabitha awarded him with a gracious smile.

"I don't understand it," Luke stammered, shaking his head in confusion.

"Why don't you come over here and see for yourself?" Mary smiled, a slender brow lifting in amusement.

Clearly hesitant, Luke looked back and forth between Mary, Peter, and Tabitha. It was obvious his mind was screaming in protest. He was completely shocked by what he had seen, unable to reconcile the miracle with the knowledge in his head.

"Well?" Mary prodded, tilting her head to one side. "Didn't I warn you that our God has been known to work a mind-blowing miracle every now and then?"

Dropping his leather physician's bag, Luke ventured cautiously toward the bed. Standing before Tabitha in disbelief, he shook his head, studying her from head to foot. Tentatively reaching out, he dragged the back of his hand along her forehead. It was cool to the touch.

"I don't understand it," he breathed, dropping to his knees before Mary and Tabitha as they sat together on the bed, hands interlocked. "She was stone cold, utterly lifeless. I examined her body myself!"

"Then you recognize you have witnessed a miracle today?" Peter asked him, exchanging a knowing look with Mary.

"Do you remember a conversation we shared quite some time ago?" Mary asked him, watching him carefully. Smiling, she noted that his expression indicated he knew what she was about to say. "I asked if you would believe that God raised Jesus Christ from the dead, if you literally saw someone raised to life. And do you remember what you said, Luke?"

"How could I argue with such an obvious display of power," Luke confessed, shaking his head in wonder. "And now that I have seen, my arguments have fallen flat, one by one."

Exchanging knowing smiles with Tabitha, Mary knew that years of prayers for this kind physician had been answered in an instant.

"I cannot deny it any longer," Luke said, his brown eyes earnest. "Mary, my faith is sealed."

***

Dorian

He wouldn't have believed it if he hadn't seen Tabitha himself. And now, all Dorian could think about was getting to his wife and sharing the news. She needed to know. Tabitha's death had ripped her heart to shreds. But her miraculous resurrection would stun and amaze every villager in Joppa, his wife included.

He made it from the Refuge to Josiah's home, where Tirzah and Martha were staying with Laurel, in record time. Giving the wooden door several hard knocks, he stepped back, wondering if he could bear the wait for someone to open the door. He was tempted to simply throw it open and walk right in.

Tirzah answered the door, her features drawn and pale, dark circles rimming her typically expressive brown eyes. "Dorian?" she asked, confused to see him.

Dorian simply smiled, a wide smile broader than she'd ever seen stretch across his handsome features.

Taking one look at his sparkling eyes, Tirzah stepped outside, slamming the door behind her. "What? What is it? What has happened?" she demanded, her heart pounding in her chest.

Tossing her another smile, Dorian offered her his arm. "Come and see for yourself."

CHAPTER 48

Tabitha

Joppa

After bathing, combing her hair, and changing into fresh clothes, Tabitha felt like a new woman. And she supposed, in a way, she was. God had miraculously restored her to life. She could hardly believe it, and yet an entire village had witnessed her death. She couldn't deny what had happened, nor did she wish to.

Her gracious heavenly Father had granted her a second chance at life, the opportunity to reach even more people for His kingdom and glory. And she intended to do exactly that. She wouldn't waste even one precious moment of the beautiful life the Lord had given her. Never again would she allow sorrow over the past to paralyze her from moving forward. She intended to make the most of every opportunity the Lord presented to her. Every single day. For the rest of her life.

And that begins today, she decided, seated in front of her vanity and gently placing her head covering over her golden hair. Gazing at her own reflection in the glass, she marveled at the strength coursing through her body. She was certain she would never take for granted the indescribable blessing of *good health.* To be able to breathe without gasping or wheezing, to swallow food without excruciating pain, to sleep through the night without burning up with fever—all these things were gifts she had previously taken for granted. But never, ever again.

"Tabitha! Good heavens, Tabitha, is it really you?"

Wheeling around, Tabitha grasped the back of her chair as Tirzah slammed into her suite, her garments fluttering, her head covering askew.

"It *is* you!" she cried, crossing the distance between them in record time and throwing her arms around her friend.

Laughing, Tabitha squeezed her back.

"I couldn't believe it when Dorian told me!" she exclaimed, her breath coming in short, excited puffs. When she finally drew back, her face was streaked with tears. "I don't know what to say, Tabitha. God was faithful, even when I was not."

"And He always will be," Tabitha smiled. "He understood your grief, Tirzah. And He's patiently waiting for you to run back into His arms."

Nodding through her tears, Tirzah intended to do just that.

Rising from her chair, Tabitha pushed it back in, pausing to cast another encouraging smile at her friend.

"You look nice," Tirzah remarked, noting that Tabitha had donned her finest garments and styled her hair. "Do you have some pressing business to attend to?"

"Actually, yes," Tabitha informed her, her bright eyes twinkling.

"Should I ask what it is?"

"I've asked Mary to arrange a meeting for me with Amal," Tabitha explained, a mischievous smile teasing the corners of her lips. "Although I've asked her not to tell him about the miracle. As of now, he has no idea I'm alive."

"Well, I'd say he's in for quite the surprise," Tirzah grinned, loving it.

"You could say that," Tabitha chuckled, headed for the door. "Let's see if he can deny God's power now."

"I want to hear how it goes!" Tirzah told her. "And don't think you've weaseled your way out of telling me everything that happened while I was gone! I want to hear all about your resurrection."

Grinning broadly, Tabitha tossed her friend a wink before slipping out the door.

***

Amal was grousing as usual as he followed Mary down the hall and through the curtained entrance to Tabitha's office. And Tabitha was already waiting for him, seated behind her desk, her hands folded casually on the smooth wooden grain.

The moment Amal emerged from the curtains, he froze at the sight of Tabitha smiling patiently, seated behind her desk.

"Great God in Heaven," Amal gasped, nearly plowing backward into Mary, who calmly observed the scene from the entrance. "What is this?" Amal demanded of Mary, his eyes wide with fright. "*What* is she? *Who* is she?"

"Don't you recognize your business partner, Amal?" Mary asked him, tilting her head to one side.

"But she's...she's *dead*!" he declared, looking as if he'd seen a ghost.

"I was resurrected by the power of the Holy Spirit, my lord," Tabitha said, wondering if he was about to turn and flee for his life. "As you can see, a believer's death is an open door to everlasting life with Jesus."

"Your Savior—the Carpenter from Nazareth—*He* did this?" Amal stuttered, his eyes widening in amazement. Daring a few steps closer, appeared to be absorbing every detail of her face.

"Yes," Tabitha nodded gently.

"But... He was crucified by Romans. Everyone knows that. He's *dead*!"

"Like I am?" Tabitha asked him, her lips tipping in a knowing smile.

"It must be some kind of delusion...a clever trick..." Amal stammered in bewilderment.

"No delusion, and no trick," Tabitha assured him. "Jesus was raised from the dead, and when He ascended to Heaven to be with His Father, the Holy Spirit was sent to dwell in the hearts of believers. And by the power of that Holy Spirit, I am alive today."

"But why?" Amal demanded, puzzled. "Why would He bring you back from the grave? To what purpose?"

"To demonstrate His might and power," Tabitha told him frankly. "Let me ask you, Master Amal: Can you truly deny the Lordship of Jesus Christ after all you have seen?"

Bowing his head, Amal appeared more conflicted than she had ever seen him. Clearly, she had given him a terrible shock. Rocking back and forth, he wrestled against his fear, grief, and uncertainties.

Rising from her chair, Tabitha came around the desk. Exchanging a knowing look with Mary, she went to Amal, placing a gentle hand upon his arm. She felt his muscles tense underneath her fingertips, but she didn't lift her hand. "Jesus is alive, Amal. Just as I am. It's time to *believe*. You cannot fight it anymore."

To her complete and utter amazement, Amal nodded his head in concession.

Tabitha didn't even realize her arms had flown around his neck until she felt him hugging her back. Weeping tears of joy, her heart swelled with thankfulness. The deepest longing of her husband's heart had finally come to fruition.

Feeling content and happy in Amal's fatherly embrace, Tabitha leaned her head on his shoulder, smiling as she imagined a blessed reunion of father and son in a glistening city with streets paved of gold.

***

Mary

Discreetly slipping from the room, Mary allowed daughter-in-law and father-in-law time to repair the bridges that had been burned between them. She knew Tabitha would be honored and overjoyed to lead Amal in prayer as he accepted Jesus as his Lord and Savior.

Traveling quietly down the hall, she smiled to herself as she recalled the various reactions of friends and fellow believers as they had learned of Tabitha's resurrection. Many were still unaware of the miracle, as Tabitha had been restored to life less than two hours prior. But it had been important to Tabitha to convene with Amal first. She had been completely convinced that *this* would be the miracle to get his attention and stop him dead in his tracks. And she was right.

She knew that Dorian and Tirzah were spreading the word now, sharing the good news with those who mourned. And Luke had retired to his suite, furiously chronicling every detail of what he had witnessed in the bedchamber on the upper floor.

Amidst the atmosphere of rejoicing and gladness sweeping over the mansion, Mary noticed that someone in particular seemed conspicuously absent. And based on recent conversations she had shared with him, she realized that she knew exactly where to find him. Turning on her heel, she changed course, headed for the lovely outdoor gardens framing the seaside estate.

CHAPTER 49

Mary

Joppa

"Shouldn't you be celebrating?" Mary asked the handsome young man seated on the marble bench near an ivy-strewn stone wall.

"Hello, Mary." Adam's smile was halfhearted, despite his effort to appear welcoming. "It was truly a privilege to meet you. You are very special to Tabitha, and I can see why."

"It was a pleasure meeting you as well, Adam."

He responded with another gracious smile.

"May I join you?"

"Of course," he said sincerely, shifting to make room for her beside him on the bench.

"I must confess, I'm a bit surprised to find you out here, rather than inside with the others," Mary said carefully, watching his reaction.

Adam appeared deep in thought for a moment, a muscle in his jaw twitching slightly. Finally, he looked at her, his honest brown eyes conveying his hurt. "She didn't even ask to see me, Mary. She was miraculously raised to life, and I never entered her mind, not even as an afterthought."

"That's quite an assumption you've made," Mary gently observed.

"I know it sounds petty, childish even," Adam admitted, shaking his head with a faint smile. "But the feelings I have for Tabitha haven't been returned, Mary, and I don't want to pressure her. I love her too much to do that."

"I understand your line of thought," Mary said. "But I wouldn't give up so easily. Tabitha hasn't asked to see anyone—except Amal."

"Amal?" Adam repeated, perplexed.

"She believed this miracle would convince him of the validity of Christ's resurrection, and she was right."

"Amal believes?" Adam exclaimed, amazed.

"Tabitha is praying with him even as we speak."

"Praise God," Adam breathed. "Tabitha has prayed for his salvation for years."

"God is good," Mary supplied, pleased. "As much as you love Tabitha, I'd think you would know that the salvation of souls has always been first and foremost in her mind. Which is why she chose to address Amal first, before anyone else."

Nodding slowly, Adam realized that Mary was right.

"And if I'm not mistaken, that is something you treasure about her," Mary dared, a knowing smile shaping her lips.

"I do treasure her heart for evangelism," Adam said, chuckling to himself. "I've never known anyone like her. She's relentless in her pursuit of the lost."

"Speaking of relentless," Mary said, "I wouldn't give up so easily, Adam. God has a way of working things out in His own good time. And she'll come around."

Encouraged, Adam resolved to take Mary's words to heart.

***

Tabitha

Basking in the wonder and joy of her father-in-law's newfound salvation, Tabitha slipped out of her office, thanking God for His abundant mercy as she stole down the corridor and nearly collided headfirst with—

"Eli!" she exclaimed, grasping his arms to steady herself.

"My lady!" he declared in awe, his eyes round with disbelief. "It's true—you're alive!"

"Praise God for His undeserved kindness and mercy," Tabitha said with great feeling. "It's only by His grace that I stand before you today, Eli."

Eli stared at in disbelief, a strange combination of emotions passing over his face—fear, amazement, relief, awe, and lastly, recognition. Glancing around as if to ensure they were alone, Eli whispered nervously, "I prayed for you, my lady."

Heart swelling with warmth for her faithful overseer, tears sprung to Tabitha's eyes. "You went to the synagogue on my behalf, Eli?"

"No, my lady," he said, shaking his head. "I joined the prayer vigil Josiah hosted in the meeting hall. And I prayed...to your Messiah...for the first time."

Clasping her hands to her heart, Tabitha somehow resisted the urge to throw her arms around him. "And then what happened, Eli?"

"I couldn't take my eyes off the cross," Eli said, nervously shuffling his feet and looking at the ground. "The wooden one mounted on the wall behind the speaker's platform. I begged your Messiah to heal you, if He had any power at all."

Eyes brimming with tears, Tabitha nodded in understanding.

"And He did," Eli stated simply, surprising even himself with his statement of faith. "Though I shall be displaced from the synagogue and publicly shamed, I cannot deny the power of God. Jesus Christ is His Son. He is the Savior. Who but God could raise the dead before my very eyes?"

"Praise God," Tabitha breathed, overwhelmed with joy and gratitude. "Welcome to the family of faith, my brother. My heart bursts with happiness for you."

"I just thought you should know."

"You've made me the happiest woman alive—literally, *alive*." She laughed, even more amused when Eli appeared characteristically unimpressed with her little joke.

Shaking her head in awe, Tabitha realized that all the pain and suffering and uncertainty leading up to her death was entirely worth it, even if the only result was the salvation of Eli and Amal.

Even so, she had a sneaking suspicion that the resurrection miracle would impact far more people of Joppa than she could possibly imagine.

***

Settling into its western bed for the night, the sun cast the shimmering waters of the Great Sea in breathtaking rose gold hues as Mary and Tabitha sat at the wrought-iron table on the balcony adjoining Tabitha's private quarters. Feeling contented and loved, Tabitha nestled her daughter on her lap, holding her close. She still smelled of cinnamon, coriander, and cumin after working closely in Josiah's kitchen with Martha for several days. Breathing deeply of the familiar spices' inviting scents, Tabitha marveled at the beauty of simply sharing a sunset evening with Mary and her young daughter on the balcony. Life was truly precious, far too precious to squander away.

"I cannot begin to explain how wonderful it's been to see you again, Mary," Tabitha said with great feeling. "I have missed you."

"And I have missed you, dear one," Mary told her. "I can scarcely believe how your little Laurel has grown!"

As if in response, Laurel giggled and squirmed off her mother's lap, scampering off to go play with the other children. Chuckling, Tabitha watched her go. "That girl has enough energy for three children combined."

"I imagine it will serve her well in time to come," Mary said with an enigmatic smile. "Especially if she stays as busy as her mama."

"Is there anything I can do to convince you to stay here in Joppa a bit longer?" Tabitha implored with earnest eyes.

"Ah, beloved," Mary smiled, reaching across the table to take her former maidservant's hand. "How I wish I could. But Luke and I must depart at first light. I have a wedding to attend."

"Oh, Mary, I can scarcely believe John Mark and Rhoda are finally getting married!"

"Frankly, neither can I," Mary chuckled. "But it's time."

"Even more than that, I can't believe that Saul—no, you say it's *Paul* now—I can't believe that Paul agreed to conduct the ceremony!" Tabitha exclaimed.

"You wouldn't even recognize him, Tabitha," Mary said. "He is on fire for the Lord. One would never believe that he once devoted his life to the destruction of the Way. Now, he's sacrificed everything—his safety, power, prestige, and position—to preserve it."

"But it's a shame he had to flee Jerusalem before he had the opportunity to officiate John Mark's wedding," Tabitha commented, considering everything Mary had told her.

"Yes," Mary nodded, amused. "Fortunately, he was able to arrange for an old friend to replace him before the believers saw him off. A former colleague of his will conduct the wedding ceremony for John Mark and Rhoda once I return to Jerusalem."

"You say his life was in danger in Jerusalem?" Tabitha asked her, fascinated.

"Sadly, yes," Mary affirmed solemnly. "The Hellenists came against him when he boldly preached

Jesus as Messiah. He'd been with us less than two weeks when we realized his life was in jeopardy, so we sent him to Caesarea. From there, he relocated to Tarsus, his hometown. I imagine he'll continue preaching there until tempers cool a bit in Jerusalem. I'm sure he'd hoped to spend more than a measly fifteen days with us."

"Your prayers of many years have been answered, Mary," Tabitha said, silently thanking God that He had enabled her to forgive her husband's tormentor. "Saul—I mean, Paul—has surrendered his life to God. And now he is a willing vessel in his Creator's hands. Who knows what the Lord may have in store for him, as well as for the great body of believers, as a result."

"It certainly is a season of miracles," Mary remarked, her gaze traveling fondly toward her beloved former maid. "And you, Tabitha, are living proof."

"I couldn't have said it better myself," Adam said, surprising both women when he stepped out on the balcony. "Have you room for one more?"

"Actually, I was just about to retire for the evening," Mary said, rising gracefully from her chair. "Luke and I must depart for Jerusalem early in the morning."

"Ah," Adam nodded, knowing she was graciously allowing him time with Tabitha. "We shall surely miss you and the kind physician, Mary."

"Though I cannot speak for Luke, I will undoubtedly return to visit soon," Mary promised.

"We would be honored by your presence, Mary," Adam told her, his expression conveying how deeply he meant it. "Will Peter be returning to Jerusalem, as well?"

"Peter feels called to remain in Joppa a bit longer," Mary explained. "Simon the tanner extended an invitation, and he will be lodging with him for a time."

"Excellent!" Adam declared, pleased. "I shall ask him to address our church gathering while he's here."

"I'm sure he would be honored to do so," Mary nodded, delighted by the thought.

"What a wonderful idea!" Tabitha exclaimed, eager to hear the apostle preach again.

"Well, I should be going now. I have a long day ahead of me," Mary said. "Good night to both of you," she added warmly, touching Adam's shoulder in encouragement before slipping away.

"Good night, Mary," Tabitha said fondly, watching her go. Turning her attention toward Adam, she rewarded him with a genuine smile.

"Well, look at you," Adam smiled back, gazing upon Tabitha in a way that made her blush. "Here you are, alive and well. Fully restored."

"You know, I wondered when you would visit me," Tabitha teased, smiling a bit shyly.

"You've had quite a long line of people eager to see you today," he reminded her, his brown eyes twinkling as he joined her at the table, lowering himself onto Mary's chair. "I wish I could say I was being noble, allowing everyone else an audience with you first. But my intentions weren't quite so selfless. I figured I'd have a better chance of having you all to myself if I waited until everyone else was preparing to retire for the evening."

"Ah, I see your strategy." Tabitha laughed, amused. "It seems to be working."

Leaning back in his chair, Adam studied her closely, shaking his head in awe. "I don't know what to say," he finally told her, his handsome features appearing softer in the waning light at dusk. "I look at you, and I see a miracle, Tabitha. What wonders our God has wrought! How marvelous are His ways."

"I've been thinking the same thing," Tabitha admitted, leaning forward and folding her hands on the wrought-iron table. "I can hardly wrap my mind around all that's happened, Adam. I know that Jesus resurrected Lazarus, a widow's son, and a religious leader's daughter from the dead. But to see Him do so *now* by the Holy Spirit through ordinary men… it truly steals my breath away."

"*You* steal my breath away," Adam said boldly, holding her gaze with earnest eyes. "When you slipped away from us, Tabitha…when I thought I had lost you…" Pausing, Adam swallowed hard before drawing a steadying breath. "I will praise our glorious God with every breath I take for restoring you to us, dear one. I never want to lose you again."

Amazed by the peace and courage welling in her heart, Tabitha met his gaze with confidence. "You won't," she told him, smiling at the look of surprise he gave her. "I'm not going anywhere, Adam."

"I'm glad to hear that," Adam said, leaning forward and gingerly offering his hand. "Because neither am I."

For a brief moment, Tabitha's gaze flitted to his open hand resting on the table between them. Glancing up at him, she saw the message conveyed in his kind brown eyes—the same tender message that had been there all along, from the first day she had encountered him at the market stalls. Gentleness. Affection. Loyalty. Friendship.

Love.

Smiling softly, Tabitha placed her hand in his, her heart fluttering nervously—but also happily—in her chest.

"You have never looked more beautiful to me, beloved," Adam whispered, his features shining with hope.

Tabitha's heart was so full she couldn't speak. But she hoped that her eyes conveyed the swelling joy she now experienced in his presence. And everything else she wished to communicate to him.

CHAPTER 50

Mary

Jerusalem

It wasn't easy leaving Joppa and her beloved Tabitha behind, especially after reuniting with her after many years apart. How Mary wished she could have stayed and learned all about the Refuge, getting to know the orphans and widows for whom Tabitha had sacrificed her life, and perhaps even witnessed a blossoming romance between the beautiful young widow and a certain handsome young deacon of the local church.

Returning to her lovely Upper City mansion, Mary was ushered inside by exuberant servants eager to welcome their mistress home. The house was aflutter with activity as the staff made all the preparations for Passover, which would be upon them in less than a week.

"My lady, you have returned!" Rhoda happily exclaimed, hurrying down the stairs with a dust rag in hand and crossing the reception hall to meet Mary near the vestibule. "We are all so grateful you had safe travels."

"Hello, Rhoda," Mary said fondly, warmed by the girl's sincere concern for her. "I see you've all been working hard to prepare for the Passover."

"We wished for everything to be perfect when you returned," Rhoda confided a bit shyly. "May I talk your shawl, my lady?"

"Thank you, Rhoda" Mary smiled, shrugging out of her warm shawl and allowing Rhoda to take it.

Folding the elegant shawl over one arm, Rhoda asked anxiously, "Has Tabitha made a full recovery, my lady?"

"Oh yes, you could definitely say that," Mary chuckled, smiling faintly in amusement. "I shall tell you and the entire household all about it very soon. You'll scarcely believe all that has happened, Rhoda."

Eyes shining, Rhoda's expression betrayed her eagerness to hear all about Mary's experience in Joppa.

"But, first," Mary said, her gray eyes twinkling with good humor, "there's something very important we must see to."

Rhoda looked up at her expectantly, always ready to be of service to her lady.

"I feel like attending a wedding this evening," Mary mused, her luminous gray eyes sparkling with fun. "Have you any suggestions about where I might find a bride and groom?"

***

Rhoda

"You look beautiful, my darling girl," Mary whispered into Rhoda's ear, stepping back so the bride could see her reflection in the full-length mirror Mary had purchased especially for this day.

Heart fluttering with nerves, Rhoda gazed at her own reflection in the glass, amazed by what she saw there. No longer did her reflection convey a skinny, wide-eyed little girl, skittish and easily frightened. No, the face that looked back at her in the mirror was that of a lovely young woman, full of faith and hopeful expectation. Gentle, dark-brown curls graced her shoulders, emphasizing her soft mouth and rosy cheeks. Gingerly lifting a hand to her throat, Rhoda fingered the delicate fabric of her cream-colored gown, marveling at the intricacy of the pattern and design. She'd never seen—much less, *worn*—something so beautiful in all her life. The fact that her beloved mistress—soon to be her mother-in-law—had also worn it on her wedding day made it even more special.

"My lady," Rhoda breathed, her eyes glued to the breathtaking reflection glimmering in the tall, gilded mirror. "I cannot thank you enough for all that you have done for me today. This gown is lovelier than anything I have ever seen."

"It was made for you," Mary smiled, carefully lifting a delicate, hand-embroidered veil and placing it on Rhoda's head.

Smiling softly, Rhoda knew that Mary had kindly tailored the gown so it would fit her future daughter-in-law. Whereas Mary was tall and shapely, Rhoda was petite and slender. Somehow, Mary had found a talented seamstress to make the necessary adjustments to the lovely gown.

Turning away from the mirror, Rhoda bravely took her lady's hands in her own, her large brown eyes searching Mary's with warmth and trust. "You have been like a mother to me, my lady," she said, her eyes misting with a faint sheen of tears. "I will never forget how you rescued me from the slavers in Cyprus, and how you brought me into your home. By the grace of God, I became part of your family that day. And I will always be thankful, always."

"Praise God for His abundant mercy," Mary smiled, squeezing Rhoda's hands in response. "You are so special to me, dear girl. And now, even more so. For when you become my son's wife, you shall also become my daughter."

Blinking back tears, Rhoda nodded, deeply touched.

"Now," Mary smiled, tenderly adjusting the girl's graceful veil. "Are you ready to marry my son?"

***

Mary

A trumpet blast pierced the air, announcing the arrival of Rhoda's bridegroom. Throngs of believers gathered in the Upper Room, seating themselves on wooden benches and waiting eagerly for the wedding to commence.

Mary sat on the front row, dressed in her finest apparel. Looking truly radiant in her ruby-colored gown and golden amphora earrings, she smiled encouragingly at a very nervous John Mark, who stood on the platform with the former priest Paul had recommended to them, flanked by the apostles Matthew, Andrew, and John, who had happily agreed to stand as witnesses to the sacred union.

"Am I late?" Luke whispered, hurriedly slipping onto the bench beside Mary. "I got held up with a patient in the Lower City."

Smiling fondly, Mary shook her head. "You're just in time," she informed him, overjoyed that the young doctor was finally counted among her brethren in Christ. "Thank you for coming, Luke."

"I wouldn't miss it."

***

Rhoda

"Are you ready, dear one?"

Releasing a nervous breath, Rhoda accepted Barnabas' proffered arm, trustingly looping hers through his.

"I do believe you are the loveliest bride I have ever seen—both inside and out," Barnabas confided, his light-brown eyes conveying his fondness for her.

Looking up at him, Rhoda's throat constricted with happy tears. "Thank you, my lord, for giving me away."

"I couldn't ask for a higher honor or privilege, my dear Rhoda," Barnabas assured her. "You are like a daughter to me. And now, even more so."

Tightening her grip on his arm, Rhoda smiled at him through her tears as he led her up the stair-case, closer and closer to the Upper Room...and her bridegroom. Emerging at the top of the marble stairs, Rhoda was scarcely aware of the sea of believers gathered to witness the blessed event. The moment Barnabas led her down the center aisle, her gaze instantly fastened upon the face of the one she adored, waiting for her upon the platform, his eyes shining with all the love and promise in the world.

Somehow, the walk down the aisle felt like an eternity even as it felt like a split second. After assisting Rhoda onto the platform, Barnabas led her directly to her waiting groom, joining their hands together in a fatherly gesture of blessing and support.

Heart nearly bursting with happiness, Rhoda gazed through her gauzy veil, joyfully beholding the one she loved. Everything else immediately faded into the background—the throng of believers filling the Upper Room, the garlands of fresh flowers strewn about the chamber, the steadily burning lamps lighting the space, and the smiling witnesses upon the stage seemed frozen in time as John Mark held her hands in his, his thumbs gently massaging her trembling fingers.

When the older priest spoke, asking the congregation to join him in prayer over the couple about to be joined in holy matrimony before God and men, she was scarcely aware of it, despite his authoritative voice that resonated throughout the entire chamber. Suddenly realizing that the priest was leading the believers in prayer, Rhoda quickly closed her eyes and bowed her head, attempting to focus on the prayer even as her heart raced ahead of his eloquent words. Once the prayer had ended and the ceremony had commenced, she had to force herself to heed the priest's words, somehow managing to respond with the customary answers at the proper times.

When the priest finally granted John Mark permission to lift Rhoda's veil, the eager young groom did so tenderly, reverently. Rhoda waited with bated breath, overwhelmed with sweet emotions. The moment their eyes locked, her heart sprang into her throat as her groom gazed deeply into her eyes with a special look reserved just for her.

"Now, in the sight of God and these many witnesses today, I pronounce you, John Mark, and you, Rhoda, man and wife," the priest said solemnly, and the entire gathering erupted with cheers and applause, as some even tossed flowers at the beaming newlyweds, rejoicing in the sacred love they shared.

Convinced that this was the happiest moment of her entire life, Rhoda smiled shyly at her new husband, and he returned her joy with gusto, taking both her hands in his, raising them to his lips, and kissing them ardently.

Flushing prettily, Rhoda allowed her new husband to take her arm, escorting her to the lavish wedding banquet prepared just for them.

CHAPTER 51

Rhoda

Jerusalem

Rhoda felt as if she was floating upon a cloud, so happy and contented was she, as early morning sunlight slanted through the large, elegantly latticed window of her bridal suite. Nestled in bed with her new husband, she lay comfortably on her side, perfectly fitted to his lean body, his arm draped lovingly over her hip.

She hadn't the slightest idea how long she had been awake. But she would have happily lain there for days, soaking up the sheer delight of her husband's nearness, the warmth of his body, and the comfort of his protective arms around her.

Their wedding night had far exceeded anything she could have possibly dared to hope for. For the first time in her young life, she realized the sacred beauty of two becoming one.

I am truly one with this wonderful man, she

thought, smiling to herself as she listened to the sound of his gentle breathing behind her. *Today, we begin our life together. Only God knows what He has in store for us, but I cannot wait to find out.*

Closing her eyes, Rhoda thanked the Lord for the gift of marriage, marveling at the goodness of her God.

***

Mary

"You did it, my dear sister," Barnabas said, joining Mary on the upper balcony overlooking the walled-in outer court as the gloriously golden sun came up. "Your son is a married man, and you now have a daughter. How are you holding up?"

Smiling wanly, Mary gripped the wrought-iron railing, casting a sideways glance toward her brother. "To see my son married to a sweet, godly bride does my heart good, even if it does ache just a bit."

"Well said, beloved."

"I marvel when I consider all that God has done," Mary said, her graceful features bathed in golden light. "Everywhere I look, I see His fingerprints. Not only has He bestowed upon His church a blessed time of peace, but He has lavished us with a glorious season of miracles, as well."

"I cannot argue with that," Barnabas agreed. "His mercies never cease, do they? It makes me wonder all the more what our gracious God will do next. One can only guess, I suppose. But I imagine it will exceed our wildest hopes and expectations."

Fondly taking her brother's arm, Mary leaned her head on his shoulder, entirely at peace.

***

Tabitha

Joppa

The morning sun rose over Joppa, bathing the quaint seaside village in ethereal light.

Awed by the simple beauty of spring, Tabitha stood upon her balcony, drinking in the glorious view as she communed with her Maker, rejoicing in His presence and thanking Him for the miracle of life. Every breath she drew was a blessing, not to be misused or taken for granted. Every day upon the earth was a sacred gift, meant to be cherished.

Righteous Father in Heaven, she prayed as her hazel-green eyes swept across the dazzling seascape just beyond the protective stone walls of Joppa. *How can I thank You for all You have done? How can I praise You enough?*

Leaning against the railing, she pondered the miracles of recent weeks—including her impossible resurrection. *Precious Lord, I would be less than honest if I didn't share something that's been on my mind,* she continued, thankful that her tender Savior invited her to pour her heart out to Him. Closing her eyes, she attempted to piece together her thoughts in a logical manner. *You raised me from the dead,*

Lord. And for that, I praise You forever. But I can't help but wonder... You raised me to life, and yet Stephanos remains buried in the grave. Releasing a steadying sigh, she added bravely, *Though I am tempted to ask why, I desire to trust You instead.*

She could hardly believe it had been nearly five years since her husband's body was committed to the earth. At times, it felt like an eternity. And then again, at times, it felt like the blink of an eye. And while the ache of loss remained, time and the mercy of God had soothed the raw pain, rather like a healing balm applied to an open wound. And while the scars would remain, the healing hand of God was undeniable.

I may not fully understand Your ways, Tabitha continued frankly. *But I know You have a plan, a purpose behind everything that's happened in my life. You desire the salvation of the world, which is so much more important than our temporary lives here on earth. Though we have but a partial understanding of Your will here and now, I can see how my resurrection has led to the salvation of countless souls here in Joppa—Luke, Amal, Eli, Martha, and Jonas will now join us in Heaven someday, because You stopped them dead in their tracks, working a miracle they couldn't deny.*

Tabitha paused, allowing herself a moment to bask in the peace her Savior freely offered. Opening her eyes, she was comforted by the familiar view of blue sky, billowing clouds, sparkling waters, sandy beaches, and dipping seagulls—all proclaiming the wisdom, might, and power of her Creator.

And even as my resurrection resulted in the salvation of dozens upon dozens of souls, Stephanos' death promoted the furtherance of the gospel unto all the world, Tabitha mused. *There was a purpose in both, Lord—my life, and his death. Even so, I recognize that my healing is only temporary. Someday, my time on this earth will end and You will call me home. But a blessed day looms before us, just as the brilliant morning sun lingers upon the horizon.* Smiling to herself, Tabitha gloried at the thought of the heavenly trumpet blast ringing through the ages when Jesus Christ Himself would return, gathering all His faithful saints unto Himself and ushering them into eternity in paradise. Death, forever banished. Pain, eternally absolved. Fear, cast out and trampled underfoot.

Oh, Jesus, how I long for that blessed day, she prayed, overwhelmingly grateful for the hope of eternity. *What a blessed reunion that will be!*

Feeling refreshed after her time spent in prayer, Tabitha left the balcony, entering her bedchamber with a bit of a spring to her step. Crossing the room, she paused before the elegant wardrobe across from the canopy bed. Grasping the bronze knobs, she opened wide the wardrobe doors, even as they creaked in protest. A lone gown occupied the space within—her Aunt Pennie's wedding gown, the one she had lovingly restored at her Uncle Joram's request. The one he had mysteriously bequeathed to her in his will, his parting gift to her.

With a secret smile, Tabitha stretched out her hand, gingerly fingering the soft, satiny folds of the creamy wedding gown. As joyous realization washed over her, Tabitha thanked her God for freeing her from the bonds of the painful past. For breaking the chains of bitterness and unforgiveness. For restoring her life, as well as her broken heart.

It's time, Tabitha decided, her heart skipping a beat in joyous anticipation.

She was ready to accept the priceless gift her loving Savior had so tenderly arranged.

A LOOK AT:
REDEEMED

In a land steeped in ancient mysteries and divine wonders—the Promised Land—a powerful love story unfolds.

Not only does this tale bring to life the enduring bond between Ruth and Boaz, but it also delves into the poignant journey of Adara and Kemuel, a young couple burdened by the heartache of childlessness. In a society where barrenness is seen as a curse, their struggle becomes a testament to the unwavering strength of the human spirit.

As these two couples' lives become entwined by the providence of God, they witness firsthand the depth of His redemption and the boundless reach of His grace.

Immerse yourself in this Biblically-inspired story of hope and discover the relentless power of faith, love, and redemption.

AVAILABLE NOW ON AMAZON

ABOUT THE AUTHOR

Rachael C. Duncan is a passionate follower of Christ. Her goal is to reach as many people as possible for the sake of Christ and His kingdom. She believes that God has gifted each of His children with different gifts to be used to strengthen the body of Christ and fulfill the Great Commission. (Matt. 28:19-20; 1 Cor. 12)

Rachael was blessed to be raised in a strong Christian home, and she accepted Jesus Christ as her Lord and Savior at a very early age. Since then, she has determined to live her life in accordance to His Word and to share the love of Christ through the gift of writing.

Rachael has been passionate about writing since she was a small child. She especially loved writing plays and short stories. At the age of fourteen, she wrote her first play, which was performed as a dinner theatre production by a local school.

She has been actively involved in both women's and children's ministries for over a decade. Currently, she enjoys teaching a weekly girls' Bible study, writing plays for a local homeschool group, and participating in local ministry outreaches for women and children.

Rachael currently resides in Texas with her husband and their first "child"—a playful rescue puppy named Riley! In addition to her writing, she is an enthusiastic "keeper of the home" and "helpmeet" as well as being actively involved in ministering to the women and children God has placed in her life. (Titus 2:3-5; Gen. 2:20-23)